3 iss
2019

WITHDRAWN

To renew, find us online at:
https://capitadiscovery.co.uk/bromley

artnership with

Bromley

BETTER
the feel good place

D0337293

30128 80401 00 2

HOW TO PROPOSE TO A PRINCESS

REBECCA WINTERS

A HUSBAND SHE COULDN'T FORGET

CHRISTINE RIMMER

MILLS & BOON

First Published in Great Britain 2019
by Mills & Boon, an imprint of HarperCollinsPublishers,
1 London Bridge Street, London, SE1 9GF

How to Propose to a Princess © 2019 Rebecca Winters
A Husband She Couldn't Forget © 2019 Christine Rimmer

ISBN: 978-0-263-27264-2

1019

MIX
Paper from
responsible sources
FSC™ C007454

FSC
www.fsc.org

This book is produced from independently certified FSC™ paper to ensure responsible forest management.

For more information visit: www.harpercollins.co.uk/green

Printed and bound in Spain
by CPI, Barcelona

HOW TO PROPOSE
TO A PRINCESS

REBECCA WINTERS

To my dear daughter Dominique, herself a wonderful writer, who cried through parts of this story with me. That told me her heart had been touched too.

CHAPTER ONE

THOUGH OFFICE HOURS for patients ended at four thirty p.m. weekdays, and the receptionist had gone, Dr. Nico Barsotti didn't say good-night to his last patient until five thirty Tuesday evening. Even after diagnosing her with strep throat and writing out a prescription, he still couldn't call it a night. Before he could grab a bite in town on his way home, he needed to check on his nine-year-old patient, Tommaso Coletti.

Once he'd said good-night to his nurse who would lock up, he walked through the Hospital of the Three Crosses in the capital city of Domodossola to the pediatric floor in the other wing. The boy had suffered a ruptured appendix on Monday evening. Dr. Sala had performed the surgery, but Nico was his physician. He needed to follow up on the course of IV antibiotics he'd ordered and study the latest lab tests.

Nico nodded to the charting nurse at the station before walking into the room. He'd expected to see at least one of the boy's parents. Instead he beheld a sight that brought him to a halt.

Sitting in a chair next to the bed reading to him was a woman probably in her midtwenties who had luminous golden hair that fell to her shoulders. She wore a light blue volunteer lab coat over a dark blue dress. He caught a glimpse of her lovely profile and moved closer to discover she was reading a book popular with children.

Adriano, il Cane di Pompei was the story of a special stray dog who saw ancient Pompei as a magical place with its archaeological sites. The smile on Tommaso's face meant he was enjoying it. Who wouldn't be mesmerized by the woman's voice? She read it with all the charm and allure of a great storyteller.

He waited until she'd finished before walking over to the other side of the bed. His gaze met hers. Between her light sea glass blue eyes and golden hair, he couldn't look anywhere else. Nico knew he'd seen that beautiful face before. But where?

The blonde knockout reminded him of a celebrity, but he couldn't think which one. She gave him an enticing smile she probably wasn't aware of. That's when he remembered. Last month she'd been eating in the hospital cafeteria with Mia Giancarlo, one of the nurses. He recalled she'd been wearing a silky print blouse and skirt, her womanly figure transformed. Her image had stayed in his mind, and he'd been looking for her ever since.

"Look who's here, Tommaso," she said. "It's Dr. Barsotti."

The boy turned his head in Nico's direction, his eyes excited. *"Dottore—"*

"Ehi, Tommaso. I can see you've been well entertained. *Come stai?"*

"Fausta has been reading to me!"

Fausta? The name rang a bell.

Santo cielo! Now it was all coming back to him. *Princess Fausta Rossiano in the flesh.*

"How do you do, Princess?" he said as he checked the IV bag and took Tommaso's vital signs. "He's a lucky boy to receive a visit from you."

"*I'm* the lucky one, *dottore.*"

"Her name's Fausta," Tommaso corrected him.

Nico smiled to himself.

The three daughters of King Victor, ruler of the small country of Domodossola that touched on the borders of France, Switzerland and Italy, were known for their beauty. During these last few years there'd been two royal marriages, and their pictures had been on TV and in the newspaper. Nico ought to know since the magazines in his office put there for the patients were filled with royal news. There'd been constant speculation that the third stunning princess would be marrying a royal prince in the near future.

He shouldn't be surprised that the yet unmarried daughter of the royal family would actually volunteer her time this way. They did a lot of admirable philanthropy for the country. Her friendliness had won over his patient.

"When can I go home?"

"You're doing much better this evening, Tommaso. I'll probably release you in the morning." He turned to put some information into the computer.

"Not until then?" the boy muttered. "I'm fine now."

"We must do what Dr. Barsotti says!"

Tommaso's father had arrived. His wife followed him inside. Nico watched their interaction. Tommaso didn't know how lucky he was to have loving parents.

Nico had grown up in an orphanage run by the nuns. For years he'd been trying to find his parents and where he'd come from with no success.

After they thanked the princess for her time, she slipped quietly from the room. He gave instructions to the parents before he left to catch up with her. Strongly drawn to her by her appeal, he wanted to get acquainted, but other than staff, he saw no sign of her in the corridor.

He approached the charge nurse. "When did Princess Fausta start reading to the children?"

The other woman's face broke into a broad smile. "She's been a hospital volunteer for several months in the geriatric department. This week she was assigned to Pediatrics. So far, all the patients have been delighted. She has a real way with them. We're excited she'll be working with us until she's transferred to another department."

"When will she be here again?"

"Tomorrow. For the time being she comes on the afternoon shift four times a week."

"I see. Thank you."

Nico left the hospital, glad he had to wait only until tomorrow when he checked on another patient. Hopefully he'd find her here.

During the drive back to the palace in the limo, Fausta relived those moments in Tommaso's hospital room when Dr. Barsotti had come in. Over the past two months she'd seen him several times from a distance when he'd come in to the hospital cafeteria. But they hadn't actually spoken to each other until now.

Fausta hadn't thought it possible to be attracted to another man after her heart had been broken four years ago. Dego Spinella had been her childhood sweetheart.

Dego's father, Tano, had been the personal chauffeur for her father over the years. He, along with his wife and two children, lived in a house on the estate. Their son Dego was Fausta's age. Along with her sisters, they'd all played outside together over the years. As they grew older, the friendship between Fausta and Dego grew into love.

They'd planned to go to the University of Domodossola together and then get married. But her dream was shattered when one day just before college started, her father told her that Dego was leaving for Rome, Italy, to attend college there. The king had made plans to pay for his lodging and tuition as his way of thanking Tano and their family for all their years of service.

In panic, Fausta had phoned Dego. "Why didn't you refuse my father so we could be together?" she cried in despair. "That's all you had to do!"

"How could I turn down his kindness, Fausta? As Papa said, this is a once in a lifetime opportunity for me. Our family doesn't have that kind of money. But you and I will phone and send letters. After graduation we'll be together again and make plans for our future."

What future? You've stabbed my heart, Dego.

Fausta's father hadn't forced him to go. It had all been up to Dego, but he hadn't fought for their love.

"Cara?" he'd prodded when she hadn't answered. "Tell me you understand. Of course I love you and am going to miss you, but he's been so good to our family and he *is* the king."

That's right, and she'd been born the daughter of a king instead of a commoner like she'd wanted to be. "I understand more than you think."

Fausta had never liked being royal and her parents knew it, but the years growing up around Dego had been idyllic. He wasn't royal and they got along so perfectly, she knew a marriage between them would end in a lasting love match. Her plans for them to get a little home in the city where they could raise a family and live a normal life with children had been her dream.

But his willingness to leave her without begging her to go to Rome with him was worse than a betrayal. She'd thought their love had meant everything to him, but nothing could have been further from the truth. Fausta had been living in a fantasy world with no substance. Many times they'd come close to making love but had decided to wait until they were engaged.

His sudden departure had left her feeling heartbroken and betrayed. Her father had known she was in love with Dego and she knew he didn't like it. But he wouldn't have stood in the way of her marrying *if* Dego had loved her enough.

The fact that Dego had left for Rome without agonizing over them being torn apart said it all. The phone calls and letters from him came less and less, killing her feelings. In time she learned he'd married an Italian girl. Dego had been subtly bribed, and more than ever she hated that she'd been born a royal.

In the last four years there'd been no other man. She knew her parents were hoping she'd end up marrying one of the princes on their short list. But that would *never* happen! *One day she'd find herself a commoner who couldn't be bought for any reason!*

Her thoughts flashed back to Dr. Barsotti.

The second she'd laid eyes on the family practice doctor with his dark fringed midnight blue eyes and black-brown hair, his image had filled her thoughts. At six foot three with a rock-solid physique and potently male, no other man could come close to him.

Just hearing about his virtues from her best friend, Mia, revealed qualities beyond his looks. Besides being twenty-eight and single, he wasn't a baron, a count, a duke or a prince. Pure and simple, he was a non-royal doctor, already a revered professional who she doubted could be intimidated, manipulated or bought at any price.

Once in her apartment at the palace, she phoned Mia because she'd promised.

"Fausta? I've been waiting to hear from you."

"I just barely got home from the hospital after my first shift on the pediatric ward. It was so much fun."

"I know how much you love kids."

"I do." Fausta adored children and looked forward to the day when she had a family of her own and an attentive husband who had no other duties than to come home at the end of the day and be with them.

"Any sightings of Dr. Barsotti?"

She gripped her cell phone tighter. "He came in to check on one of his patients while I was reading to Tommaso."

"How did that go? I guess the doctor went into shock to see Princess Fausta Rossiano working there."

Fausta's breath caught. "I hope it was a good one."

A small laugh escaped her friend's lips. "Do you honestly know a man who wouldn't be thrilled to get near you if he could?"

"*Mia—*"

"Stop pretending when you know it's true."

"The good doctor didn't seem to care that I left the room. I could have been wearing a quarantine sign for his lack of interest."

"Don't be ridiculous. You're the daughter of King Victor, *that's* why he played it cool. He doesn't want to presume. Felipe is the same way when it comes to you."

"I know." Dr. Felipe Peletti, a friend of Dr. Barsotti's in the same medical group, had been dating Mia. The two were in love. "There are certain lines they won't cross."

"I'm afraid most ordinary people, men in particular, have the same problem when it comes to your *royalness*," Mia teased.

Fausta's friend had never had that hang-up. They'd met in high school with no secrets between them. She was one of the few nonroyals who'd treated them like equals and Fausta loved her for it. "You mean my *untouchableness*."

"If only the masses knew what a fun, easy person you are to be with."

"Ditto. Now I'd better let you go. I know you have to be at the hospital first thing in the morning. See you for lunch at Babbo's." It was a trattoria around the corner from the hospital.

"Absolutely."

"Ciao."

* * *

Wednesday after office hours, Nico was elated to find the princess comforting his ten-year-old patient Gina. The girl suffered from a form of childhood absence epilepsy. Each seizure lasted ten to twenty seconds and ended abruptly. Two out of three children responded to treatment and the seizures usually disappeared by midadolescence.

He'd had her brought in for tests before he ordered medication for her. She was holding on to a new stuffed animal for dear life.

The princess looked up at him when he entered the room. She was a vision in a soft orange blouse and skirt beneath her lab coat.

"Here's Dr. Barsotti, Gina."

The girl looked frightened. "Are you going to give me a shot?"

He shook his head. "No. I just came in to see how you are doing."

"Her mamma will be right back," her visitor said with an entrancing smile.

Nico nodded before checking his patient's vital signs. "In the morning you'll be able to go home."

"You see?" the princess assured her, patting her other arm.

"Am I going to die?"

"Of course not," Nico answered her. "I believe this condition is going to go away by your midteens. Don't be frightened by things some kids say to you. They don't know what *I* know."

A small smile broke out on her cute face. "Fausta

brought me this white Lagotto hunting dog." Fausta again. "She says her father has one." That didn't surprise Nico. The king was known to hunt. "I love him."

The princess's compassion and generosity impressed him. "I'd like to be a patient so she'd bring me one just like yours, Gina."

"I might be able to arrange something," their royal guest drawled without looking at him. She stood up as Gina's mother came back in the room. "I loved spending time with you, Gina. Do everything the doctor says and I know you'll get well too."

"Do you have to go?"

"There's another patient I have to visit, but I'll keep you in my prayers."

"Thank you for the dog."

"You're welcome."

"Bless you, Princess," her mother whispered. Their visitor was winning everyone over.

Like last evening, the princess slipped out of the room before Nico could stop her. He spent a few more minutes talking to his patient, then he left to find out where the princess had gone. The charge nurse said she was seeing a patient down the hall.

Nico waited and made phone calls for twenty minutes until she appeared and walked toward him. The second their eyes met, he realized how much he'd wanted to see her again.

He'd never been so drawn to another woman. That was the hell of it. She was a princess and had to be off-limits to a man who wasn't of royal birth. At least he assumed as much, knowing her sisters had married royalty, plus listening to the speculation in the media of a royal marriage in her future. But he didn't see an engagement ring on her finger.

"That was a generous gift you gave my patient."

"I brought one for all the children and was happy to do it, but you have to know that what you said to her relieved her fear. It's obvious you have a way with children."

"You have your own magic." He shifted his weight. "How much longer are you on duty?"

"I'm off now. *Buona sera*, Dr. Barsotti."

He watched her walk away on those long slender legs. Unable to help himself, he followed her. "Princess?"

She turned around. Her exquisite blue eyes lit up. "Yes?"

"I'm headed for the cafeteria for a bite to eat. Would you care to join me before you leave the hospital? Or is there someone waiting for you?" Might as well find out right now.

"There's no one. In fact, I'm headed to the cafeteria myself to get some work done. But first I need to get my laptop from my locker in the cloakroom off the cafeteria. If it's all right with you, I'll meet you there in five minutes."

"That sounds perfect."

Curious to know the nature of her work, he headed for the cafeteria. After going through the line, he found them a table. When she came in minus her lab coat, everyone stared at her. Whether she was a princess or not, her beauty drew attention, especially his.

She acted oblivious as she made her way to the table and put her computer on another chair. "I'll be right back after I go through the line." Upon her return he noticed she'd chosen coffee and a sandwich too. The second she sat down, she started eating. "Forgive me. I'm starving."

"I can relate."

Her gaze met his. "This afternoon I dropped in to see Tommaso and bring him a stuffed dog like the one in the story, but he wasn't there. Obviously you released him this morning."

Nico nodded as he drank his coffee. "If you'll give it to me, I'll pass it on to him when he comes in the office for a checkup. That'll make his day."

"He made mine. Thank you for offering. I'll give it to you before you leave this evening. It's in my locker."

"I have a better idea. Why don't you bring it to the pediatric floor tomorrow and leave it at the nursing station? I'll meet you there after your shift has ended and take it with me. If you're free, we could eat here in the cafeteria again."

Her lips curved into another of those smiles he felt reach inside him. "I don't normally have plans after work and would enjoy that very much."

She radiated a warmth that crept under his skin, causing his pulse to race. How could it be that she wanted to be with him when she could have any man she desired?

"Bene." He needed to focus before he got lost in those blue orbs. "Are you liking your volunteer assignment?"

She lit up. "I love it. If I'm blessed enough to be a mother one day, I plan to have a lot of children."

Nico found himself envying the prince who would turn out to be her fortunate husband and father those babies. "What kind of work do you do that requires your laptop after volunteering here half the day?"

"I help fund-raise for my younger sister, Lanza. She's in charge of setting up low income housing for veterans and others and setting up soup kitchens for the homeless. I spend my mornings calling on potential donors like CEOs who believe in helping with a financial contribution. In the evening I send them information and set up more appointments. That's what I'm going to do right now."

Nico finished the last of his sandwich. "I can't think of a worthier cause." He actually couldn't and found her remarkable for caring so much. The male CEOs she met probably fell madly in love with her and would grant her what she asked for without thinking about it.

If he weren't paying off a debt while he hired people to search for his parents, he would make a donation. "I suspect you're anxious to get busy, so I'll leave you to your work and see you tomorrow at the end of the day."

"I'll look forward to it, *dottore*."

He hoped she meant that because the last thing he wanted to do was put distance between them. "*Buona sera*, Princess."

Thursday evening Fausta's pulse was racing as she left her last patient and walked down the corridor toward the nursing station. But the doctor wasn't there waiting for her and her heart plummeted to her feet. She couldn't believe how disappointed she was as she approached the charge nurse. How could she care about him this fast? What was wrong with her?

"Do you still have the stuffed dog I left here when I came on duty?"

"No. Dr. Barsotti took it and said he would meet you in the cafeteria."

After struggling to recover, she thanked the nurse and left for the cloakroom. Once she'd hung up her lab coat and pulled out the laptop from her locker, she was so eager to see him, she could hardly catch her breath.

A chuckle escaped her lips when she saw him seated in a stone colored summer suit at the same table as yesterday drinking coffee. What a gorgeous man! He'd propped the dog on its backside in the chair next to him, like he was a diner too. Her eyes met the deep blue of the doctor's and they both laughed. He had an imp inside him that played havoc with her emotions.

"You were amazing to find this terrier for Tommaso, Princess. He looks like the dog painted on the book cover."

"I think he does too." She left her computer on the other chair. "I'll be right back. What are they serving tonight?"

"I hear it's chicken and rice, but I think we should give it a miss." He took a deep breath. "If I asked if you'd consider having dinner with me elsewhere, what would you say?"

She cocked her head, causing that golden mesh to swish against her shoulders. "*Are* you?"

"Am I what?"

"Asking me out to dinner?"

His adrenaline surged. "Yes." Why not. This would probably be the only chance in his whole life to spend an evening away from the hospital with this stunning princess. Naturally she would have to be free of any commitments in order to accept.

"I'd love it" came the response, which astonished him again. She really wasn't involved with someone? Earlier she'd told him there was no one, but he had to be sure.

"Are you honestly telling me there's no prince in your future?"

"Nico—it's true I'm under constant pressure to marry a prince on my parents' short list, especially now that both of my sisters are married." He knew it! "And of course, there's continual speculation about my marrying a prince in the media. There will always be gossip. But in all honesty, I swear to you there's no prince in my life and there *never* will be!" she said with such emotion, he knew she'd meant it.

Before he could say anything else, she blurted, "What about a woman in yours? How come you're not going home to someone important this evening?"

"I date on occasion, but so far there's been no one special."

She smiled. "I'm going to take you at your word. Thank you for being truthful with me. Now that we have that settled, where shall we go? I don't know about you, but I'm hungry."

"How about Babbo's?"

Her heart leaped. He'd just invited her on a date. "I'd love it."

"Then let's go."

As she reached for her laptop, he picked up the dog and they left the hospital.

Fausta couldn't believe he'd asked her out and was literally floating as they walked the short distance to the trattoria. For a while she could be the commoner she'd always wanted to be, going out to dinner with a fabulous man who wanted to be with her.

This was the normal life she'd always wanted! The way the women stared at him during their walk, she knew they'd give anything to be in her place.

When they reached Babbo's, Nico found them a booth and they both ordered lasagna. After they began eating, she asked, "How was your day?"

"Busy. A fifty-year-old male patient of mine had his gall bladder removed this morning. His surgeon didn't want to release him until tomorrow. Though he should do well, I need to know if there are any complications before I go home."

"Where would our world be without doctors like you? I know my father relies on his. We're all indebted to him."

Nico blinked. "What's wrong with him?"

"A bad heart. These days my brother-in-law Prince Stefano is helping him more and more with the load."

"I'm sorry he's not well."

She sighed. "I am too and shouldn't have said anything. No one outside the family knows."

"Don't worry. Your secret is safe with me."

Fausta finished her coffee. "I believe you." She'd lost her trust in men four years ago, but somehow she felt she could trust this doctor who took her breath away and had a bedside manner that instilled confidence in his patients.

One dark brow lifted. "Did you find any new bene-factors this morning?"

She welcomed the change of subject. "Not today. Maybe tomorrow. Fund-raising takes time, but I had such a wonderful afternoon with the children, I can't complain about anything."

"Nor I."

Suddenly his phone rang and he answered. When he hung up, he said, "I was afraid of this and need to check on my patient now. Tell me something. How do you get home at night?"

"Don't worry about me. I call for the limo. The driver will pick me up here."

"I'm sorry I have to go." He got to his feet and picked up the dog. "Do you work tomorrow?"

Her pulse picked up speed. "Yes. Tuesday through Friday."

"Unfortunately I have a two day seminar that will prevent me from meeting you. If you're free Sunday evening, I'd like to see you again."

"I want that too." Her swift response thrilled him. "When you come to the palace, drive around to the left entrance and I'll be there waiting for you. Just name the time."

"Six thirty?"

"That sounds perfect. Thank you for dinner this eve-ning."

"I'm the one wanting to thank you for coming with me." After reaching for the dog, he glanced at her. "I don't want to leave, but work calls."

"Don't apologize. I bet your patient can't wait to see you walk in his room. I know that's how I would feel."

If she didn't miss her guess, she sensed he would rather stay with her. Heaven help her but she hated that the evening had to end so fast. Sunday sounded so far away.

"I'll see you soon, Princess. And I'll make certain Tommaso receives his gift when he comes in for his checkup."

"Grazie. A presto, dottore."

CHAPTER TWO

NICO LAY AWAKE half the night. He kept seeing the princess's incredible light blue eyes staring into his, holding him spellbound. The words that she wanted to be with him too haunted him throughout the two days of meetings. But his insecurity over not knowing who his parents were made him feel less worthy of her interest. It was hard for him to believe she wanted to be with him.

The women he dated on occasion didn't come close to her kind of compassion or understanding, let alone her beauty. She was unique in ways that made him hunger to know her better. Much better.

On Sunday evening he drove to the fifteenth century palace and followed her instructions that led him to the side entrance. She stood outside the doors next to a guard waiting for him, dressed in a wispy blouse and skirt in a heavenly shade of hyacinth.

Her flowery fragrance filled the interior of his car as he helped her inside. Within seconds he drove his car out of the parking area and the estate onto the street.

"Fasten your seat belt, Princess."

"I will if you'll do me a favor and start calling me Fausta."

"You're sure?"

She let out a gentle laugh he loved hearing. "Since we're going to be seeing each other more often from now on at the hospital, it sounds too formal. Do you mind if I call you Nico?"

"Do you have to ask?" It didn't seem possible that they were on a first name basis. Excitement shouldn't have rippled through him.

"What do you ask the patients to call you? That is *if* they don't recognize you."

"Even if they do, I introduce myself as Fausta, as I did with Tommaso. My full name is Vittoria Eugenia Fausta Rossiano, but I prefer Fausta."

He filed that information away for future reference and turned onto another boulevard, but the traffic was heavy everywhere. "With your many responsibilities as a princess and fund-raiser, how do you have time to volunteer too?"

She turned to him. "Mamma has always said that charity never fails. By balancing my priorities raising funds for the homeless shelters Lanza is in charge of, I have time to volunteer. I envy my friend Mia for working at the hospital. When she mentioned a new volunteer program being started a few months ago, I jumped at the opportunity to indulge myself if there was an opening."

"Indulge?" he asked, full of admiration for her willingness to serve.

"Yes. You don't know how much fun it is to listen to older people talk about their past or read stories to the children when they're too sick to do anything else but listen. Lanza has an adorable baby boy, Ridolfo. He's eight months now and I already read to him. As you know, she married Prince Stefano of the Kingdom of Umbriano. Luckily they live here.

"As for my eldest sister, Donetta, she's married to King Enrico of the country of Vallefiore and is expecting. I'm excited about another niece or nephew coming along."

He smiled. "I remember reading in the news about their marriages."

She nodded. "Maybe they'll have a cute little girl or a boy like Ridolfo or Tommaso."

"You made his day. I listened while you finished reading to him."

"I'm the one who loved it. He asked a lot of questions about Pompeii, especially when I told him I'd been there and described some of the things I'd seen. He said he wanted to go there. He's a bright boy."

"I agree. In the beginning, did he recognize you as Princess Fausta?"

"If he did, he never let on. Children are wonderful. They don't set up boundaries."

Like you have, Barsotti. The fact that he'd even asked the question revealed his amazement that she continued to want to be with him. "I think most every adult has that problem who meets a royal like you."

"It shouldn't be that way. From the first time I realized I was born a royal, I fought against it and wanted to be a commoner. Though I can't change my heritage, I live my life like an ordinary person as much as possible."

That revelation came as a surprise to him. "Why do you feel that way?"

"You don't know how difficult it is to grow up not

having your father around when you need to talk to him. It's not natural to have to make appointments to see him. If you want to know the truth, I wouldn't wish my royal life on anyone."

"I had no idea." She sounded so completely serious, he had to believe her. Yet it still didn't change his wonderment that she wanted to be with him.

"I guess you've already noticed I'm always ready for a meal."

He grinned. "By the lovely look of you, no one would guess. I'm starving too. What do you like?"

"Anything. Surprise me. I'd like to see where the renowned Dr. Nico Barsotti goes for a meal after an exhausting day." *Renowned?* "I'm always looking for a good spot to eat."

"That doesn't sound like you spend much time at the palace."

He felt her eyes on him as he headed for the old part of the city with its narrow cobblestoned streets. "How many hours a day do you stay in the place where you live?"

Nico knew where this conversation was going. Once again he'd left himself wide open with a statement that showed how off the mark he was over the life of a royal. "I sleep there. That's about it."

"You've just described my life."

Except that her world was full of activity he knew nothing about and wished he didn't want to know. There was no way he could ever have a romantic relationship with her. Though she insisted there was no one and she was free to be with him, he believed her parents would eventually prevail on her to marry some important prince. Again, he reminded himself that her sisters had married royalty. Why would it be different for her?

"There's a small restaurant around the next corner that serves one of my favorite dishes. Have you ever eaten *maialino allo spiedo*?"

Her eyes sparkled like blue diamonds. "Roast pig? I'm sure I have."

"But this recipe is different and you're in for a real treat."

After a minute he found a parking space along the ancient street, but it turned out to be a tight squeeze between cars smaller than his. He slid from the car and hurried around to help her.

Soon people were staring at her, but she seemed oblivious. He noticed that men couldn't take their eyes off her. No doubt they wished they were in Nico's shoes as he ushered her inside Prospero's, a small dimly lit *cantina* over two hundred years old.

The owner saw Nico and hurried toward him with a wide smile. He couldn't take his gaze off Fausta. "*Dottore*—are my eyes deceiving me?" he whispered.

Nico chuckled. "No, *amico mio*. Prospero Gallo? May I introduce Princess Fausta Rossiano?"

"I *knew* it! *Benvenuto*, Your Highness!" He beamed. "I've never been so honored."

"Just call me Fausta, Signor Gallo, and I'm the one who feels privileged. Nico tells me you make the best roast pig in Domodossola."

Nico could tell by the way the owner seemed at a sudden loss for words that her compliment had thrilled Prospero. But after a moment he recovered and led them past several other diners to the best table of the house in the corner, where they were seated.

"We don't need a menu, Prospero. Just some white wine and your wife's *rigotoni alla carbanara* to go with the *maialino allo spiedo* followed by coffee."

"*Al vostro servizio*, Nico." His gaze switched to Fausta. "Princess," he murmured before hurrying to the kitchen, unable to call her by her first name.

By now the staff had to be aware of their illustrious visitor. Nico knew that a visit from a member of the royal family had made Prospero's night. Being with her had made Nico's night and he intended to enjoy it to the fullest.

"The owner is charming. Has he been a patient of yours?"

"No. We met in an entirely different way. When I moved to Domodossola eighteen months ago and joined the hospital staff, I asked around to find out what restaurants served roast pig. I tried several places, but they were a disappointment. Then I came to Prospero's and now I never go anywhere else when I'm in the mood for it."

"Why is that dish so special to you?" She'd just sipped the wine one of the waiters had brought to their table. Her lips glistened from the liquid, causing him to think thoughts he shouldn't be having, like how she would taste right now if he were to kiss her. His instant attraction to her was growing in leaps.

He drank some of his. "They use an old recipe that reminds me of the years I lived in Biella."

Her eyes searched his. "You mean Biella, Italy?"

"Have you been there?"

"Once years ago, with my mother and sisters. Mamma loved it because it was hilly with old *castellos* she'd visited as a child. As I recall, we had lunch there with a friend of my father's cousin. I remember walking up the steep, narrow streets to the citadel."

"I did it many times myself."

"So you're Italian! You must be here on a visa. Now that you're a doctor here, do you think in time you might apply for Domodossolan citizenship? Quite a few people from other countries hold dual citizenship."

"That's true—"

But before he could answer her question, Prospero brought their food to the table. He nodded to Nico then said, "*Buon appetito*, Princess."

"*Grazie*, signor. It looks delicious. So does the *rigotoni alla carbanara*."

Nico eyed her after Prospero walked away. "He cooks the meat. His wife makes the pasta with *guaciale*."

She looked surprised. "Doesn't that mean 'cheeks'?"

He chuckled. "In this case pig's cheeks. Normally the pasta is made with pancetta, but the meat is too crisp. *Guaciale* melts in your mouth." All the time they talked, he couldn't stop admiring the mold of her face and the way her eyes danced. There wasn't another woman like her in existence and he didn't want this evening to end.

The waiter brought coffee as they started eating. After a few minutes she leaned toward Nico. "This food is divine. How do you know all this? Were you a five-star chef before you became a doctor?"

"Not exactly. From the age of twelve to eighteen I

was a pig farmer on an estate on the outskirts of Biella before and after school."

"You're kidding!" she cried with excitement. "You got to play with all the little piglets?"

Her comment tickled him. "You like pigs?"

She smiled. "Yes! Sometimes my sisters and I would visit a pig farm on the palatial estate and I always wanted to take one home and turn it into a pet like my rabbit. My parents forbade it, but— Oh, they're so adorable!"

So was she. Already Nico realized he was falling hard for her. "For the most part they're well behaved as long as you don't separate them from the sow. There were times when I had to help a runt so it would thrive, and the vet would come. They have to be given antibiotics to prevent infection, and you have to put iodine on their navels. But sometimes the runts died. That was the hard part."

"How sad that must have been for you. When the wild rabbit I found and nursed back to health eventually died, it took me a long time to get over it. I'm surprised you didn't become a vet."

Nico finished his wine. "There was another experience earlier in my life that influenced me to go into a different kind of medicine, but I'll never regret my time on that farm."

"I think you were lucky."

"For many reasons I agree." *Right now I'm the luckiest man on the planet.* "The family I lived with were good to me and cooked roast pig at least twice a week. We ate well, which was a blessing because I was always hungry. Whenever I get homesick for those days, I come here to eat."

"I can see why. Do you ever go back to Biella?"

He was flattered and humbled by her interest in his life, as if she really wanted to know. "About every two months since I moved here. I enjoy the trip and visit friends, some of whom need medical help."

"How fortunate for them to have you looking after them." After she'd finished her meal, she swallowed the rest of her wine. "Where is *your* family?"

The inevitable question, reminding him of the separation between them. For a little while he'd forgotten. After sitting back, he studied her through narrowed lids. "I've been wanting to know the answer to that question since my first remembrance of life."

She studied him. "I don't understand."

"Someone like you whose royal pedigree goes back thousands of years would have a hard time relating."

"Please can't you forget my background and just talk to me like I'm a normal woman?" she persisted. Her endearing sincerity got to him.

Nico slowly drank his hot coffee. "I'm here on a temporary visa that has to be renewed on a regular basis. I have no idea of my true nationality, which is why I couldn't answer your question about citizenship."

A slight frown marred her brow. "But your parents—"

He lowered his cup. "I think around five years of age I must have asked someone where my mamma was because there was a painting of the bambino Gesu with his mamma in the big room.

"Apparently I understood some Italian and remember a lady in black patting my head. 'Only God knows,

figlio mio. While you are here, we shall call you Nico.'
Later I learned I'd been placed there with the nuns at
the age of two, but I have no memory of it. The orphanage is in a village near Biella."

A look of compassion and other emotions less de-
finable pooled in the celestial blue eyes of the princess.

"Now I've told you more than I've told anyone else in
years. You have that rare quality of being a good listener.
I'm not surprised you were hired as a volunteer. The sick
children won't mind being in the hospital with you there
for comfort. Would you like dessert before we leave?"

"No, thank you," she whispered, clearly moved by
what he'd told her.

Already he'd learned she had a sensitive nature that
made her even more desirable to him. It set off warnings that he'd be a fool to get any more involved, even
if she were amenable, but it was too late. She'd already
walked right into his heart. But even if he dared to
imagine a future with her, how could there be one? She
was the daughter of a king and queen. No matter what
she'd claimed, he was convinced her future would be
settled by them when the time was right.

"Then I'll drive you back to the palace so your bodyguard seated near the entrance to the restaurant can
go off duty and stop worrying that I'm going to whisk
you away."

An orphan.

To think she'd been complaining about waiting for
her father's attention growing up when Nico had been
raised in an orphanage!

Already crazy about him, her heart went out to him.

She wished the handsome, hard-muscled man who was so much more than a doctor would drive her to a place where they could be completely alone to talk some more.

Nico had stunned her by what he'd revealed of his life so far, but she'd only scratched the surface. After he'd taken her into his confidence, there were endless questions she wanted to ask.

Instead he'd reverted to treating her like a princess, which put distance between them when it was the last thing she wanted. Tonight had been magical. Having to go home was the part she hated.

After paying for their delicious meal, he said goodbye to the owner and walked her to his car, clinging to her hand. The small intimacy filled her with longing to get closer to him. Soon they would reach the palace and this glorious evening together would be over. She couldn't bear it.

If she invited him in to her apartment so they could talk further, would he turn her down flat because he couldn't allow himself to cross that line? She'd told him there was no other man in her life.

As they entered the estate, she guessed she'd find out because she didn't want to say good-night. Already he'd become of vital importance to her in every way. He followed the road around the palace to the side entrance. Another minute and he pulled to a stop. "Home safe and sound."

Fausta prayed he would want to stay in the car to talk with her for a little while, but no such luck. He got right out and walked around to her side to open the door.

Their arms brushed as she alighted, sending darts of awareness through her body.

"Would you like to come inside, Nico?" Her heart was pounding so hard it had made her voice throb. *Please say yes.*

"Thank you, but I'm afraid I still have to return several calls after I get home."

Don't react, Fausta.

"I forgot about that. Thank you so much for the ride and a dinner I'll never forget."

"Neither will I, believe me. Before you go in, I wondered if you would like to go to a film with me Tuesday evening after work? We'll grab a bite on the way."

His question caught her off guard so completely, she almost fainted with happiness. "I can't wait and haven't been to a movie in ages."

"Neither have I. We'll leave after your shift. In case an emergency crops up, let's exchange cell phone numbers."

When that was accomplished, he said, "*Buona notte,* Fausta."

She smiled. "*Alla prossima,* Nico."

Fausta headed for the entrance where a palace guard opened the door for her. Without looking behind her, she went inside and dashed up the staircase to her apartment.

Her gambit to prolong their time together tonight had failed, but he wanted to see her again on Tuesday evening. When he'd first turned her down, she'd feared he'd decided she wasn't that interesting after all. But his next question had sent her spirits soaring. He *did* want to be with her, hopefully as much as she craved to spend time with him.

She found herself dancing around as she got ready for bed. When she came out of the bathroom, her cell phone was ringing. She reached for it and checked the caller ID. It could be any one of her friends who worked on fundraisers with her. Seeing who it was, she clicked on. "Mia!"

"Wow! Do you ever sound happy."

"I am. Nico and I went to dinner tonight, and Tuesday night we're going to see a film."

"Wait. Tell me all that again. Go slowly."

She clutched the phone tighter. For the next few minutes she explained how things had happened at the hospital, their meal in the cafeteria and Babbo's, plus their subsequent dinner at Prospero's. Remembering that Nico had said he hadn't told anyone else about his past in years, she kept that information to herself.

"The dinner was over too soon, and he drove me home. I asked him if he'd like to come in, but he said he still had work. I was afraid I'd ruined things by pushing too hard, but then he asked me to go to a movie with him."

Mia chuckled. "What did I tell you? The guy's smitten."

So was Fausta. So smitten she knew she'd never get to sleep. "Tonight he found out how much I wanted to be with him, like I was a desperate woman."

"If anything he probably couldn't believe that you, Princess Fausta, would actually ask a nonroyal man to spend private time with you inside the palace. In most people's minds, it just isn't done because it's such a great privilege."

"I don't want to hear that. He's such an incredible man, Mia." Her voice shook.

With the background he'd come from, he was even more remarkable than anyone knew. "Being with him tonight has let me know I've lived a very sheltered, uninteresting life as a royal."

"Don't be ridiculous."

"I'm being honest. The woman who wins his heart will be the luckiest woman alive."

"Fausta—"

"Sorry, Mia. It's late. I'll see you on Monday. If you can make it, let's meet in the cafeteria on your lunch hour before we both go on duty and we'll talk."

"That sounds good. But do yourself a favor. Don't assume anything. To him you have to be the most fascinating female on earth."

"You think?"

"I know."

If only that were true. Tonight he'd revealed he didn't have a clue about his origins. But there was one thing she understood above all else. Whoever his parents were, he'd inherited qualities and genes that put him head and shoulders above other men. She adored him.

"Ciao, Mia."

"Ciao."

Fausta hung up. Tuesday evening couldn't come fast enough for her.

CHAPTER THREE

SINCE THE DINNER with Fausta on Sunday evening, Nico had been out of sorts. She had everything to do with his restlessness, but it wasn't something he wanted to talk about with anyone, not even Felipe.

The women he dated knew nothing concerning his background. When or if the right one came along, that would be different. However, Fausta had been such a good listener, she'd drawn him out.

Their conversation at Prospero's had caused him to open up about his life in a way he'd never done since moving to Domodossola. He decided it was because in the end, nothing could come of his association with her. That's why he'd felt comfortable telling her certain facts. Maybe he even enjoyed shocking her a little about his work on a pig farm, but she didn't act shocked.

In truth, he was the one who'd been stunned when she'd invited him in to her apartment at the palace. There was nothing he'd wanted more than to get closer to her. He knew she wouldn't have asked him inside if she hadn't wanted it too. But it wouldn't have been a good idea because he desired her in all the ways a man could want a woman.

It was one thing to enjoy a few meals at or near the hospital with her. But to take her to Prospero's before returning her to the palace had opened the floodgates for him. Now he'd invited her to a movie.

Little by little he was fanning the flames with a royal princess whose life had been mapped out from birth. Though she wished she were a commoner and insisted she would never marry a prince, Fausta had admitted that her parents were constantly pressuring her. Of course he believed her, but Nico didn't feel... worthy of her.

He was a child who'd grown up abandoned by his parents and had become a realist. Though Fausta might not be in a relationship right now, she'd just told him her parents had royal plans for her. All he could imagine would be an affair with her, which would be impossible to hush up, something he couldn't let happen.

There was another factor too. It wouldn't be fair to go on seeing her when he might not stay in Domodossola much longer. That all depended on finding his parents, and he was expecting some news of them soon. For that reason, he hadn't bought a home and settled down here.

The small Italian-speaking country of Domodossola was only two hours away from Biella on the northwestern Italian border. His parents could have lived within that radius before he was taken to the orphanage. But so far a thorough investigation here in this country as well as the region around Biella hadn't turned up any information. At this point he'd been investigating elsewhere.

When or if he did find his parents, or discover his origins or where he belonged, and he discovered it was in another country, hopefully one or both his parents would want to get acquainted with him. It might be that he'd make a permanent move to be with them.

Then again, they might not want anything to do with him. Though he was taking a huge risk, he'd nursed the hope of a reunion for years. Certainly he wouldn't expect a woman he was involved with, especially the princess, to deal with a future as uncertain as his.

All this was on his mind as he and Fausta exited the theatre. She looked gorgeous in a summery print dress. "Let's get some gelato around the corner before I take you home."

Their bodies brushed as they made their way through the crowds. The warm, beautiful early summer night brought out his longing to find a private place and kiss her into oblivion. So far he hadn't touched her. He didn't dare, or he wouldn't want to stop.

They both chose strawberry gelato and made their way back to his car. On the drive to the palace his mind flew ahead to the next time they would be together. Right now, he couldn't imagine his life without seeing her every day. He decided it would be safer to continue to be with her in public places where they would be around other people.

Nico drew the car around to the side entrance before turning to her. "I enjoyed being with you tonight more than you know. Thanks for sitting through that action film. It wasn't as good as it was purported to be." He took her empty gelato cup and put it in the bag.

"I agree, but I didn't care because I had a wonderful time. Since you probably have to go, will you wait long enough for me to run inside? I have something I want to give you."

She had something for him? He couldn't imagine. "Of course I'll wait."

"Be right back."

Within five minutes she'd returned carrying a white Lagotto hunting dog, the same kind she'd given Gina. After opening the passenger door, she placed it on its backside and put the seat belt around it.

She grinned. "You said you'd like one. His name is Giorgio. He works on a local pig farm. Now you won't be lonesome on your drive home because you'll both have a lot to talk about. *Buona notte*, Nico."

He burst into deep laughter as she shut the door and disappeared inside the palace. No one had a personality like Fausta's. Everything about her had enamored him to the point he wanted to take her home with him and throw away the key.

Barsotti? You're in huge trouble.

After he reached his apartment, he phoned her, hoping she'd pick up.

"Nico? Is Giorgio giving you problems already?" she teased.

He closed his eyes for a moment. "I'm calling because you ran inside the palace before I could thank you. Your gift has special meaning for me.

"When I first started working on the farm, people came who didn't know me and just called me Giorgio. I asked Angelo about it and he said it meant 'farmer.' Trust you to know that. Thank you again. See you tomorrow after your shift is over?"

"Absolutely."

When Wednesday evening rolled around, Nico didn't have a patient in the hospital, so he had no excuse to visit the pediatric ward. But that didn't stop him from racing over there after hours to find Fausta. The long overnight wait to see her again had been deadly.

She came walking down the hall ten minutes later and broke into a smile to see him by the nursing station. "*Ehi*—how's Giorgio?" Her hair shone like a pot of gold in the sunlight.

"We've become best friends. I've made him my guard dog while I'm at work."

"I'm glad you like him."

"I hope you realize I like the woman who gave him to me." He heard her breath catch. "Shall we head for the cafeteria for dinner?"

"I have a better idea. I brought a picnic for us and thought we could eat it on the grass behind the hospital."

She'd planned a picnic?

Today she was dressed in a yellow top and print skirt beneath her lab coat. He loved the way she looked. He loved everything about her. "I love the way you think."

"Give me a second. I put the bag in the fridge of the nurses' lounge."

He felt an adrenaline surge as she darted back down the hall for their meal. Fausta never ceased to captivate him. When she returned, she was carrying a plaid blanket along with a bag of food. No one had planned a surprise like this for him before.

He took the sack and they made their way through the halls and down the staircase to the door leading out back. It was another beautiful balmy evening. She found them a spot and spread out the blanket.

They sank down and emptied the sack. Soon they

were both munching and drinking soda. "Where did this meal come from? It's fabulous."

"I asked one of the palace chefs to make me a picnic."

"No wonder I've never eaten such delicious sandwiches and salad before."

"Jeanne is a great cook and my friend. Sometimes I take her to lunch to give her a break."

"That sounds like you," he said in a thick-toned voice. "Unselfish and generous to a fault." He'd never known anyone so easy to be with. She never pouted or acted upset.

Fausta blushed. "Thank you for saying that, but it's not true."

"I have proof to the contrary before my very eyes." He continued to stare into those light blue pools until she looked away. "What's your agenda this week?"

"Tomorrow I have to go back to the palace by three o'clock to help entertain some foreign dignitaries for the evening. Papa insists on it."

Maybe it was a prince her father wanted her to meet, but Nico had to stop worrying about that or he'd go crazy.

"On Friday morning I have an appointment with the head of the Tocelli cell phone company. I've been pushing him for a commitment and believe he's going to help fund one wing of the new veterans' hospital."

"Bravo." Fausta's charisma could turn a man inside out.

"What about you?"

"No seminars for several months, *grazie a Dio*."

She laughed quietly. The urge to take her in his arms and kiss her had become a viable pain he couldn't endure much longer. So much for his plan to slow things down. Driven by his desire to be with her despite his reservations, he brought up an idea he'd promised himself he wouldn't do.

"Fausta? Before I have to go back in and check on a new hospitalized patient, I wanted to ask if you have plans for this coming Saturday."

She'd started to clean things up. "That depends," she said with an alluring smile that made his heart thud.

"I wondered if you'd like to drive to Biella with me. While I call on my patients, we'll visit the pig farm."

Her blue eyes danced. "There's nothing I'd like more than to see some cute little pigs!"

You've done it now, Barsotti. But he didn't care. Insane as it was, he needed to be alone with her away from their world. "It'll be a two-hour drive both ways. Can you be ready by nine? We'll stop to eat along the way."

"I'm always up early and will wait outside the entrance."

"Bene." He got to his feet and picked up the sack. She folded the blanket and they went back inside as far as the cloakroom. When she lifted her eyes to him, Nico could see a nerve throbbing in the base of her throat. "See you on Saturday."

After they said good-night, he conferred with his colleague over a patient, then drove to his apartment and phoned Enzo, who sounded ecstatic to hear from him.

Knowing that he would be with her all day Saturday was the only thing that helped him get through the rest of his week.

After letting the older man know he'd be driving to Biella and would be bringing someone with him this time, Nico got ready for bed, almost feverish in anticipation of being with Fausta.

When he drove up to the side of the palace on Saturday morning, there she was with molten gold hair, dressed in jeans and walking boots. She'd worn a long-sleeved kelly green pullover that revealed the feminine mold of her body. She carried a jacket over her arm and looked like she was ready for a day in the country. Every exquisite detail about her spoke to him.

Nico jumped out of the car and walked around to open the passenger door for her with the palace guard looking on. "*Buon giorno*, Fausta." He put her jacket on the back seat before getting in behind the wheel.

"I'm so glad you asked me to come with you today. I'm thrilled to be getting out of the city."

"After the antiseptic halls of the hospital, I am too."

They took off and headed for the highway taking them out of the city. He was aware of security following them, but he didn't care. This morning she smelled like wildflowers in a meadow. Nico had never been with a woman like her. Moreover, he'd never done anything this exciting. She'd wanted to come with him. Nothing else mattered.

All the way to the border and beyond, the trees were in blossom with pink and white petals. She let out a sigh. "It's a beautiful June day already. Only a few white clouds are hanging in the sky. Everything is green and lush. I can't tell you how happy I am to be out in nature like this."

Her words painted a picture. "You took the words out of my mouth." They traveled past manicured farms that displayed a picture-book quality. "Does your family know you're with me?"

"I'm sure they do."

By now they probably knew all about him and didn't approve. Nico didn't want to think about it, but it was hard to look past the demands of her royal background. "I don't know about you, but I'm hungry. Let's stop in the next village and get some food we can eat in the car."

"I was hoping you'd suggest it."

They came to a hamlet and found delectable rabbit quiche with rosemary, black raspberry fruit tarts and sodas at a little local deli.

"This food is divine." En route she ate and drank with the same relish he did. "I know we're traveling to Biella. You said the orphanage wasn't that far from there. Could we see it too?"

He sucked in his breath. "You want to go to Mottalciata? The population is only about fifteen hundred people."

"You really did grow up in a small village, but it's part of your childhood. I'd love to at least drive by it."

"If you want, then we'll go there first."

Before long they reached the village in question. "This place, plus the Barsotti farm on the outskirts of Biella, made up my only world until I went to the university in Turin, Italy."

She looped some of that diaphanous hair behind her ear. "I haven't been to Turin in years. By now it's probably grown to a million people."

"Most likely."

"To go to the university there must have been a revelation to you."

He nodded. "When I wasn't studying, I walked and walked, marveling at everything."

Her eyes played over him. "I can just imagine the wonders that filled your young man's vision of everything."

They smiled at each other in understanding.

"Where's the orphanage?"

"It's in part of the old Romanesque church. We're coming to it now."

"Would it be hard for you to go in? I'd love to see where you grew up."

"Not hard, but I don't imagine things will be the same. I haven't been inside it since I left to attend the university."

Her gaze implored him. "It'll be fascinating to find out."

She was right about that. "Just coming here again, seeing the village through my outsider eyes at this point, brings back haunting memories."

Alarm filled Fausta's expression. "If it hurts too much, we should turn around."

He heard what she was saying, but they'd arrived. Nico pulled up in front of the church and shut off the engine.

"I'm not in pain, Fausta. At that time in my life, I grew up bewildered. So many children with no mothers or fathers. I was full of questions. Where were all our families? Where was *mine*? How did I end up here of all places? Didn't my parents want me?"

Her light blue eyes misted over. "We don't have to go in."

"I want to. After telling you about my past the other

night, I feel a need to revisit this place now that we're here."

After a pause, she asked, "Would you rather go in alone?"

His dark eyes impaled her. "I wouldn't have come to Mottalciata without you."

The intensity of Nico's words penetrated to her insides, causing Fausta to tremble. She got out of the car before he opened her door. Together they entered the church vestibule and followed the sign to the orphanage entrance.

Nico knew exactly where to go. An elderly nun in black seated at a desk greeted them as they walked through the door to the office.

"*Buon giorno*, signor. How can I help you?"

"My name is Nico Barsotti. This is my friend Signorina Rossiano."

It pleased Fausta that he didn't refer to her as a princess. The nun didn't appear to recognize her and that was fine with Fausta.

"From the age of two to twelve I spent my life here. A year ago, I learned from a friend that the holy mother who looked after me passed away. I'm sorry that I found out too late since I wanted to thank her for everything. The sisters were very good to me."

She smiled at him. "I'm sure she knows, signor."

For Nico's sake Fausta hoped so.

"Would it be possible to go into the common room for a moment, or should we come back?"

"You may go in now. The children are at lunch."

"*Grazie.*"

Fausta followed him through some double doors into the large room he'd told her about. A big beautiful painting of the Madonna and child took up part of one wall. Next to another wall stood an upright piano. There were shelves with well-worn toys and books. Seeing this place gave her the idea to send the orphanage some donations, but they would have to come from her own personal money.

He reached for her arm and they gravitated toward the painting. Nico studied it for a long moment. Fausta knew he'd gone back in time. "How remarkable. Nothing here has changed after all."

This was where he'd spent his early childhood. Pain stole through her for his heartache. "I'm thinking about the children in the other part of the orphanage, Nico. I'll pray they grow up to be happy and become as successful as you are."

He squeezed her arm before letting it go. By tacit agreement they walked through to the office. Nico approached the nun still seated at the desk.

"Thank you for letting us visit. We'll be leaving now."

"Come anytime. You'll always be welcome."

Fausta left with him. They walked out of the church in silence. She feared this visit would trouble him for a long time. But when they got in the car, he turned to her, his dark blue eyes alive.

"There was an old doctor who came from Biella once in a while when one of us was sick. He seemed like a magician to me and could fix anything. Every time he showed up, I followed him around and asked questions.

I thought how wonderful if I could do something like that one day."

Realizing that Nico had been thinking about the doctor who'd set him on his course, she could hardly swallow for the boulder in her throat. "So, *he's* the reason you became a physician. Do you think he's still alive?"

"I wish he were so I could thank him, but no. He too died after I left the orphanage." Nico started the engine. "Are you ready to visit some pigs? I come here every couple of months. The Barsotti farm is about two miles from the main square here."

"I've been thinking about playing with them ever since you mentioned it at the hospital."

His good spirits were contagious. Nico would never know what it meant to her to be let into his life, allowing her to see beneath the surface. He drove on while she drank in the bucolic landscape.

When they came to the Barsotti farm, Nico pointed out the farmhouse and the many outbuildings. The large property looked well kept. Several long buildings housed the pigs.

Nico pulled up to the office. "I'll run inside and see if I can find Angelo. Be right back."

"Take all the time you need."

She got out to wait, loving seeing the place where he'd worked, loving being with him like this.

A few minutes later Nico reappeared with an older farmer who was dressed in overalls and wore a huge smile on his mustached face.

"Fausta? I'd like you to meet Angelo Barsotti, the man who transformed my life after taking me out of the orphanage. I owe him and his wife everything. Today she's visiting their daughter who just had a baby, so you won't be able to meet her."

"I'm sorry about that."

The farmer removed his cap. "Princess." His gaze swerved to Nico. "Looks like you've done right well for yourself."

"Nico has sung your praises, signor. I'm very happy to meet you. Last week we went out for roast pig. He told me about life with you and how kind you and your wife were to him."

"Nico was a good boy and a hard worker."

"He's an excellent doctor now, but it's obvious he hasn't forgotten those years with you. Would it be possible to see some of your piglets before we leave?"

The farmer grinned. "He said you wanted to play with them. One of our sows just had a litter. Come with me."

Delighted, she followed them to one of the long buildings containing the individual grilled stalls to house all the pigs.

Inside she saw several workers walking up and down the aisles. He led them to a section where the new mother was tending her litter. There were seven spotted piglets who stuck their noses toward them.

"Oh—look, Nico! Aren't they adorable?" She ran over to the fencing. "Can I hold one, Signor Barsotti?"

He laughed. "Go right ahead."

Fausta leaned over and picked one up from the straw. "You sweet little thing," she crooned as it made snorting sounds. Soon all the piglets were making noises, causing her to laugh. The men laughed too. Her gaze fused with Nico's. This was a moment of pure joy she'd never forget.

She walked around with it for a minute, but before the sow got too upset, Fausta lowered the piglet back to the straw. "If I could, I'd take all of you home with me."

They left the building and walked back to his office. "There's a restroom inside, where the two of you can freshen up, Princess."

"Thank you. I'll be right back."

She went inside first. It thrilled her to have met the man who'd given Nico a real home and family until he'd turned eighteen. Fausta thought him and his wife remarkable people.

To give them time alone, she went back to the car and reached for another soda while she waited. The two of them talked and laughed. She got another lump in her throat when she saw them pat each other's shoulder.

"You made a hit with Angelo," Nico said after he got back in the car and they drove away.

"He was so nice. I can understand why you love visiting him. How do you have his last name since you haven't referred to him as your adoptive father? Or did I miss something?"

"They wanted to adopt me even though they had four children. I told them I'd rather not belong to anyone because I wanted to find my birth parents. Deep down I didn't feel worthy of love when my own parents didn't want me. People just automatically thought I belonged to them and the name stuck."

Whoa. He didn't feel worthy? Fausta was only now beginning to understand how much being an orphan had impacted him. Not many children would have turned down the opportunity to be adopted yet go on repaying them for their kindness.

He glanced at her. "I wouldn't blame you if you think that was strange and ungrateful of me, but I assured them I'd work triple hard for them to earn my keep until I could leave at eighteen. I've been sending them money ever since I became a doctor."

"Not strange, Nico. Just amazing that even at the age of twelve, you were so fiercely independent. It's made you into the man you've become." His comments had raised more questions she wanted answers to, but now wasn't the time.

Nico eyed her. "From here we're going to visit a couple. I want you to meet Enzo and Pippa. They're expecting us and have done everything for me since I started working for Angelo. In truth Enzo has been my savior and mentor."

"Savior?"

"He owns the land where Angelo works the pig farm, but let me back up. Angelo came to the orphanage to find a boy he could train who would help on the farm. He chose me and was given special permission to let me live with his family on the farm and go to school with his children.

"I was chosen, but I had to be interviewed by the owner before I could be hired. It seemed that one of the owner's grandsons had died at the age of twelve. I guess I was a reminder of him and he developed an interest in me. He often dropped by the farm to talk to me and we became friends."

"That's very touching."

"In time he took me to his home for visits and saw to

it that I got the best schooling. After I turned eighteen, he paid for me to attend college and medical school in Turin. He and his wife have always had a doctor to take care of them, but I made him a promise that I would also be their personal physician for life after I graduated."

Fausta was dumbfounded by what he'd just told her. It answered so many questions about how he'd gotten from A to B. "Where does he live?"

"In the foothills of Biella not far from here."

They'd reached the outskirts. "So, *they're* the people you take care of."

His dark eyes gleamed. "I visit them every couple of months and always look forward to it."

They drove through the town and up a winding road through the lush foothills to a picturesque estate. When an imposing *castello* appeared through the trees, Fausta drew in her breath.

"I've been here before!" she cried softly.

He'd pulled up in the courtyard and had turned off the engine before looking at her. "I know. You told me you'd been to Biella the night we went to dinner."

"But I mean *this* is the estate where my mother brought me and my sisters for a visit. I recognize the distinctive crenellated walls and the belfry."

Nico's eyes played over her. "You're sure? How old were you?"

"I was around ten. Donetta was thrilled because the owner had some beautiful horses and let us ride. Of course, I'm no champion like my sister. She has a room full of trophies."

"It's true Enzo *is* a great horse lover. Let's go inside."

But no sooner had Nico opened the passenger door

for her than a man with white hair who was probably in his eighties wearing casual clothes came outside to greet them.

"Nicolo—" she heard the man call out before hugging him fiercely. She was struck by the love between the two of them.

As the old man turned to her, he let out a strange sound. "When you told me you were bringing someone with you, I didn't know you meant Princess Fausta Rossiano!"

"Am I missing something here?" Nico looked confused.

The older man moved toward her. "The last time I saw you and your sisters, you were just young girls. It must have been fifteen years ago." He smiled. "The older one rode like the wind."

Fausta smiled back. "I just told Nico I remember coming here. You're Duca Enzo Frascatti of Piedmont, the local magistrate of the area. You're the good friend of Prince Lorenzo, my father's cousin!"

Nico stared at her in wonder.

"Indeed I am. Lorenzo and I are the best of friends. He's the one who advised me to buy a new Sanfratellano stallion from the king's stables in Vallefiore. To think your sister is now the new king's wife! It's a small world, my dear."

"It certainly is. I'm thrilled to meet you again after all this time."

Enzo reached for her hand and kissed the back of it. "This is a joyous day. Come inside and we'll all catch up. My wife, Pippa, and I have lunch waiting for you. She's in a wheelchair and not doing that well, but she's always eager for the next visit from our Nicolo."

Fausta's gaze fused with Nico's. She could tell he was bursting with questions. So was she!

Nico grabbed his medical bag. Together they followed Enzo inside. He walked them through to the main dining room of the sumptuous *castello* Fausta remembered, where his wife sat in her wheelchair at the table. Nico led her around.

"Pippa? Do you remember Princess Fausta? She's the person I brought with me today."

The white-haired older woman studied Fausta out of eyes dimmed by the years. "You were a precious little girl who loved all the animals. My how you've grown up into a beautiful woman."

Fausta blushed. "Thank you, Duchessa. It's so kind of you to have us for lunch."

"Nonsense. Nico is like a son to us. Why don't you be seated so we can talk."

Nico held a chair for Fausta. After they sat down, the staff served them lunch.

The *duca* raised his wineglass. "This is a very happy day. I'd like to make a toast to our Nicolo and the princess. To your health and other things."

After they'd sipped their wine, Pippa eyed Fausta. "When our grandson died, Nico came into our lives and brought us happiness. Did he tell you we wanted to adopt him?" Fausta's eyes met Nico's for a moment. Everyone loved him. "But he was so stubborn, he wouldn't hear of it."

Except that Fausta knew the real reason. Nico's origins had made him feel unworthy of love.

CHAPTER FOUR

THIS OUTING HADN'T turned out as Nico had expected. Fausta fit in seamlessly with Enzo and Pippa. They were all of the same world.

Except for having been born to an unknown man and woman who gave him life, Nico had been beholden to the nuns at the orphanage, the farmer and the *duca* for being allowed to thrive on this earth. Even though he was now a doctor and could earn his daily bread from here on out, Fausta's father was still pressuring her to marry a prince. It didn't matter to him that his daughter had been dating Nico.

For the rest of lunch he talked about his practice and answered their questions about how he and Fausta had met at the hospital. Afterward he gave Enzo and Pippa a physical before he and Fausta left to drive back to Domodossola. Her bodyguard's car followed at a distance.

She turned to him. "Are you able to tell me what happened to Pippa?"

"Last year she fell in the shower and broke her hip. The fall injured both knees and she's in a lot of pain."

Fausta decided she shouldn't ask about Enzo.

"What would they do without your help? You can tell they love you so much."

Nico flashed her a glance. "The feeling's mutual. Luckily their married children live close by and take them to Turin to see their regular doctor when it's necessary. I like to look after them because I love them."

"They're lovely people."

"I know they enjoyed your company and remember your visit years ago. Did you see the way Enzo beamed when he saw you?"

She nodded. "But Angelo was so kind too. Imagine him and his wife taking you to their hearts! It's a wonderful thing they did for you. Their generosity makes you believe in the goodness of the human spirit."

Nico smiled. "Angelo couldn't get over the way you, a princess, gathered that piglet in your arms like it was a baby."

"It *was* a baby." They both chuckled.

The extraordinary woman seated next to him blended in wherever he took her. Today had been a day out of time. Fausta was such great company, he could wish it would go on forever and he had to face the truth. He'd never been in love. But after meeting and being with Fausta for the last two weeks, he knew he'd fallen in love with her. It had happened so fast, he couldn't believe it.

Yet in acknowledging it to himself, it only made him more conflicted. They were relishing each other's company now, but even if she accepted him for who he was, her royal heritage hung between them like a barrier that could prevent them from moving forward.

Before she got out of the car, he needed to tell her what was on his mind. She needed to understand that the visit with Enzo had underlined a problem he could no longer ignore. He pulled in the parking area and shut off the engine. Two other cars were outside, but no one was around except the palace guard.

Her eyes darted to him. "You've been quiet for the last little while. I can tell something's on your mind. I would invite you in so we could talk. But since I know you'll turn me down like you did before, I won't."

He eyed her in frustration. "Fausta—"

"I saw the look on your face when you realized my father's cousin had a connection with Enzo. I know what you're going to say," she interrupted him. "Before long my father will learn through Lorenzo that you and I spent a whole day in the country together and visited Enzo."

His lips thinned. "That's right. Say what you want, but I'm *not* a person on the king's short list of possible suitors for his daughter."

"No, you're not. But that's all nonsense to me. I've told you how I feel about living a normal life."

"Even so, you'll understand why I'm reluctant to go on spending more time with you when we know your parents couldn't be happy about it."

She bowed her head. "I understand more than you think. Thank you for a beautiful day I'll always remember. When we see each other at the hospital, we'll agree to nod and walk on." In the next breath she got out of the car faster than he could believe. "*Addio*, Nico."

As she walked toward the palace doors, he jumped out of the car and hurried toward her. "Wait, Fausta!"

She wheeled around, her features taut. "Why are you prolonging this when you're afraid to be with me?"

"Afraid?" The breath caught in his lungs.

"Well, aren't you?" she asked.

He let out a sound of exasperation. "It's not fear! To continue pursuing you would be pointless for several reasons! But I didn't mean for what I said to come out the way it did. *Per l'amore di Dio*, will you come back to the car and let me explain?"

At first he didn't think he was getting through to her. He stood there in agony until he saw her expression change. "I will for a few minutes."

"Grazie," he whispered.

After opening the car door for her, he got back in his side and turned to her.

Fausta cocked her head. "What is it you want to say that I don't already know?"

"On the day I first met Enzo, Angelo came out to the pen where I was feeding the pigs. He said the owner of the property had come to interview everyone who worked on his land.

"I didn't know Angelo wasn't the owner. He said Duca Frascatti was a great man whose family descended from a former Italian king and had riches I wouldn't be able to imagine. He'd hired Angelo from the village to come and run his pig farm for him. It was a great honor. As such, Angelo told me I had to honor the *duca* like he was a holy person."

"Did that frighten you?"

Nico frowned. "No, but it made me nervous. I didn't want to say anything wrong for fear I'd—"

"Commit a sin?" She smiled. "I saw the cross on the wall in Angelo's office. I imagine the nuns put the fear in you. You poor thing."

Fausta understood a lot. "When the *duca* came, he talked to everyone, but when he interviewed me, he started to weep. I thought I'd done something wrong until he told me I looked like his grandson who'd drowned."

"That's what Pippa said."

"What he said made me very sad. From then on, he asked if he could keep coming to see me and be friends with me. No one had ever taken a personal interest in me that way in my life. With Angelo it was different because I worked for him in a business-type arrangement. He wasn't looking for another son."

"But he wanted to adopt you."

"I know, and I'll never forget. Angelo was the best. As for Enzo, he was the one who talked to my teachers at the village school and took interest in everything I did. One day I was invited to the *castello*. When I look back now, I know Angelo didn't like it, but he had no choice except to let me go."

"I bet he gave you a talking-to before you left," Fausta surmised.

Nico nodded. "He told me it was a great privilege no one was given unless they were also born of a king. He said that I had to be the one exception, but I mustn't presume anything or expect such a gift to ever come my way again."

She stirred. "So *that's* when you learned that there was a line drawn between a commoner and a royal, one you could never hope to cross."

"Exactly. You can imagine how Angelo must have felt today when he came face-to-face with Princess Rossiano, who'd driven here with me. I know he's still trying to figure it out."

"He handled his shock very well. So did you when you found out I'd been to the *castello* before."

Nico nodded. "When I first saw the *castello* and entered it as young teen, I thought I'd died and gone to heaven. But instead of obeying Angelo's counsel, I waited for the attention Enzo showered on me and went there many times.

"Then came a day when he told me my grades at school were excellent, and he was sending me to the university in Turin. I couldn't wait to go. I was overwhelmed by his generosity to me."

"Angelo probably couldn't believe it," she murmured.

"I know he wasn't happy about it. I admit I was surprised he didn't want me to take advantage of the scholarship. He said I'd presumed too much and hadn't learned my lesson. When he warned me that I could never belong to the *duca*'s world, it pierced me with pain and guilt."

"Of course it did!"

"I knew he was jealous of the *duca* who could do things for me he couldn't. It really hurt him when Enzo talked with Prince Lorenzo, who arranged to find me a position at the hospital in Domodossola."

"*That's* why you ended up in my country? I had no idea. How wonderful for you."

"I'm indebted to Enzo in so many ways, you can't imagine. And even though I told Angelo I loved him and would always repay him for his kindness, I knew it was hard on him. But I saw the division between the two men in countless ways and knew what Angelo had said was true about that invisible line."

Fausta let out a deep sigh. "It *is* true, Nico. I found it out in my own painful way four years ago."

"What do you mean?"

"Forgive me if I accused you of being afraid. It's because of an experience in my life that changed the way I look at everything now."

"Go on," Nico urged. "I want to hear it all."

"Let me go back to the beginning. Tano, the chauffeur for my father, lives on the estate with his wife and children. His son Dego was my age. My first memories of childhood include them and my sisters. As we grew up, my friendship with Dego turned to love. We were excited to go to the university here in Domodossola together and eventually marry.

"One day my father told me he'd sent Dego to Rome, Italy, to attend the university there."

A groan escaped Nico because he knew what was coming.

"It turned out my father offered to the pay the college tuition and lodgings for Dego as a thank-you for their service to our family. With tears in Tano's eyes, he praised my father for what he'd done. But the man had no comprehension that he might as well have cut the heart out of my body."

"Fausta—" With every revelation she was removing the scales from Nico's eyes about her perfect life. It answered one question. She'd been in love with a commoner before. Deeply in love.

"I was desolate, knowing immediately what had happened. My father had arranged everything. My sisters had warned me Papa would find a way to separate me and Dego, but I didn't want to believe he could do anything so terrible. Within a year Dego had met and married a girl from Italy."

"I'm so sorry," Nico whispered.

She lifted her eyes to him. "It's all in the past. When I got over the first wave of pain, I was furious with Dego because he didn't fight for me. In my naivete, I'd thought he'd loved me so much, he would have found a way for us to be together and get married no matter what my father did. I hated it that he'd been so afraid.

"In time I realized he couldn't have loved me the way I needed to be loved, otherwise he would have stayed in Domodossola and married me. My father wouldn't have prevented our marriage if Dego had insisted on it. At that point I stopped living in a fantasy world. It taught me a huge lesson."

Nico rubbed his forehead. "I hear everything you're saying," he commiserated, "but as you told me, your father hasn't stopped pressuring you to marry someone he has picked out for you. Palace security knows every move you make and keeps him informed where I'm concerned."

Her head reared, causing her molten hair to float against her shoulders. "He can pressure until doomsday, but I'll do what I want."

"I believe you, but if you defy him, he could cut you off in a way I'm not sure any princess would be prepared for."

"When that day comes, I'll deal with it. Since I now have a greater understanding of how *you* feel, I won't put you in a position that will make you feel guiltier than you already do."

He grasped the hand closest to him. "You have no

comprehension of how I feel," his voice grated. "Guilt has nothing to do with it. The reality is I don't want to make things more difficult for you."

She stared into his eyes. "Do you want to be with me, Nico?"

"You *know* I do."

"I feel the same way. Can't you tell?" Her voice throbbed.

"Yes." He caressed the side of her face. "If you don't have any plans for Monday evening, I'd like to take you to dinner. Your choice. I want to know what Princess Fausta does when she mixes with the commoners."

Her eyes lit up an electric blue. "You're on."

"I'll wait for you out in the parking lot after you go off duty."

"Perfect."

After she'd given his hand a long squeeze he felt through his whole body, she let go and got out of the car. He watched until she'd disappeared inside the palace. On the drive back to his apartment, he didn't know how he was going to wait until Monday evening when they'd be together again.

Realizing he needed a few groceries, he stopped at a local *mercato*. Once he reached home, he showered and got ready for bed before phoning the patients who'd called his service earlier.

With that accomplished, he sat down at the computer in his bedroom and checked any emails that had come in. He'd been paying investigators to find out how and why he'd ended up in an orphanage at the age of two. For the last year he and Enzo had covered northwestern Italy, parts of France, Switzerland and the country of Domodossola with no clues.

Frustrated that nothing had turned up yet, he'd hired other investigators to cover northeastern Italy, including pockets of Austria, Slovenia and the country of La Valazzura. If those searches didn't come up with something substantive, he would be forced to look farther south in Italy.

After going into the kitchen for a snack, he went in the living room, where he'd pre-recorded a soccer game between his alma mater, Torino, and Florence at the Stadio Olimpico Grande Torino. The team had quite a few losses. They were probably going to lose this one too. He didn't really care because he couldn't concentrate. His conversation with Fausta was all that filled his mind. She'd suffered trauma of her own.

Right before the end of the match, his phone rang. He picked up and said hello.

"Nico?"

That breathless voice couldn't belong to anyone else. His heart thudded too hard. "Fausta—are you all right?"

"I am now."

"Be honest with me. Is there something wrong?" Certainly the news that they'd been together all day had reached her father's ears.

"Yes. I had such a wonderful time today, I can't settle down, so I thought I'd bother you. What are you doing?"

"I just finished watching a boring soccer match and my old college team lost. Your call has saved me from severe depression. After our conversation in the car, if you had invited me in your apartment this evening, I wouldn't have said no."

"*Now* you tell me!"

Her answer was totally unexpected, filling a hungry place inside him that had never been fed until she'd come into his life.

Her quiet laugh enchanted him. "Do you mind if I pick your brains for a minute?"

She was a constant surprise to him. "Fire away."

"I haven't been able to get the visit to the orphanage off my mind. How many children does it house?"

He hadn't been expecting that question. "Anywhere from thirty to thirty-five."

"I want to make a donation that will be meaningful. I realize the place needs all kinds of supplies, which I plan to provide. But I'm also thinking about individual gifts that will thrill the children."

Touched beyond words by her generous nature, he sank down on the couch. Visiting the orphanage today had given him ideas too about lending his services to them every time he came to take care of Enzo and his wife.

But the possibility that the investigators might find his mother or father soon stopped him from making a commitment he might not be able to keep. If he tracked down his parents and one of them wanted a relationship, he would relocate if he had to.

"Fausta—it's enough that you want to do this, but your family does too much charity for you to incur such an expense for one facility."

"This will come from my own personal fund, so let me worry about that. Try to imagine what you think the children would want in today's world. What would mean the most to them?"

He took a deep breath. "I'll reflect on it and tell you on Monday when we have dinner. Have you decided where you want to eat?"

"Yes. It's down in the university district. I'm sure you'll love it if you haven't been there before. Now I'm going to get off the phone and give you room to breathe. See you Monday."

His hand tightened on the phone. "Fausta?"

"*Si?*"

The last thing he wanted to do was hang up. "Thanks for the phone call."

"You're a busy doctor. I promise I won't make a habit of bothering you. *Buona notte.*"

CHAPTER FIVE

THE DOMO GRILL featured a live band made up of university students while the clients danced.

The place was always crowded. Over the last few years Fausta and her friends had spent many an evening here. She knew the owner and most of the staff. They treated her like they did everyone else and made her feel totally comfortable.

"If it isn't the *deliziosa* Fausta! I see you've brought another lucky admirer with you. When is it going to be *my* turn?"

"*Buona sera*, Fabbio. We want your signature chicken Parmesan sandwiches with basil and melted provolone, and beer," she said to the fun-loving, cheeky waiter.

"Local or imported?"

"Local," Nico declared before she could speak for him. When the waiter moved away Nico said, "The guy meant it."

She laughed. "Maybe, but I happen to know he has a wife and baby at home. Fabbio is putting himself through college by working two jobs. I'll leave him a big tip."

His eyes played over her. "Want to dance?"

This was one time she couldn't wait to get in her partner's arms. She smiled. "I thought you'd never ask." Fausta had purposely chosen this *cantina* so they could get closer to each other.

They got up and walked over to the packed dance floor. Every woman in the place fastened her eyes on gorgeous Nico in his silky blue sport shirt and trousers. No man compared to him. He put his arms around her and pulled her close. She'd wanted this for so long. After Dego had left four years ago, she never expected to desire a man again.

Fausta inhaled the scent of the soap he'd used in the shower. They moved around other bodies as best they could to the soft rock music. This was heaven with her head against his shaven jaw, his hand splayed across her back as if she were precious to him.

She knew she'd fallen fathoms deep in love with Nico. The man was perfect to her and the fire for him was growing out of control. When he eventually danced them over to their booth, she didn't want to let him go, but she had no choice. They sat down and started to eat.

His penetrating eyes watched her. "The food and beer are excellent. I can't believe I haven't eaten here before now."

"If you'd attended college in Domodossola, this would have been one of your hangouts."

"No doubt."

She finished her sandwich. "Have you decided what kind of gifts I can have sent to the orphanage?"

"After holding you in my arms, I confess the mention of orphanage donations is the last thing on my mind."

Heat filled her cheeks. "I keep thinking about that place."

"All right—since the students attend public school, I think it would be wonderful to set them up with a few computers that can be used at playtime this summer. The nun we met at the orphanage was using one, but I'm sure that's the only one. It would mean a company will have to go out to install them."

"I had thoughts along those lines too, Nico, and plan to arrange for everything. If I bought ten of them, that would allow three or so students on a computer. They could take turns. Time on the computer could be a real incentive to do well in school. What do you think?"

Her generous heart was a constant revelation. "I think I would have given anything to have one when I lived there."

"Good. Then that's what I intend to do. I'll also purchase ten special desks to house them and ten printers and paper so they can print off what they like. I'll arrange for several technicians Lanza and I have used setting up shelters to spend several days downloading the software and showing them how everything works."

"You don't need to do that too."

"I want to. Someone has to show them how. The little children will love to do playtime on them. There are coloring and painting programs for them. The older ones can do science experiments and study the planets."

His penetrating eyes bore into hers. "Your gifts will revolutionize the orphanage."

"Exposure is everything. Besides having fun, they need to be conversant with technology. It will help them get good jobs and go to college if that's what they want."

"You're an extraordinary woman, Fausta."

"Why do you say that?"

"It's evident you love children, but it reveals the measure of your character that you want to do something to better their lives."

"I don't hold a candle to you or your kindness, Doctor Barsotti."

He shook his dark head. "We're not talking about me."

"*I* am. When Angelo said that Enzo had made you an exception to all the rules, he knew what he was talking about. Whoever your parents were, they created a special child."

Nico scoffed.

"It's true!" she declared. "Angelo chose you from the other children in the orphanage to work for him. Enzo picked you out of all the other workers to befriend. It wasn't just your looks that reminded him of his grandson. Both men wanted to adopt you. You carry an aura that sets you apart."

His expression grew solemn. "What am I to say to all that?"

"Nothing. I'm as impressed by you as everyone who so far has had the privilege to be your friend, and I wanted you to know."

"If you've finished eating, why don't we leave here and take a drive." He put some euros on the table. "It's a beautiful night."

Yes! Fausta couldn't wait to be alone with him. Dancing with Nico had only increased her hunger to get closer to him. "I'm ready."

They left the grill and walked to his car in the parking lot. He drove out to the street and headed for the foothills where there was an overlook with the city spread below them. Nico pulled to a stop and turned off the engine. She felt him turn to look at her.

"If I do what I want to do with you, I'm afraid I won't be able to stop."

She angled her head toward him. "If you *don't* do what I'm dying for, I won't be able to stand it."

In the next breath Nico reached for her and lowered his compelling mouth to hers. At the first contact she moaned with desire, needing him like she needed air to breathe. Her arms wound around his neck and she clung to him as they tried to feed their needs that were bursting out of control.

"I've wanted to do this since the first time we met," he admitted, kissing every feature of her face.

She pressed a hot kiss to his mouth. "I've wanted this even before we met." Being with him like this was better than she'd imagined.

"What do you mean?"

"After I was hired, I saw you in the cafeteria several times before you even knew I existed. Mia told me who you were. From then on I hoped we'd meet."

"I remember seeing you too and couldn't get you out of my mind."

"When you came in Tommaso's room, I almost had a heart attack from excitement."

"You weren't the only one," he half growled the words and cupped her face, kissing her with increased passion. "You're the most beautiful thing to come into my life, Fausta. I'm afraid you're becoming far too important to me."

"*Nico*—don't you know that's how I feel too?"

Once again he swept her away, filling her with ecstasy. Then suddenly he lifted his mouth and turned his head. "Another car has pulled behind us. If I don't miss my guess, it's one of your bodyguards taking pictures."

Damn them, she cried inwardly.

"We're getting out of here." In one quick movement Nico let go of her and turned on the engine. Within seconds he took off so fast she heard the squeal of tires.

Fausta knew they were headed for the palace and didn't try to stop him. He wasn't used to being surveilled and she didn't blame him for being frustrated. When they drove around the palace to her private entrance, he turned off the engine and looked at her. In the semidarkness, his eyes blazed. "Are you free Friday evening?"

Her heart pounded with sickening force. "I'll make sure I am."

"Good. I'll pick you up at six and drive you to my apartment, where I plan to cook for you."

His home was the one place where she could be truly alone with him. Joy of joys. "I'll help."

"It'll be enough just to have you there with me. Now I think you should get out, so we don't provide any more entertainment."

She looked over her shoulder and saw the headlights. "Agreed."

He leaned over to give her another hungry kiss before she slid out of the car. All the way past the guard and up the stairs to her apartment she rejoiced that Nico had made the decision to fight for her. She'd known he'd been born exceptional and he was proving it!

* * *

Thursday proved to be a hectic day with overbooking that prevented Nico from walking over to the pediatric ward in time to see Fausta before she went off duty.

Upset because it meant he wouldn't be seeing her until Friday, he phoned her later. To his chagrin, he had to leave a message on her voice mail. He told her he was sorry he'd missed her today because of complications with his schedule. But he would wait for her outside the hospital after work and drive her to his apartment.

She returned his call later, apologizing for not being able to phone him until now. They chatted for a moment about Mia and Felipe, who were planning to get married. How lucky for Felipe that he could marry the woman of his dreams with no complications.

Unfortunately a permanent relationship with Fausta wasn't grounded in reality. He knew it deep in his soul and couldn't go on pretending something that wouldn't happen. When Friday night came, he knew what he had to do to stop what he'd started by pursuing her in the first place.

"See you tomorrow, Fausta. *Buona notte*."

"*Sogni d'oro*, Nico."

When he went to bed, his dreams weren't sweet. They were dark. In the middle of the night he woke up in a cold sweat, disturbed that he was putting Fausta in jeopardy with her family every time they were together.

She wanted a man who would fight for her, but at what price to her? If he were to ask Fausta to marry him, would she be able to handle making the ultimate sacrifice that could mean being cut off from her family? She said her father was a reasonable man, but so far she hadn't fully tested him.

Family was sacrosanct to Nico and had to be to her and her family. Nico didn't want her to have to give up everything in the royal sense in order to be with a man her parents could never approve of. He was tortured by the thought of not seeing Fausta in the future, but he didn't see how they could be together.

Underlying his torment was another more immediate concern. He would never stop trying to find his parents. Nico had to have come from somewhere and felt in his gut he was getting closer to discovering his origins.

In the end he made coffee and planned out some new strategies on the computer using maps until it was time to get ready to go to his office at the hospital. He'd leave the office early enough to hurry home and get dinner started before he picked her up.

"Mmm… Something smells delicious." Nico had just let Fausta inside his miniscule apartment in the university area of the city, the kind most students rented.

"It's my own version of manicotti casserole, one of the few easy dishes Angelo's wife showed me how to make while I lived with them. But the *panfocaccia* comes from the *paneterria* on the corner."

She chuckled. "Here I thought you'd spent all day cooking."

Now that they were alone, she was waiting for him to pull her into his arms. It was all she'd been able to think about. Instead he gave her a five second tour of his sparsely furnished one-bedroom place with its tiny living room and kitchen featuring a square table for two. He'd already set it and had made coffee.

After pulling out a chair for her to sit, he served up the food and brought their plates to the table. "I realize my apartment is probably smaller than the cloakroom off the hospital cafeteria. I hope you don't suffer from claustrophobia."

"Several friends of mine live in apartments this size. Everything's cozy."

He darted her a glance. "In my case it's colorless, but it serves my needs."

Nico's behavior puzzled her. He'd been distant since she'd run out to the car after he'd picked her up. Something had to be bothering him. He hadn't even tried to kiss her. Maybe a scheduling problem hadn't been the real reason for his not showing up on the pediatric ward Thursday evening. She started to feel anxious.

"It hasn't hindered your ability to make us a feast." She drank her coffee. "This *manicotti* is fabulous, Nico. I've had seconds of everything. But now I want to know what's on your mind. Since picking me up, you've been different. I don't believe it has anything to do with my being a princess, or that my bodyguard followed us here and you feel threatened."

He sat back in his chair with his coffee, eyeing her steadily. "You're right. The truth is, I haven't been completely honest with you."

Her heart thudded. "About what?"

"About my life."

She kneaded her hands beneath the table. "I don't understand." Fausta cocked her head, causing her hair to sway against her face. "What exactly are you saying?"

"The facts are that I've always considered my time here in Domodossola to be temporary."

Her expression sobered. "Why? You're an established physician."

"That may be true, but since I earned my first paycheck as a doctor, I've been actively looking for my parents."

She blinked. "Are you serious?"

"Yes. I'm praying to find one or both of them and make them a part of my life if it's possible."

"You mean all these years, despite everything, you've continually hungered for them?"

"That's the right word. When you and I first met, you asked me if I had applied for Domodossolan citizenship. I should have told you then that I planned to put down roots in the country where my parents had been born, where my mother gave birth to me. It's been my goal in life."

"I had no idea, but how hard life must have been for you to feel such an emptiness without them."

He nodded. "You can't imagine. Every day I go to my computer or answer a phone call in the hope that today will be the day I hear the news I've been wanting for years. I have so many questions.

"In what country will I find them? Who was my father? How did my parents meet? Were they the same nationality? Are they both still alive? Had they been married, or had they simply slept together? Had she been a single woman who'd been left abandoned?"

"Oh, Nico," she whispered, lowering her head.

"I've always come back to the notion that my mother could have been like other penniless girls in their teens who was forsaken and had to give up her baby. To my mind that seems the most plausible reason I ended up at an orphanage. If that's the case, I want to find her and help take care of her if she's still struggling and wants to be reunited."

Fausta's eyes had grown misty. "My heart aches for you, Nico. How did you know where to start?"

"I've only been able to work with two available clues. The first was that the Mother Superior told me I'd come to the orphanage at the age of two understanding a few words in Italian. That meant I'd been raised by at least one parent who spoke Italian."

"Of course. What was the second?"

"She told me the exact date I was put in the orphanage. I arrived with five other toddlers at the same time. Why an influx of six children at the same time on the same day, with all of us were wearing the same nondescript clothing?"

"That's all you've had to go on?" she asked.

"It's worse than looking for a needle in a haystack and takes a lot of money to pay the investigators to do the research. That's the reason I live here in a modest, low budget furnished apartment. I keep out enough money to pay for expenses and recompense Angelo. The rest is used to fund the inquiries that so far have turned up nothing, forcing me to go further afield."

"Where have you looked?"

"One of the reasons I decided to be a doctor here was because I thought it was a good place to start my search."

"You mean you might not have come to Domodossola if you hadn't been searching for them?"

"No."

She shook her head. "Then we would never have met."

"I can't imagine it either," he admitted and grasped her hand. "But since your small Italian-speaking country of Domodossola on the northwestern Italian border is only two hours away from the orphanage on the outskirts of Biella, it sounded possible.

"My mother or parents could have lived within that radius before I was put in the orphanage. Unfortunately, a thorough investigation here in this country as well as the region around Biella and Turin hasn't turned up information. At this point I've been investigating elsewhere. The chances are that I could have been born somewhere in northeastern Italy, or parts of Austria, or even in Slovenia or La Valazzura.

"But nothing promising has turned up yet. Right now I'm focusing on the fact that my parents could have come from any country where Italian is spoken. I've been whittling down the possibilities because I refuse to give up."

"You're a truly amazing man."

"Why? Because I want to know my parentage?"

"No, because you don't let anything get in your way."

He drank more coffee. "Angelo has told me he thinks I'm foolish to keep spending my time and money looking for them. The other day he told me that finding my parents wasn't meant to be, that I should accept the situation."

"But Angelo doesn't know your heart," she said with her incredible insight.

"You're right. I'll never give up searching. Enzo has

continued to encourage me and has backed me financially in order to help."

"He's a remarkable man."

"I couldn't agree more. If I should find out that I was born in Domodossola and that one or both of my parents still live here, I'll keep my position at the hospital and live out the rest of my days here. But so far the fruitless searches have proven to me and Enzo that I came from some other part of Italy or Italian-speaking country."

"But you don't know that positively!"

"That's true. What I want you to understand is that once I stumble onto my history and family, whenever that might be, whoever they are, wherever they live outside Domodossola, I could be leaving here and my job for good to be near them. That's assuming they might want to be with me after all this time. In that case, it wouldn't be a good idea for us to go on seeing each other."

A gasp escaped her lips. "Why do you think that?" Her head flew back. The way he was staring at her out of those midnight blue eyes, she knew he meant every word he'd just said.

"Please don't look at me like that, Fausta. I can't promise where I'll be next week, a month, a year, five years, ten years from now. Every day my money goes to pay for researchers doing the footwork for me. I live my life a day at a time and wouldn't ask anyone to share it with me."

She leaned forward. "Why can't you continue making your life here so we can be together? Why is it imperative that you uproot yourself as soon as you learn about your beginnings?

"If you should catch up with your parents—if one

of them or both want to be with you—couldn't you visit them often, or help them to come here to be with you? You could do whatever it would take without turning your whole life upside down," she argued. "And mine…"

He didn't answer right away. Instead he let go of her hand and got to his feet. "Come on. Let's move to the living room, where we can talk and be more comfortable. I need to explain that I don't want to force you to live in limbo while I wait for that day."

Fausta left the kitchen first and sat down on the end of the couch. To her chagrin he sat on a chair opposite her and pulled it closer, clasping his hands between his knees. This evening he'd dressed in trousers and a dark blue polo shirt. She couldn't take her eyes off him.

"What else aren't you telling me, Nico?"

"I learned something about myself when I did my internship. Part of the year I did a rotation in psychiatry. I did that on purpose, not only to get a better perspective on my patients, but to find out what made me tick."

"I can understand that," Fausta murmured.

"Dr. Neri, the director of the psychiatric program for my unit, had long talks with me after hours about my particular situation. He said the uprooting of a child's first emotional attachment from within a family group can be catastrophic.

"According to him, the particular shortcoming of institutional care like the orphanage means that a child like me didn't get the continuity of care no matter how well-meant."

"I'm sure that's true." Her heart was pained for him.

"He said it's almost always impossible to maintain

any kind of continuity because of the high ratio of children to staff. There's always the speed and frequency of staff turnover and the nature of shift work to consider."

She moaned. "You saw that borne out when the Mother Superior and the doctor at the orphanage both died."

Nico nodded. "As the director went on to explain, institutions like the church orphanage have their own culture, which is often rigid and lacking in basic community and family socialization. A child like myself had difficulty forming relationships, even with the other children. I wanted the security I'd been torn from."

"Then why did you refuse to be adopted when it would have given you security?"

Their gazes fused. "Dr. Neri told me my early sense of loss had made it close to impossible for me to trust people. He felt I'd been traumatized to a greater degree than some of the other orphans. I couldn't respond normally to the hand that reached out to me.

"All I wanted was my parents. No one else would do. I grew up and slowly learned to care for Angelo and Enzo, but I never outgrew the need for my birth parents. My loss made me more cautious, even fearful of strangers, and caused me to avoid touching them or accepting affection.

"Though Angelo and Enzo became steady elements in time, he said I'd suffered too much damage early. Thus finding my parents and roots became the paramount driving force of my life. He said I was an unusual case."

She fought the tears stinging her eyelids. "What if you can't ever find them? What if—"

"They're dead?" he finished the question for her

and stood up, putting his hands on his hips. "Dr. Neri warned me about that too."

"What did he say?"

"He suggested that I go in for psychiatric counseling to accept that I might not find answers and enjoy the life ahead of me."

Fausta couldn't agree more. "Did you get help?"

"No. Once I started my next rotation as a general practitioner, I didn't have time. As soon as I graduated, I left for Domodossola to interview for my job at the hospital. I've been inundated with work ever since. But I'll be honest. I readily accepted the position at the hospital because I'd hoped to find my parents here in your country."

His eyes traveled over her. "Instead something else happened. What I never expected was to meet you, the daughter of the king and queen of Domodossola no less. Any more time spent with you puts you in double jeopardy."

Her chin lifted. "And if I were a commoner?"

"But you're not one, Fausta. Whatever happens, I'm on a journey that has to be taken alone. The day could come soon when I'll have to leave Domodossola on a moment's notice. Depending on the circumstances, I might never be back. For this reason, there's no way I can promise you where my life is going, and that's not fair to you when your life is here. You're a princess of the realm."

"If you only knew how I wish I weren't!"

"Listen to me, Fausta. Meeting you has been the most wonderful thing to happen to me in my life. But I've been filled with guilt that I haven't been totally honest with you about my unknown future. You deserve so much more."

"I don't deserve anything! All I want is to be with you. Can't you accept that?"

He rubbed his chest absently. "I want to be with you too, but I'm worried about us getting any more involved. If we stop seeing each other now, there's no harm done."

Suffocating with pain at this point, she shot to her feet. *No harm done? When I'm madly in love with you?* Fausta's heart cried.

Every word had driven the knife a little deeper. Ice had to flow through his veins for Nico to say something like that to her. She would never have thought it possible.

"Are you telling me you can walk away from your patients too? And what about Felipe's wedding? He thinks you're going to be his best man. I thought you'd made a commitment to Enzo and Pippa to take care of them."

His features hardened. "I plan to follow through with everything for as long as I'm still here."

While Fausta was capable of functioning, she opened her purse, unable to handle what he'd just told her. Pulling out her cell, she started to call her limo driver, but Nico took it from her and hung up. The touch of his hand sent waves of desire through her. He'd read her mind.

"I picked you up and I'm driving you home." His fierce tone stopped her from arguing.

"Then I'd like to leave now."

Fausta reached for her purse and walked out the apartment door first. In exquisite pain, she struggled not to break down as they headed for the parking area at the side of the building.

He helped her in the car. After shutting the door, he got behind the wheel and they took off for the palace at the north end of the city. "I should never have reached out to you. Nobody had to tell me I was playing with fire. I don't dare touch you again and you know why."

"You don't owe me any explanation. Once again, I've made a mistake over a man. I don't believe your reason for breaking up with me, Nico, but that's your affair. You and I have both been fools to spend time together."

The tension between them was palpable. So was the silence.

When they reached the palace, she brushed some hair out of her face. "Just so you know, I intend to carry out my idea to have computers installed at the orphanage. You won't have to do deal with any of it."

"Fausta—"

"Please don't say anything, Nico. I get it that you're on a quest for your life. Interestingly enough, so am I. More than ever in fact." She couldn't stay in Domodossola as long as Nico was still here.

The second he pulled up to the side entrance, she opened the door and got out. Before she shut it, she said, "I hope to heaven that one day your dream will come true. *Addio per sempre.*"

CHAPTER SIX

AFTER TELLING NICO goodbye forever, Fausta rushed past the guard and up the stairs to her apartment. No sooner had she entered her room than her cell phone rang. In her heart of hearts, she wanted it to be Nico. She pulled it out of her purse. To her surprise the caller ID said it was her sister Lanza.

She picked up. "Lanza?"

"I'm glad you answered."

"I just got home."

"I know. Stefano and I had taken Ridolfo to visit with the parents when security let them know you'd arrived. I'm afraid you're going to be getting a visit in a few minutes, and I'm sure you know why."

Fausta had told Lanza she was dating a doctor from the hospital, but she hadn't told her anything else. "I do."

By now Enzo would have told Lorenzo about her visit to the *castello* with Nico. It had been only a matter of time before the news reached her father's ears. Fausta drew in a deep breath. She was ready for them.

"Thanks for the heads-up."

"If you want to talk later, call me."

"You know I will."

"Remember I'm on your side."

"Love you, Lanza. Give little Rufy a kiss for me." That was her nickname for him.

"I've already given him dozens when Stefano has given me a chance." She laughed.

After clicking off, Fausta changed into a nightgown and robe while she waited for her parents. Until they talked, she didn't have the luxury to break down sobbing. Not yet.

Before long Fausta heard a familiar knock and hurried to the door to let them in. She gave them both a hug. "Lanza told me you were on your way up. Come in."

They walked into her living room and sat down on the couch opposite her. Her father smiled. "We haven't seen a lot of you lately. When we learned you'd come home, we thought we'd drop in for a few minutes."

"I presume you've had a talk with your cousin Lorenzo, so I can guess that's why you're here."

Her parents glanced at each other before her father said, "I must admit we've been surprised to learn you've been dating a Dr. Nico Barsotti from the hospital for some time."

Her mother sat forward. "We were even more surprised to learn that you drove to Biella with him and spent time with Enzo and Pippa. It would have been nice if we'd known about your association with this doctor before hearing about it from cousin Lorenzo. How did you meet him?"

Fausta sat on her legs in her favorite chair. "I've been doing a little part-time volunteer work at the hospital four days a week on the pediatric ward. He's a family practice doctor who was checking up on a patient and we became acquainted." That was the simplified version.

"I'd say it's more than an acquaintance at this point," her father asserted. "I understand you spent time at his apartment in town this evening."

"Yes. Nico made dinner for us."

A frown marred his features. "If the press finds out, the publicity won't be good for the doctor, whom Lorenzo tells me he helped get taken on at the hospital last year. As for you, any mention in the media could color your prospects for the kind of royal marriage we'd like to see for you."

Her cheeks grew hot. "Don't worry, Papa. You don't have to find a new position for Nico in Rome to keep us apart. He would never accept your money to get him settled in order to salvage his reputation or mine." Once he had a lead on his parents, Nico would leave the country on his own.

Her mother looked pained. "I can't believe you spoke to your father like that, Fausta Rossiano."

Neither could she, considering his heart condition. For the first time since she learned he had heart trouble, she'd forgotten because she was in so much pain over Nico. But never again!

"I'm sorry, Papa, and meant no disrespect. I hope this hasn't distressed you too much. The fact is, neither of you needs to be concerned. Earlier tonight Nico and I ended our relationship."

When he did come over to the pediatric ward to look in on a patient, he wouldn't find her there. She'd leave fifteen minutes early every evening to escape.

"Mia figlia—" Her father eyed her soulfully. "Why

is it you continue to refuse the suitable men who've wanted to get to know you? All your mother and I want is your ultimate happiness. Prince Cesare is very anxious to spend time with you."

Fausta slowly got to her feet. "I know that, but I have to be attracted, Papa."

"Darling," her mother spoke up. "If you'll give some of them the opportunity to be with you, I know you'll meet one who will steal your heart."

If only her parents knew. Tonight her heart had already been ripped out of her body...

Right now, she was in such agony, she was desperate to be alone. "If you don't mind, I have a headache and need to get to bed." *I need to phone Aunt Ottavia and get away from here.* "Please forgive me."

Her father stood up first and gave her another hug. "Don't be upset with me, *dolcezza*."

"I'm not, Papa. You need to know I never want to hurt you or Mamma." She kissed him and her mother before walking them to the door. "See you tomorrow. *Buona notte.*"

The second they left, Fausta ran to her bedroom and reached for her cell phone. Her whole body was shaking. Thankfully her aunt answered.

"Fausta, darling—how wonderful you're calling me!"

"I hope you'll still think it's wonderful when I ask if I can come tomorrow and stay with you for a few days."

"Nothing would make me happier! I can tell something's wrong, but I won't ask right now. You can tell me after you get here."

Tears had started to gush down her cheeks. "You're a

lifesaver, Zia. I'll let you know my arrival time as soon I've made arrangements." She had to let the hospital know she wouldn't be able to volunteer her services for the next week. Something unavoidable had come up. "Love you."

"Love you, *cara*."

Fausta hung up and threw herself across the bed, utterly gutted by what Nico had told her. To never know his love because he felt he had to take his journey through life alone? It would surprise her if she were still alive by morning, let alone physically able to fly far away from the man who'd changed her world forever.

Late Monday afternoon a fragmented Nico had just dealt with his last patient when his cell phone rang. It wouldn't be Fausta. He'd made certain of that by the brutal way he'd broken off with her. Though ending their relationship had been the only fair thing to do, he'd been in agony since driving her back to the palace on Friday night. Another minute in his apartment and he would have taken her to bed.

Nico was aching for Fausta and didn't dare be around her now. Otherwise that whole speech he'd made that they couldn't be together anymore would have been for nothing. Aware she was his weakness, he'd promised himself that if he had a patient admitted to the hospital today, he would ask Dr. Silvio from the medical group to make the rounds.

He glanced at the caller ID and frowned. It was the *duca*. Something had to be wrong for him to phone this soon after the last visit to Biella.

"Enzo?" he blurted after clicking on.

"I'm glad you answered, *mio ragazzo*. Since I know you're busy, I'll make this fast. Can you come to the *castello* tomorrow? I wouldn't ask if it weren't of the most vital importance."

Nico's hand tightened on his cell in reaction. "Did Pippa fall again, or are you having trouble breathing? Tell me the truth."

"Calm yourself. It's nothing medical, but we *must* talk."

Maybe this call had to do with the fact that Enzo had been chatting with his friend Prince Lorenzo. By now the king knew about Nico and Fausta. Enzo could be warning him there was trouble ahead. That made the most sense, but after Friday night, Nico had already taken care of the problem and was one step ahead of him.

"Enzo—why don't you just tell me what's on your mind right now?"

"No, no. I have to see you in person." *Why?* Nico didn't understand. "Can you get someone to cover for you for the day?"

His brows lifted in reaction. Enzo was being surprisingly mysterious and insistent. "Yes, of course." After all the older man had done for him over the years, he could never turn him down. "I'll come first thing in the morning."

"*Grazie*, Nicolo."

The click sounded before Nico could even say goodbye.

Curious and intrigued by the nature of Enzo's unexpected call, he hurried out to the front desk.

"Dina? An emergency has arisen, and I'll have to be

out of the office until Wednesday. Would you call the patients scheduled for tomorrow and make other appointments for them? If one of them needs to be seen immediately, ask Dr. Silvio's nurse to fit them in." The two doctors helped each other when necessary.

"I'll take care of it, *dottore*."

He nodded and left the building. After grabbing some dinner and doing errands, he drove to his apartment and checked any new emails before getting ready for bed. The urgency of Enzo's strange request had happened at a vulnerable moment for Nico, who needed to keep busy.

If that phone call hadn't come when it did, he might have found himself walking over to the pediatric ward. His pact with himself was so fragile, he knew every honorable intention would have been lost the moment he'd seen Fausta.

Eventually he went to bed, but sleep was lost on him. He'd put Giorgio on his dresser, but the sight of him was so painful, he put him in the closet. At five in the morning he rolled out of bed to shower and shave before taking off for Biella. He brought his medical bag just in case.

During the trip, he relived that day with Fausta in the country. The unforgettable memories of her while they visited the orphanage and the pig farm made him groan with longing for her.

By seven thirty a.m. he arrived at the *castello* full of questions. A limo with smoked glass was parked in the courtyard. Something was going on. Nico expected that Enzo was out for his morning horseback ride. Curious, he walked around the rear to the stable first. Sure enough, he found his mentor emerging from the stalls with a trim, distinguished-looking, well-dressed man.

Silver threaded his dark hair and clipped beard. He was of average height and probably in his early sixties. Nico had never seen him before.

Enzo hurried toward him. "Nicolo—you're here even sooner than I'd expected!"

"After your phone call, I almost came last night."

While they hugged, he could feel the other man's steel gray eyes riveted on him as if in disbelief. It gave him an odd feeling.

After letting him go, Enzo turned to the other man. "What do you think, Signor Bruno?"

The visitor walked around them while he kept studying Nico. "The resemblance is uncanny, Signor Frascatti. There can be no mistake. Even without a DNA match, he's the one without question."

The man spoke Italian with a noticeable Slovenian accent. What did he mean "he's the one"? Nico's gaze darted back to Enzo for clarification.

"Dr. Nico Barsotti? May I introduce you to Signor Basil Bruno. He's the head of the secret service for the country of La Valazzura who has been our visitor at the castello."

What kind of business did Enzo have with this man? "How do you do." Nico shook hands with him. La Valazzura bordered Italy and Slovenia. That explained his accent.

"You have no idea how pleased I am to meet you at last, Dr. Barsotti. I'm here on official business for my country."

Nico shook his head. "What am I missing here?"

"I understand you've been searching for your parents since you were old enough to ask the Mother Superior of the Sant'Agate Orphanage where your mamma was."

Nico's heart started to thud. No one knew that information except Enzo, and more recently, Fausta.

"It pains me that over all these years, your heritage has had to remain a complete secret in order to save your life."

What? "Are you saying they're alive?" The mention of Nico's family filled him with an excitement he'd never known before.

"No. I'm sorry to have to tell you they are not." Just as quickly, Nico's spirits plummeted. "Your mother, Nedda Corelli, living on her own with you far from the capital in the village of Mesecino near the Slovenian border, died soon after you turned two years old."

The news shook Nico to his core. The woman who'd brought him into the world and had raised him for his first two years was gone? Just when her existence had been revealed? He couldn't bear it. In his dreams he'd imagined a reunion that would make up for the years he'd missed.

"And my father?" he asked in a hoarse voice.

"He died ten days ago in the capital city of Azzura after being bedridden with heart failure for the last six months."

Only ten days ago he'd been alive? Nico was aghast.

"With his death I've finally been able to bring you out of hiding."

What in heaven's name was the man saying? "Are you sure *I'm* the person you should be telling this to?"

"Without question, but let's begin at the beginning. Yesterday I flew here to meet with Duca Frascatti."

Sick with pain and shock, Nico looked at Enzo. "How long have you known about all this?"

"I knew nothing until last evening, Nicolo."

"The *duca* has been in the dark like everyone else," Signor Bruno explained. "But through my sources, I've known about his association with you for years. Last evening we spent hours talking about you and the remarkable life you've led so far."

Nico shook his head. "Forgive me if I'm still incredulous."

"Who wouldn't be? However, I've shown him all the documentation he needed and he can vouch for me."

A warm sun shone down on Nico, but he felt a chill. "I trust Enzo with my life, which means I'm willing to hear you out."

"I'm glad you said that because now that you've arrived, I have the great honor to fill in the missing facts about your origins and heritage. But for both your sake and the *duca*'s, maybe we should go inside and sit down to talk. This will take some time."

Nico didn't move a muscle. "Who am I, signor?"

The man smiled. "You're very direct and so much like your father, who was my close friend, it's uncanny." Maybe Nico was dreaming. "You were legally christened Massimo by your mother, a fitting name for you since it means 'the greatest.' You were her treasure and the joy of her life."

With those words Nico found it difficult to swallow.

"To fully answer your question, you are the illegitimate, only born, living child of Carlo Umberto Fernando di Savoia, king of La Valazzura."

King Carlo had been Nico's father?

He staggered in place while the world reeled on its axis. Nico remembered hearing something about the king's recent death on the news. He thought he must be hallucinating.

Stupefied by what he'd just been told, he glanced at Enzo for verification.

A smile lit up his mentor's eyes that was unmistakable. "You're King Carlo's son, all right. From a photograph I've been shown, you look so much like he did in his twenties, I thought I was seeing double."

"It's true," Signor Bruno corroborated. "Here. You can keep this." He handed Nico a two-by-three-inch black-and-white photo from his breast pocket.

With a trembling hand, Nico reached for it. After one look at the man in the picture, he gasped aloud. Enzo had spoken the truth. Nico and King Carlo were father and son all right. Same height. Maybe not mirror images, but incredibly close in coloring and bone structure.

Nico cleared his throat. "Do you have a photo of my mother?"

"I do. This is yours too."

In the next instant Nico found himself gazing at a young, beautiful dark blonde woman in a skirt and sweater. Right away Nico saw certain resemblances to himself. He could well understand his father's attraction to her.

"You have some of her facial features. It's hard to tell in that picture, but her eyes were a light brown. However, yours are a piercing dark blue like your father's."

Incredibile! "Did my mother have royal blood?"

"No. She was a commoner."

Like me.

Nico still felt like one as he held the photos side by side. For twenty-eight years he'd longed for the sight of the two people who'd brought him into this world. His father had been a married man and a king who'd had an affair with a nonroyal. Nico had been the result. He was still trying to take it all in.

"Sadly, his Majesty died ten days ago. He has left his childless wife, Queen Liliane, on the throne. With her consent, I flew straight here to talk to you once the funeral was over."

So much news staggered Nico. He could only stand there staring at him. Enzo's firm hand gripped his shoulder. "Come inside, Nicolo. You've had the shock of your life."

The three of them walked to the side entrance of the *castello* and went inside to the main floor *soggiorno*. Nico had no remembrance of how they got there. Pippa had joined them.

She wheeled herself over to the couch where he'd sat down. "We always knew there was something exceptional about you. Angelo told us the same thing after observing you at the orphanage. When I spoke with the Mother Superior, she predicted you'd been placed there by God for a unique reason. She claimed that one day all would be revealed."

Tears filled her eyes. "That day has finally come, and we couldn't be happier for you. You're the son of a great king. It all fits."

"Pippa—" He struggled to say her name, but he was

too overwhelmed to think, let alone talk. After studying the photos once more, he put them in his shirt pocket.

"There's much to tell you," Signor Bruno broke in. "I understand you've never traveled to La Valazzura. The name of our beautiful country comes from its many blue lakes hidden in the mountains that are covered in pine trees. In the fifteenth century it was a free imperial enclave of self-ruling and autonomy, represented in the imperial diet, subordinate only to the Holy Roman emperor."

Unable to stay seated, Nico walked around for a minute while he attempted to process what he was hearing.

"Our country speaks Italian and some Slovenian. It has undergone a civil war started by your father's cousin almost thirty years ago. Giuseppe Umberto, now sixty-three, has tried many times to bring about a coup that would take your father down. He never succeeded, but there was an interminable amount of suffering that cost thousands of lives. There were many attempts on the life of your father.

"For a short time at the beginning of the rebellion, your father had a mistress, who conceived his child at a time when his marriage to the queen went through a bad period. They couldn't have children. Though she wanted to adopt, he wanted a child of his own body. Like you, he wanted his own blood. No one else's."

Nico's eyes closed tightly for a minute.

"The two of them became estranged because of it. For a short time he sought comfort elsewhere. When Carlo learned Nedda was pregnant, he had her installed in her own apartment in Mesecino on the other side of the country and provided for her needs.

"He didn't want to embarrass the queen, whom he loved despite their problems. Naturally he wanted to protect Nedda and you, the only son he would ever have.

"But when full war broke out, Carlo begged me to take both of you out of the country where you and your mother would be far from danger. Unfortunately, she was severely injured and died in the hospital before she could be rescued. I had her buried there, then I brought you to the orphanage here in Italy."

"Did my father know I was still alive?"

"No. I didn't dare tell him, or he would have insisted on my bringing you back to the palace. It wasn't safe at that time. The queen could never have handled it, and both of you, maybe all three, could have been assassinated by followers of Giuseppe."

The story was stranger than fiction, but it was Nico's story. By now he was riveted.

"There were many refugees. I decided to take five other orphaned children who'd lost their parents to safety with you. Since then, all five have been adopted. But apparently you didn't want to belong to anyone except your own parents."

"No," Enzo conceded. "As you've discovered, Nicolo was always his own person."

The other man chuckled. "Just like your father. You have to understand that the king was a target for years. His evil cousin wanted the power. Word got out that your father had a mistress and a baby. For that reason, no one could know where you'd been put in hiding for fear of assassination. Not even the church in Turin or the Mother Superior ever knew they were housing the son of King Carlo."

This was all too much. "What about the queen?"

"Incredibly the secret stayed intact from her. But now the prime minister of our government is calling for a new king. On one side, Giuseppe wants desperately to attain the throne and has been the root cause of the unrest. He's super ambitious and doesn't have the love of the country, but he commands his own army. The second your father's funeral was over, I took the queen aside and told her you were alive."

Nico groaned. "I'm the love child she could never have. How she must despise me!" he bit out.

"Not despise. Like everyone else, Liliane believed you'd died with your mother. To learn that there's a part of him alive in you has come as a tremendous shock. Their inability to have children caused real trouble in their marriage. I'm sure her pain over his affair will continue to stay with her, but she believed in him and the monarchy.

"The fact is, your father was well loved and she knows it. No matter her bitterness, if you—his son— are equal to the task and have his same remarkable genes, she'll sense it after meeting you. If she thinks you could fill your father's shoes after the parliament guides and helps you learn how to rule, her opinion will weigh heavily with them because she's revered by most of the people too."

A strange sound escaped Nico's throat. "I'm sorry, but I don't know how she can she feel anything but the fiercest resentment of me. It wouldn't surprise me if she wished I were dead."

"That's for you to find out if you decide to meet her."

"*Cara Dio!* Did the queen know my mother?"

"She met her once."

"I can't imagine any good coming out of this."

"Would you rather I hadn't contacted the *duca*? Do you wish you didn't know anything?"

His jaw hardened. "I don't know if I have an answer to that question."

"Again, your frank honesty reminds me of your father. Will you do me the great honor of flying back to La Valazzura with me today, Your Highness? That's who you are to me even though you're still the uncrowned Prince. I've already arranged for your bodyguards."

Out of all the possibilities Nico had entertained when considering his origins, he could never have made up a scenario like this.

"The royal jet is waiting at the airport in Turin. Every moment we hesitate, your father's cousin is attempting to mount another coup that is gaining momentum. But the arrival of King Carlo's son could change the tide."

"How can the queen possibly be okay with this?"

The other man shook his head. "It's important for you to know Carlo mourned the loss of his precious little dark-haired Massimo every day of his life. He was there at your birth and took you to his heart. If your father were alive, he would beg you to carry on his legacy. With training and advisers to help you, you're the only man on earth who can."

Me? The illegitimate son? A doctor with no credentials to govern? A grieving queen who has been betrayed in the most cruel of ways?

A shudder racked Nico's body. How did all that work?

"Since the *duca* has told me how you've longed to

know your parents, then now's the time for you to meet with the one person who knew your father far better than anyone besides me. If nothing comes from your visit and you wish to return to the life you've made, Liliane can at least answer the many questions you've had in your heart all these years."

Nico stopped pacing. Only four days ago he'd bared his soul to Fausta.

Whatever happens, I'm on a journey that has to be taken alone. The day could come soon when I'll have to leave Domodossola on a moment's notice. Depending on the circumstances, I might never be back.

The three day visit to Ottavia in Rome accomplished one thing Fausta had needed to put one foot in front of the other again. Her aunt encouraged her to follow through with her idea to give computers to the orphanage. Doing something of worth for those children would force her to set aside her heartache over Nico for a little while.

Fausta flew from Rome to Turin to meet with officials at church headquarters. They were delighted that Princess Rossiano from Domodossola wanted to donate such a gift to the Sant'Agate Orphanage and they talked with the Mother Superior to make the arrangements.

After receiving the necessary permission, Fausta flew home to Domodossola to touch base with her contacts. The next day she drove to Mottalciata and booked a room at one of the village's hotels. She knew she'd have to be there for quite a while.

The Mother Superior couldn't have been more excited. Since there was so little room at the orphanage, she had the desks with the computers and printers set up in the large common room. Five were placed at one end. Five others were put at the opposite end with the piano and toys in between.

As soon as more electrical outlets had been installed, two men set the computers up with the software and they were in business. Since Fausta was computer savvy, she planned to stay in the village for as long as it took to work with each student. She wouldn't leave until they were competent enough to have fun on them without help.

When everything was ready, the Mother Superior took Fausta into the big dining room and introduced her. The children were finishing their dinner. They had no idea who she was or that she'd been the one responsible for the gifts. That was the way Fausta wanted it.

The Mother Superior clapped her hands. "Children? I'd like you to meet Signorina Rossiano. She's the person who is going to show you how to use the computers and printers that were donated to us."

The children shouted with excitement. They attended the local school during the school year and were dying to get their hands on them. Fausta remembered Nico telling her he'd have given anything to work on one.

As she looked at each of the children, she could picture Nico, who'd spent ten years eating meals in this room, and felt a fierce tug on her heart. At the moment there were twenty-nine children from the ages of six to fourteen.

"You'll have to learn how to use them in shifts. Right now we'll start with Emilio, Eva, Nicoletta, Paolo, Sergio, Remo, Teresa, Guido, Maria and Nicolo."

Just hearing that last name caused Fausta's pulse to pick up speed.

"Follow Signorina Rossiano to the common room. Once your turn is over, more of you will be called until everyone has had a chance before it's bedtime."

Teaching the children how to work on the computer turned out to be pure joy for Fausta. She'd never had so much fun in her life.

Since school was out for the summer, she was able to work with the children in shifts throughout the day. They were smart and caught on fast.

By the following Monday she realized it wouldn't be long before they didn't need her anymore. That put her in a panic. As long as she kept busy, she couldn't agonize openly over Nico until she went to bed.

Fausta decided that when she went back home in a few more days, she would do a fund-raiser to buy more computers and have them installed in other orphanages around Domodossola. Finally she had a cause of her own, separate from Lanza's.

The children's hunger to learn the latest technology convinced her it was a worthy cause in many ways and would help her deal with her pain. But she'd never get over losing Nico. That wasn't possible.

CHAPTER SEVEN

AFTER NICO'S TRIP to La Valazzura, he returned to Domodossola the next Monday morning and drove straight to his office. But this time *he* was the one who had a contingent of bodyguards from La Valazzura following him.

The dozens of messages both on his phone and email account would have to wait. Several were from Felipe and Dr. Silvio. None of them were from Fausta of course.

After working through a full day's schedule of patients, he hurried over to the pediatric ward to find her. Fausta had been burdened with his personal pain and had felt it. He wanted her to know her prayer for him had been answered. His long search to find his parents had been miraculously realized.

If she'd already gone home from the hospital, he'd drive to the palace and wait for as long as it would take to see her. He'd been reborn into a new world he had no affinity for. There was only one person he wanted to talk to about the tumult going on inside him and he needed her.

He stopped at the nursing station. "Where can I find Princess Fausta?"

The nurse looked up. "She's not here. Last Monday Signorina Vitale told us that the princess now has a royal commitment that prevents her from doing any more volunteer work for the hospital for an indefinite period. It's a shame because she's the children's favorite person."

That was Nico's fault. Feeling as if he'd been stabbed, he thanked her and left the hospital. En route to pick up a quick meal he phoned Fausta, but could get only her voice mail. After asking her to call him back immediately, he drove home and went to the kitchen to make a pot of coffee. He might be up all night waiting to hear from her and needed fortification. Maybe he'd done too much damage and no amount of persuasion would get her to call him.

Before he'd left the baroque palace in Azzura, he'd made a solemn promise to the prime minister and Basil. In one month's time he'd tell them if he wanted to try and fill his father's shoes. But it all depended on the queen. She had yet to consider if she could accept him, let alone back him.

Until he heard from Liliane, Nico needed the next thirty days to do the most serious soul-searching of his life. But he couldn't do any of it without talking to Fausta.

A few minutes after nine his phone rang. He grabbed it. When he saw who was calling, he almost had a heart attack before clicking on. "Fausta?"

"Nico? What kind of emergency would require you

to talk to me when we said our goodbyes over a week ago?"

"Something earthshaking. I tried to find you on the pediatric ward and was told you weren't there. You should know that the nurse said they're all in mourning you can't come in to volunteer for a while. You were their favorite."

"That's very kind of her."

"Because it was the truth! Are you still in Rome?"

After a silence she said, "No. Why do you ask?"

"Because I have to see you in person. When will you be back at the palace?"

"Not for a while."

He took a quick breath. "Where are you?"

"Mottalciata."

He rubbed the back of his neck. "What are you doing there?" As if he didn't know.

"I've been here for close to a week doing business with the orphanage."

No doubt having computers installed. She'd said she planned to make it a priority. He stifled a moan. "Where are you staying?"

"At a hotel in the village."

"Which one of the two?"

"Nico—"

"It doesn't matter. I'll find you because I'm coming right now." He hung up and flew out of his apartment after throwing a few necessities into a bag.

Two hours later he drove by the first hotel, trailed by his bodyguards. He saw several cars parked outside. Because one was unmarked, it had to be her bodyguard. He jumped out and hurried inside to the front desk.

But before he could ask the man who'd just come out to the counter to ring her room, Fausta emerged from the staircase, her golden hair flouncing. She had to have been watching for him. With a face and body like hers, she was so gorgeous it took his breath away. She'd dressed in beige pleated pants and a tan colored crew neck top with short sleeves.

"I don't care if it's close to midnight." He spoke first. "I need to talk to you. We can go out to my car or up to your room. The choice is yours."

She rubbed her hands over womanly hips in what he perceived was a nervous reaction. "Follow me."

On the way up to the second floor, he had to stop himself from reaching out to pull her against him. Her room was the second one on the right, adequately furnished with a TV. If the owner downstairs had any idea who she was…

"Sit down, Nico." She indicated one of the chairs at the table before she sat on the other one and crossed one elegant leg over the other. Her suitcase lay open at the end of her bed. Through the bathroom door he could see a robe hanging. The room smelled faintly of her flowery fragrance.

"You look wonderful," he murmured.

"So do you. When I heard this was an emergency, I figured you couldn't have driven here if you were incapacitated. Since I've worked with children all day and am exhausted, why don't you tell me why you drove here so I can go to bed? I don't think the hotel is full in case you need a room."

"Fausta—I received a call from Enzo. He demanded I cancel the appointments with my patients and come to the *castello*. I couldn't imagine what he wanted, particularly when he insisted it wasn't for medical reasons. When I arrived there the next morning, I found him with a visitor who'd come from La Valazzura to see him."

Her blue eyes flickered. "That's interesting. Papa wanted to fly there for the funeral of King Carlo, a ruler he admired who died recently, but the doctor wouldn't okay it."

Nico couldn't help but wonder if that admiration would influence Fausta's father for good when the truth came out about him. "I'm sorry he didn't get the opportunity." *I'm sorry I didn't either.*

She eyed him steadily. "You haven't told me about your emergency yet."

"The man who visited Enzo was Basil Bruno, the head of the secret service for King Carlo and Queen Liliane."

Her eyebrows furrowed in a gentle frown. "What did he want with Duca Frascatti?"

"He knew Enzo was my mentor."

Fausta sat straighter. "Why did that matter to him?"

This was it. His heart pounded extra hard. "It was Signor Bruno who placed me in the Santa'Agate Orphanage when I was two."

A cry escaped her lips.

"My legal name is Massimo. During the beginning of their civil war, I was taken to safety and am the only living son of King Carlo Umberto Fernando di Savoia."

The world stood still for a minute.

"Nico—" Her gasp filled the room.

"For the last week I've been in La Valazzura learning

as much about the lives of my parents and my heritage as I could absorb before flying back. You were the one person I wanted to see, but you weren't at the hospital. I never meant to hurt you. It killed me to learn you'd stopped volunteering because of me."

"None of that matters." She wiped her wet face with the backs of her hands. "Nothing is as important as knowing that in the last week you've found your life! You have answers to all your questions. There couldn't be a greater gift! You're the son of King Carlo? How absolutely fantastic. Who would have imagined?"

"Certainly not Angelo."

"No," she said with a laugh as more tears escaped her lashes.

"Especially when he learns I'm the *illegitimate* son."

The smile slowly faded from her face. "What do you mean?"

"My father betrayed the queen during a bad time in their marriage. They could never have children. He had an affair with my mamma, who was a commoner. Her name was Nedda Corelli."

"Oh, no," she half groaned. "Did you spend time with her?"

"That would have been impossible. She was killed during the war that swept the country. To preserve my life, I was taken to the orphanage in secret by Signor Bruno."

Fausta got up from the chair and came to kneel in front of him. "I'm crushed you never did get to meet either parent." She grasped his hands, lifting those iridescent blue eyes to him. "Do you wish you'd never found out about your life?"

After a long pause he said, "Basil asked me the same question. I told him I didn't know how to answer him. I still don't."

She let go of his hands and got up to sit on the side of the bed. "That's because you're grieving over the parents you never got to know."

"It's more than that, Fausta. Every time Queen Liliane looks at me, she's torn apart all over again, hating the horrible truth that her husband had carried on an affair with my mother. I'm the son who should have been Liliane's. It's a monstrous scenario."

"I agree," Fausta said in a quiet voice, "and I can't imagine her pain or yours. But if you will look beyond it for a moment, you now know who you are and where you came from. You don't have to go through the rest of your life wondering and waiting."

He stared into her eyes. She was making sense. "That's true."

"After I flew to Rome to be with my *zia* Ottavia, I unloaded on her. As we talked, I began to realize it was selfish of me to be hurt by your decision that we end our relationship. All these years you've been on a journey that needed to be taken alone. I understand that better now. I'll admit I didn't like it, but I refused to wallow in my pain and decided to concentrate on helping the orphanage."

There was no one like Fausta. "So you don't mind my trying to reach you tonight?"

Her chest rose and fell visibly. "I would *never* have forgiven you if you hadn't." The fierceness of her tone convinced him she'd meant it. "What's going to happen now?"

Nico got up from the chair and walked around for a minute before turning to her. "Since my parents have died and are buried, I can go on with my life being a doctor here in Domodossola."

She lifted her head to look at him, but her sober expression gave no indication of what was going on inside her. "Or?" she prodded. "You're being pressured to become the next king."

Fausta hadn't grown up the daughter of a king for nothing. "I've been approached by Basil and the prime minister to consider it."

"That isn't surprising. A while back at breakfast I remember Papa saying how tragic it was that there was no son to inherit the throne of La Valazzura."

"Your father spoke the truth. Unfortunately, it's criminal that the only one is the bastard love child who is infinitely unqualified to be the head of the country."

"I don't know." A smile broke out on her beautiful face. "You've been a pig farmer. That has to count with all the farmers who need their king to understand the industry that feeds its citizens."

"Be serious, Fausta."

"I'm being very serious. You're a doctor at a time when health care is the chief concern of every head of state on earth. No one could know more about it than you. For that matter, who could dictate immigration policies or understand the plight of war-torn orphans and refugees of this world better than a king who'd grown up in an orphanage to survive?"

"Fausta…"

"It's true. The more I think about it, I can't conceive

of a man in today's world who would suit the demands facing your country more than you do."

He scoffed, though he was deeply touched by her words. "You forget the faction of government that didn't like my father's policies. There's a cousin of my father's, Giuseppe Umberto, who started the war thirty years ago and is waging a campaign to be put in as king by the parliament."

"There's always an opposition party with someone overly zealous and ready to take over. Does this Giuseppe know you exist?"

"I'm afraid he does now."

"How does the queen feel about it?"

"I have no idea. She hasn't had enough time to get over the shock that I'm alive."

"You mean she didn't know?"

"She knew there'd been a child but thought I had died too. She was never told I'd been taken to safety. When Basil walked me in to the palace to meet her, she took one look at me and almost fainted. There's a strong resemblance between me and my father. I'll show you."

He pulled four photos from his breast pocket and handed them to her. Two of them were the ones Basil had given him. The other two were of his father, one when he was older, the other just before he died.

As she studied them, she shook her head. "How utterly incredible! You don't need a DNA test. No wonder the queen went into shock." Fausta kept scrutinizing them. "Your mother was so lovely. There's a look around her eyes that reminds me of you. How hard for you that you never got to know them." She put the photos on the bed. "I don't know what to say," she murmured in a tearful voice.

"I'm afraid that's *my* dilemma."

"Of course it is—" she cried with infinite understanding.

Nico needed to hold her more than he needed life itself. In the next instant he reached for her. They clung to each other before he found her mouth and began kissing the daylights out of her. Tonight he'd discovered she was his rock.

"I've missed you so terribly, Nico."

"Tell me about it." Their need for each other was off the charts. He couldn't get enough of her. "You've got to stop me, Fausta. I need to go downstairs and get a room. I was assigned bodyguards before I left La Valazzura. Combined with yours, our every move is being watched."

She kissed his features. "Now you're going to find out what it's like to be royal. I've always hated it, Nico."

"Understood," he whispered. "What an irony of ironies," he said against her luscious mouth before devouring her all over again. His need for her was out of control and always had been since the evening they went to Prospero's. But eventually he was forced to call on every atom of self-control to let her go.

"In the morning I'll come by your room and we'll go to breakfast before driving over to the orphanage. I want to see what magic you've performed."

Fausta hugged him harder. "I don't want you to leave."

"You think *I* do?" His voice shook. "But I know we

can't do this right now. Too much is at stake, above all your reputation."

She made a sound of exasperation and eased out of his arms. "I've told you before that I'm not concerned about what my parents want."

"I'm afraid I am."

Her expression closed up. "You're thinking like a royal already."

He shook his head. "I'm thinking you and I have a lot to talk about in the next thirty days."

"Why thirty days?"

Nico let out a troubled sigh. "That's when I have to let Signor Bruno and the prime minister know if I've decided to return to La Valazzura and take on my father's mantle."

"I see."

"The queen will have to be in agreement before I'm presented to the parliament for a vote. Even then Giuseppe could be the one who prevails in that fight. Until then, all options are on the table. Now I need to get out of here before I can't!"

Fausta couldn't stand it to watch him tear out of her hotel room, but she had no choice. If he only knew he'd left her so unsatisfied physically, she was in pain and clung to the back of one of the chairs for support.

What did he mean that all options were on the table? There were only two. Either he remained a doctor in Domodossola, or he embraced his destiny in La Valazzura.

She spent the rest of the night in absolute turmoil. When he'd driven here to see her, she'd thought he'd come to tell her he was in love with her and wanted to marry her. If he never found his parents it didn't matter, because he didn't want to continue his journey without her. And if one day he did get the information he'd been looking for, Fausta would be with him and the future would take care of itself.

Together they'd fight any opposition from her parents and settle down in an adorable house with a picket fence and children. They'd be a married couple with a whole life ahead of them until circumstances changed for them. Fausta had gone crazy waiting for him to show up at the hotel so she could tell him she loved him more than life itself.

Nothing in a million years could have prepared her for his astounding news after he arrived. It was one thing to learn he'd found his parents. But to be told he was the undeclared, beloved son and heir of King Carlo Umberto of La Valazzura had turned her inside out.

The noble part of the orphaned boy engrained inside Nico would be overjoyed and want to honor his father by following in his footsteps. Everything that had happened to him in his life until the arrival of Signor Bruno had been a preparation. Fausta believed it and had pointed those things out to him because she knew he'd already made the decision in his heart.

But *her* heart wasn't in it. How could it be when she'd wished she hadn't been born a royal? The restrictive life had brought her little pleasure. At Enrico's coronation, Fausta had told Donetta she planned to marry a commoner and nothing would ever change her mind. Her sister had replied, "Be careful what you wish for."

A shiver racked her body now.

In making that wish, the commoner she'd fallen head over heels in love with had turned out to be the son of a king. She couldn't be happy about it, not for him or for herself.

With this knowledge, Fausta's world had forever changed because Nico would always be the love of her life. But sadness had enveloped her because he wasn't who she thought he was. It changed everything.

Fausta tried to shake off her sadness as they drove over to the orphanage after eating at a trattoria. She had to keep reminding herself that this entire situation was about him, not her. It was beyond selfish of her to feel this torn up.

He'd achieved the goal in his life to find out who he was and where he came from. But when she'd fallen madly in love with him, little did she realize what rivers of sorrow she would have to cross as a result.

When they arrived at the orphanage, the children were out in the back courtyard playing. Nico followed Fausta inside.

"What do you think?" She was anxious to know his reaction.

He walked into the common room with her, dressed in a linen shirt and khaki trousers. She found him so handsome, it hurt.

After looking at all the equipment and their placement, he whistled. "The room has been transformed." One of the nuns had set up a mobile bulletin board on wheels with a lot of pictures the children had run off on the printers. They'd signed their names. Fausta watched him study each one.

"*Ehi!* Here's a robot designed by my namesake."

Fausta smiled. "Nicolo is a cute little seven-year-old redhead who is crazy about everything related to the computer and doesn't want to do anything else. Maybe he'll be a big tech genius one day."

Nico raised his eyes to her, enveloping her with heat. "You'll be the reason why. I can't tell you how impressed I am. You're a wonder."

Her pulse raced. "It has been so much fun to teach the children. They're smart and have learned fast. I should have become an elementary school teacher."

He moved toward her. "Why didn't you?"

"That's not the kind of thing one of my father's daughters is allowed to do."

A frown marred his striking features. "How much longer are you planning to stay here?"

"Today's my last day."

"The place will fall apart without you."

She chuckled. "Oh, no. The nuns have been learning too, and they help the children."

"It won't be the same."

"You're right. I'll miss them terribly, but not for long."

"What do you mean?"

"As soon as I get back to Domodossola, I'm going to make visits to the various orphanages. I have no idea how many exist. When I've done my homework, I'm going to set up new fund-raisers and use the proceeds to buy more computers and printers. It's going to be my project from here on out. All children are hungry to learn."

Suddenly a whole group of children came running in the room and hurried to the computers.

"Children? Before you get started, I'd like you to meet Dr. Barsotti. He used to live here at the orphanage too."

"For how long?" asked Teresa.

"Ten years," Nico answered.

"Did you get adopted?"

The unexpected question touched her to the core. She could only imagine how Nico felt at this point.

"No. Still, I had several good friends who watched out for me. But we never had computers or a teacher like Signorina Rossiano."

"She's not a nun," Sergio blurted.

Nico grinned. "Is that good or bad?"

"Good. She's fun!"

"You're right." Nico's eyes wandered over her. "Your teacher is not only fun, she has the sweetest nature of anyone I've ever known."

Heat swept into her cheeks. "Children? Dr. Barsotti is a good friend," Fausta interjected. "We're here to help you learn how to cut and paste." She darted him an impish glance. "Shall we get started?"

He got right into it with her and was too wonderful. After two hours had passed, she made the announcement to this first group that today would be her last day with them. "But I'll be back to check on you in another month."

She hadn't forgotten what Nico had told her about orphan institutions where the staff had large turnovers. She was already starting to feel a bond with these children. Fausta would love to adopt all of them.

"How come you have to go?"

"So I can help at other orphanages, Maria."

"Oh."

One of the nuns escorted the children from the room. Then another group came running in and the whole routine began again. By five in the afternoon she'd said goodbye to the last session. The second they disappeared out the door, she buried her face in her hands, overcome with emotion.

Nico's arms came around her from behind. He buried his face in her hair. "I wouldn't have missed this day for the world. You've touched their lives and they'll never forget you."

"They've touched mine." She wiped her eyes and turned around. "Thank you for helping. To see you working with the children when you were once a resident here…"

She couldn't finish what she was going to say because his mouth covered hers. He kissed her with so much hunger, she forgot where they were and wanted it to go on forever.

"Signorina Rossiano?"

Fausta pulled away from him, embarrassed to be caught in his arms.

Maria, the eight-year-old with the long dark hair, had come in the room. "I wish you didn't have to go." She ran over to hug her around the waist.

"I don't want to, but I'll see you again before summer is over."

"Do you promise?"

"I promise." She kissed her forehead before the girl left the room.

"Oh, Nico—"

He put his arm around her shoulders. "Come on.

Let's leave for the hotel and freshen up. Then we'll go out for dinner in Biella. Afterward we'll go back to the hotel. It will give us time to talk before we return to Domodossola in the morning."

CHAPTER EIGHT

NICO SAT BACK in the chair to drink his wine while he feasted his eyes on Fausta in the candlelight. Could any woman be more gorgeous?

"I remember passing this *ristorante* when I explored Biella for the first time at the age of fourteen. So many finely dressed people sat out on this patio eating foods I'd never dreamed of. They didn't seem to have a care in the world. I couldn't comprehend living their lives."

She flashed him a sad smile. "And soon, other teenage boys in La Valazzura will see their new king riding through the city in a carriage after his coronation. They won't be able to comprehend *your* world."

Her words disturbed him. He put his half-empty glass on the table. "You think I've made my decision already?"

"Haven't you?" Fausta was always direct. That was one of the many qualities he loved about her. "Your parents may no longer be alive, but your legacy is there waiting for you."

"I'm not at all sure about that."

Those blue eyes studied him intently. "I remember your telling me that if you found out your parents were from Domodossola, you would stay. But if you found them elsewhere, their country would be your country and you would put down roots. I happen to know you meant those words with all your heart."

Nico groaned softly. "I didn't count on another woman being tormented that I'm alive."

She cocked her head. "In all honesty, the queen *did* know about the affair. At this point you must have some idea how she feels about you deep inside."

"It doesn't help that I look so much like my father. Try to put yourself in her place."

He could hear her mind working. "Were they in love in the beginning, or was it a marriage of convenience?"

"Their marriage was arranged, but in time they fell in love. Basil confirmed it was a happy marriage until they realized there would be no children."

After a prolonged silence she said, "If that's true, and then he had an affair…" She shook her head. "If that had happened to me, it would have killed me and any love I'd had for him. I would have gone away and asked for a divorce. I'm afraid I know myself too well. It would destroy me to see the child of their love ascend the throne when I couldn't have a baby with him."

"That's what I thought you'd say."

She leaned forward and grasped his hand. "I'm sorry, Nico. I didn't mean to hurt you."

"You've only spoken the truth, Fausta, and that's what I want. In order to counteract my pain, both Basil and the prime minister have told me what a great man he was. But to do that to his wife… Far be it from me to judge any man, but—"

"But he *was* your father," she broke in with heartfelt

emotion. "You wanted to love who he was, whatever his faults. He was the man you'd idolized somewhere in your psyche without knowing anything about him."

"Your understanding is a revelation to me, Fausta. It isn't just my father I'd ascribed with numberless virtues. How could my own mother have brought herself to get involved with a married man?"

"Then you believe she knew he was the king?"

He nodded. "Liliane told me all about it. They'd been fighting because she wanted to adopt and he was adamant that he didn't want to raise someone else's child. During that difficult period, he left to make visits to several military cemeteries across the country and honor fallen heroes. It was in winter and he came down with the flu that caused him to collapse."

"Oh, no."

"My father was taken to the hospital in Mesecino and had to stay down for close to a week. A young nurse took care of him. As soon as she could, Liliane rushed to his side. But the moment she entered his hospital room, she knew something had happened. My father was more distant, and it became clear he and the nurse had become involved."

"That story is too painful," Fausta whispered.

Nico agreed. "Liliane said the clandestine affair lasted for about a year before he came to her and confessed to everything, including the fact that they'd had a baby son. By then full war had broken out."

A moan came out of the woman seated across from him.

"He begged Liliane's forgiveness for his weakness, insisting that he loved her and always would. He also promised he would never see my mother or the baby again and kept that promise, although he made provisions for them to be taken care of through Basil. My father did keep his promise to Liliane, but nothing was ever the same between them."

"No. It couldn't be. So what are you saying, Nico?"

He finished his wine. "Basil and the prime minister want me to take my place as the heir apparent to the throne and believe the parliament would be behind me. They insist the queen has no vote politically and couldn't stop me. But I told them that if she can't get past her pain—and I don't see how she can—then there's no way I would consider murdering her heart again. My father already did it once."

"Nico—please don't let what I said influence you in any way."

"You didn't. I was sickened the moment Liliane spoke frankly with me. I left La Valazzura with this proviso: unless I hear from Liliane herself before the thirty days are up, and she can see a path for me that wouldn't destroy her, then I'd think about it. The palace is her home since she left her father's palace in Slovenia years ago to be married. For the time being she's a figurehead no matter who ascends the throne."

"That poor woman. My heart aches for her." Fausta's head lifted. "My heart aches for *you*. I wish I could take away your pain."

"You already have by just being you. I needed this day with you and am looking forward to getting back to work as long as you're free at five o'clock every day and weekends for us to be together. Once you tell your parents the truth about me, they might even add me to the bottom rung of their short list of acceptables."

Nico thought she would smile, but the opposite was true. "Do you mind if we go back to the hotel?"

"I didn't mean to say the wrong thing."

She refused to look at him. "You didn't, but I'd rather continue the rest of this conversation when we don't have an audience."

Several people had probably recognized her. "Would you like dessert?"

"I couldn't, but please order for yourself."

"I'd rather be alone with you." He paid the bill and they left the restaurant for the car.

When he pulled in next to her car in the hotel parking lot, he turned to her. "Why did my mentioning your parents bother you so much?"

"I'd rather not talk about it."

"Fausta—you and I don't have secrets from each other. I don't want to start now."

She suddenly looked at him. Her eyes glittered with unshed tears. "I've spent my life wishing I weren't royal so I could be like all my friends, able to make choices without worrying about the royal rules governing what my parents have outlined for me. I've said it before, the difference between the classes is indecent."

"I'm aware of how you feel," he whispered.

"Do you have any idea how strange it is to hear you of all people say that you're probably acceptable to my parents now that you have a pedigree that goes back thousands of years? It angers me when I think of how Angelo spoke to you about crossing lines. No human should have to worry about being good enough to associate with another human."

"Fausta…" He pulled her to him and kissed the tears off her cheeks.

"After that lovely dinner, I'm sorry for being so upset, Nico. Forgive me, but so many things pain me. I wish you could enjoy your parents' love story. They must have been attracted to the point they couldn't deny themselves. How hard it must have been for them to part. He never got to see you again." She buried her face in his neck and wept quietly.

"I'm presuming it was even harder to face his wife with the truth while continuing to rule," Nico murmured. "I'm glad I knew nothing until now."

She raised her head and looked into his eyes. "Thank heaven you were taken to safety! Your parents would be so proud of you if they knew what an amazing man you've become. Maybe they do know."

"Bellissima—" Nico embraced her harder.

Fausta ran her hand through his hair. "Isn't it amazing that after all the searches you made and would continue to make throughout your life, it was Basil who came to you with the information only he could have provided? Does he know if your mother still has relatives living? It's possible you have aunts and uncles who might be able to tell you more about her."

He took a deep breath. "We didn't have time to talk about that yet. He and the prime minister tried to cram a hundred years' worth of their country's history into my brain over those five days."

"I can imagine. What about your father's family?"

"Aside from the cousin I told you about, all the relatives have passed on due to the ravages of war."

"I realize I'm brimming with so many questions, it's driving you crazy."

"I love it, otherwise I wouldn't have driven here the second I flew home. I need you to help me make sense of everything. Let's go back to your room. We have all night to be together before leaving for Domodossola in the morning."

"That wouldn't be a good idea, and I'm not talking about our bodyguards keeping watch. I don't trust myself alone with you, so it's better if we talk here in the car."

When she tried to ease away from him, he wouldn't let her go. "Don't you know how much I want you? You have no idea how I've longed for you."

"Your father probably told your mother the same thing before they lost their heads. Look what happened! Their lives were ripped apart. You and I can't afford to do the same thing."

"You're not making sense."

"Oh, yes, I am. Anything could happen in the next thirty days. I'm convinced you'll hear from the queen. She loved your father once. In the end she'll want you to return to La Valazzura and go before the parliament endowed with the many qualities that made him a great king even my own father admired."

"Then you have a lot more faith than I do."

"Please listen, Nico. Don't you know how tragic it would it be for Basil and the prime minister to receive a message that the still unwed Princess Rossiano of Domodossola is the mistress of the commoner-turned-uncrowned-king before the throne is even his? The people would fear a potential pregnancy. If you can't imagine it, I can. *Like father, like son. It must run in the genes.* The press will go ballistic with glee and tear you apart."

"Don't," Nico begged and crushed her to him. "Surely by now you know how deeply I'm in love with you."

"Actually I *don't* know," she fired back, her face awash in tears. "You couldn't tell me how you feel until now because you didn't dare say the words to a princess. Angelo really got to you. You've always felt you didn't deserve to be with me. But now that you've found your life and we're equals, you're suddenly entitled to speak those forbidden words of love?"

"Fausta—" He tried to kiss her, but she wouldn't let him.

"Do you have any idea how much I needed to hear you say you loved me when we were at your apartment, *before* you knew who you were? I would have done anything for you. But you couldn't say the words. That's why a relationship based on what we've had up to now is thin as air."

"Don't talk that way, *amore mio.*"

"Nico, we've spent borrowed time together for a short while. You believed it had to end and broke up with me that night at your apartment, telling me you were on a search for your parents that had to be taken alone. The real reason was that you couldn't see us ending up together. I thought I was going to die and couldn't believe I was still alive the next day."

He smoothed the moisture off her cheeks. "You'll never know what I went through."

"Does it matter? When you leave for La Valazzura, and I know you will, a royal world will await you complete with a list of princesses dying to meet you. At that point all things will be equal. You'll have the time you need to find the right woman for you, one who will hold your heart and give you children. There'll be no baggage and you'll be a revered king."

"Listen to me, Fausta. You're the woman who holds my heart. I want children with you and no one else. Whether I become a king or remain a doctor, there's no one else in this world for me but you."

She shook her head. "I believe you mean it, but you're a man suspended high between two worlds. I'm watching in agony from below."

"Mia amata—" He cupped her face in his hands and kissed her with such passion they were both breathless. "Whatever world I choose, I need the answer to one question. Will you marry me?"

Nico reached in his pocket and pulled out a ring. "This is a blue diamond, close to the color of your eyes. I bought this after we spent that day in the country together. Tonight, I intended to give it to you. That's how real my love has been for you from the beginning."

A gasp escaped her lips. He felt for her left hand, but she wouldn't cooperate. "I—I can't accept it," she stammered.

"In the name of heaven, why not? Have you decided you don't love me?"

Her cry resonated in the interior of the car. "Don't be

ridiculous. I'm so in love with you, I've been half out of my mind since the first evening you took me to dinner."

"Then why won't you let me put it on you?"

She threw her head back. "If you were the doctor from the hospital asking me to spend the rest of my life with you, I would put it on myself and never take it off. But you're not Nico Barsotti. Your name is Massimo Carlo Umberto, the future king of La Valazzura, and you're going to have a remarkable reign."

"You don't know that!" he cried in frustration. "Hell, I don't even know what I'm feeling yet."

"You're still too close to it, but I feel it in my bones. Unlike you, I've known who I was and have known my own feelings from the time I was a young girl. I knew I was a loved princess who had to sit still for the royal family pictures and wait all the time to see my father for a few minutes. I didn't like that life then, and I don't like it now. I want to marry a man with a normal life like the magnificent family practice doctor I fell so hard for."

"Fausta—"

"When you fixed dinner for us in your apartment, I thought you were going to propose to me. I'd been picturing our life together. I even went so far in my thoughts to imagine that if we couldn't have children because either one of us had a problem, we'd go to the orphanage and adopt a little Nicolo or Maria. The dreams I've had…"

She pressed her lips to his. "Those dreams will keep me warm in my old age. Years from now tonight I'll remember that the great king of La Valazzura once asked me to marry him. And now I'm going to say good-night and goodbye. Please don't see me inside the hotel or call me. I need to be by myself."

"What am I going to do, Enzo?"

Nico had driven to the *castello* on Wednesday morning after watching Fausta leave the hotel in her car. He hadn't slept all night. His heart had gone with her, leaving him in agony.

His white-haired mentor eyed him with a solemn expression after Nico had poured out his soul to him. "I wish I could help. The only advice I have for you is that you don't make your decision hastily then live a lifetime of regret if it's the wrong one."

"That's my biggest worry. I only have a month before I must act one way or the other. There are so many unknowns, Enzo. Fausta has brought me the greatest happiness I've ever known. Whatever I do, there can be no joy in my life without her. She lights up my world and everyone else's."

"Indeed she does," Pippa chimed in. "Even as a girl she had a spirit and vivaciousness we noticed immediately. According to Lorenzo, she's been a worry to her parents because she's not biddable like her sisters and has rebelled over being a royal. She knows her own mind."

Nico clung to the back of a damask chair, unable to sit. "She made that painfully clear last night when she refused the ring I bought her."

Enzo sighed. "Fausta is Victor's daughter and wise beyond her years. Not only has she shown her superb taste in falling for you, she has learned the lesson of not jumping into the fire too soon. Give her time to assimilate what you've told her."

"If you'd heard her last night, you'd know there's no hope."

Pippa smiled at him. "There's always hope when there's love."

"I've got to pray you're right, Pippa."

"Don't forget she's been imagining being the wife of a doctor at the risk of estranging her parents. She's been comfortable with that idea and has figured out how she's going to keep you close to her so the two of you can have a wonderful life together. But now you've thrown her a huge curve."

"A royal curve she doesn't like," Enzo concurred.

Pippa wheeled herself closer. "Fausta needs time to get used to the fact that you might become king of another country, one foreign to both of you."

"I'm still having trouble comprehending it."

"Just remember that she has watched her mother deal with being her father's queen since she was a toddler. I believe her fear stems from a lot more than living a royal life with you if she has to."

"What do you mean?"

"Fausta has been there and done that while she too has been forced to wait for her father's attention. It's no mystery why she has grown up wanting marriage with a man who comes home from work to her at five every evening."

Pippa's comment were beginning to make sense.

"What terrifies her most is that the two of you will

rarely have time together when you're king. Over the years she has watched her mother waiting, waiting, waiting for those precious times to be alone with her husband. I can't say I blame Fausta for dreading that same scenario for herself."

"Pippa's right, *mio figlio*. So be patient while Fausta starts working out how she as queen can get you to herself more often and keep you in love with her."

"I'll love her beyond life," Nico ground out.

"I believe you will," Enzo murmured. "What's your plan at the moment?"

"To get back to the hospital. Dr. Silvio has doubled for me and I owe him. If or when I hear from Queen Liliane, that will help determine how I proceed."

Nico's white-haired mentor eyed him with a solemn expression. "I wish I could help. Once again, the only advice I have for you is that you weigh your decision carefully. But when you only have a month before you must act one way or the other, that sounds ridiculous, doesn't it?"

"Above all, don't leave Fausta alone," Pippa added. "No matter what she said, she really doesn't want you to stay away from her. You do understand that in her heart, the sun rises and sets with you. I saw it while the two of you were here."

"I want to believe that, Pippa." He walked around and kissed them both. "What would I have done without you two? All the time I was looking for my parents, I had you. I've been blessed. The second I know anything, I'll drive here to give you checkups and we'll talk. Stay well. I need you."

He left the *castello* for Domodossola. All the way to his apartment he pondered their remarks and advice.

Don't give up on me, Fausta. Per l'amor di Dio, *don't give up.*

CHAPTER NINE

FAUSTA CRIED SO hard all the way back to Domodossola, her blouse was soaked with tears and her face looked ravaged.

When she reached the palace, she swept past the guard on the way up to the apartment with her suitcase. There were eight text messages on her cell phone she'd ignored while she'd been driving home.

Adrenaline gushed through her body when she saw that four of them were from Nico sent at various intervals. She sank down on the side of the bed in pain. Fausta had said goodbye to him and she'd meant it.

At first she couldn't look at them, but finally she caved and read the first one.

I love you, Fausta. It happened when I walked into Tommaso's hospital room and heard you reading to him.

Tears dripped down her cheeks. She read the second one.

We were meant to be together. I felt it when we visited the orphanage the first time and know you felt it too.

Fausta's heartache deepened and she jumped off the bed before reading the third one.

I'll never say goodbye to you, so don't think you're going to get rid of me. That wouldn't be possible.

"Nico—" she cried out in anguish and pressed the phone to her chest. But the last message was still calling to her. With trembling fingers, she opened it.

Fausta. I meant it when I said you were the only woman for me. From the very first moment you spoke to my heart. That only happens once in a lifetime. I'm not giving up, so be warned.

Completely torn up inside, she needed her sister and phoned her.

Lanza had just put Rufy down for his afternoon nap and said she'd come right away.

The second she knocked and walked in, Fausta ran to her and they hugged.

"Tell me what's wrong. You sounded frantic on the phone."

"There's so much to tell you, I don't know where to start."

"This is about Nico I'm sure."

She nodded. They ended up on the couch in her sitting room. "What I'm about to tell you can't go beyond these walls."

Lanza's brows lifted. "It's that bad?"

"It is for me."

"Fausta—don't keep me in suspense."

"All right. Here it is. Nico was put in an orphanage at the age of two and was never adopted, though he'd had two opportunities. The point is, a little more than a week ago he found out where he came from and who his parents are."

By now she had Lanza's complete attention. "Was his mother a single mom who couldn't take care of him?"

"No." Fausta twisted her fingers together. "She was a young nurse in Mesecino, La Valazzura, who took care of a man in the hospital with a virus. They fell in love and had an affair. It turns out Nico's real name is Massimo Carlo Umberto Fernando, the only son of King Carlo di Savoia."

Lanza's eyes widened. "King Carlo who died recently?"

"The very one."

"Dr. Barsotti is his son?"

"The illegitimate son. King Carlo and his wife, Queen Liliane, couldn't have children. Nedda Corelli was Nico's mother and the king's mistress, but she died during the war over there when Nico was only two."

Too late Lanza tried to cover a gasp with her hand.

For the next few minutes Fausta told her his history, the reason he'd been put in an orphanage, everything. She included the fact that the prime minister and the head of the secret service wanted him to go before the parliament as the heir apparent.

"They're convinced he'll be voted in and crowned king in his father's stead. But he'll only agree with the queen's approval because he recognizes her deep pain."

"Good heavens, Fausta!" Her sister got to her feet.

"This is all unbelievable! So, if she can get past her pain, Dr. Barsotti will be the next king of La Valazzura."

Fausta looked up at her through the tears. "Yes. Here I thought I'd found the man I'd been wishing for all my life. Instead he has turned out to be the one thing I never wanted."

Her sister eyed her intently. "Has he asked you to marry him?"

"Yes, but only after he found out he was the son of King Carlo."

"Come on, Fausta. You know why. That's because he didn't dare ask you to marry him believing you're destined to marry some prince. The media has talked nonstop about your royal future."

Her jaw hardened. "Do you have any idea how angry that makes me feel? I told him I couldn't marry him and refused the diamond ring he tried to give me. He said he bought it after our first trip to Biella, but he didn't propose then."

"*What?* You mean he bought you a ring before he knew about his heritage? Are you crazy to turn down such a courageous act when you're madly in love with him?"

"I don't want to marry royalty. You more than anyone in this world besides Donetta know how I feel about that."

Her sister frowned. "I'm afraid I do. But this particular king happens to be the man you adore."

Fausta swallowed hard. "I know. I was an idiot."

"I think it's destiny. The parents will be overjoyed when they find out. I know for a fact they'll give you their blessing. Papa holds Nico's father in high esteem. He talked about him at breakfast."

"I remember, but that doesn't help my situation. I'll be sitting in a palace for the rest of my born days while Nico runs the country and manages to eke out a little time for me." Fausta got to her feet. "No, thank you. I'd rather remain single."

"Don't forget there'll be children."

"Don't forget that Stefano lets you travel with him when he has to go to the gold mines. I envy you that."

Lanza reached for her hand. "Come and sit down with me again." Fausta did her bidding. "Tell me something. When you found out that Nico was an orphan, did that make you love him less or more?"

"I—I don't know how to answer that." Her voice faltered. "I admit that I admired him for making such a success of his life, but I fell in love with him at the very beginning and didn't care about anything else."

"Since you loved him not knowing anything about his birth parents and background, then it meant you accepted him just as he was, an orphan who became a busy doctor. So now that you've found out he's the son of a king, why does that make a difference?

"He loves you and wants you to marry him. Isn't your love more important than what he's going to do in the future as long you're with him?" Lanza used her brilliant logic to get to the heart of the matter in a hurry.

"I don't know."

"As I recall, you've always maintained that marrying a commoner would make a marriage between the two of you more interesting. Remember that he *was* a commoner until just a week or two ago. Learning that he's a future king really spices up your whole relationship. Think about that for a while before you push the greatest love you'll ever know out of your life. That kind of love only comes once in a lifetime."

A shiver passed through Fausta's body. Nico had texted those exact words to her.

Lanza kissed her cheek. "I love you and know you'll work it all out. Now I have to get back to Rufy."

"Bless you for listening to me."

When her sister disappeared, Fausta walked around, trying to come to grips with what Lanza had just said. But her sister had been kind about it.

What she'd really implied was that Fausta was being selfish, always dreaming about what she wanted. She expected Nico to stay in Domodossola for her sake when the life he was born to happened to mean he was the uncrowned Prince of La Valazzura. The orphan boy was the son of a wonderful king. Nico could also do great good for his country and honor his legacy.

Yet he *had* dared to love her! He'd let her into his life and had told her all his secrets. He'd fought for her. He'd declared his love and had even bought her a ring he probably believed wouldn't be good enough for her. And what had she'd done? Thrown it all back in his unforgettably striking face.

When she put herself in Nico's place, she realized that in rejecting him, she'd done the worst thing anyone could do. To expect so much of him would mean holding him back from his destiny if he wanted to follow in his father's footsteps.

Throughout the rest of the afternoon Fausta did a lot

of soul-searching. By evening she was done with tears and realized that life without him was no life at all.

She checked her watch. By now he was probably on his way home from the hospital. Though she could phone him, that wouldn't be enough. She needed to see him face-to-face and tell him how much she loved him, beg his forgiveness for the way she'd been reacting. He needed to know all the secrets of her heart she'd kept from him.

After she took a shower and dressed in a sleeveless white sundress, she left the palace and drove to his apartment in the other part of town. On the way she picked up some food at her favorite deli for them to enjoy.

Since she knew his car, she parked along the street and would wait until she spotted him, then follow him inside. Fausta was sick with excitement and running a fever at the thought of being with him. Once she got her arms around him, she'd never let him go.

Nico's last patient didn't leave until ten after six p.m. He had half a dozen calls to return, but he'd make them after he drove home. He'd texted Fausta during the drive to Domodossola and didn't expect to hear from her. But he was following Pippa's advice and wouldn't leave her alone.

Tomorrow night he planned to drive over to the palace and call her from outside her private entrance. He'd keep after her until she responded. These thoughts and more filled his mind as he reached the parking area of his apartment and hurried inside.

It was a hot night. No sooner had he gone into the

kitchen for a cold glass of water than he heard a knock on the door. That was a surprise. Maybe it was Felipe.

He hurried to the door and came close to going into cardiac arrest to see Fausta standing there in all her golden glory. She held a sack in one hand, her purse in the other. In that filmy white dress with the spaghetti straps, he thought he'd never seen anyone so breathtaking.

"Nico—" Her anxious blue eyes searched his. "Will you forgive me for bursting in on you like this? I was sitting out in my car waiting for you to come home. I brought dinner if you want some, but if you'd rather be alone—"

"Come here to me." He pulled her inside. In an instant he relieved her of the purse and sack, then picked her up in his arms and carried her over to the couch. She half lay against him as he hungrily covered her mouth with his own.

Nico no longer had cognizance of time or surroundings. The fire that had been kindling over the weeks burst into flame. Her kisses intoxicated him. She held nothing back.

"I love you more than you'll ever know, Nico. I want to be your wife," she cried breathlessly. "Forgive me for being so cruel to you."

He lifted his head. "Cruel?"

"Yes, my darling. I'm ashamed of the way I've treated you. I've had issues and hang-ups about my life as a royal and I've let them come close to ruining my relationship with you."

"What's made you change since last night?"

"Lanza."

"I don't understand."

"Today she asked me a few salient questions that made me realize what a selfish creature I've been."

Nico burst into laughter. "I've never known anyone less selfish than you."

She shifted in his arms so she could look into his eyes. "That's because you don't know the real me. Since I met you, I've wanted everything my way. When I found out you were the son of a king, I hated it. I wasn't thinking about you and how ecstatic you were to have found your parents and your roots.

"Oh, no. I was only thinking of myself and how that knowledge affected me. I desired the fictional man I'd dreamed about all my life. A commoner. He'd take me to his cottage with a picket fence. We'd have perfect children and live a blissful life. The first time I saw you, I knew you were the man of my dreams, and I set out to capture you no matter what I had to do."

"You accomplished your objective." Nico kissed her long and hard. This was the warm, giving woman he adored.

Tears smarted her eyelids. "I can't believe I didn't accept the ring when you asked me to marry you. I was so entrenched with my own pitiful vision of royal life, I ruined what should have been the most magical, thrilling moment of our lives. I don't know why you didn't slam the door in my face a little while ago."

He kissed her throat. "I have a confession of my own. On my way home, I stopped to talk to Enzo and Pippa. They told me I had to give you time. I've been hanging on to their advice for dear life."

"They're wise and wonderful. So is Lanza. I wish it

hadn't taken the questions she asked me for me to wake up and realize what a fool I've been. Oh, Nico. Please tell me it's not too late." She put her arms around his neck. "I love you with every breath of my body. I don't care what you do for a living as long as I'm there with you. We'll make it work."

"You're reading my mind." Nico reached in the front pocket of his trousers and pulled out the ring. He found her left hand and slid it home on her ring finger. "You're mine now, *bellissima*. There's no going back."

"I don't want to go back."

Their hunger knew no bounds as they began devouring each other all over again. Later when his cell phone rang, he groaned. It was probably the service. He hadn't called his patients yet.

"You need to get that," she whispered against his lips.

"I'm afraid I do." Nico eased himself away from her and stood up before answering it. He was still trembling with desire for her.

She got to her feet on those elegant legs of hers. While he was on the phone, she took the sack of food into the kitchen and warmed everything up in the microwave.

He stood in the doorway watching her every movement as he returned calls to patients. Talk about a vision in white and gold.

By the time he'd finished, she'd put their food on the table. The aroma of the coffee she'd made reminded him he was starving. Nico kissed her succulent lips before sitting down with her to eat. "How come I'm so lucky?"

"I've been asking myself that question since the evening you asked if you could drive me home from the hospital. My feet don't touch the ground anymore."

"I know the feeling."

When they'd finished eating, he reached for her hand and pulled her up against him. "Nothing's changed since last night." He smothered her with kisses. "I want you in my bed, so I'm thinking we should get married now. When the time comes to decide the course of my life, I want us to be man and wife already so we can make the decision together. I've found I don't want to do anything without you."

She moaned against his mouth. "I feel the same way. But that would mean going through a ceremony right away."

"That's the whole idea. How does tomorrow sound? I don't need anyone's permission. Naturally I'd like your parents' blessing. Shall we call them now and tell them our plans?"

He heard her sharp intake of breath. "*Nico*—be serious!"

"You think I'm not?"

"But getting married that fast would be impossible!"

"Not so. Enzo will arrange it."

"How?"

"As *duca* of Piedmont, he has magistrate power to waive the rules and ask the priest to marry us in the *castello* chapel. He's done it for several others on a moment's notice. Once our marriage is a fait accompli, we won't have to worry if word gets out that we're expecting our first child. What do you say?"

She clung to him, staring into his eyes with a hint of anxiety.

He kissed the end of her nose. "Now who's afraid."

"If I'm afraid, it has to do with your future. Everything's up in the air where the queen is concerned. If we're going to do this, don't you think you need to let her know?"

Nico rubbed his hands up and down her silky arms. "Where the love of my life is concerned, it's no one else's business. Protocol be damned! Are you ready to take the plunge with me, *tesora*? Yes or no."

By the way her eyes lit up, he could tell she was excited at the thought. "You honestly believe Enzo can arrange everything by tomorrow?"

"All I have to do is get him on the phone. The decision is yours. What about your parents?"

Fausta looked dazed. "I think it would be better if we call them after we say our vows."

"Are you sure? I don't want you to do something that could sever your relationship with them forever."

"It won't."

"You don't know that."

"My parents will be overjoyed when they learn that I married the son of King Carlo."

"But you'll be denying them the pleasure of watching the ceremony."

She chuckled. "I'd rather avoid the pomp. Think of the money that could be used for a good cause, like the other wing of the veterans' hospital. Honestly I know my parents will be so happy I married a prince, they'll get over it."

"Even if I'm illegitimate?"

"That won't worry my parents. If they had known

you'd been available all these years, I can promise that *you* would have been the first name on their short list."

A burst of laughter poured out of Nico. *Happy* didn't begin to describe what he was feeling. It killed him to let her go, but he had to. "In that case I'll walk you out to your car in plain sight of our bodyguards."

They left the apartment. When they reached the car she'd parked on the street, she turned to him. "Aren't you going to give me one last kiss?" He'd already opened the door for her.

"I don't dare. Looking the way you do right now, it's a miracle I'm letting you go. Starting tomorrow, life will be a different story morning, noon and night."

Heat suffused her face. "How can you be away from the hospital again?"

"Let me worry about that. Be ready at six in the morning when I come by for you, *bellissima.* Wear casual clothes. By afternoon I'll deliver you back to the palace and the bodyguards will think I was paying a house call on Enzo and Pippa. I'll take my doctor bag with me. No one will know anything happened. It'll be our secret, at least for a while."

Her eyes swam with tears. "I love you so terribly, Nico, I don't want to leave you."

He felt her love to the marrow. "We badly need to be married, Fausta." He blew her a kiss and shut the door. After she drove off, he returned to his apartment and phoned his receptionist at home.

Nico told her he wouldn't be coming in until one tomorrow. He asked her to move the morning appointments to the afternoon schedule and he'd fit everyone in somehow. Then he got on the phone with Enzo.

"Nicolo—what's going on?"

"How are you feeling?"

"Never been better."

"That's good because I'm getting married tomorrow morning and need the help only you can provide if you grasp my meaning."

The older man laughed. "I'm glad to hear you took Pippa's advice. As for mine…"

"I'm in love and can't wait, Enzo."

"Obviously Fausta can't either. I'd better get on the phone to the priest. How soon can we expect you?"

"We'll arrive at the *castello* at eight a.m. Can you arrange for the priest to meet us in the chapel for a quick ceremony? You and Pippa will be our witnesses. When we've said our vows, we'll have to get right back to Domodossola so no one suspects anything, not even Fausta's parents. That was her decision, not mine."

"Sounds like her. That girl knows what she wants. What I want to know is, how long do you expect your marriage to remain a secret?"

"Only until she tells her parents. But the point is, I decided to take your sage advice about weighing my decision. That's why I want Fausta to be my wife first. Together we'll choose whether to stay in Domodossola or leave for La Valazzura when the time comes."

"Bravo, figlio mio."

"Once again you're saving my life, Enzo."

"You saved mine the day I interviewed you at the farm. Pippa and I decided you'd been sent to us in our grandson's place."

Nico's throat swelled with so much emotion he couldn't talk.

"It will be our joy to see you married to the adorable Fausta. Knowing what I do about her, she'll make the kind of loving companion Pippa has always been to me."

When Nico could find the words, he said, "I couldn't ask for more than that. *Ci vediamo domani.*"

At five to six the next morning, Fausta came out of the palace doors carrying her purse. Nico was already there. She climbed in his car, wearing jeans and a soft pink cotton top with short sleeves. His piercing dark eyes devoured her before he drove away. "How did you sleep?"

"I've been so excited, I couldn't."

"You look fabulous anyway."

She laughed. "Thank you. I'm glad you like my wedding dress. It's a Fausta original."

A grin broke out on his handsome face. "I've got food and coffee in the back seat when you're ready to eat."

"Goody! I'm hungry now. I'll feed both of us."

"I was hoping you'd say that."

Fausta reached around and put the sack and thermos in her lap. "You're going to make the most satisfactory husband on earth."

"Tell me that again in fifty years and I'll believe you." His gaze darted to her hand. "Where's your ring?"

"In my purse."

"I'll need it to put on your finger during the ceremony."

A small moan escaped. "I don't have one for you yet. I wanted to ask Lanza for help but didn't dare." She took it out of her purse. He put it in his breast pocket.

"Don't worry. Enzo will find something for you to give me."

Fausta poured coffee in the cup and handed it to him. She couldn't stop staring at her breathtaking fiancé. He smelled wonderful as always. Today he wore a tan jacket covering a button-up white shirt and dark trousers.

"What did Enzo say when you called him?"

"He and Pippa are overjoyed with our news."

"They don't think we're crazy?"

He smiled. "I didn't say that, but they're happy for us."

"I hope he doesn't tell Lorenzo."

"He won't, but let's not forget you came to my apartment last evening. Your parents couldn't be happy about it since it was your second visit to enemy territory. This evening after work you'll be driving to my apartment again. I wouldn't be surprised if they send security to my door."

Fausta handed him a ham-filled croissant and took one for herself. "Then we'll phone the parents tonight and give them our glorious news. That is if our bodyguards haven't caught on to our devious scheme before then."

"Who knows?" After they'd eaten, he put a hand on her arm. "Any regrets?"

Her crystalline blue eyes clouded over. "How can you even ask me that? I'm so in love with you, it's indecent."

"That makes two of us. Do you know when I saw you in the cafeteria with Mia, I thought you were a celebrity because you seemed familiar? Your beauty, everything about you drew me in. The next time I saw you in Tommaso's room, I couldn't believe my eyes.

"But when he called you Fausta, my heart almost failed me because it was then I realized you were Princess Rossiano. By the time I'd recovered my wits, you'd left too fast for me to be able to catch up to you. I was haunted by you until your next visit to the ward. At that point I'd lain in wait for you. No way was I going to let you get away from me again."

The intensity of his deep voice found its way to the deepest recesses of her soul.

"I didn't want to get away. You were the most amazing man to come into my life. When you turned down my invitation to come to my apartment, I told Mia I'd made a huge mistake with you."

"You know that's not true."

"I do now, but that night I was afraid I didn't measure up to you. I worried that you didn't find me interesting enough. Let's be honest. In many ways I've led a sheltered life compared to yours. More than ever I hated it that I was a royal. I feared that you wouldn't be back. The torture I went through." She shook her head.

"You didn't witness the torture I went through. While we ate at Prospero's *cantina*, I sat there thinking that I'd met the woman of my desire. No other woman had ever come close or ever would. Prospero's eyes lit up to see that the princess of the realm had honored him by eating at his restaurant.

"For that night you were *my* princess. I was the happiest man alive until I drove you back to the palace that represented the dividing line between us. For a time I'd forgotten. When you asked me inside—"

"Every lesson Angelo had tried to teach you got in the way," Fausta broke in. "I didn't know how to fight it."

"You didn't have to. You already had me hooked body and soul, and now you're about to become my wife. Whatever happens, wherever we end up, I swear I'll love you forever, Fausta."

Too touched by his words, all she could do was clutch his hand for the rest of the drive to the *castello*.

After they arrived and Nico had parked the car in the courtyard, he grabbed his doctor bag and opened Fausta's door. Enzo, looking sporty, was waiting for them at the entrance with a huge smile on his face. He hugged Nico before turning to her.

"You're right on time for your own wedding. *Congratulazioni*, Fausta." He gave her a warm hug, which she reciprocated. "Nico says you're on a tight time schedule, so the priest has been warned. Since I'm taking your father's place to give you away, I'll walk you to the chapel where Pippa is waiting."

"Thank you so much, Enzo."

"It's an honor."

Nico left the bag in the foyer and they proceeded to walk down several hallways of portraits and tapestries to the small chapel on the main floor. With candles lit, the interior dazzled the eye like a jewel. Fausta adored everything, including the beautiful statues, but she didn't see the priest yet.

Pippa sat in her wheelchair near the altar. While Enzo took Nico aside, she tugged on Fausta's hands and pulled her down to kiss her cheek. "You're marrying a veritable prince, but you already know that."

She nodded. "He's the prince of my heart."

"You've caught the eye of a most amazing and wonderful man. I know you're both going to be very happy."

"Dear Pippa—*grazie* for arranging this for us."

"We wondered if we would ever see this day. Nicolo seemed so determined to find his parents, I feared he would never find true love. Then he brought you inside the *castello*. The look in your eyes told me everything I wanted to know."

Fausta struggled for breath. "He's my life."

Pippa handed her a man's gold band. "This is the wedding ring I gave Enzo. He wants you to give it to Nico for the ceremony."

"I can't take this."

"Yes, you can. It means the world to my husband. He loves Nico like a son."

"You two are so dear."

As she put it in her blouse pocket, the priest walked in. He was young and quite handsome. No doubt he was surprised she was wearing pants. Not even a veil.

"Father Pietro, allow me to introduce Princess Fausta Rossiano of Domodossola."

"*Principessa*. I understand this must be a secret, quick ceremony. I'll do my best."

"You're very kind to perform the service, let alone this early in the morning. We're indebted to you."

Enzo and Nico moved toward them. "Father? I'd like you to meet Dr. Nico Barsotti. How do you wish to proceed?"

"If you'll sit by your wife, I'll ask these two to stand in front of me. Dr. Barsotti, if you'll take the right hand of Princess Rossiano?"

Fausta could hardly believe this was really happening. Nico gripped her hand, holding it fast, but her heart was pounding much faster.

CHAPTER TEN

"DEARLY BELOVED, Nico and Fausta. Marriage is the most important of all earthly relationships. It should be entered into reverently, thoughtfully and with full understanding of its sacred nature. Your marriage must stand by the strength of your love and the power of faith in each other and in God."

Fausta believed that to the core of her soul.

"Love is very patient and kind, never jealous or envious, never boastful or proud. Love is never haughty, rude or selfish."

Except that she'd been selfish, but never again.

"Love does not demand its own way. Love is never glad about injustice but rejoices whenever truth wins out."

Truth had finally won out and Nico now had full knowledge of his parentage. Fausta knew the news he'd waited for a lifetime had released him and had made him free.

"If you love someone," the priest spoke on, "you will be loyal to them no matter the cost. You will always believe in them, always expect the best in them and will always stand your ground in defending them."

Those were vows she would defend with her life.

The priest eyed Nico. "Knowing what is expected, do you, Nico, take Fausta to be your lawfully wedded wife?"

Nico answered in his deep voice, "I do."

At that point the priest looked at Fausta. "Knowing what is expected, do you, Fausta, take Nico to be your lawfully wedded husband?"

"I do with all my heart," she avowed.

A small smile broke out on the priest's face. "You will now exchange rings."

Fausta met Nico's glance before they reached in their pockets. He put the diamond ring back on her finger and squeezed her hand. She followed by placing Enzo's ring on Nico's finger with trembling hands. He had to have been surprised but didn't let it show.

"In as much as you have given each other these tokens of abiding love in the sight of witnesses, then by the power invested in me by the Church, I pronounce you man and wife. What God has joined together, let no man put asunder."

He blessed them. "In the name of the Father, the Son and the Holy Spirit. Amen. You may kiss your bride."

The short, almost surreal yet perfect ceremony had come to an end.

She was so insanely happy she raised her head to Nico, whose eyes burned with desire for her. He pulled her closer and gave her a husband's possessive kiss, thrilling her in every part of her being. Fausta clung to his hard, fit body, giving him everything she possessed to show him what he meant to her.

"Every dream of mine has come true," he whispered

before drowning her in passion that filled her with indescribable rapture. "We have two hours before we have to drive home. Come with me."

Blind with love, she went where he took her. They left the chapel and ascended the staircase to an apartment on the second floor. After picking her up in his arms, he carried her through to the bedroom and followed her down on the bed.

"Mia moglie—" Nico cried against her mouth.

She really was his wife now! They couldn't get close enough fast enough. No kiss lasted long enough.

"It should be a sin how beautiful you are. Love me, Fausta."

"That's all I've ever wanted to do since I first laid eyes on you, *amore mio*. Don't ever stop loving me."

"As if I could."

The divine sensation of lying in his arms for the next two hours and knowing his possession sent her into ecstasy. Fausta had been able to only imagine what it would be like to know her husband's possession. But her imagination hadn't given her a clue of what really went on with this incredible man, who made her feel loved and immortal.

They groaned in breathless protest when the house phone rang. Nico didn't pick up. They both knew it was Enzo reminding them they needed to leave for Domodossola if Nico wanted to keep his afternoon appointments at the hospital.

"We need to get up," she whispered against his lips, but she couldn't bear to move out of his arms.

"Not yet, *squisita*." His mouth kissed every feature of her face as a prelude to making love all over again.

But when the phone rang a second time, they both knew what it meant.

Fausta slid out of bed, provoking another groan from him, and hurried to the bathroom to shower and dress. Nico followed suit before engulfing her in one long kiss in the doorway before they left the bedroom. "This will have to last until tonight."

Together they flew down the staircase to the salon where their two favorite people were seated. While Nico removed the ring and handed it back to Enzo, Fausta put the diamond ring back in her pocket. They all hugged.

"You'll never know what you've done for us. This is the happiest day of our lives," Fausta told them.

Pippa beamed. "To see you two this deliriously in love is pure joy for us. I have a gift for you. Open it when you get home."

"You shouldn't have."

"When you open it, you won't feel that way."

Fausta kissed her again and put the small sealed sack in her purse. "I'm embarrassed we didn't get to say goodbye to Father Pietro. Please tell him how much we appreciated his doing the service for us. We'll send him a note and be in touch with you soon."

After signing all the marriage documents, they rushed out to the car. Enzo brought Nico the doctor bag and saw them off, smiling at both of them. "You lucky people. I envy you. Let the adventure begin."

After starting the car and driving out of the courtyard, Nico reached for her hand. "We're on an adventure all right," he declared. "I'll never forget this day or the fact that Enzo let you put his wedding ring on my finger."

"He loves you like a son."

She heard him suck in his breath. "He and Pippa made it possible for us to become man and wife today. Are you happy, Signora Barsotti?"

"I think you know the answer to that. Do you have any idea how much I love the sound of my new name?" she cried emotionally. "I wish—"

"I know," he broke in. "The last thing I wanted to do was leave the *castello*. We need weeks and weeks to be alone together. I'm in more agony now than ever before and would never suggest putting a two hour time limit on the wedding night."

"No." She squeezed his hand hard.

His car ate up the miles as they sped back to Domodossola. He darted her a glance. "We need all night tonight. After work I'll come straight to the apartment."

"You'll probably be late seeing patients. I'll need a key so I can bring some of my things over early and have dinner waiting."

"I'm not sure I'll be able to eat. One sight of you and everything else will go out of my head except to take you in my arms."

"I don't honestly know how I'm going to wait long enough for you to come home."

"Tell me about it."

As he drove over the speed limit, she looked at her watch. They were nearing the city. "If you're supposed to be at the hospital at one, then don't drive me to the palace. That'll take too much time. I'll go inside with you and call for the limo. It'll look more natural since I've often gone there to meet with Mia."

"Are you going to tell her about us?"

"I won't say anything to anyone until you and I feel it's right."

"Your parents must be told first."

"Agreed. We'll talk about it tonight."

Before long he pulled into the physicians' parking lot and parked in his spot. Fausta got out on her own and walked inside the hospital behind him. Once inside the doors, he pulled a key off his key chain and handed it to her.

Their gazes fused with longing. "Until tonight, *tesora*."

While he walked away, she put the key in her purse and pulled out her cell phone. In a few minutes the limo pulled up to the entrance. The driver opened the rear door for her.

Fausta climbed in, secretly overjoyed that she was now Dr. Barsotti's wife. Was she ever! Visions of what had happened a couple of hours ago when he'd taken her to another realm of existence robbed her of breath. If the bodyguards following them knew about the marriage already, it didn't matter.

She put her head back and closed her eyes, dreaming of the night to come. If Nico's mother had been this in love with his father, Fausta couldn't imagine the pain they would have gone through to say goodbye.

Thank heaven Fausta didn't have to face a permanent separation from Nico. They were husband and wife forever. As the priest had said, "What God has joined together, let no man put asunder."

Nico was just leaving his office at seven thirty p.m. after a packed schedule when Felipe showed up at the door. The two men gave each other a hug.

"I'm glad to see you back, *amico*. Let's get together. Want to go out for a beer right now? I want to tell you about my wedding plans."

Stifling a moan, Nico said, "There's nothing I'd like more, but I have to go out on an emergency house call. Can we do it tomorrow night? Five thirtyish? I won't let anything get in the way." He hated lying to his buddy, but he had no choice.

"Sure. You have a sick patient?"

"Very sick." *I'm the patient and need to get back to Fausta or I'm not going to make it.*

"Then I won't keep you. Until tomorrow night!"

Nico patted his friend's arm and dashed for the stairs. A whole evening and night to make love to his wife. Was there ever a more beautiful woman alive, inside and out, or one more loving?

He drove to his apartment and parked the car, eager to get her to himself. She'd left the door unlocked. Something smelled delicious. After hurrying inside, he found her in the kitchen by the stove wearing a white lace negligee that caused him to gasp.

"What took you so long?" She flashed him a seductive smile that melted his insides. "Our dinner is ready to be eaten. Why don't you freshen up and then join me at the table for our first meal together as a wedded couple." She'd set it with glasses of red wine and a vase of white roses.

He could hardly think, let alone make a sound. Finally, he managed, "I'll be right back." A quick trip to the bedroom to change into his robe and wash his hands, he returned to the kitchen.

"Sit down, *amato*, and open your gift first."

In a daze, he unwrapped the tiny box by his glass and pulled out a man's gold band. "We'll get it inscribed later. Try it on and see if it fits."

His heart thudded. "I need your help."

"No, you don't, or this roast pig from Prospero's will go to waste."

Fausta...

"I guess we can't have that." He put it on.

"You're mine now and I'll adore you forever."

Forever.

She put their dinner plates full of food on the table and sat down. While he was trying to take in her beauty and all that she'd created here, she lifted her wineglass. The blue diamond ring was back on her finger. "To the husband who has made me thankful I was born." There were tears in her voice.

Nico lifted his glass. "To the wife who made an orphan feel like a king and has literally transformed my life."

He clinked her glass and they drank the liquid, which glistened on her lips, reminding him of the first time at the *cantina*. He would have sold his soul to kiss her that night. Tonight he intended to kiss the two of them into oblivion.

Her eyes feasted on him as they ate. "Roast pig has become my favorite meal. Every step of your life has enamored me. I guess you saw Pippa give me a gift before we left the *castello*. They were little photographs of you taken from the time you were twelve. I studied them for hours."

He took a quick breath. "Trust Pippa."

"You have no idea how precious they are to me, but she knew what they would mean to me. What a darling boy you were! No wonder you captured their hearts. I'm going to have each one framed." She stared into his eyes. "Tonight, I'm putting in an order for a baby who looks just like you."

"I already put in one earlier today, for an enchanting princess with hair of gold and jewel blue eyes, but I'm more than eager to accommodate you this very minute." He got up from the table and pulled her after him.

Nico could see she'd already inhabited his bedroom. Her feminine items draped around had turned his apartment into a love nest. Giorgio had come out of the closet and sat on the chair. Overcome with emotion, he crushed her to him. He'd never imagined happiness like this was possible.

"I need you, *squisita*—I want to love you and never let you go." In the next breath they lay down together. Throughout the hours of the night they gave in to the passion consuming them. His ardent lover thrilled him.

Enzo had called her adorable. Fausta was that, and so many other things—he was blown away by her womanly magic. He would never be able to get enough of her. Toward morning they both fell asleep with their legs entangled, her face burrowed against his shoulder.

When he heard a phone ring, he knew he couldn't ignore it. A patient might be calling who needed him. But Fausta was one step ahead of him.

"It's my phone, Nico. I'll get it. You sleep." She reached for it on the bedside table, but by now he was awake. For someone to call her at five thirty in the morning concerned him.

She sat up to talk. All he heard her say was "Lanza." After a minute, she thanked her and hung up.

"What's going on, Fausta?"

"I think you can guess." She put the phone on the table and returned to his arms.

"So, our secret is out."

"Yes. My bodyguards saw us go in with your doctor's bag. Then they saw the priest leave the *castello* and knew something was wrong. They caught up to the priest and said they were on the king's business. He told them he'd performed a marriage service for you and me. That's all they needed to hear.

"Lanza wanted to give us a heads-up that the parents are now in the know. They wanted to find out what she knew. I'm glad she couldn't tell them anything."

"So am I, Fausta, but we need to talk to them before I have to leave for the office. My first appointment is at nine. Let's get dressed right now and drive to the palace. What we need to tell them has to be said face-to-face. They deserve to know everything. I want them to know how much I love you."

She threw her arms around his neck. "It's going to be all right, Nico. I promise."

"I'm not worried about me, *tesoro*. It's you."

"Don't worry about me. I have *you*."

Her faith in him was humbling. He recalled a certain conversation with Felipe.

I'm thankful I'm not in your shoes. When the time comes, I don't envy you. But for what it's worth, I defy the king to find a better man for his daughter than you.

"Mamma? Papa? I'd like to introduce you to my husband, Dr. Nico Barsotti, who is a family practice physician at the Hospital of the Three Crosses."

Fausta's parents had been waiting for them in the salon following her phone call to them.

Nico bowed with infinite composure. "Your Majesties. It's a great honor to meet you at last." With his tall, rock-solid build and dark hair, he looked fabulous in his tan suit and tie. She loved him so terribly, her heart hurt.

"How do you do, Dr. Barsotti." Her patrician father and mother made imposing figures, but she could always count on them to be kind. They'd faced difficult situations with her sisters' marriages. "Why don't you and Fausta be seated."

"Thank you."

She reached for Nico's hand and they sat on the love seat opposite her parents.

"Lanza phoned us at Nico's apartment earlier this morning. We imagined the news would leak out but hoped to have a chance to tell you before you heard it from anyone else. Since it's too late for that, we want you to know why we didn't come to you before now. Nico has an amazing story to tell. I'm going to let him explain."

Fausta's beloved husband sat forward and began his incredible tale, starting with life at the orphanage. As the revelations continued to unfold, she watched her parents' somber expressions change to ones of disbelief and eventual awe.

Her father was the first to shake his head. "You're the son of King Carlo and definitely look like him. How amazing, and how sad that you didn't get to meet him."

"As Signor Bruno explained, he didn't dare bring me out of hiding until he felt there was no threat."

"Your father was a remarkable king who had to rule

under the very difficult circumstances of war. I would have attended his funeral if I'd been physically able."

Her mother had put a hand over her heart. "You never got to meet your mother either. I'm so sorry."

"So am I. Where the queen is concerned, I don't know what's going to happen. Fausta and I wanted to be married before I have to make a decision, but we just don't know what that decision will be until she reaches out to me."

Fausta felt her father's eyes on her. They were smiling. "You always knew your own mind. Are you still angry with me that I sent Dego and his sister to school in Italy years ago?"

"Funny you would ask me that, Papa. Last night as I was getting our dinner ready at the apartment, I found myself thanking you for preserving me for Nico. He's my life." Her voice shook.

"That's the way it should be, *figlia mia*."

"I truly did want both of you at the ceremony, but the fuss of a royal wedding isn't for me. I know a worthy cause where we could donate the money."

Her father nodded. "I'm grateful for Enzo and Pippa."

"So are we!" she cried. "They were wonderful to help arrange for the priest to marry us."

Nico nodded. "They've been like parents to me. I owe them so much I can never repay them. Perhaps the day will come when you'll forgive us for getting married in private."

"That was my fault," Fausta blurted. "Nico wanted to tell you, but—"

"But you wanted to do it your own way," her mother said with a smile. "You always did, and now you've married the man who has set you on fire. We couldn't be happier. Welcome to the family, Nico. Whether doctor or king, you've made our daughter happier than we've ever seen her."

"I'm the one who's happy. Fausta is a gift, one I'll treasure all the days of my life."

Fausta got to her feet. "I wish we could talk longer, but Nico has to get to the hospital."

Her parents stood up and walked over to Nico to give him a hug. It thrilled Fausta's heart to watch the three of them embrace.

"Walk me out," Nico whispered a minute later against her neck. When they reached the foyer, he gripped her upper arms tightly. "I never met such gracious people in my life."

"I told you it would be all right."

"No wonder you're the way you are. Thank heaven your father got rid of Dego. Thank heaven for Angelo. Thank heaven for Enzo and Pippa. Thank heaven for Lorenzo, who got me a position at the hospital. The day I met you was the beginning of my life, Fausta."

"And mine. What time can I expect you home?"

"I promised Felipe I'd go out for a beer with him after work. He wants to tell me about their wedding plans. Expect me by seven."

"After you tell him we're married, maybe you might make it by eight?" she teased and pressed a kiss to his lips. "I won't be able to breathe till you get home."

Later that evening Felipe came in to Nico's office at quarter to six. They left in their cars for a favorite pub that served sandwiches and local beer. After ordering from the bar, they found a booth. Sports reviews were on the TV closest to them.

They talked about Felipe's wedding set for August 5. There would be a rehearsal dinner the night before.

Nico was about to tell Felipe everything when there was a news flash that interrupted the latest scores of soccer matches.

"We interrupt this program to bring you breaking news from the royal palace. In a secret wedding ceremony, twenty-five-year-old Princess Fausta Rossiano, middle daughter of King Victor and Queen Ginata, was recently married to commoner Dr. Nico Barsotti. More details will be forthcoming on the ten o'clock news. Now back to our regularly scheduled program."

Felipe let out a whoop everyone in the pub could hear. A grin broke out on his face. "You sly fox. I knew something's been going on. How come I had to hear it on the news?"

Nico lowered his beer glass. "You would have been the first person I told, but Fausta and I still hadn't talked to her parents and that didn't happen until this morning at the palace. I'm positive they didn't release this news to the press, so of course there's been a leak." Which meant Basil and Queen Liliane had heard about it too.

"Where did you get married? When?"

In the next little while Nico told him everything. His friend studied him in sheer amazement as his story unfolded.

"Santo cielo! Over the years you've been looking for your parents, when all this time you've been the son of

King Carlo? And now you're the heir apparent to the throne of La Valazzura? This is the most incredible thing I ever heard."

Nico nodded. "I'm still trying to deal with it. If I didn't have Fausta with me…" He finished the rest of his beer. "Nothing's final. It can't be until I hear from the queen. My father's evil cousin, Giuseppe Umberto, wants the throne for himself. A battle is waging for control over there."

"Would you hate me if I said I hope you stay in Domodossola for the rest of your lives? Mia adores Fausta. It'll be a loss neither of us will get over."

Those words warmed Nico. "How could I hate you when you've been the closest thing I'll ever have to a brother?"

"Amen."

"I love being a doctor, Felipe. I'm not sure I can give it up." He let out a troubled sigh. "But whatever happens, I promise you we'll be here for your wedding. It'll be my privilege to be your best man."

"Is it all right if I tell Mia?"

"She's probably heard already."

"But not *your* story. I'm sure you want to get back to Fausta. You're still on your honeymoon. Let's go."

After another hug, they parted company at their cars. Nico drove home knowing Fausta was there waiting for him. She was all he could think about as he hurried inside the apartment, breathless to sweep her in his arms.

He thought he'd find her in the bedroom since he'd returned later than he'd meant to. Instead he saw her sitting in the living room still dressed in casual clothes. His normally radiant wife looked worried. She wasn't alone. Signor Bruno was with her.

La Valazzura's intelligence agents worked with a speed that didn't escape Nico.

CHAPTER ELEVEN

"BASIL?" HE WALKED over and shook his hand, then sat next to Fausta and grasped her hand. "I take it you've heard the news about our wedding."

The older man nodded. "What's more important, the queen has her spies and your marriage has caused such a serious problem for her, she has sent me here to talk to you personally. Perhaps your wife should be the one to explain to you since I've told her everything."

Nico turned to her. "What's going on, *tesoro*?"

"The queen made the decision that she wants you to be the next king. Since she's Slovenian, she has a young cousin, Princess Anne of Slovenia, who will make you the perfect wife. A marriage between the two of you will keep the ties close between your two countries. Therefore, she wants our marriage dissolved as if it had never been.

"For the sake of the crown you should listen to him, Nico. I'm an impediment. We've only been married for two days and could end it just as quickly."

Angrier than he'd ever been in his life, Nico got to his feet. "When I met with her, Basil, I was a single man. We didn't discuss my marital state, nor did she lay down any conditions."

"Nevertheless, she has now set the rules. I'm here to present them to you."

"Do you mean to tell me that even though she knows I've just married my heart's desire, she could cold-bloodedly ask me to divorce my new wife in order to gain the throne?"

Basil stood up, composed as ever. "She knows your chances could fail if you arrive with a foreign-born wife. It could create more problems for our paranoid nation. She fears the parliament would have great difficulty accepting the situation or trusting it."

Nico didn't believe any of these reasons were the major force driving the queen. She was still unforgiving of what Nico's father had done to her. But it would give her some satisfaction to know he would have to take a new bride he didn't love in order to fill his father's shoes. Somehow, she would have her revenge if he divorced Fausta.

His body tautened. "Thank you for delivering her message to me. You can return to La Valazzura and tell her that no earthly throne is more important to me than a celestial marriage. I plan to live with Fausta through eternity."

Basil's eyes studied him for a long moment. "You'd make a remarkable king. Your cousin will never be able to fill your father's shoes, but I know you could."

"Thank you for the vote of confidence, Basil."

The cousin of Nico's father was banging on the doors of the Azzura palace, ready to burst them down. Let him.

"Thank you for being so gracious, Princess."

As Basil had discovered, Fausta was the epitome of all those exceptional Rossiano qualities. Nico had never loved her more than he did at this moment.

"I'll convey your decision to the queen." Their visitor bowed to both of them and left the apartment.

"Bellissima—" He swung around to embrace her, but she stood at a distance, all closed up. Nico knew that look. "The waiting is over, *grazie a Dio.* Our new life is ahead of us. Come to bed with me. I'm aching for you."

She took another step back. "We have to talk first."

He took a deep breath. "There's nothing to talk about. We're staying here in Domodossola for the rest of our lives."

"Nico—you've just been told that Queen Liliane wants you to be the new ruler of your country and take over where your father left off. We know it's what he would have wanted if he were still alive."

"Except that she wasn't honest with me and had her own secret agenda. I'm a married man now and that disqualifies me."

"But we can get a divorce."

His brows furrowed. "I'm going to pretend I didn't hear you say that."

"You have to listen to me! You've been on a path your entire life to discover your identity. I believe with all my heart that you're supposed to be the new king. There've been too many little miracles along the way that prove to me you're the one who's been destined to be the head of the country."

Her words gutted him. "Does our love mean so little to you that one word from the queen and you're willing to destroy everything between us so that I can be king?"

"No. I'm not saying this right. Please, darling, I—"

"I think you are," he cut her off. "Is it possible that my becoming king at any cost is more important to you than I am? How many times have we talked about the class difference between us? I'm beginning to see that there truly is a gigantic gulf that separates our thinking."

She shook her head. At this point tears were spilling down her pale cheeks. "I need to explain what I meant."

"I heard you loud and clear. You're from the aristocracy. You people really do march to a holy drum. Angelo was right. Queen Liliane has decreed what she deems necessary, and you fall on your sword. But where does that leave me? According to you, there is no *us*! Our wedding ceremony can be discarded for the greater good. Is that it?"

"Yes!" she cried. "Because you're a magnificent man, one who's destined for greater things than most men on this earth. It's your birthright! You heard Basil. I saw the way he looked and spoke to you. He holds you in reverence and you can't deny it."

"I deny nothing. But I'm beginning to wonder how you can consider making such a sacrifice, *unless* our love pales in comparison to the love you had for Dego. Is that what this is about? This morning your father asked if you'd forgiven him for sending Dego away. I find it amazing that after all this time, his name was still brought up. Is *he* the one you'll never be able to forget? Is that why you're able to consider letting me go?"

"No, darling. You have this all wrong."

He headed for the bedroom. "Nothing you could say

is going to take away my pain. Drive safely when you go home."

She followed him. "I'm not leaving. This is my home."

"I don't think so. We might not have signed papers yet, but I already feel divorced."

"Don't you know I only said these things because I don't want to be the one who holds you back from your real purpose in life?"

He wheeled around. "I thought we were going to make all our decisions together! I'm not at all certain what my real purpose in life is except to be your husband and the father of our children! I thought that was what you wanted."

"*It is*, or I wouldn't be your wife right now. But, Nico, I was with you that day we drove to Biella and visited the orphanage. You revealed the secrets of your heart to me. I visited with those who loved you. You're a unique man who has gifts the world needs."

"Needs my own wife can give up for the whim of the queen?"

"How can you say it's a whim?"

"She found a way to get back at my father by making a decision she knew would tear me apart. But the only person who has torn me apart is you. I'm going out for a while, but I'll be back."

"Please don't leave—"

"Just give me a little time."

He heard her call his name, but his pain was too deep, and he kept walking.

Nico, Nico. At two thirty in the morning he still hadn't come home. Beyond sick, Fausta paced the floor.

When she heard the ding on her phone she checked the text message.

I've gone to the office. Won't be home until after work.

This was a Nico she didn't recognize. She'd done this to him.

Beyond tears, she lay awake until midmorning, soul-searching. As she sorted through their conversation, it stunned her that he thought she still loved Dego. He couldn't be jealous of him!

But the more she dug for answers, the more she understood that the orphan boy hadn't owned anything of his own. He didn't want to belong to anyone but his own parents. Everything he'd received while growing up had been given to him by well-meaning strangers. He didn't have anything of his own until he'd earned his first paycheck as a doctor. Even then he sent money to Angelo.

All his life had been a fight to compete and survive. Then he'd met her, and another kind of fight had ensued. He'd overcome the great obstacle in his mind to marry her knowing she was royal. Yet no sooner had they gotten married than Basil had shown up with the queen's proposition. And what had Fausta done?

She'd flung Nico's love for her in his face when it was the last thing she'd ever meant to do. To tell him she'd give him a divorce after the two days of joy they'd just shared was so cruel, she couldn't believe she'd said it. Fausta needed to repair the damage before any more time passed.

The first thing she did was call his work. His receptionist answered. "Dr. Barsotti's office."

"Hello? My name is Eugenia Santi. This is an emergency. Could the doctor see me at the end of the day? It's a female problem that's getting much worse."

"Are you bleeding?"

"No, but the pain is severe."

"I see. Has he seen you before?"

"Yes, but it was a house call."

"He has another late patient too, but why don't you come at five thirty p.m. and I'll see if he'll fit you in after that. Otherwise you may have to go to the ER."

"Thank you."

The second she hung up, she showered and washed her hair. Then she put on a filmy dress in a blue and yellow print with flutter sleeves. With blue forget-me-not earrings and a splash of her favorite fragrance, she felt ready to take on her unsuspecting husband.

Her heart was thudding so hard she was afraid the patients waiting for him could hear it as she entered the reception room and reported to the receptionist. The woman stared hard at her. "I'm afraid it's going to be a wait, Signora Santi." She'd noticed the blue diamond ring Fausta was wearing.

"It doesn't matter as long as I get to see him."

After an hour the receptionist told her she could go in. This was a whole new experience for Fausta, who'd never visited him here. Her excitement was off the charts when she entered his impressive-looking book-lined office.

He wore a white lab coat and had been putting something into the computer. When he turned to her, the look on his face was worth all the trouble she'd gone to to surprise him. His eyes devoured her inch by inch.

"I told your receptionist I was having female problems," she began before he could say a word. "But I lied because it's a heart problem. The worst kind there is, and it's so painful no pill or operation can fix it. You see, it's my husband. I hurt him so terribly, I don't know how to win him back. At this point my pain is unbearable.

"Please tell me you can help me. Maybe if I explain, you can give me some advice. You see, he has had to fight for everything all his life. He fought for me against all odds. But when it was my turn to fight for him, I told him I wouldn't stand in his way if he wanted something more. It was the wrong thing to say. All he wanted was me and he has proven it over and over again.

"*Dottore?* How do I prove that all I want in this life is his love? How do I convince him that what I once felt for a boy from childhood was simple puppy love? I didn't know the meaning of love until I met my husband. If I don't get help soon, I'm not going make it."

Nico's expression didn't change as he buzzed his receptionist and told her she could go home.

"If you'll step into the examining room, I'll listen to your heart and we'll go from there."

Holding her breath, she followed him into the other room.

"Let me help you sit on the table." He put his hands around her hips and lifted her with ease. Their bodies brushed together, sending a thrill through her. She waited breathlessly as he reached for his stethoscope and started listening to her heart. His jaw was pressed against her cheek. He smelled divine.

"You're right. A lot of damage has been done. It's pounding way too hard to be healthy. I want you to lie down."

Heat swept over her as she lay back. He slid his hands up her arms and pinned her there. His eyes were like lasers as he examined her features. "Your poor husband. You're so beautiful. He must have a heart attack every time he lets you out in public. My advice is that you go home and make love to him. Never let him go, not even after you've convinced him that you love him the way he loves you."

"I promise," she whispered. "Kiss me, Dr. Barsotti, or I think I'm going to pass out from wanting you too much."

"Well we can't have that. Not in my office."

His mouth found hers and he kissed her close to senseless. Tears beaded her lashes. Her husband had forgiven her. She couldn't ask for anything more.

"I have news, *bellissima*," he murmured. "This afternoon I had a phone call from Basil. After he reported to the queen, she said that she'd only been testing me to see if I was an honorable man. If I hadn't passed the test, that would have been it. But because I loved you more than I loved anything else, she says she wants me to fly to La Valazzura with you.

"Basil told me she'd like to meet the woman who was prepared to put me first if that's what you wanted for me, even if it meant a divorce. With that kind of unselfish love, she feels you'll make the perfect queen. I guess I have some serious rethinking to do where the queen is concerned."

"Darling—the room is spinning. I really think I'm going to pass out."

"Keep holding on. Don't faint on me. We need to go home and talk about what we want to do. Our world is out there waiting, whichever one it is."

EPILOGUE

THE SMALL ROYAL dining room of the palace had been lit with candles. A fragrance from the pink roses filled the ornate room. Fausta knew her mother had picked and arranged them for this delicious roast pig dinner to welcome Nico into the family. Jeanne, the head chef at the palace, had really outdone herself as a favor to Fausta to honor her new husband with his favorite meal.

Her parents sat at one end. Lanza and Donetta sat across from each other with their husbands. Fausta and Nico had found their places at the other end. Their family had sat around this table all their lives, but tonight everything was different for Fausta. For the first time since she was a little girl, she no longer felt conflicted about being royal and enjoyed a sense of belonging that was new to her.

Falling in love with Nico had changed her perspective on life. She knew a sense of completeness and was so full of joy she could hardly contain it.

Her father tapped his wine goblet with a spoon and got to his feet. "What a glorious sight! Our three precious daughters married to husbands they love and who love them. What father or mother could ask for more, especially when they are the finest men Ginata and I know."

Fausta smiled at her husband, who squeezed her thigh beneath the table.

"Nico—that's how we know you—welcome to the family," her father continued. "Whatever path you and Fausta choose to take, whether you remain Dr. Barsotti here in Domodossola, or Crown Prince Massimo in La Valazzura, we support you and wish you joy.

"Our Fausta followed her dream to marry a commoner. You got your wish, poppet. We got our wish too, because he makes you so happy. And…it doesn't hurt that he's the son of King Carlo, a sovereign I always admired."

While everyone chuckled, Fausta's eyes filled with tears.

"Ginata and I are content and looking forward to enjoying our Rufy and soon-to-be born grandchildren for years to come. Therefore, we've decided now is the time for me to give up the crown. It will be conferred on Stefano, who is Lanza's beloved and has been my rock since he joined the family.

"The coronation will take place in a week because Enrico must soon get back to Vallefiore to run the affairs of his kingdom. Before he and Donetta leave, we want our whole family together to sustain Stefano as the new king of Domodossola."

Everyone clapped for Stefano, who hugged Lanza.

When everyone had congratulated him, her father added, "If Nico decides to step in to his father's shoes, then we'll all fly to La Valazzura to see his coronation whether the doctor gives me permission or not."

"Papa!" the girls cried in fear.

Suddenly her mother stood up. "Don't worry. He may have been in charge all these years, but now that he's stepping down, it's my turn to lay down the law and I'm not letting him out of my sight! We're not going anywhere. If necessary, we'll watch Nico's coronation on television."

Fausta squeezed Nico's hand before hurrying to the other end of the table to hug her parents. Her sisters got there first.

When she finally turned around, she saw the husbands huddled in one corner of the dining room talking quietly. It thrilled her that Nico was already bonding with his brothers-in-law. As she approached, Nico saw her coming and started toward her. Talk about a blinding light of happiness. Like Fausta, her husband had found peace.

*****

A HUSBAND SHE COULDN'T FORGET

CHRISTINE RIMMER

For MSR, always.

Chapter One

The accident never should have happened. And it wouldn't have happened if Alyssa Santangelo hadn't let herself get distracted by thoughts of the past.

With a long stay in her hometown ahead of her, Aly had promised herself that this time, she would not try to keep a low profile. This time, she wouldn't be slinking around town like a heartsick fool, trying to avoid any chance she might run into the guy who'd lied and broken her heart and had her served with divorce papers after making zero effort to work things out.

And there. She'd just done it. Let her mind stray into dangerous territory. She wasn't going to do that. She would not think about *him*.

And she *wasn't* thinking about him. Not really.

She was only reassuring herself as to how this visit

would go, only bolstering her resolution to stand tall and be strong. With a deep breath and a determined smile, she focused on the road ahead of her.

The drive from Portland International to Valentine Bay was a beautiful one. They called this section of US Route 26 the Sunset Highway. It wound in and out of the national forest, working its way west toward the setting sun.

It was just twilight on a warm Saturday evening in July. Aly had the windows down in her rental car and the air smelled of spruce and fir. Of Oregon.

Of home.

And her thoughts…

Her thoughts just wouldn't behave. They kept drifting, wandering, pretending to stay in the present, and then circling back again.

To her ex, to Connor Bravo.

Really, she hardly thought of the guy anymore—or if she did, she reminded herself firmly to *stop* thinking of him, to count her blessings instead.

And her blessings were many. She had a job she loved at Strategic Image. The ad agency had hired her as an assistant to an assistant straight out of the University of Oregon. She'd started at the bottom of the ladder, but she'd moved up fast. She'd made friends, good friends, the kind a woman can count on. Her current apartment in Tribeca was perfect, a small space, but with a huge closet for her fabulous wardrobe. She was living her dream in New York, New York.

Only one thing was missing—the right man to share her life with.

It wasn't as though she hadn't tried to find him. She

put herself out there, dating guys her friends had introduced her to and guys she met via Match and Coffee Meets Bagel. Somehow, though, that special something was always missing. Her relationships never lasted that long. The most recent of those had ended a couple weeks ago. Kyle Santos was a great guy. He just wasn't the *right* guy. It had seemed wrong to drag things out, so she'd broken it off with him.

And seriously, what was she brooding about? She was only twenty-nine and mostly focused on her job. She would find the man for her, eventually. And she would get it right the second time around.

Coming home, though...

Well, it was tough. The memories were everywhere she turned. She and Connor used to drive this stretch of highway together several times a year, going back and forth from OU in Eugene. They would stop at rustic, logging-themed Camp 18 for burgers and to give their phones a workout snapping pictures of each other, mugging it up with the chainsaw sculpture of Big Foot at the entrance to the gift shop.

Those were the good times. The *best* times.

Too bad Connor had screwed everything up, lying to keep her and then refusing to even try the life he'd sworn he was eager to live with her.

She blinked and refocused and reminded herself yet again to cut it out.

Didn't work.

Seven years since he'd divorced her, and still it took only an hour on the Sunset Highway for the memories to come flooding back.

Did he ever think of her?

Oh, I don't think so...

During one brief visit home five years ago, she'd seen him down on Beach Street with a blonde. They'd looked like a Ralph Lauren ad, Connor and the blonde, both of them all tawny, tanned and fit. Aly had ducked into a leather goods store before he could spot her, but the damage was done. The sight of him with another woman had cut her to the quick.

Aly clutched the steering wheel more tightly. She swallowed hard and blinked against the hot pressure of rising tears.

Seriously. What was the matter with her?

Seven years since her marriage ended. She hadn't spoken to the man once in all that time and she never would. She really was over him, definitely.

"You're doing it. Again," she whispered at the windshield, her voice disgustingly breathy, weighted with despair. She flexed her fingers to relax them. It was years ago. It didn't matter. She wasn't coming home for him.

"Woman up," she muttered to the empty car.

If she saw him, she saw him. *Get over it. He has.*

Up ahead, headlights gleamed. It was weird, in the fading light. The oncoming vehicle almost looked as though it had swerved into her lane.

Scant seconds later she realized the horrible truth. The headlights *were* in her lane.

With a sharp cry, she jerked the wheel hard to the right to avoid impact—too hard, she realized too late. The thick trunk of a Douglas fir reared up beyond the windshield.

A split second later, the world went black.

* * *

Voices.

They seemed to come from all around her. Voices and sirens and strange sounds—air escaping, metal creaking. Her chest felt like someone had whacked it with a hammer. And the skin of her face, which was buried in something that smelled like singed baby powder, burned as though she'd face-planted on asphalt.

She heard a groaning sound. It came from her own mouth.

A man's voice near her left ear said, "She's coming around."

Another groan escaped her. Gritting her teeth, she willed her body into action and somehow managed to flop back away from the smelly thing that covered her face—an air bag! The smelly thing was an air bag.

With yet another groan, she put it together. Somehow, she'd been in an accident, and it looked pretty bad...

Carefully, she turned her head to meet the worried eyes of the state trooper staring at her through the wide-open driver's-door window. Red light from a light bar reflected on his face in strobe-like flashes.

"It's okay," the trooper promised, in that tone people use when it really isn't, but what else can you say? "We're going to get you out of there. Can you talk to me?"

"I...yes. Of course."

"How are you feeling?"

"Uh." She tried to decide. "I think I'm all in one piece, at least."

"Good girl. What else?"

"There's...some pain. My chest aches. And my

face..." It really did feel as though someone had taken a cheese grater to her cheeks and forehead.

"That's from the air bag," the trooper said.

Aly shut her eyes and dropped her head to the seat rest again. "Everything hurts, but I don't think anything is broken..." Or maybe she was just in shock and didn't even realize she was almost dead.

"Hold tight," the trooper said. "I promise we're going to get you out of there as quickly as we can..."

It took a while. They brought out the Jaws of Life and sawed her free of the ruined car, which had folded itself around her like a big metal pretzel.

The EMTs moved in. They talked about how lucky she was—her face a little scratched up, a big bruise forming like a beauty pageant banner diagonally across her chest from the seat belt. On her left knee, she had a cut that would need stitches.

And she'd sustained what they called a mild traumatic brain injury—seriously, who even knew you could use the words *mild* and *traumatic brain injury* in the same sentence? One of the EMTs said they estimated she'd been unconscious for less than ten minutes. Patiently, they guided Aly through the basic vision and consciousness tests.

She passed, the paramedic reassured her. She was going to be fine. The woman patted her shoulder gently. And Aly felt such gratitude, like a warm wave washing through her aching chest.

So what if everything hurt? She was lucky to be alive and relatively unharmed.

The EMTs gave permission for her to talk briefly to another state trooper, a woman this time. Aly tried to remember. She recalled passing Camp 18, but after that, it was all a blur.

"I don't know, really, how it happened, or why I hit that tree. I think there were headlights, maybe, coming at me, in my lane…"

The trooper nodded. "We have a witness, a woman in a vehicle who wasn't far behind you. She saw the other car in your lane and barely swerved in time to avoid a collision herself. She's the one who called 9-1-1. Unfortunately, her description of the oncoming car is too vague for identification. She said she thought it was a dark sedan."

"So, whoever it was will get off scot-free?"

The trooper gave a shrug of regret. "It happens—too often, sad to say."

Aly put her hand to her head. "I'm sorry. My head really hurts."

The officer was sympathetic. "I'll let you go, then." She gave Aly a card. "Call this number if anything more comes back to you."

"What about my things? They're still in what's left of the car."

The trooper gave her another card with a number to call to get her stuff once what was left of the car had been "processed" and "cleared."

And that was it. The EMTs loaded her into an ambulance and off they went to Valentine Bay Memorial.

At the hospital, she kept telling everyone that she felt fine, just a little banged up with a headache. She asked to call her parents. The request brought soothing noises and promises that she could make the call "soon." They took her vitals and examined her more thoroughly for any new and potentially worrisome symptoms from her head injury. The air bag burns were declared minor and treated with a gentle cleaning and antibiotic ointment.

In the end, the doctor in charge prescribed a night at the hospital for observation. Barring complications, he promised, she would be released the next morning.

They moved her to a regular room and she used the phone by the bed to call her mom, who answered on the second ring with, "If you're a telemarketer, hang up now."

Her cheeks still hurt, but Aly smiled anyway. "Hey, Mom. It's me."

Catriona Santangelo said nothing for a slow count of three, after which she stated carefully, "You're not calling from your phone and we expected you two hours ago."

"Yeah, well…" Alyssa let her head drop back to the pillow with a sigh. "Can you believe I don't even know where to start with this?"

"What's happened?"

"I'm fine, I promise you. Are you in bed?" Aly's mom was forty-eight—and seven months pregnant with her fifth son. In recent weeks, her blood pressure had climbed. She'd had cramping and some bleeding and the family doctor had put her on modified bed rest—which was why Aly, who never came home for more than a few days at a stretch, had taken an extended leave from her job in Manhattan. At a time like this, Cat needed her only daughter at her side and Aly needed to be with her mom.

Cat scoffed, "Of course I'm in bed. I hardly dare to get up to go to the bathroom. The men in this family will be the death of me, I swear. *Overprotective* is too tame a word for your father and your brothers, let me tell you."

"And yet here you are, having another one."

"God never gives us more than we can handle—plus, well, you know your father." Ernesto Santangelo was a plumber by trade. He was strong and fit at fifty and he loved Aly's mom with a fiery passion, to say the least. Cat's voice grew husky. "Impulsive and so romantic. What can I say? I could never resist him."

"La, la, la—I don't want to hear about your, er, private life, Mom."

Cat started laughing and then Aly was laughing, too—until she gasped at the pain around her ribs. "Ouch!"

"All right, Alyssa," her mother said sternly. "What is going on?"

"It's nothing that serious. I was in a little accident, that's all. My rental car was totaled, but I'm going to be fine."

More dead air on the line. Alyssa's mom never got hysterical. Cat was the strong, silent, effective type in any emergency. "Tell me," she finally commanded. "Tell me everything. Now."

Aly explained what she could remember about the accident, finishing with, "I don't really remember why, exactly, I veered off the road and hit a tree, but when I came to, the car was a goner."

"Thank God you're all right—but a *mild* TBI? That's still a concussion, right?"

"Yes. And do not get out of bed, Mom. Do not come to the hospital."

"But are you sure that you're…?"

"A little battered and very relieved to be all in one piece. That's where I am on this. They're keeping me overnight, but only for observation. It's nothing serious and I'll be home with you in the morning."

After another unhappy silence, Cat promised to stay put. "Your father and your brothers will be there soon," she said. "Give me the number there in your room."

Aly rattled it off.

"I love you, Alyssa Siobhan."

"I love *you*, Mom." She said goodbye.

Twenty minutes later, her dad appeared. He kissed her carefully on her forehead and called her Bella, the way he always did. She reassured him that she was doing fine.

Within the next half hour, her four brothers filed in. They surrounded her, a wall of Italian-Irish-American testosterone, their thick, dark eyebrows scrunched up with worry for her. She reassured them that it looked worse than it was and the doctors were only keeping her till tomorrow to be on the safe side.

Her dad announced that he and the boys would be staying at the hospital with her. The nurses brought extra chairs and the men settled in to keep her company. They took turns visiting the cafeteria and the beverage machines in the waiting area for refreshments. Her head was aching a little and she started to feel really tired.

"Go to sleep," urged her dad, his warm, rough hand

gently squeezing her arm. "We'll be here when you wake up."

"Dad, really. You guys don't need to stay."

He patted her hand. "Just rest. Close your eyes and let it all go…"

She followed his whispered instructions. But before she could drift off, a nurse came in and shooed the men out to take her blood pressure and her temperature, to test her pupil reaction and ask her about her level of pain, which was minimal.

When the nurse left, her dad and her brother Marco returned to sit with her. They talked a little. Marco reported that he'd enjoyed his first year at OU. Her dad reassured her that her mom was safe at home, tucked into bed per doctor's orders, with her brother Pascal's wife, Sandy, looking after her.

Aly's eyes drifted closed again and her father's deep voice faded to a low drone in the background…

She woke late in the night, with no idea where she was. Startled, she popped up straight in the strange bed and sent a bewildered glance around the dark room.

She saw her oldest brother, Dante, slumped down asleep in the bedside chair. Something must have happened to her…

She glanced across the room and saw the institutional clock on the wall. There was a bed tray and rollers next to her bed—a hospital bed.

An accident. I've been in an accident—haven't I?

Her knee throbbed dully, her cheeks and forehead burned and she had a mild headache. Every time she took a breath, her chest hurt—from the seat belt, most likely.

She must have made a noise, because as she sagged back to the pillow again, Dante flinched and opened his eyes. "Hey, little sis." He'd always called her that, even though she was second oldest, after him. "How you feelin'?"

"Everything aches," she grumbled. "But I'll live." Longing flooded her, for the comfort of her husband's strong arms. She needed him near. He would soothe all her pains and ease her weird, formless fears. "Where's Connor gotten off to?"

Dante's mouth fell half-open, as though in bafflement at her question. "Connor?"

He looked so befuddled, she couldn't help chuckling a little, even though laughing made her chest and ribs hurt. "Yeah. Connor. You know, that guy I married nine years ago—my husband, your brother-in-law?"

Dante sat up. He also continued to gape at her like she was a few screwdrivers short of a full tool kit. "Uh, what's going on? You think you're funny?"

"Funny? Because I want my husband?" She bounced back up to a sitting position. "What, exactly, is happening here? I mean it, Dante. Be straight with me. Where's Connor?"

Now Dante sat very still, as though he feared the slightest movement might set her off, make her do something dangerous.

And she *felt* dangerous. A scream of fear and longing crawled up her throat. She swallowed it down and demanded, "I want Connor. Go get him and tell him I need him. Now." Her headache was worse, pounding so hard, a merciless hammer inside her head.

Dante patted the air between them, trying to soothe her, to settle her down. "Aly, you have to—"

"Connor!" She practically shouted. "Get me my husband, Dante. Bring him in here to me. Now."

"Okay." Dante leaped to his feet. "Take a deep breath and try to relax. I'll be right back…" He raced out the door.

She pressed a hand to the sore spot on her head as it throbbed all the harder. "Connor," she whispered, shutting her eyes, *willing* him to come to her. *Connor, I need you. I need you so much…*

A nurse bustled in, Dante close on her heels. "What can I get for you, Alyssa?"

"My husband," she demanded. "I want you to get my husband in here now."

Chapter Two

Wednesday morning, just as Connor Bravo was about to leave for work, the doorbell rang.

Connor dropped his briefcase on the floor by the stairs leading down to the garage and went to answer, half expecting it to be Mrs. Garber from next door looking for Maurice. The lean, black cat was always getting out. He would strut around the neighborhood, his skinny tail held high, like he owned every house on Sandpiper Lane—and the people in them, too.

But it wasn't Mrs. Garber.

"Hello, Connor." Dante Santangelo, dressed in Valentine Bay PD blues, stuck his fists in his pockets and gave Conner a barely perceptible nod.

"Dante." What was he doing here? Once, they'd been best friends. But for the past seven years, they'd both taken pains to steer clear of each other.

Alyssa? The name ricocheted in his brain, a boomerang with sharp edges.

Had something happened to her? Just the thought had him widening his stance to keep from staggering where he stood. "What?" he heard himself ask, the single word ragged, overloaded with equal parts fear and regret—fear for whatever could be so bad it had brought her brother to his door again.

And regret for all the ways that he, Connor, had messed up. He'd been a complete ass and he knew it, a selfish kid who'd screwed up his marriage to the most amazing woman in the world—and then refused to even try to fix what he'd broken.

How many times had he wished he could have another shot?

Too many.

But he didn't deserve another shot. He'd thrown away what he wanted most. And when he'd finally admitted to himself what an idiot he'd been, it was a long way past too late.

The hard fact was that the best thing he could do for Aly was to leave her the hell alone, let her live the life she loved in New York City and find a better guy than him.

Dante's expression gave him nothing. "We need to talk."

His heart in his throat and his gut twisted into a double knot, Connor stepped back and gestured his ex-best friend inside.

Dante refused Connor's stilted offer of coffee. In the living room, Aly's brother stood by the slate fireplace and flatly recited the scary facts. "Four days ago, driving home from Portland International, reportedly in an effort to avoid an oncoming car, Aly swerved and ran into a tree. She wasn't speeding, but she was going fast enough that her rental car was totaled."

Connor's heart, still stuck in his throat, seemed to have turned to a block of solid ice. "What are you telling me? My God, is she…?"

"She's alive, but she's pretty banged up. And she had a concussion. She was knocked unconscious, though not for that long."

Connor's heart slid down into his chest again and recommenced beating—too fast. "So then, you're saying she's okay?"

"Not exactly…"

Connor shoved his hands in his own pockets to keep from grabbing Dante and shaking more information from him—or worse, punching him a few times until he finally explained what had happened to Aly. "Is she okay or not?"

"At first, we thought she was going to be fine."

"But…?"

"She woke up before dawn the morning after the wreck, and asked for you."

For a split second, he was the happiest man on the planet—until reality hit him. "She hates me. Why would she ask for me?"

Dante looked at him kind of warily. "Look, man. Maybe you ought to sit down, you know?"

"Just answer the question."

"Suit yourself. It's, well, it's some kind of weird amnesia."

"What? Wait. Amnesia? What are you telling me? You're making no sense."

Dante glared. "I'm trying. But you need to shut up long enough for me to explain."

Connor winced. "Sorry." He forked his fingers back through his hair. "I'll keep my mouth shut. Go on."

Dante eyed him with skepticism, but then laid it right out there. "My sister is firmly convinced that the two of you are still married."

Still married. Him and Aly? "That's crazy."

"Now you're getting the picture." Dante's expression was bleak. "We've tried everything—arguing, reasoning, begging, pacifying. Nothing seems to get her past it. She will not accept that you two have been divorced for years."

"But…her doctors, they must have some idea of what to do, how to handle this."

"They've tried. There have been CT scans and MRIs, long visits with a therapist—and with Father Francis, too."

Father Francis. The name brought back memories. Of the little Catholic church on Ocean Road where all the Santangelos had been baptized. Of Aly, a vision in white, coming down the aisle to him. Their wedding had been small, just the families, and put together quickly because they wanted to be married more than they'd wanted all the trappings of a big ceremony and a fancy reception. Father Francis had led them through their wedding vows.

Dante continued, "The brain imaging tests revealed nothing out of the normal range. Father Francis keeps reminding us that God will find a way. The doctors predict that over time she will remember she's not married anymore and hasn't been for years. Her real life will come back to her."

"But…what about right now? How is she now?"

"She's suffering." Dante's dark eyes accused him. "She keeps demanding to see you. At first, she cried and carried on, refusing to listen when we told her that you'd divorced her years ago. Now, she just quietly insists that she doesn't believe us and she needs to talk to you. We're kind of out of options at this point. And she's only getting calmer—and at the same time, more scarily insistent. She says that if you won't come to her, she'll hunt you down and demand to know what's going on, why you've suddenly deserted her."

Connor swore low and sank to the fireplace seat.

Dante went on, "It got worse this morning. She's started to think that something bad must have happened to you. She's staying at my folks' house. Mom called me a half an hour ago to tell me that at breakfast Aly called Dad a liar right to his face. About broke the old man's heart. I mean, she *is* his favorite. She told Dad she needed him to tell her why we were all keeping the awful truth from her. My mother's pregnant, on bed rest. She doesn't need the extra stress of worrying that Aly's going to climb out a window and run off in search of you."

"Of course not." Connor had always liked Aly's mom. "Cat's having another baby?" She had to be almost fifty.

Dante sneered at him. "Didn't I just say that?"

Connor put up a hand. "Can you dial back the hostility a notch or two, maybe? It's not helping."

"Yeah, well. Let's just be honest here. I don't trust you. You bring out the worst in me."

"What do you want me to do, Dante?"

Aly's brother shook his head. "I hate it. I don't want you anywhere near her. But she really needs to see you. She needs to hear the truth from you."

"No problem." He'd deserted her once. This time, he would be there when she needed him. "I'll go to her. You said she's at your parents' house?"

"Yeah. They discharged her from Memorial day before yesterday."

"I'll go over to your folks' house right now." He stood.

"You'll talk to her new shrink first," growled Dante. "And you'll do what the doctor tells you to do."

Connor put up both hands in complete surrender. "However it has to be, I'm in. Where do I go to see the psychiatrist?"

"*You* don't go anywhere. I'll drive you there."

"Why?"

"The family won't have you taking this over, trying to run this show. You're not her husband anymore. You've got no claim on her and if you want to help, you'll do it our way."

A spike of adrenaline had Connor on the verge of saying something he would almost certainly regret. But he wasn't the same hotheaded, self-centered kid he'd been when he'd ruined his marriage to Aly. This wasn't about him. It wasn't about Dante. It wasn't about their lifelong friendship that had been tested more than once and ended up turning into something hard and dark and ready to explode.

This was about Aly. Connor *would* remember that. "Fine. I'll ride with you." He took his cell from his pocket. "Let me just call Daniel." The oldest of Connor's siblings, Daniel ran the family company, Valentine Logging. Connor was CFO.

Dante eyed him with furious suspicion. "We don't need the family business on the street. What's your brother got to do with this?"

"For God's sake, chill. I need to let Daniel know I won't be in today."

Dr. Serena Warbury had her office in Valentine Bay's downtown historic district. She'd taken a room on the second floor of a rambling two-story Craftsman-style house repurposed for professional use. Connor and Dante sat in the downstairs waiting room until Dr. Warbury was ready for them.

Dante didn't even try to make conversation. He sat with his elbows on the chair arms, fingers laced together between them, and never once even glanced in Connor's direction.

Connor thumbed through a dog-eared *Sports Illustrated*. When that got old, he stared out the window and tried not to worry too much about Aly. Eventually, the therapist came down the stairs and led them up to the second floor.

Right off, Connor liked Dr. Warbury. She was smart and direct. It took her no time at all to figure out that Dante's hostility toward his ex-brother-in-law wouldn't help the situation. She sent Dante back downstairs to wait. He wasn't happy about it, but he went.

Connor refused a cup of herbal tea. He took a chair

by a window with a partial view of the Pacific a few blocks away. The therapist repeated what Dante had already told him about Aly's condition and how it would most likely fade over time on its own.

She went on to explain, "Right now, we want her to take it easy. That's unlikely to happen until we can reduce the anguish and confusion she's suffering, with her brain telling her one thing and everyone else insisting otherwise. She needs a lot of rest and as little excitement and stress as possible."

"I get all that. But what can I *do*?"

"To help her, you will have to be patient and kind—and honest, too. The whole point is to reassure Alyssa that everything will work out, while at the same time never giving her any less than the truth. You can't 'humor' her or go along when she insists something's true that isn't. You have to be frank. You are divorced and have been for several years. If she tries to insist otherwise, you must quietly and firmly tell her that's not true."

"No lies. I can do that."

"And you mustn't indulge your own emotions, either. You have to be calm and steady. Let her lead the conversation. And no matter what she says, you must not become defensive or angry. This is not about you, not an opportunity for you to justify your past actions, whatever they might have been. I'm not privy to the details of your divorce, but I understand from what members of her family have said that it was not amicable."

"They're right. I was a dick, okay?"

"Well." Dr. Warbury seemed to be hiding a smile. "Don't be overly hard on yourself, either."

"I get it. I honestly do."

"If you're going to become upset, you will upset Alyssa."

"I won't upset her," he vowed, and wondered at himself to promise such a thing. Anything could happen. She might take one look at him and realize he really just pissed her the hell off, no matter how bland and even-tempered he managed to be.

Dr. Warbury smoothed her yellow skirt. "I believe it could be helpful to her, to see you and reassure herself that you are all right, to hear it from you that you two are divorced. But if you don't think you can keep control of your emotions, please say so now and I will recommend to you and to her family that you stay away."

By then, he was seriously considering backing out. If seeing him ended up only making it worse for her, he would never forgive himself.

But at the same time, he really wanted to help—and he needed to see her, to find out for himself just how bad off she was, to do whatever he could to make things more bearable for her. She'd always been so strong and focused, so totally in charge of herself and her life. It must be killing her to have her own mind betraying her, to have everyone telling her that reality was not as she believed it to be.

He had no illusions. There was no possibility of a future for them, together, anymore. They'd had something real and true and beautiful. All that was gone now, broken beyond repair, mostly by him. He didn't want to fix it. He didn't believe it could be fixed.

He just wanted Aly to be whole and happy. He wanted her to be ready, the way she'd always been, to take on the world. He wanted to be able to picture her living the East Coast life she'd created for herself, making it big in New York, New York.

"I'll follow your instructions," he said. "Please tell her brother it's all right that I see her."

The ride to Cat and Ernesto's house was as silent as the one to Dr. Warbury's office had been.

Dante seethed. Connor had the feeling that anything he said might set him off. He and Dante were the same age, both of them two years older than Alyssa.

It was sad, really. What they'd come to. All through elementary school, middle school and high school, it was Connor and Dante, joined at the hip, the best of friends. Alyssa had been off-limits to Connor then. A guy didn't put moves on his best friend's little sister—no matter how much he wanted to.

Aly hadn't helped. She'd done everything in her power to get him to give in and make a move on her.

She'd started crushing on him when she was thirteen. By then, she already had serious curves to go with her beautiful face, her thick, dark hair, cobalt-blue eyes and milk-white skin. She started wearing shorts and tight T-shirts every chance she got, just to drive him crazy.

But he'd pretended he didn't notice. His mom and dad had died that year, the year Aly was thirteen. They'd drowned in a tsunami during a vacation in Thailand, of all the awful ways to go. He was all broken up about it, like everyone else in the Bravo family. Whenever Aly tried to get close to him, he would think of his lost parents and nurture the ache inside himself, the feeling of bitter loneliness to be without his mom and dad. He'd always felt a little guilty that he used his parents' death to protect himself, to keep from getting too close to Dante's gorgeous little sister.

After a year or so of trying really hard to get his attention, Aly seemed to get the message that he wasn't going there. She went totally the other way, completely ignoring him. He'd told himself that all he felt was relief. She was Dante's precious sister and Dante was his best friend in the world. He didn't need that kind of trouble.

Not long after she turned fifteen, Aly started hanging out with her first boyfriend, Craig Watson. Connor had managed to keep his cool about that, but barely. He'd had a lot of violent fantasies wherein he beat the crap out of Craig. Somehow, he'd managed not to act on those fantasies.

Over time, he'd even succeeded in convincing himself that everything was cool between him and Aly, that he thought of her as an honorary little sister and nothing more.

Until they met up at OU. She was a freshman and he was in his junior year, and Dante was miles away at Portland State. At first, they pretended to each other that they were just friends, that Connor was looking out for her, taking the big brother role while she adjusted to college life.

That pretense died fast.

They were lovers within a week, and by the second week of classes, they were inseparable. Dante completely lost it when he found out. He came after Connor. They fought hard and dirty. Connor broke Dante's nose and ended up busting the metacarpal bone of his little finger in the process.

But their injuries healed. In time, Dante forgave him and agreed to be best man at the wedding.

Everything was pretty much perfect. Except for Alyssa's dream for her future, the one Connor had pretended he shared.

Cat and Ernesto Santangelo still lived in the big two-story house where they'd raised their family. Their four sons were all grown up. Pascal and Tony were married, with kids. Dante was divorced with twin daughters. Marco, the youngest, would be nineteen now. Last Connor had heard, Marco still lived at home.

Dante parked in the big graveled turnaround in front of the house, filling an empty space between two other vehicles. A mud-spattered quad cab was parked several yards away. Had all the Santangelo sons shown up for this?

Dante turned off the engine. "Mom and Aly are both fragile right now," he warned. "You give either of them the slightest hint of grief and you will be dealing with—"

Connor cut him off with a wave of his hand. "I get it. Let's go in."

In the house, the full gauntlet of Santangelo men waited for him in the big living room. All four of them—Ernesto, Pascal, Tony and Marco—stared at him through identical angry, coffee-brown eyes. Dante, too, for that matter.

Ernesto, as the patriarch, did the talking, his voice

low and carefully controlled. "We don't want you here, but what else can a man do? My Bella won't quit asking for you. You'd better not screw this up or we'll make it a family project to rearrange your face for you."

Okay, the threats were getting really old. He was here, wasn't he? He'd promised to keep himself under control. What more did they want? About now, it was getting pretty hard not to imagine how much he would enjoy mixing it up with a Santangelo or two.

Aly, he reminded himself. *She's why you're here.*

Connor kept his voice calm and said what Dr. Warbury had warned him to say. "I'm not here to cause trouble, only to help."

Several seconds of cold stares ensued. Finally, Ernesto nodded at Marco. "Go on, get your sister."

"Wait a minute," Connor put a lot of effort into keeping his voice low and easy. "I'm guessing Aly would rather meet with me in private. I have promised before and I'll promise again to behave myself. I'm just thinking she'd rather do this without her father and her brothers breathing down her neck."

"Forget that," Ernesto and Dante said almost in unison.

Ernesto went on, "You know nothing about what my daughter would rather do. It's happening here, in the open, where we can keep an eye on you. You will tell her that you're not married anymore, that you haven't been married for a long time and that's gonna be that."

Connor let a shrug speak for him. He'd tried. At this point, it seemed counterproductive to push the issue.

Marco vanished into the front hall. Nobody spoke. An endless couple minutes ticked by.

And then, at last, Aly appeared in the open doorway to the foyer, with Marco right behind her. She had bruises on her pale arms and two black eyes. A white bandage covered a spot on the left side of her head. The gorgeous, milky skin of her cheeks and forehead was scraped raw and scabbed over. Cuts and scratches marred the soft column of her neck. Only her glorious mane of dark hair appeared unscathed, except for that shaved area on the left side. It was covered with a white bandage. She looked like hell—and so damn beautiful it hurt.

She gasped at the sight of him. He probably did the same. It rocked him, rocked him deep, just to see her again.

There was a moment, endless and so sweet. They stared at each other. God, it was good. A complete lie, yeah, but perfect nonetheless. She was looking at him the way she used to before he screwed it all up. Like he was everything that mattered, the center of her world.

As the seconds ticked by, he grew more and more certain that she would throw herself into his arms. He could not wait.

She didn't do it, though. Instead she came forward with her head high and held out a hand. Every nerve in his body on fire with hopeless yearning, he took it.

"Come on," she said, and turned for the foyer again.

"Hey!" Dante started after them as the other Santangelo men let out a chorus of protests.

"Aly, no…"

"Aly, stay here."

"You're not leaving this room," said her dad.

Still holding tight to Connor's hand, Aly stopped

in the doorway. She turned and pinned them all with a look. "I will talk to my husband *alone* if you don't mind."

Dante froze where he stood.

And Ernesto, who never could refuse her anything, gave in. "Let them go." Suddenly, he looked old.

Not another word was spoken. Aly led Connor across the foyer and up the stairs. She entered the second room along the upstairs hall, the room that had been hers when she was growing up.

He remembered that room. Even after they got married, her mom had kept it for Aly, with her purple satin bedspread and black lacquer furniture. Pictures of him and Aly and of her school friends had remained stuck beneath the mirror frame of the vanity table.

Not anymore, though. Cat had redone it—as a guest room, apparently. The walls were a tan color, the bedspread a soft blue.

He heard Aly shut the door, and turned from studying the room to face her.

"Oh, God," she whispered. "Connor. At last."

And then she did throw herself at him.

Heedless of the rules not to encourage her, he opened his arms and grabbed her close. She hopped up, the way she used to do, and wrapped her arms and legs around him.

"Aly..." He tried to be careful of her, to remember her injuries. But at the same time, he couldn't crush her close enough. She felt like heaven and the ginger scent of her was so sweet, so well remembered. It filled him with longing and regret.

"Connor..." She lifted her head from where she'd

buried it against his shoulder. "Oh, Conn…" Tipping her chin high, she offered her mouth to him, surging up higher, eager to meet his lips.

He'd never wanted anything so much in his life as to steal a kiss from her right now.

But he couldn't do that. It wouldn't be right.

"Hey, now…" Reluctantly, and much more gently than he'd grabbed her, he eased her thighs from around him. Setting her carefully down, he stepped back.

She stared up at him, shattered. "Tell me." Bright red stained her battered cheeks. "Say it."

"I'm sorry, I…" Words failed him.

She'd always been the stronger one. Now, she said it for him in a flat voice. "We're not married. You filed to divorce me seven years ago. I live in New York and I have a fabulous career. And you and me, we're just… *not* anymore."

He blinked down at her. "So then, you do know? You remember now?"

She laughed then, a wild laugh, and tossed her midnight hair. "No, I do not remember." She put both hands to her head, as if to steady her brain after shaking it. "But it's what everyone keeps telling me. It's what I see in your eyes when I look at you." She held up her left hand, poked her thumb at her ring finger. "Bare. That's a big clue, right? My laptop is toast, but they recovered my purse and phone from the wreck of my rental car. I have a New York driver's license. It says my last name is Santangelo. And I'm on social media. I've seen a bunch of great pictures of me with my friends and colleagues in Manhattan. I wear a lot of black and I have amazing shoes." She put her hands to her head again. "Also, everything's pretty fuzzy in here. I *believe*, I'm absolutely certain in my heart, that you and I are still married. But I don't really *remember* much specifically—about you and me and our life now. I can't tell you where we live or what we do, together, day by day…"

"Because we aren't together." The words came out of him sounding cold. Cruel. He tried for a gentler tone. "Not anymore. Not for seven years."

"My family has explained it all to me, over and over, that we broke up because you wanted to stay in Oregon and I was determined to have a career with a major advertising firm. That you divorced me when I took a job in New York."

"That's right," he said gently. "That's what happened. That's the truth, at least basically."

She sneered at him. "Basically, huh? So then, what is the deeper truth, Connor? Tell me about that."

He'd come here to be honest with her, but still he hesitated, reluctant to admit what a rotten jerk he'd been. "You really don't remember any of it?"

She raised her hand and laid it carefully over the white bandage on the side of her head. "Just…random images. Nothing makes sense."

He stared down at her. Where to even start?

"Tell me," she demanded again.

He made himself do it. "From the first, when we were at OU together, you were all about getting out, getting away. No small-town life for you, you told me. And I went along with you, I *agreed* with you. I said I wanted what you wanted, that I would go with you. I would get a job in finance. We would take New York by storm. I pretended to be all gung ho about it. You interviewed with your dream company in Manhattan and they hired you. We even signed a lease on a postage stamp of an apartment."

"But you didn't really want to go?"

He shook his head. "We were packing for the move when I finally admitted I didn't want to do it. I wanted a life here in Valentine Bay, working with my brother, building the family business."

She seemed more confused than before. "You lied because...?"

"I didn't want to lose you. I told myself you'd change your mind, that deep in your heart, you didn't want to go, either."

"But I really *did* want to go?" It wasn't quite a question.

"Yeah. You did. You really did. Still, when I finally admitted I wasn't going, you were...patient with me. You tried to compromise, begged me just to try New York for a year and then we would reevaluate."

"And you?"

"I dug in." He couldn't meet those bruised blue eyes. "I said forget it, I wasn't going. I was so sure that when it came right down to the wire, you wouldn't leave me, that you would give it up and stay home."

"But I didn't."

"No. You went. I didn't reach out. You didn't, either. Two months after you left, I had you served with divorce papers."

"Connor."

He looked at her then. Her eyes were wide, full of wonder—or maybe just complete disbelief.

"Nothing?" she whispered. And then her voice

gained strength. "You gave me nothing for two months and then, without so much as a phone call, you filed for divorce?"

"That is exactly what I did."

"You were an assh—"

"Yes, I was. And that's not all. I scrawled a note on the envelope the divorce papers were in. I wrote, 'Or you could just come home.'"

She blinked. "Wow. You make yourself sound even worse than what my brothers told me."

"Yeah, well. You signed the papers and wrote your own little note. Two words. *'Or not.'*"

That brought a low, husky laugh from her. "Good for me."

"I can't say I thought so at the time, but yeah. Good for you."

"So then what you're really saying is that you were a total douche-basket who threw me and our marriage away?"

He held her gaze and told the painful truth. "That is exactly what I was and what I did."

She just stood there looking at him for the longest time. He had no clue what she might be thinking, though he was pretty sure it wasn't anything good.

And he was having a little trouble not surrendering to his insane compulsion to drop to his knees and beg her for another chance.

He didn't give in to that. He had no right. It was way too late for second chances, for big, dramatic gestures. He was here to help her, not add to her confusion.

In time, she would remember her real life in Manhattan. She would realize that she had everything she'd ever wanted, that she was better off without him.

"I don't know what more to say, except that I am so sorry. And if there's anything I can do now, anything at all to make it better for you, just let me know, okay?"

"Anything." She scoffed. "You'll do anything for me."

"I just want to help."

"Well, okay then. Thank you for coming, Connor. As for what you can do for me, you can get the hell out."

Chapter Three

"Love you and miss you. Lots. 'Bye, Sibbie." Cat Santangelo hung up the phone.

Aly, nice and comfy in the wing chair by the window, with her feet propped on the plush ottoman, asked, "How's Aunt Siobhan?"

"She thinks she needs to be here. I talked her out of coming. Your uncle Albert just had back surgery. She's got enough on her plate taking care of him. She sends her love." With a fond smile, Cat patted the empty side of her new king-size adjustable memory-foam bed. "Come on. It's a giant bed and it's super comfy. Get up in here with me."

Aly pushed the ottoman out of the way, rose and went to stretch out on the bed with her mom. "Is he kicking?"

Cat rested a hand on the pillow next to Aly's head.

Aly felt her gentle touch as she fiddled with a lock of Aly's hair. "He's more of a puncher, I would say."

Aly turned on her side—the good side, without the bandage—and rested her hand on her mom's big stomach. "Nothing, not even a nudge."

"Yeah, he never punches me except when we're alone. I think he has a shy side."

Aly stroked her mom's belly, soothing Cat and herself and maybe the baby, too. It felt good, to spend time with her mom again. A lot of women had issues with their mothers. Not Aly. She and Cat had always banded together, presented a united front. With five strong-willed men in the family, they needed to have each other's backs.

There was a hopeful whine from the floor on Cat's other side. Aly and her mom chuckled together and Aly said, "Tuck wants up."

"Come on." Cat patted the mattress and up came Tucker, a wire-haired terrier mix her mom had adopted from the local shelter a few years before. The dog made himself comfortable, cuddling up close to Cat.

"Did it help?" asked her mom. "To see him, to talk to him?"

"In a way…" Aly indulged herself and pictured his face. His hair had darkened to a golden brown over the years and the dent in his sculpted chin was as sexy as ever. And those eyes. He could break her with those cool blue eyes.

Tuck's tags clattered cheerfully as he gave himself a scratch.

"What way?" asked Cat.

Aly considered blowing off the question, but then couldn't. "Don't judge."

"Never."

"Seeing him made me more certain."

"Of…?"

"That he loves me and I love him, and whoever's fault it was, we should be together."

"Did you tell him that?"

"Are you kidding? He explained what a complete jackass he'd been, that he'd thrown me away—thrown *us* away. After he was finished, I mostly just wanted to punch him in the face."

Her mom was watching her, a little smile teasing at the edges of her mouth. "And yet you're still in love with him."

"Smug, Mom. That's how you sound."

"I am smug," replied Cat. Smugly. "I always knew that someday you two would get back together."

"Ha! You ever tell Dad that?"

"Dear heart, there a few things your father just doesn't need to know. Men are so simple." She faked a deep voice. "Bring home the bacon. Protect the women." She chuckled. "Connor hurt you and that makes him the bad guy in your father's eyes. I see it more in shades of gray."

"You always had a soft spot for Connor."

"Your dad wants you safe. I want you to have what your heart most desires."

Aly snuggled in closer. She whispered to her unborn brother, "Hey, handsome. How you doin' in there?"

Cat asked, "So what are you gonna do about what your heart most desires?"

"We are so over, Connor and me."

"Yes, but that wasn't my question."

"Fine. What *can* I do?"

Cat gave her a look both teasing and conspiratorial. "Your dad and your brothers are still worried you're going to climb out a window and go after that man."

Ever since her rude awakening in the dark hours of Sunday morning with her mind all turned around, the men of the family had repeatedly explained to her that she'd come home for one reason—to take care of her mom until after the baby was born. "Uh-uh. I'm here for you."

Cat grunted as she shifted to her side. She pressed a kiss in the middle of Aly's forehead and then retreated to her own pillow with a sigh. "Show me the law that says you can't do two things at once."

Connor spotted Alyssa as he turned into his driveway. She sat on the front step wearing a pair of those black, tight-fitting legging things that came to midthigh, silver sandals and a clingy white shirt that made her full breasts look even more spectacular than they had the day before. She was petting Maurice, who slinked in a figure eight at her side, arching his skinny back in pleasure, black tail held high.

The garage was under the house, with retaining walls on either side of the sloping driveway. When she raised her hand to him in a wave, Connor almost ran into the wall on the passenger side. At the last second, he straightened the wheel and rolled the Land Rover safely inside. The garage door glided down behind him and he let his head droop forward until his forehead met the steering wheel.

What's she doing here? What's going on?

He shouldn't allow himself to be so stupidly happy at the mere sight of her beautiful, banged-up face—and none of his questions would be answered while he hid in his car.

He ran up the steps to ground level, growing breathless all out of proportion to the short climb. Dropping his briefcase on the bench in the block-glass window nook beside the door, he paused, swiped his hair back off his forehead and straightened his shoulders.

After yesterday he had figured he would never see her again—at least not on purpose, certainly not sitting on his front step waiting for him to come home.

She was standing at the threshold when he pulled the door open, Maurice at her feet. He noticed that the bandage on the side of her head was gone. She'd combed her hair over the bare spot. "I like your cat," she said.

With a low, entitled "Reow," Maurice strutted inside. Connor didn't try to stop him. The cat went where he wanted to go. "Maurice belongs to my next-door neighbor. He just *thinks* he owns the whole block and everyone in it."

"Maurice," she repeated. "It suits him. He's friendly and affectionate and he has a lot of confidence."

"Too much confidence, if you ask me."

And that was it. They'd run out of words. Several seconds dragged by.

Finally, she spoke again. "Is it okay if I come in, too?"

"Uh, sure. Of course." He stepped back and she stepped forward. He shut the door.

"It's a beautiful house," she said. "I love the weathered gray shingles." Her impossibly thick black eyelashes fluttered up as she glanced at the vaulted ceiling. "What kind of wood is that?"

He blinked to make himself stop staring at her. "Hemlock."

"Gorgeous. I noticed there's even a big porthole window upstairs."

"Yeah."

"Kind of beachy and nautical. The perfect house for Valentine Bay."

He really didn't give a damn about his house at this particular moment. "What's going on? Is everything…? I mean, are you okay?"

"I'm fine—well, I still have the, er, major memory problem, but it's not any worse."

Relief made him realize he'd forgotten to breathe. He drew in air and let it out with slow care. "So…?"

She folded her pale hands together in front of her and licked those amazing, pillowy lips of hers. The sight sent a bolt of lust straight to his groin, which annoyed him no end. He tried really hard to think about unsexy things—getting his oil changed, power-washing the driveway…

Finally, she spoke again. "My mom gave me your address. Don't freak out, but she admitted she's kind of kept tabs on you since we split up—not in a stalkerish way, I promise."

"Why?"

"Long story. Let's just say she always liked you."

A Santangelo who still liked him. Who knew?

Aly glanced away. She seemed really nervous now. And then she huffed out a breath and faced him again. "Look, Connor. Can we talk?"

He put out a hand toward the raised living area behind him. She went where he indicated, taking a seat on the gray leather sofa. Maurice jumped right up beside her and started to purr.

Connor hesitated midway to the armchair. "I can make coffee or something…"

She shook her head. As he sat down in the armchair, she asked, "You live here alone?"

"Yeah."

"Got a girlfriend, Conn? Someone special?"

"No." And what did it matter to her if he was seeing someone exclusively? "I've got a question for *you*, now."

"All right."

"Should I expect your brothers to show up any minute, eager to beat the crap out of me?"

She smiled at that. "Don't worry. My mom will handle my brothers." She concentrated on petting Maurice, her bruised hand moving in long, slow strokes. "Actually, I came to ask you a favor."

Whatever it was, he would do it. Maybe he could make up at least a little for all the ways he'd messed up back when. "Name it."

And just like that, she dropped the bombshell. "I'm on an extended family leave of fourteen weeks to take care of my mother, or so my dad and brothers have repeatedly explained to me since the accident. I want to move in here. I want to live with you until I go back to New York."

Live with him?

Had she really just said that?

And why was his heart beating so hard against the walls of his chest? "What about your mom?"

"What do you mean?"

"You just said it. You're here to take care of Cat until after the baby's born."

"I am, yeah. And I will. I'll spend my days with her, be with her any other time she needs me, too. But if you say it's okay with you, I would, um, have a room here, if you have an extra one. So that I could spend time with you, too."

He was really trying to get his mind around this. "You want to live with me?"

"Isn't that what I just said?"

"Yeah. And I don't get it. I really don't."

"I, um…" She brought a hand to her head at the place where the bandage had been. Her sleek black eyebrows were all scrunched up.

"Alyssa. Are you okay?"

She rubbed the spot. "I am, yes. It's just that when I get tense my head hurts sometimes. A little."

"Are you sure that you…?"

"I'm all right," she insisted. "It's just what it is. Stress reaction after trauma. I'm not going to go crazy on you or anything, I promise."

A scary thought occurred to him. "Did you drive yourself here?"

"Ungh." Now, she pressed both hands to the sides of her head, as though his question had almost caused her brain to explode. "You sound like my dad, you know that? And yes, I did drive myself. It's all worked out with the rental company. The blue Mazda out front is mine for the rest of my visit here. I'm cleared to drive, so you don't have to worry I'm going to run into another tree or anything." Her eyes sparked with equal parts irritation and determination. "And as for my staying here with you, I would pay rent."

"Aly, forget about rent. It's not about that."

"Listen, I'm not asking to share your room or anything. It's a pretty big house and you said you live here alone. You have to have a spare room."

"I just don't get it. We're divorced. It wasn't friendly. And it's not like we've kept in touch."

"I know that. I understand the actual facts of the situation, I promise you. All I want is a chance to..." She made a small, frustrated sound as the words trailed off. He waited, giving her time to collect her thoughts. Finally, she offered a sad little shrug. "Look, I get it, I do. Having me underfoot for three months does not make you feel warm all over."

She had no idea how wrong she was. "I didn't say that."

"You didn't *have* to say it. It's right there on your face."

"Alyssa. I want to be up front with you."

"Yes. Please. Be up front with me—and say you'd love to have me stay in your house while I'm in town."

He braced his knees wide and bent to lean his elbows on them. "I'm trying to do the right thing here, okay? And I just don't see how your moving in with me could possibly be good for you. Our marriage is over."

"I know that." She said it through clenched teeth.

"But you told me yesterday that you didn't really believe it."

"Connor. I do believe it. Yeah, my head's a little screwed around right now, but I still have all my faculties. I know we're not married. I have no illusions that I've somehow fallen down a rabbit hole and when I finally emerge, we'll be married again and everything between us will be like it was eight years ago. I'm not Alice. There is no Wonderland. I get that. I do."

"But you don't *believe* it."

She touched her head again. "I *do* believe it. I just *said* I believe it. I know my own brain is lying to me."

He sat back in the chair and spoke as softly as he could manage. "I'm upsetting you."

She put up both hands. "No. Please. You're not. You're really not. I am *allowing* myself to become upset—and I'm stopping that. Now."

"It just seems like a bad idea. How are you going to find your way to fully accepting the truth if the two of us start playing house?"

"Playing house is not what I asked for," she replied in a carefully modulated tone. "I asked you to let me stay with you while I'm in town. As a renter or a houseguest, whichever works better for you."

The thing was, he wanted it. Wanted *her*. Still. He always had. It was his problem. And he accepted it. No one compared to her. He doubted that was ever going to change.

But that didn't mean he should take advantage of her now. She needed to stay away from him, not start living in his house.

Major fail so far, Aly was thinking.

Connor was in no way convinced. He seemed to view

her request to move in here as yet more proof that her injured brain wasn't operating on all thrusters.

So what? He could think what he wanted. She had a goal and she was pulling out all the stops to attain it.

The accident had not only scrambled her memories. It had stripped away seven years of denial and foolish pride, brought her face-to-face with herself, shown her what she really wanted most in the world, held a mirror up to all the ways she'd failed in courage and in love.

She said, "Forget about all the reasons you believe it would be wrong for me, *bad* for me to move in with you. It won't be bad. It will bring…understanding between us, peace between us. It will give us a chance to work out our issues with each other, which we never did."

He still wasn't buying. "Face facts. It's long past the time when we could have worked anything out."

"I disagree."

"Aly, it's years too late."

"For us to piece our marriage back together, maybe. But it's never too late for us to learn to put all the bitterness and sadness behind us."

He regarded her steadily, those steel-blue eyes probing. "Is that really what you want, what you think you're going to accomplish? That we can make peace and then let each other go?"

It wasn't. No way. In spite of everything, she wanted it all with him. She'd never gotten over him; she understood and accepted that now. She still felt so powerfully drawn to him. She had it bad—bad enough that her injured brain had rebelled on her and tried to rewrite the past.

Her heart had never really moved on from him and

she was finally willing to put her pride aside and let her heart lead the way. She wanted to try again.

And she needed to tell him that.

Just not right this minute.

"What I want is to spend time with you."

"It's a bad idea."

"Oh, yeah?"

"Aly. You know it is."

"And yet just a few minutes ago, and yesterday, too, you promised me that you would do whatever I needed you to do."

"Yes, I did. And I meant it both times." He stood. "Just…not this."

Her head ached. She longed to grab the fancy glass dish on the coffee table in front of her and chuck it at his heartbreaker-handsome, infuriating face.

But her doctors had explained that she shouldn't get herself worked up, that she should try to stay calm, that in the near future, headaches and emotional outbursts were likely if she let herself get stressed out. Getting overexcited would slow the healing process down.

Aly put her head in her hands and made herself suck in several slow, deep breaths. It helped. The ache in her head lessened and the frantic feeling of losing control eased.

"Aly…" Connor came toward her. He stopped a foot from where she sat.

"It's all right," she said, breathing slowly and evenly. "I'm okay, honestly."

"I've upset you. Again. Aly, I'm so sorry."

"No. Really." She met his eyes, saw his remorse, felt his regret for causing her pain right now and in the past.

"Don't beat yourself up—I mean, you *should* be sorry for what you did seven years ago. But as for right now, it's your house. I get it. If you don't want me here, well, what else is there to say?"

"I didn't say I didn't *want* you here. I said I thought it would be a bad idea for you to stay here."

Was he giving her an opening? "So…you *do* want me here?"

"Aly…" He seemed not to know what to say next.

Maurice was curled in a ball against her thigh, purring contentedly.

Connor picked up the cat, set him on the floor and sat down beside her. "This is just crazy."

"Tell me about it." She watched Maurice strut away, tail held high. And then, with a tired little groan, she let herself sway toward the man sitting next to her.

The most beautiful thing happened. He wrapped his arm around her.

It felt so good, just to lean against his solid strength. And he smelled the same. Clean and manly, like soap and cedar branches. She breathed him in and felt better about everything. The proximity of his body, his heat, the weight of his arm across her shoulders—it all added up to contentment, somehow. Having him close made her world a better place.

He rubbed her arm, soothing her.

With a sigh, she gave in to the comfort he offered, resting her tired head on his hard, warm shoulder, relaxing in the cradle of his embrace.

He stroked her hair. She wished he would never stop. "I'm only trying to do the right thing here," he said, his voice low, rumbly. Intimate in the best sort of way.

The right thing...

How could he not know that *this*—his arm around her, his hand caressing her hair—was just about as right as it ever got? She leaned more deeply into his strength and flat-out reveled in having him hold her again.

Years. It had been years since he'd held her. That seemed simply impossible. How could she have let the distance and the silence between them go on for so long? Whatever he'd done, whatever the facts were, her heart knew the truth. Her mom was right. They needed this time together, she and Connor.

And in the end, if it *didn't* work out, well, at least she would know that she'd finally given her all to take back what they had together.

He bent closer. She felt his lips in her hair, reveled in the warmth of his breath on her skin. Every part of her—body, mind and soul—rejoiced at the contact.

And then it was over.

He lifted his arm from across her shoulders and moved slightly away.

She shifted to face him. Looking straight into his wary eyes, she asked again for what she wanted. "Please help me, Connor. I don't want you to lie to me or pretend you're my husband when you're not. I only want to spend some time with you, to stay in your house and to be with you. Not as lovers, not as husband and wife. As who we are right now."

A frown creased his brow as he stared at her for the longest time. She tried to brace herself for his final refusal. What more could she do? She'd pretty much pulled out all the stops, and if he still wasn't going for it, she would need to accept his decision.

But then he said, "Your dad and your brothers will probably kill me."

Was that a yes? It sure sounded like one. Her heart lifted. "Did you just say that I can stay here with you?"

His frown only deepened. "I don't want your dad and brothers pissed off. You don't need that kind of stress."

"I can deal with them."

"You need time to heal. What you don't need is a lot of family conflict right now—and neither does your mom, with the baby and all."

"My mom may be on bed rest, but I would bet on her against the men in my family any day of the week. As for me, I meant what I said. I will deal with them. It's up to me where I stay and they're going to have to accept that."

"Yeah, well. You know that doesn't mean they're going to be happy about it."

"Connor."

"What?"

"It can all be worked out with my family. This isn't about them. I want some time with you. Tell me you just said yes. Tell me I can stay here."

He looked at her probingly now. "You're sure?"

"Positive."

"All right, then. My guest bedroom is yours."

Chapter Four

Connor watched the glowing smile take over her face.

He could hardly believe it. Three months of the two of them sharing a house. It seemed impossible.

Impossible in a dream-come-true sort of way—only not. Because who was he kidding? He had doubts, serious doubts as to the wisdom of this decision.

But he'd agreed and they were doing it. He just had to remember that the main goal was for them to make peace with each other.

Peace. Closure. Learning to get along. Putting the past behind them once and for all. That kind of stuff.

They were *not* trying again. They were practically strangers now and he *would* remember that. She was only doing this because of the bump on her head. She wouldn't be anywhere near him if she hadn't been in an accident that had turned things around in her brain.

She said, "I know this will help me. I can't thank you enough."

His arms ached to reach for her, to yank her close. He needed to slam his hungry mouth down on hers.

But he caught himself just in time.

Oh, man. This was a bad idea. Way too risky. For both of them.

He should back out. Now.

But when he opened his mouth, what came out was, "So. I'll show you your room, then?"

He led her upstairs to the room at the front of the house. It had a queen-size bed and its own bath.

"It's beautiful," she said. "I love the big windows and the little balcony…" They stood at the foot of the bed she would sleep in, staring at each other. "Weird, huh?" she asked, her eyes so blue and wide open, staring into his.

"Yeah." He said it way too softly. "Weird."

The past was suddenly a living thing, rising up in the air between them.

He remembered. Everything. Too much.

Aly, as a little girl, her hair in pigtails, wearing red shorts and a white shirt with a grape juice stain on the collar, her little fists planted on her hips, giving Dante a serious piece of her mind. *"Why can't I play with you and Connor? Mommy said to be nice to me and you're not and it's not fair and I hate you. I hate you both…"*

Aly at thirteen, already curvy, so damn beautiful and totally forbidden, flouncing away from him when he told her to get lost.

And that first day on the Memorial Quad at OU.

She'd turned around and blinded him with a teasing smile.

"Connor. Imagine meeting you here..."

He knew then. There was no way he could keep his distance from her, not with both of them away from home, together—and Dante nowhere nearby.

He knew that she would be his. And he would be hers.

And Dante would just have to get past it and move on.

She called him back to the present, saying, "I should probably get going. I need to check on my mom and pack up my things..."

Downstairs, he gave her a key. "I'll follow you."

A puzzled frown drew those gorgeous lips down at the corners. "Why? All my stuff will fit in the Mazda."

"Your dad's not going to be happy."

"So? He doesn't make my decisions for me."

"Aly. I'll be dealing with him one way or another. Might as well just do it now and defuse the situation as best I can right out of the gate."

"But it's not your problem. I said that *I* would deal with him and my brothers." She tipped her chin high and pulled her shoulders back.

"Can we get real about this?"

"But I *am* being real."

"No, you're not. Ernesto's not going to like this, and one way or another, he's going to find me and let me know exactly how he feels. Why not be proactive about it?"

She might be almost a stranger to him now, but he

could still read her. She was actively restraining herself from giving him an eye roll. "I can handle my dad."

"Yeah. You can. He'll give in to you—and then come looking for me. Can we cut all that down to one step? Please?"

"Hmm. I guess I feel guilty for dragging you into this."

"And yet you've done it anyway." He was razzing her and enjoying it far too much.

She chewed on her lower lip as she considered her response. "Well, I'm not backing out. So you can get that idea right out of your head."

"I'm going with you, Aly."

They shared a mini stare-down. In the end, she blinked first. "Fine." Which meant it wasn't, but she was through fighting him on it.

He quelled a grin of triumph. "We might as well just take the Land Rover. Plenty of room for whatever you need to bring over."

"See how you did that? I started out going in my rental car by myself and ended up in your car with you behind the wheel."

Whatever he said next would only bring on another argument. He kept silent and gestured her ahead of him down the stairs to the garage, Maurice trailing behind.

When Connor opened the garage door, Mrs. Garber was standing on the sidewalk at the top of the driveway. Maurice ran to meet her. She bent to pick him up, then stepped out of the way of Connor's vehicle, giving them a jaunty wave as he and Aly drove off.

* * *

At the Santangelo house, Aly paused in the foyer to remind him once again that she would handle her father.

Connor kept his expression neutral. "Whatever you say." He would do what he had to do. No point in standing there arguing about it.

They followed their noses to the kitchen. Ernesto, in a white T-shirt, Carhartt dungarees and an apron, stood at the stove stirring red sauce in one pot while pasta boiled in another.

"Hey, Dad."

Ernesto was smiling as he turned—but then he spotted Connor in the doorway behind Aly. He scowled at his only daughter. "Why is he here?"

Connor opened his mouth to take control of the situation.

Aly beat him to it. "He's with me, Daddy. I've asked Connor to let me stay at his place and he's generously said yes."

"What did you just say?" Ernesto brandished his big wooden spoon. Aly opened her mouth to answer, but he cut her off before she could get a word out. "Don't tell me. I heard you. You'll give me a heart attack and you are doing no such thing. What is the matter with you?"

"There is nothing the matter with—"

"Stop." He shoved his spoon in her direction. "What can you be thinking? You can't just—"

A hissing sound interrupted him.

Behind him on the stove, the pasta had boiled over. The water sizzled and foamed as it ran down the sides of the pot. Aly's dad swore a blue streak as he spun around to turn off the fire. The water settled a little. He turned the burner back on and carefully adjusted the flame before facing the two of them once more.

"Bella," he said, his voice more controlled now, still angry, but also tender. "You can't go and live with *him*."

"I can, Dad." She went to him and pressed her hand to his tanned, rough cheek. "And I'm going to. I'm here to get my things."

"You're here to take care of your mother."

"And I will. Just you watch me."

"You've had an accident and you are not yourself."

"Oh, no. That's not true. I'm all banged up, yeah. But I know fact from fantasy and I am very much myself." She kissed him, a brush of her lips at his jaw. "Now, I'm going to go and see how Mom's doing. Then I'll pack up my stuff and Connor and I are out of here." She turned and came toward him in the doorway, leaving her dad scowling after her. "Try not to kill each other," she advised.

And then she was gone.

The silence hung heavy between him and his ex-father-in-law. Ernesto turned to his pasta and sauce.

"I couldn't say no to her," Connor offered to the older man's broad back.

Ernesto shrugged. "At least you had the balls to show up here and admit it."

Connor tried to decide what he should say to that. Nothing, he decided. Better to quit while he was ahead. He kept his mouth shut.

"Stay for dinner," Ernesto said flatly. "There's plenty."

Marco arrived a few minutes later. There was more or less a replay of the confrontation with Ernesto. But

Aly's father had already given his reluctant blessing to the situation, so Marco unhappily fell in line.

Cat came to the table to eat with them. She looked really good for a hugely pregnant older lady. And she seemed blithely unconcerned that Aly was moving in with him. Cat spent most of the meal quizzing him about his family—about his sister-in-law Keely's six-month-old baby girl, and his sister Aislinn and brother Matthias, each of whom had gotten married within the past year.

Connor felt so comfortable around Aly's mom that he almost started blabbing about Madison Delaney, who had married local shipbuilder Sten Larson the month before. Madison, a bona fide movie star, was the newly found member of the Bravo family. She'd been switched at birth with Aislinn twenty-seven years before.

So far, the switched-at-birth story hadn't gotten out to the media. Madison and Sten wanted to keep it that way, so they'd all agreed not to mention their relationship to America's Darling outside the family.

And yet, even with Ernesto and Marco barely speaking, radiating disapproval and sending him dark looks, Connor almost revealed Madison's secret right there at the Santangelo dinner table—because of his soft spot for Aly's mom.

Cat looked like an older version of her only daughter, and she could wrap a man around her finger same as Aly could. Way back when he and Dante were kids and Aly was just Dante's bratty little sister, Connor had considered Cat like a second mom. When his own mom had died suddenly in that tsunami in Thailand, Cat had been right there for the Bravo family, bringing over the baked ziti and lasagna and lamb stew, ready to help out wherever help was needed.

It came to him sharply as he shoveled in Ernesto's excellent pasta that Aly wasn't the only one he'd lost due to his own pigheaded unwillingness to admit what an ass he'd been, and make an effort to work things out. He'd missed her mom, too. And Dante, his lifelong best friend… What the hell, he'd missed all the Santangelos. He'd wrecked so much that was precious and irreplaceable. Maybe Aly thought they could somehow make it all right again.

But the way he saw it, some doors were closed to him now and forever.

"You're quiet," Aly said on the drive back to his house.

He didn't want to talk about it, didn't even want to glance her way. No woman had a right to look that beautiful—even with peeling air-bag burns covering most of her face. "Just tired," he lied.

At the house, he helped her carry her things inside, said good-night and retreated to the master suite. He had a little trouble sleeping, so he got out his laptop and caught up with email and a few minor loose ends that needed tying up at Valentine Logging.

In the morning, he was up and showered and dressed at six, figuring he would head straight to Warrenton and the company offices, stopping off at a diner he liked for breakfast on the way. Was he hoping to avoid any chance he might run into Aly?

Absolutely. He'd spent too much of the past sleepless night regretting giving in to her. She shouldn't be here. It wasn't good for her to be here—and not good for him, either. It was over between them. They shouldn't be kidding themselves that they could somehow make everything right.

And yet yesterday, he'd given in to her. He'd let her do that thing she did so well—let her convince him that what she wanted was good for him, too.

Well, fair enough. He'd blown it, said yes when he should have firmly told her no, and now she was living in his house with him. But he was drawing the line at that. She could stay as long as she needed to stay to make peace with the past or whatever she thought she was doing here. She could have it her way, take care of her mom and sleep in his guest room.

And he would go on with his life as before.

When he pulled open his bedroom door, he smelled coffee, heard a cabinet door shut and a spoon clink against a cup. Evidently, Aly was already awake. The reality of that—of her actual presence, here in his house—hit him all over again, causing an exasperating lifting feeling in the cage of his chest.

Not good.

He needed to get out of the house and behind the wheel of his car. Unfortunately, the open-plan living area downstairs would make it just about impossible for him to escape to the garage without her spotting him.

Like a tongue-tied kid afraid to face the prettiest girl in school, he hovered on the upstairs landing. Pathetic.

She was staying for weeks. He couldn't be freaking out at just the idea of coming face-to-face with her. It was going to happen. On a regular basis.

When he finally made himself descend the stairs,

she was sitting across the room, at the table by the windows in the living area, drinking coffee. Her midnight hair fell in thick, loose curls down her shoulders and she wore a tight pink shirt and black capri pants. The woman was too damn delicious for his peace of mind.

She held up her mug to him. "Love that pod coffee maker you've got."

He crossed the room to her but didn't take a chair. Instead, he stood by the table, his briefcase still hooked on his shoulder, ready to make his escape. "You're up early."

She sipped from the mug. "I woke up at five. I think I'm still on New York time."

"You slept okay, though?"

"Great, thanks—and I've checked the fridge, found the eggs and that Olympia Provisions chorizo you always loved. Want some breakfast before you go? I'm cooking and I can make it fast."

He shook his head and lied, "Thanks, but I need to get going."

That sinful mouth of hers kicked up at the corners in a hint of a smile. Her eyes said so what if he thought they were strangers now? She didn't buy that crap. She knew him, those eyes said, knew him so well. "I was thinking that on the way home from Mom's today, I'll stop by Safeway, pick up a few things. I'll fix you dinner, if you're available."

Margo. The name popped into his head, flashing red.

He couldn't believe it. He'd forgotten all about Margo.

Two lines drew down between Aly's periwinkle-blue

eyes. "Okay. You look like you just got some bad news. What's going on?"

"Uh. Thanks for the offer, but I can't make it for dinner tonight."

She just sat there and looked at him, waiting for him to bust to whatever it was.

There was absolutely no reason for him to feel like a guilty cheater.

But he did. "I've got a date."

She set her mug down. They stared at each other. It went on for several seconds, until she said cautiously, "I don't want to assume anything."

What did that even mean? "Good."

"But you did say there was no one special."

There wasn't. With Aly on his mind, he'd forgotten all about Margo James—and whatever he said next, he would sound like a jerk. Probably because he was one. "This is the second time we've gone out, Margo and I. We set the date for tonight before your brother knocked on my door Wednesday."

She made a little humming sound. "I see. You couldn't have mentioned this date last night?"

There was no good answer to that one, so he just told the truth. "I'm sorry. Until just a minute ago, I forgot all about it."

She pinned him with a cool stare. "You forgot that you had a date."

"Isn't that what I just said?"

She did that humming thing again.

He couldn't read her. She seemed fine with him going out with some other woman—or if not fine, accepting. More or less.

And why shouldn't she be fine with it? They weren't married anymore. They weren't…anything.

All of a sudden, he was furious at her. And at himself, too. It was a completely irrational fury and he would damn well keep it to himself.

She asked, "So, will my being here cramp your style?"

"No. Of course not." Yeah, he had planned to bring Margo here after their date. Last Friday night they had come here—to his bed. But last Friday night was a million years ago. No way would he bring another woman here now. He added lamely, "I just, well, I could be late getting back."

"Okay, then." She gave him another ghost of a smile. "I'll see you when I see you."

"Good enough." He turned to go.

"Connor?"

Four steps from the table, he stopped and faced her again. "Yeah?"

"We never exchanged numbers. We should probably do that, don't you think?" She pulled a phone from her pocket.

"Right." He rattled off his phone number.

She punched in the numbers and tapped out a short text. His phone buzzed. He took it out. She'd written, "Tell Margo your ex-wife says hi."

He gritted his teeth. "Funny." And he turned and got out of there.

"A date?" Cat set down her strawberry smoothie a little harder than necessary. It made a definite *clunk* when it hit the table. "Connor has a *date* with someone else tonight?"

They were in the Santangelo kitchen, Cat with her feet up on a chair while Aly stood across the table folding a pile of laundry. "Yeah. He told me this morning as he was going out the door."

"That man." Cat glared into the middle distance. "Just when I dare to get my hopes up that he's finally going to stop being a bullheaded idiot, he does something like this."

Aly shook out one of her dad's T-shirts with an angry snap and replied with way too much snark, "I thought you had a soft spot for him, Mom. I thought you were on his side."

Cat made a humphing sound and rubbed her big belly. "I'm on *your* side is what I am. I want to think that he deserves you, that he's grown up a little and can finally appreciate a woman like you. But he doesn't make it easy, now does he?"

Aly folded the shirt and moved on to the next one. She tried to stick with the snark and not descend into weepiness, but since the accident, it was always way too easy to get emotional. "I don't know, Mom…" It came out sounding disgustingly sad.

"Dear heart." Cat reached out. Aly met her halfway. They clasped hands across the table. Cat gave Aly's fingers a reassuring squeeze before letting go. "I really don't know what to say. I'm so disappointed."

Aly pulled over the nearest chair and sank into it. "I can't help thinking that I should just go to his place, get my stuff and come back here where I belong."

Her mom had the smoothie halfway to her mouth.

She set it down again, minus the clunking sound this time. "Don't be hasty."

"Mom. He's going out with someone else tonight. I hate it. But I also know I have no claim on him."

"Oh, yes you do. You always have. Connor Bravo doesn't want anyone but you, not really."

Aly groaned. "Please."

Catriona O'Leary Santangelo had been with Aly's dad since she was sixteen years old. At seventeen, she'd married him. Dante came along five months later. Neither Cat nor Ernesto had ever so much as looked at anyone else in a romantic way. Cat believed in fate and love that lasted a lifetime.

"I say this with all the love in the world, Mom. But you have no way of knowing what Connor Bravo really wants. I can't help but wonder if anybody does."

"Did you tell him to call that other woman and say he's not available, after all, and he won't *be* available— ever?"

"No. But I sent him a text. 'Tell Margo your ex-wife says hi.'"

"Cute. But not direct enough. You've got to tell him what you want up front. Men are—"

"*Simple creatures.* I know, I know." She pushed the load of laundry toward the center of the table so she could prop her elbows and brace her chin between her hands. "I can't do this. It was a bad idea."

Her mom looked troubled. "You think it's something serious with this other woman?"

"He did say that he'd forgotten all about her until this morning…"

Cat brightened. "Well, see then? That's because all he can think about is you."

"Oh, come on. It's a *date*. A *second* date. Things are different now. People can hook up so easily. Generally, men don't go on dates that often—and definitely not on second dates—unless it's someone they really like and want to get to know better."

Cat was frowning, deep in thought. "Connor would, though."

"Mom. You're kind of creeping me out. How can you possibly know what Connor would do?"

"He's a nice boy. Even if this woman is just for a good time, he would still take her out for a decent dinner first. He's that kind of man."

"Ew." Aly got up, grabbed a sock and searched for its mate in the pile. "Uh-uh. Either way—if he really likes her or it's just a booty call with dinner thrown in—*I* don't like it. It makes everything *wrong*, somehow. He's got his life and I've got mine, and I have to stop trying to pretend that my scrambled-up brain knows the truth and reality doesn't matter. I've got to stop kidding myself. Sometimes things end. They end all wrong and you wish with all your heart that you'd done things differently. But you did what you did and you can't go back and do it over again."

The offices of Valentine Logging were housed in a barnlike manufactured building at the Warrenton docks on the Columbia River.

Valentine Logging was still a family-owned company, one that had almost gone under when George and Marie Bravo died in Thailand sixteen years before. But

Connor's great-uncle Percy Valentine, who had been in his sixties at the time, had pitched in to help Daniel learn to run the place.

By nine years ago, when Connor came on board, the company ship was considerably steadier. Another few years after that, and they were back on course. Since then, they'd expanded, increasing their profits three times over.

Once a week at least, Daniel joined Connor in his office to go over the calendar, review the jobs in progress and the ones coming up, making sure they had everything on schedule and under control.

That day, at a little after five, they were just finishing up the weekly review.

"So, we're looking good," said Daniel. "On schedule with both projects."

"We're good, yeah," Connor replied.

He was supposed to pick up Margo at six thirty. They had reservations for seven at his favorite steak house in nearby Astoria. He liked Margo, he really did. She was smart and fun and neither of them was looking for anything serious. Since his marriage imploded, he didn't do serious. It was just better that way.

But more than once that day he'd almost called Margo to beg off. He didn't want to go out with her. It felt all wrong to go out with her.

He needed to go home to Aly, eat that dinner she'd offered to cook for him, look into her lavender-blue eyes and ask how her day had been, how her mom was doing, how she, Aly, was feeling. If she'd had any more headaches, if she'd thought it over and decided she still hated his guts, after all…

Daniel, across the desk from him, shut his own laptop. "Okay. What is up with you?"

His brother would find out soon enough, anyway. Might as well get it over with. "Aly's in town for the next few months. Cat's pregnant and Aly's here to help out."

Daniel took a minute before he replied, "So...you've seen Alyssa, spoken to her? Is that what you're telling me?"

"More. Much more."

"Connor. Just explain yourself."

Connor cracked his neck and raked both hands back through his hair. Then he laid it all out for his older brother—the accident, Aly's strange partial amnesia, her request to stay in his guest room for as long as she was in town. "I said she could stay. She moved in last night."

"Wow," Daniel said.

"And I've got a date tonight with someone else."

His brother, who rarely swore, said a bad word.

Connor grunted. "I don't want to go, but I feel like a jerk to call her and cancel so late."

"Need advice?"

Connor turned his mesh swivel chair sideways, slumped down in it, stuck his feet out in front of him and stared at his boots. "Make it good."

"You want another chance with Alyssa?"

"I keep telling myself it's too late."

"If you go out with someone else tonight, it just might be."

Connor slanted Daniel a dirty look. "I had a feeling you'd say something like that."

"Hey. What are older brothers for?" He picked up Connor's phone from the edge of the desk and held it out to him. "Call your date and cancel."

"I feel like a schmuck. Aly walks back in my life and I forget everything but her. I didn't even remember I had a date tonight until this morning, when Aly offered to cook me dinner."

"Okay. I agree with you. You're a schmuck." Daniel waved the phone at him. "Don't be a weenie, too. Make the call."

It was still kind of weird to Connor, how much his big brother had changed. In the past year or so, the always serious, usually glum Daniel Bravo had developed a sense of humor and become downright cheerful. The guy was happy with his family—his new wife, Keely, and their baby, and the twins from his first marriage.

"Smart-ass." He took the phone.

Daniel got up and left him to it.

Margo picked up on the first ring. "Hi, Connor." She sounded worried, which didn't surprise him. He would have texted her with any minor change of plans. A call didn't bode well for the evening itself.

It was an awkward conversation. Because he really was a schmuck. He should have called her earlier; even that morning, when he'd first remembered about the date, would've been better than now. He made a lame excuse about how "something" had come up and he was going to have to cancel.

She said she was disappointed and then, her voice a low purr, asked, "Next weekend, then?"

And he knew he would have to be more direct with her. "I'm sorry, Margo. My ex-wife is back in the picture." It pissed him off to have to say it, to have it mean so damn much. Life without Aly had been a lot simpler. He avoided getting too close, kind of skated on the surface of things. After the first couple years without her, he'd started telling himself life was better with no strings.

"Whoa," Margo said. She was not purring now. "You're getting back with your ex?"

"I don't know what's happening, really. But in the past week, everything's changed."

"In the past week? And you couldn't have called to let me know earlier?"

"Listen, I'm sorry. You are so right. I should have called you earlier."

"Yeah, well." She spoke curtly. "You didn't."

"Again, I apologize."

"Goodbye, Connor." Margo said frostily. The line went dead.

Connor called the restaurant and canceled his reservation. Then he stuck his phone in his pocket and put his laptop in his briefcase.

He felt more like a jerk than ever. But he was also relieved. He'd called it off with Margo and now he could go home to Aly. Maybe she would still be willing to cook him that dinner she'd offered. And they could talk.

Except that, when he got home half an hour later, the key he'd given her waited on the kitchen counter. The scrap of paper beneath the key read, "Never mind. I realize I can't do this, after all."

Chapter Five

It had been a quiet dinner, just Aly and her parents, with Tuck lurking under the table, hoping to catch any fallen treats. Marco was out with his friends.

No one mentioned Connor, but her mom knew what had happened. Cat might or might not have enlightened Ernesto. Aly didn't even want to know what the two had said to each other concerning Aly's fragile mental state and the way she'd moved in with Connor and back out again in the space of approximately nineteen hours.

Cat had returned to the master bedroom and Aly was straightening up the kitchen after the meal when the doorbell rang. She loaded the last plate in the dishwasher, shut the door and grabbed the sponge to wipe down the counters.

Her dad appeared in the doorway to the dining room.

"Connor's here. I would've slammed the door in his face but your mother warned me ahead of time that I better not try that. So I just shut it on him. Quiet-like. How did your mother know he was going to show up here?"

Connor's here. Her pulse raced and her face felt hot. It was a little before seven. He must have called off his date...

Her dad pinched up his full mouth and narrowed his eyes at her. "That kid's got a nerve on him. Just tell me to tell him to fuggetaboutit, that if you never see his face again, it'll be too soon."

"Dad."

"What?"

She stepped in close, kissed his cheek and handed him the sponge. "I love you. Back off." Straightening her shoulders and aiming her chin high, she headed for the front door.

When she got there, she could see him, his face only slightly distorted by the etched glass in the top of the door. They stared at each other for several seconds before she pulled the door wide.

He held a huge paper cone of dahlias—big ones in a bright rainbow of stunning colors. Nothing compared to dahlias grown in Oregon.

She stepped over the threshold as he backed up enough that he wasn't crowding her. "What do you want, Connor?" She pulled the door shut behind her so her dad couldn't hear.

"I canceled my date," he said solemnly. "I'm not seeing her again. Or anyone. No one but you. And Aly, I'm not taking anything for granted. I don't know what will happen with us—or maybe I do know and I don't want to think about it. I just know I want you to please come home with me now."

Home.

She closed her eyes—and she could see it, that little house they'd lived in together on Fir Avenue. She was still at OU then, so they spent too much time apart during the school year. But summers belonged to them, together, at home.

Summer evenings like this one, they would sit out on their little postage stamp of a front porch and watch the night come on. Dahlias grew in fat clumps on either side of the porch steps—anemone dahlias, waterlily dahlias, collarette and pom-pom dahlias.

"Aly," he whispered. "I'm sorry. When I made that date, I had no clue that you would be back in my life again a few days later. And then I forgot all about it because all I had on my mind was you."

She opened her eyes and accepted the bouquet of flowers from his outstretched hand. "They're beautiful. Thank you." She lowered her nose to them and got what she expected: nothing. Dahlias had no scent. It had always seemed so wrong to her that something so beautiful had no discernable smell.

He suggested, "Cat might like them."

That softened her heart even more. "She would love them. I'll arrange them in her favorite cut-glass vase and put them in her bedroom to make her smile."

"And then will you come home with me?"

She felt so strange, suddenly. Kind of quivery. Shy. Instead of answering his question, she asked another one. "Isn't it a little early for dahlias?"

"It's been a warm year." He gave her that smile—the secret one, the one for just between the two of them.

She'd missed that smile, hadn't she? Missed it so much, in those seven years without him. All those seven years of life she'd lived on her own in the big city...

For a tattered fraction of a moment, she stood at the corner of Fifth Avenue and West Thirtieth Street. It was summer. She could almost feel the heat coming up through the sidewalk. She heard horns honking and a sharp, high whistle—some guy signaling for a cab. She smelled apple fritters and frying sausage from a food cart nearby...

"Aly?" A hand on her arm.

She looked down. *Connor's hand.* She would know it, always; could easily distinguish it from any other. The broad, strong shape of it, the lean fingers, the perfect dusting of golden-brown hair to just a little below the sculpted wrist...

"Hmm?" She let her gaze track up until she looked into his gray-blue eyes.

"Come back home with me. Tonight."

She still wanted him. So much. Maybe too much. She should probably stick with the new plan, stay here at her mom's, not tempt fate any more than she already had.

But what she *should* do? To hell with that. Her heart had its own plan and that meant there really wasn't anything to say but, "All right. Come on in."

Inside, Connor got the dark glare of death from Ernesto. But at least Aly's dad left it at that and returned his attention to the game on the big screen mounted over the fireplace.

Connor followed Aly into the kitchen.

He said no to coffee and took a chair at the table as she reached for a giant vase from the top of a cupboard and proceeded to arrange the flowers he'd brought.

"I'll be back," she said, and went off with the flowers. He sat there, feeling strange and out of place in the kitchen where he used to feel right at home. Growing up, he and Dante had had the run of the house. Cat had always catered to them, serving up hot dogs and cupcakes and peanut butter sandwiches on demand.

Aly returned and stood in the doorway to the dining room, a battered, blue-eyed angel with all those acres of black hair he burned to bury his hands in again. Maybe he'd get lucky, steal a kiss from her tonight.

"Mom loves the dahlias. She says thank you."

Cat would have said more. "And what else?"

"She said to tell you to be good to me—or else."

He nodded. "Now, that sounds like your mom."

"You want to see her?"

"Yeah. If she's feeling up to it."

"Come on, then."

He followed Aly up the stairs.

She led him to the door of the master bedroom and tapped on it. "Mom? Connor wants to say hi."

"Sure."

Aly ushered him in ahead of her.

Cat, somehow looking even more pregnant than she had the evening before, was sitting up in bed with her scruffy little dog snoozing at her side. "Connor. My flowers are beautiful."

"I'm glad you like them. How're you feeling?"

Cat gave him a slow smile. "Much better. You had me worried, though."

What was he supposed to say to that?

Before he could come up with the right words, Cat said in a warm tone, "Goodnight, Connor."

"Goodnight," he said, and they left it at that.

He joined Aly in her room, where she was repacking her suitcases.

Downstairs again, she kissed her disapproving dad goodbye and they were out of there.

At his house, Connor hauled everything back up to the guest room and left her to settle in for the second time.

In the kitchen, he made himself a ham sandwich and ate it standing by the sink. He drank a bunch of water and then poured himself some Bowmore over ice.

Still standing by the window that looked out on Mrs. Garber's tiny side yard, he sipped his drink until there was nothing left but an ice cube. Aly didn't come down and the house was too quiet. He could almost be alone all over again.

Aly needed checking on, he decided. She'd suffered a head injury, after all.

He climbed the stairs and found the door to her room wide open. She was sprawled faceup, sound asleep on the bed, still wearing that fitted pink shirt and black pants, but minus her shoes. He stood in the open doorway to her room, drinking in the sight of her, watching her full breasts rise and fall in an even rhythm, admiring the dark halo of thick hair spread out on the pillow.

She seemed okay, her expression relaxed. Peaceful. He should close the door and let her rest.

Quietly, he took off his boots and set them by the door. It was still light out, but she'd turned on the lamp by the bed. Silent in stocking feet, he went to her and switched off the light.

She stirred a little but didn't wake. He put a knee to the mattress. With a soft little sigh, she rolled away from him onto her side, conveniently making room for him next to her.

He took shameless advantage, lying down beside her, wrapping himself around her, ready to jump up and start apologizing if she objected to his being there.

Damn. She smelled so good. Warmth and woman and ginger spice. He pulled her closer against him, burying his nose in the dark cloud of her hair.

She fitted herself into him, snuggling her gorgeous, round bottom back against his groin. It felt like heaven—and now he was sporting wood. Desire was an ache spreading all through him. He pulled her in closer, bringing his knees up, making a cradle for her thighs.

Holding Aly. Nothing compared.

She took his hand and snuggled it between those beautiful, soft breasts of hers—awake, after all? Evidently. The softest little chuckle escaped her. "I'm not having sex with you tonight, so get that idea right out of your head."

He nuzzled her hair out of his way and brushed his lips along the side of her neck. "But I can stay?"

She took her time answering. He was certain he would be sent packing. But then she sighed. "Yeah. Stay."

When Aly woke around midnight, Connor was gone. She got up, took off her wrinkled clothes and padded to the bathroom to wash her face and brush her teeth. Back in the bedroom, she put on a sleep shirt. Smiling to herself, she climbed under the covers.

He'd ended whatever it was with that other woman. And he'd admitted that he wanted to be only with her.

Things could be worse.

Maybe she and Connor wouldn't end up together. Maybe she would wake up one morning and remember with clarity all the things about the past seven years that everyone else said were true. Maybe the time would come that she would be eager to return to her life in New York.

But in the meantime, as long as her ex-husband was willing to put up with her, as long as he looked at her like he craved a whole lot more with her than he thought he had a right to ask for, well, she had a plan, and the plan was to do everything in her power to get up close and personal with him.

The next morning, she woke to the smell of breakfast cooking. Downstairs, Connor handed her a mug of coffee and pulled out a chair for her at the table.

She went off to her parents' house smiling. Connor wanted her in his house and it felt absolutely right for her to be there.

In the evening, they cooked together. She tossed a salad and fixed saffron rice while he grilled marinated chicken. It was good, just to be with him.

Good, but not enough.

And didn't he seem kind of cautious now? He was careful not to get too close. When she brushed against him, he moved away. As soon as they'd cleaned up after the meal, he disappeared into his home office upstairs.

Was he having second thoughts about the two of them taking their current status as roommates to the next level? She reminded herself not to rush things. She had weeks and weeks left in town—maybe longer. Maybe the rest of her life. It was so hard to say at this point.

That night, she dreamed of Strategic Image. Of her office, where framed prints chronicling campaigns she'd worked on over the years filled the wall behind her glass desk, testimony to her success and to how much she loved her job. When she woke in the morning, she had a mild headache.

She also remembered that dream.

Just as Dr. Warbury had predicted, her memory was beginning to return. Bits of her past had already come back to her. Not many yet—well, only two: that moment out on Fifth Avenue and now the dream of her office. It felt like a giant puzzle with all but two pieces missing.

But at least it seemed fully possible that, in time, she would know what she needed to know about the years since Connor had had her served with divorce papers.

Sunday, while she was alone in her mom's kitchen mixing tuna salad for lunch, her phone buzzed with a text.

Going to Daniel's for dinner tonight, Connor wrote. Just wanted you to know. Thought you might want to go ahead and eat with your folks.

She frowned at the screen as she tried to decipher his message. Seemed to her he wasn't inviting her. And she would bet he'd known that morning or even the day before that he would be at Daniel's tonight.

Foolish man. If he refused to invite her, he was going to have to say so.

She texted back, Who all will be there? I want to come.

It took him forever to answer. She grinned down at her phone and waited him out. Finally, he reported that it was kind of a standing thing—Sunday dinner at Daniel's. He wasn't sure how many of his brothers and sisters would show up.

Connor had started out with eight siblings—four brothers and four sisters. One brother, Finn, had disappeared at the age of eight during a family trip to Russia, never to be seen or heard from again. That left him with three brothers and four sisters, some of whom were married now. Daniel had three children. It could be a big group. She really wanted to see them all, find out how they were doing.

She texted back her demand. Invite me.

The phone rang in her hand. She put it to her ear. "Well?"

"You really sure you want to go?" He sounded kind of worried. But hopeful, too.

They needed to talk. It seemed that he still felt he should keep his distance from her. Wrong. "Yes, I'm sure I want to go. I'll meet you at your house. What time?"

"Five?"

"I'll be there."

The Bravos didn't seem all that surprised to see her. Connor must have filled them in on the situation. They welcomed her with big smiles and lots of enthusiasm. His sisters hugged her; his brothers did, too. They asked how she was doing after the accident and they didn't seem to blame her at all for the divorce.

Connor might have lied to keep her, but he must have been honest with his family about why the marriage ended. At least he hadn't turned them all against her.

Had she done that to him? Turned her dad and her brothers against him?

Due to the holes in her memory, she wasn't sure what she'd said or done back then.

But she had no doubt that she'd cast Connor as the villain. Why wouldn't she? Even he frankly admitted that he'd been the bad guy in their breakup, the one who lied about his intentions and then refused to compromise in the slightest to try and work things out.

She needed to have a talk with Dante and her dad, at least—and before them, with her mom. Find out what she'd said to them seven years ago about the dissolution of her marriage—find out, and then do what she could to end the hostilities.

It kind of astonished her how much had happened in her years away. Daniel's first wife, Lillie, had died three years back of complications from lupus after giving birth to twins, Frannie and Jake. Those two were adorable, happy and playful, talking nonstop, throwing a ball for the family basset hound, Maisey, and giggling in delight when the dog brought it back.

Then, a year ago, Daniel had married Lillie's cousin, Keely Ostergard. Daniel and Keely had a six-month-old, Marie. Aly also met Matt Bravo's bride, Sabra. Matt and Sabra lived on her family farm just outside Astoria. Aislinn, oldest of the Bravo sisters, introduced Aly to her husband, Jaxon Winter.

Dinner was a crowded affair. The table in the dining room was a long one, but there were a lot of Bravos to fill it. It was potluck, with everybody bringing something. At her mother's that day, Aly had baked chocolate chip cookies, so she'd brought a couple dozen of those.

They had coffee after the meal, and a pineapple upside-down cake Sabra had brought. The cake and Aly's cookies were gone before anyone asked for a second cup of coffee.

It was after nine when she and Connor said their goodbyes and climbed into his Land Rover.

"Tired?" he asked, as he drove them through the quiet, dark streets of their hometown.

"A little." Since the accident, she tired more easily, though her stamina did seem to be increasing, day by day.

At Connor's house, Maurice had somehow managed to slip into the garage. The cat was waiting for them on the steps leading to the inside door.

"I'll take him home," Connor said. He scooped up the cat and carried him up through the house to the front door. "Go on to bed," he instructed before he went out. "Get some rest."

She did no such thing. She was waiting on the sofa in the living area when he returned five minutes later.

"I thought you were going to bed," he said over his shoulder as he locked the front door.

"Wrong. You *told* me to go to bed." She slipped off her sandals and folded her legs up to the side on the couch cushions. "But it just so happens I'm not that tired."

He came up the single step to the living area and went on into the kitchen, where he got down a bottle of Scotch and a glass.

It simply wouldn't be right to let him drink alone, now would it? "Got vodka?"

He gave her another glance over his shoulder. "Where do your doctors come down on drinking?"

"Should I get hammered? No. Can I have a drink now and then? Absolutely."

He took down a second, taller glass. "Tonic or cranberry juice?"

"Tonic would be great."

He poured their drinks and brought them into the living area. "Here you go."

She took the tall glass and patted the couch cushion. "Sit with me."

He gazed down at her, hesitating. But then he gave in and folded his tall frame into the space beside her. She hid a smile. Poor man. Trapped by his ex-wife, who wouldn't just give up and go to bed when he told her to. "It's good, thank you," she said, after taking a sip. "And it was great to see your family again."

"They always loved you."

"I love *them*." She had another sip. "They didn't seem surprised to see me."

He'd put a single large ice cube in his Scotch. It clinked against the glass as he drank. "I told Daniel pretty much the whole story, about the accident and your partial amnesia, your mom and the baby and your coming to stay with me."

"And the family grapevine took care of the rest?"

"Essentially."

She set her drink on the coffee table and held out her hand to him. "Here. Give me yours."

He frowned at her. "Why?"

By way of an answer, she snatched his glass from him and set it with hers. He didn't object. But he did watch her, eagle-eyed, his expression equal parts wary and predatory.

Sadly, the wariness would keep him from making any kind of move—and so be it. She'd never been the shy type. She would do it for him.

She leaned closer. Now she could smell his cologne and feel the tempting heat of him. Best of all, he didn't back away.

She leaned even closer and said more softly, "Friday night you came and wrapped yourself around me. You slept with me—for a while, anyway." There were no more than a couple of inches from his lips to hers. His breath caressed her, warm and scented with Scotch. "Since then, though, it's definitely felt like you've backed off, like you're trying to keep distance between us."

He took several seconds to frame his answer. "It's a bad idea to get carried away," he said in a careful, measured tone. But those eyes of his, they said something else altogether. Those eyes weren't measured. Those eyes burned.

They burned for her. They always had and both of them knew it.

"Uh-uh," she replied, allowing herself a smug little smile. "It's a *good* idea. Coming here to stay with you is the best idea I've had in seven years. I'm so glad I got whacked in the head."

"Don't even joke about it." His voice was deliciously low and rough and hot.

She leaned that fraction closer, eliminating the last bit of distance between them. Their lips met—lightly. Gently.

That first contact brought a happy sigh from her. His lips were so soft, in perfect counterpoint to the slight scruff on his cheeks. "Oh, Conn…" She breathed the words into his mouth.

He inhaled sharply. "Aly…"

And finally, he broke. With a low, desperate sound, he reached for her. His lean, hard arms came around her, dragging her close as he kissed her.

Heat bloomed in her belly and a shiver skated down her spine. His kiss was everything she yearned for, all the promises that mattered most, the promises they'd both failed so completely to keep.

It had been years—and all right, she still didn't remember those years, exactly. But, oh, she did feel them, feel the loss of him, feel that core of emptiness inside her since they'd turned away from each other.

She *had* missed him. In the deepest, most punishing, lonely sort of way. Every cell in her body had been starved for him in their years apart.

And now, at last, he was holding her, his hungry mouth devouring hers. She shifted, turning in his arms until he cradled her across his lap. He started to lift his mouth from hers.

No way.

Wrapping her hand around the back of his neck, she

pulled him down, surging up at the same time to keep him from breaking the contact. With a groan, he sank back into her and the kiss went on—glorious. Magical.

Her greedy fingers danced across the hard musculature of his shoulders. She threaded them up into the close-trimmed hair at his nape. His tongue came out to play and she was only too eager for that sort of game.

As the kiss got deeper, his touch grew bolder. His hand glided along the curve of her hip, palming her waist, moving higher. He cupped one breast.

She moaned in gleeful encouragement and he plucked at the nipple through her shirt and bra. That made her ache in the most delicious way.

Oh, it was perfect. Everything she wanted, all that she craved, what she needed so much. Conn, holding her, kissing her, stroking all the places only he knew how to touch.

His kisses were the best kisses. They always had been.

Even their first kiss, all those years and years ago, remained unforgettable to her. It was forbidden, that kiss—because his loyalty then was to Dante and it was understood, a secret code, between Connor and Dante, that Connor wouldn't mess with his best friend's little sister.

But that day, he'd broken loyalty with Dante, if only for one brief, beautiful moment…

That day, she was thirteen and he was fifteen, and it was summertime in Valentine Bay.

It was a warm day, with a slight breeze. It felt like Southern California had come to visit the Oregon coast.

Conn and Dante and three of their buddies had gone out to Valentine Beach. One of the guys had a license, so they'd taken his truck. Aly had begged to go, but they only mocked her the way they always did. They didn't need Dante's little sister tagging along after them.

But she knew where they were going and rode her bike, locking it to a bike rack a few blocks from the beach and running the rest of the way. Stopping at the higher dunes a good distance from the water, she dropped her pack and her towel in the sand and watched what was going on down on the beach. It didn't take her long to spot the five boys she'd come looking for.

For a while, she just watched them, spying on them as they fooled around on their bodyboards. The water never got much above sixty degrees and they didn't have wetsuits, so they couldn't stay in for long. They spent more time showing off for giggling groups of girls than catching waves.

Bitter, that was pretty much her attitude that day. As always, her brother and the boy she wanted so desperately to impress had called her a kid. They'd mocked her for wanting to go with them.

Well, screw them. Especially Connor. She already had breasts and she looked really good in her red string bikini—a little pale, maybe. She had her mom's Irish coloring. But still. She definitely looked old enough to be Connor Bravo's girl.

Too bad he absolutely refused to see that they were meant to be together.

The sun was warm. In the dunes, she spread her

towel, slathered on sunscreen and stretched out under the sun. It seemed she closed her eyes for only a minute.

But when she opened them again, Conn was there, alone, standing not ten feet away from her, all tanned skin and golden windblown hair. There was sand sticking to the side of his neck and in a circle on his lean shoulder.

"You're gonna burn," he said, in that scornful tone he used with her constantly.

She sat up and held out her tube of sunscreen. "Do my back?" Her voice was perfect, calm and unconcerned.

He gulped. His cool blue eyes weren't so cool now. She stared right at him, watched his tongue dart out to lick his lower lip.

All her sulky bitterness vanished. He *did* like her. He liked her a lot. He could knock himself out pretending that he wasn't interested. But today, for the first time, he was letting her see how he really felt.

Today, for the first time, he'd given himself away.

Her body seemed to pulse with power, every nerve ending firing, shooting off sparks. One way or another, however long it took, Connor Bravo would be hers.

Totally calm, cool as someone much older—fifteen or sixteen at least—she turned her back to him, smoothed her heavy hair out of the way with one hand and held the tube of sunscreen up over her shoulder with the other. "Come on. Help me out."

He couldn't resist her. Could. Not. Resist.

Triumph made her blood surge superfast through her veins as he padded across the sand and dropped to his knees behind her at the end of her towel. He accepted the tube from her fingers. She faced front and concentrated on controlling her breathing as she felt his hot, slightly rough hand on her back.

It took only a moment or two for him to spread the sunscreen on her skin. But it was one of those times a girl never forgets. Her skin felt electric, her body on fire.

And in the end, she couldn't resist turning her head back to him again, capturing his gaze.

He said her name in a frantic, desperate whisper.

And she replied, equally breathless, "Connor."

And then it happened. He leaned that fraction closer and their lips touched.

They gasped in unison.

He pressed his mouth harder against hers, hard enough that their teeth clacked together—and that did it. The spell was broken. He jerked away.

Her eyes popped open and they were staring straight at each other. Beneath his tan, his face had flushed deep red. "I gotta go." He leaped to his feet and ran off toward the beach.

She stared after him, transported. Victorious.

Connor Bravo had kissed her.

Oh, it was happening. He would be hers. Dante could just get over himself, give up his big-brother overprotectiveness. Conn would choose *her*. He would be her boyfriend, at last.

What an optimist she'd been.

After that one, too-brief kiss on the dunes at Valentine Beach, Connor never touched her again.

Not for six long years…

* * *

Thirty-one-year-old Connor lifted his head and stared down at her through heavy-lidded eyes.

Aly blinked up at him, slightly dazed.

She'd gotten gloriously lost—in his kiss and the memory of that other kiss sixteen years before. The past and the present had all swirled together, sweeping her away. "Don't stop."

His gold-kissed eyebrows drew together. "It's not a good idea."

"Really?" She scoffed. "You're going to go there? Connor, it's why I'm here."

He shook his head. "No. It's about peace, remember? You're here so that we can make peace with each other. So that when you go back to New York, you'll have figured everything out."

Sadness curled through her. "You make it all sound so cut-and-dried."

"It is what it is. It just didn't work out for us. The point is that you need to accept the way things really are."

"*Your* point, maybe. Not mine." She reached up and lightly brushed her fingertips against his forehead and up into his hair. Her body buzzed with desire.

And another recent memory revealed itself to her.

A memory of the last guy she'd tried to make a real relationship with.

Kyle. That was his name. Kyle Santos.

She remembered sitting across from Kyle in her favorite coffee place not far from her apartment in Lower Manhattan.

Her turkey club sat untouched on the blue plate in

front of her. Her flat white was growing cold. She told Kyle she was sorry, that it just couldn't work.

Her heart ached as she watched him get up and walk away.

"Aly?" Connor gazed down at her, frowning. "You okay?"

"I'm good." She focused on how right it felt to be held in Connor's arms, on making him see that anything was possible if they just put their hearts and minds into it. "Connor, you have no way of knowing what will happen in the next thirteen weeks."

"I know what's most likely."

There was no point in lying there spread out across his lap if he wasn't going to give her the kisses she craved. She sat up and flipped her hair back over her shoulder with a sigh. "You always were way too stubborn for your own good."

"*I'm* stubborn?" He picked up his drink from the coffee table and stood.

"Wait. Where are you going?"

"Upstairs." And he started walking.

It was not in her nature to quit. She took one more crack at the problem. "You just said peace is the best we're ever going to do here. How are we going to make peace if you keep running away every time we start trying to talk about what went wrong?"

He paused in midstep. From that angle, she could see the hard bulge at his fly. They might not be any closer to working things out—to finding peace *or* each other—but there was no question the fire still burned whenever they touched. "I don't think there is any fixing it. Good night, Aly."

For a while after he disappeared upstairs, she sat there on the sofa, sipping her vodka tonic and wondering what it was about him that made him the only one for her.

Yeah, he was hot. But a lot of men were hot.

Connor, for her, was so much more. She'd always felt that he *knew* her in the deepest way, that he saw all of her—good points, flaws and all the parts in between. He saw her and understood her, as she understood him.

He had that certain something that made her yearn for him and him alone, made her want to do whatever she had to do to break down any barriers between them.

Until it all went wrong and her pride took over and she'd signed the divorce papers instead of coming home.

Apparently, she'd tried for seven years to turn her back on him, to forget him and move on, to find someone else that her heart could beat for. A wry chuckle escaped her. Judging by everything she'd learned since the accident, forgetting him had not gone well.

She'd had happiness with him once, though. Happiness, full and rich and ripe, with the promise of a lifetime together.

She stared off toward the dark windows across the room.

He had walls, Connor did. And from the age of thirteen, she'd known she was the one to bust through them, to tear them down.

So, then.

He wasn't willing at this point to talk through the issues that stood between them.

Maybe she needed to go at this a different way.

Idly, she lifted a hand and touched her lips. They were still warm with the sweet, wild pressure of his kiss.

Would it be wrong to actively seduce him, to let their bodies do the talking—at least at first?

She smiled to herself. "Whatever it takes," she whispered to the dark window across the room.

Chapter Six

Connor sat on his bed and called himself ten kinds of a wimp for running away from her.

But he really didn't want to talk about the past, about all the ways he'd screwed it up, all the ways he'd been a stupid, pigheaded kid who wanted things his way and wouldn't know a compromise if it kicked him in the ass.

What he needed was to kiss her some more, touch her some more, explore all the ways she felt just like she used to under his hands—just like she used to.

Only better.

He'd finished off the last of his Scotch and plunked the glass down on the bedside table when she tapped on his door.

"It's open."

The door swung inward. She leaned into the doorway, crossing her arms under her beautiful breasts, her sandals dangling from one hand.

And all at once, he was glad. That she was braver and stronger than he was, that she'd come after him when he walked away.

Glad for her presence in his house. Glad just to have her near again, for as long as she remained in town.

She asked, "Remember our first kiss?"

He nodded. "In the dunes at Valentine Beach. I will never forget that red bikini. I thought I was going to lose it when you handed me the sunscreen. And when I finally got my mouth on you, I knew I would die."

Her smile was slow and painfully sweet. "You ran away."

He asked drily, "Just like tonight, you mean?"

"Yeah. Like tonight. Are you afraid of me, Conn?"

He answered honestly. "Terrified. Always have been. Of how much you meant to me. Of losing you."

"You did lose me."

"Exactly."

She looked down at her bare feet and then up at him through her raven-black eyelashes. "But here I am again. I'm not that easy to lose—at least not in the long run." She laughed. The sound, husky and warm, made an ache in his chest *and* in his pants. "Good night." She reached over and grasped the door handle, pulling the door closed again, leaving him alone.

The next day, before heading over to her mom's, Aly dropped in at Valentine Bay Urgent Care to get the stitches out of her knee. After that, she spent an hour with Dr. Warbury. The doctor seemed pleased when

Aly reported the little bits of memories that had come back to her.

Aly explained that she was staying at Connor's, that it was really helping her to spend time with him. She kind of wondered if her doctor would disapprove of her moving in on her ex. But Dr. Warbury just listened and nodded and let it be.

When Aly joked about stalking herself online to learn more about who she had become during the seven years she'd lost in the accident, the doctor suggested she try reaching out to some of her New York friends. Maybe connecting with them would encourage more of her recent life to surface.

The idea of reaching out scared her. Those people thought of her as a friend. And she did feel a tug of familiarity when she studied their Facebook and Twitter feeds, when she pored over their Instagram posts. But so far, she didn't know the things a friend would know about them.

"What about Kyle Santos?" asked Dr. Warbury. "You just described a memory of him."

Aly chewed her lower lip over that. "I don't know. I mean, what I remembered was breaking up with him. I'm somehow positive I really meant it when I ended it with him. I don't want him to think I'm hoping to get back together with him or anything."

"Well then, just tell him that it isn't about trying again. Be honest with him."

She twisted her hands in her lap, still uncomfortable with the idea.

Dr. Warbury asked, "Is your reluctance to contact

Kyle actually about your ex-husband? You moved in with him, you said. Do you want to try again with *him*?"

Aly puffed out her cheeks with a hard breath—and told her therapist the truth. "Yeah. I do. I really do."

Dr. Warbury only nodded, and suggested, "Then try another friend from New York, a girlfriend maybe?"

Aly said she would consider it.

On the way to her mom's she started thinking about work, about what might be going on at Strategic Image, about how she kind of wanted to touch base there, but it didn't seem all that wise to admit that she'd forgotten the seven years she'd worked there.

They wouldn't be contacting her, at least not for a while yet. She'd always been a driven, dedicated employee, one who rarely took time off. She was due a long break and they understood that her mom really needed her. They wouldn't be distracting her with work-related issues.

And how did she know all that?

Because yet another memory had floated to the surface of her conscious mind. She remembered her last conversation with Jane Levelow, SI's director of marketing. Aly had reported that all her projects were reassigned and in good hands. Jane had said that it wouldn't be easy getting along without her, but that it was good thing for her to have some time for herself and her family. Jane also wished her well and promised not to bother her for at least the first few weeks.

Aly parked in the turnaround in front of her parents' house, next to Dante's police cruiser. She ran up the front steps feeling pretty good about everything. Her bumps and scrapes and bruises from the accident were healing—and day by day, she remembered more of the years she'd lost.

Things weren't exactly fabulous between her and Connor. But he'd kissed her like he meant it last night. And he hadn't asked her to leave yet, so the situation with him definitely could have been worse.

She opened the door to find Dante right there in the front hall, his dark eyes stormy, a muscle ticking in his jaw. "Shouldn't you have been here a couple of hours ago?" he demanded. "I got here and Mom was all alone in the house."

So much for how great everything had seemed to be going. "Is she all right?"

His frown just got deeper. "That's not the point. You're supposed to be here for her, taking care of her."

"Translation—Mom is doing fine, but you're pissed off at me, so it doesn't matter that Mom's okay, you're telling me off, anyway."

"You shouldn't be staying at *his* house. It's getting in the way of the job you came here to do—not to mention it's bad for you. *He's* bad for you. You may not remember it, but that jerk divorced you."

"*He* has a name. And I am fully aware that Connor and I are divorced. I'm also completely cognizant of your feelings about my ex-husband. There's no need to share them with me again." She recalled what she'd promised herself last night at Daniel Bravo's house— that she would be more honest with the men in her family about the past, about her breakup with Connor. "And I was to blame, too, when we broke up. It wasn't all Connor's fault."

"You remember, then? It's come back to you?" Anger

and hope warred on Dante's face. He was still so pissed off at Connor. But that she might be remembering was good news.

And she didn't remember their breakup. That was still a blank to her. "Mostly, I realize that I didn't even try to work it out with him."

"Why the hell *should* you have tried? It was all his fault."

"It's rarely all one person's fault, Dante. You've been married. You know that. And as for my being late, I got my stitches out and then I had an appointment with Dr. Warbury. Mom knew I was going to be late. Marco said he would hang around until I got here."

"I can hear you two!" Cat called down from upstairs. "Stop it and get up here, the both of you!"

Dante glowered at her. She glared right back. They'd always had a love-hate relationship. All her life, he'd tried to boss her around. He'd felt driven to protect her as his little sister. But she didn't need his protection and she chafed under the weight of it. She could take care of herself and she was fully capable of making her own decisions, thank you very much.

"Now!" Cat shouted.

They dragged themselves up the stairs like a couple of guilty kids.

"What am I going to do with the two of you?" Cat asked when they stood on either side of the bed, where she sat with Tucker curled up at her side and a fat novel spread open against her giant baby bump. She turned her chiding gaze on Dante. "I told you that Marco was here with me. He left maybe ten minutes ago. I sent him off to work because I knew Aly would be here soon, and if anything did go wrong, I have everyone in the family on speed dial. You're making a huge deal out of nothing, Dante Ernesto. Stop."

She turned on Aly and said a little more gently. "Don't argue with your brother. He only acts like that because he loves you."

He only acts like that because he's a control freak, she thought. She said, "Right. Love made him do it."

Cat clucked her tongue. "Both of you. Say sorry."

Aly said it first—as always, "Sorry, Dante."

Dante muttered, "Yeah. Me, too." He said it so sulkily that she couldn't resist making one more point.

"You should make peace with Connor."

He just stood there and seethed at her across their parents' fancy new adjustable bed.

And she simply couldn't leave it at that. "He was your best friend. And he could be again. You two need to work it out."

He said nothing. But his eyes? They said it all, reminding her that it was his loyalty to her and his need to protect her that had always been the issue between him and Connor.

Cat said gently, "Aly. You've made your point."

Aly gave an elaborate shrug. "I don't think so, not really."

"Shut the hell up anyway," her mom commanded.

They left it at that.

Before heading back to Connor's that evening, Aly detoured to the Staples up in Warrenton. Her phone buzzed with a text as the clerk was bagging up her purchase.

It was Connor. You okay?

Was he worried about her? She felt all warm and fuzzy at the thought and texted back, Sorry. I should have let you know. I'm at Staples buying a new laptop. Be there soon.

I'll wait to put the steaks on.

Thanks.

Such an ordinary exchange to make her feel so pleased with the world and everything in it. She beamed the clerk a giant smile as he handed over her new Microsoft Surface Book 2.

They ate on the small deck off the kitchen. It was nice outside, a little breezy, the air cooling as evening came on.

She felt so good, just to be with him. He seemed relaxed and happy to be spending time with her, too.

She asked him how things were going at Valentine Logging. He explained how the business had grown in the years she'd been away.

She sipped her red wine slowly and thought about the past. "You didn't want to leave Daniel, did you—I mean, when we split up?"

He sat back in his chair and looked anywhere but at her. She thought he wouldn't answer. But then he said, "When we lost my parents, Daniel was a rock—a boulder. A damn mountain."

"I remember," she said softly. Daniel had been eighteen when George and Marie Bravo died. Connor was fifteen. It was the same year she and Connor shared that first forbidden kiss—but the Bravo family tragedy had happened earlier, in the spring.

At the loss of their parents, Daniel had stepped up— in every way. He married his high school sweetheart, became like a second father to his siblings, and ran Valentine Logging with the help of their great-uncle, Percy Valentine.

Connor said, "It wasn't Daniel's fault that I refused to go to New York, not in any way."

"I know. That's not what I meant. I meant that he'd done so much for you and your brothers and sisters. You didn't want to leave him to run the business alone."

He stared at his half-finished glass of wine, but didn't pick it up. "We were a team, Daniel and me—still are— when it comes to the business. The others might pitch in, work for a summer, whatever. But he and I were the only ones who wanted to keep it going, to expand the operation, make it more than when our dad ran it and our mother's dad before him."

"You liked working with your brother and you also felt an obligation to him."

He looked up from the glass and straight into her eyes. "I didn't want to go, Aly. I didn't want to go, but I wanted *you*. Always. I was a dumb-ass, selfish kid and I blew it. I knew you loved me. A lot. And I loved you. We were happy. I liked being happy with you. It was just…easier, not to get into it. To pretend I wanted what you wanted. I thought that when I finally had to admit to you that your dream and my dream weren't the same, I could use your love for me to make you do things my way."

A burst of laughter escaped her. "Connor. Have you *met* me?"

"Yeah, well. How many ways can I say it? I had my head up my ass in a big way."

She set down her wineglass. "I've thought about it a lot this past week and you know what? I forgive you, I really do."

He gazed at her kind of doubtfully. "Now I don't know what to say."

"Don't say anything. Start working on forgiving yourself. Also, think about making up with Dante."

He braced his elbows on the chair arms and folded his hands together over his lap. "You don't ask much, do you?"

"Think about it, that's all I'm suggesting. You made up before, back when you and I finally got together. He swore he would kill you and he ended up being your best man."

"You're dreaming if you think that your brother and I will ever be friends again."

"See? That." She pointed her finger at him. "That's pure fatalism talking. You need to give that crap up and start thinking positive."

It was fun, Connor decided.

Too damn much fun, being with her.

He'd forgotten how good it was, doing all the simple, everyday stuff—cooking and eating and sticking the dishes in the dishwasher. Every single mundane activity kind of had a glow around it when he and Aly did it together.

They streamed a movie. She sat beside him on the

sofa. They kicked off their shoes. Before it was over, she was leaning on him and he had his arm around her.

He shouldn't have let her get so close.

But it just felt so good. So right. She smelled so amazing. He kept nuzzling her hair, just to feel the thick silk of it against his skin and breathe in the scent of her.

A little later, they turned off the downstairs lights and walked upstairs together—well, she led the way. He followed close behind, trying not to stare at the gentle sway of her amazing butt, those full cheeks cradled in skinny jeans that probably ought to be outlawed to save all men from descending into sexual insanity.

At the top, she turned to him.

They stood facing each other on the landing, having sex with their eyes.

He wasn't really sure how it happened. One second she was a foot away, and the next, she was plastered up against him and his arms were banding around her.

That kiss.

Her kiss.

It was as good as the kiss last night—scratch that. Better.

Her mouth tasted of coffee and the Twizzlers she'd snacked on during the movie. He could kiss her forever, their tongues sparring and twining, the feel of her exactly right, soft and hot and lush and curvy under his roving hands.

It was a long kiss. But still, it ended way too soon.

He did that—ended it—at that last possible second before he would have scooped her high against his chest and carried her to his bed.

"Not gonna happen," he muttered, breathing fast,

pressing his forehead to hers, exerting every ounce of willpower he possessed not to claim those plush red lips again.

She was the one who stepped back. She gave him one of those scorching looks from under the thick fringe of her black eyelashes. "Let me know if you change your mind." And then she turned and left him. Strolling off along the upstairs hall, hips swaying maddeningly, she disappeared into her room.

It took him a really long time to get to sleep that night.

She cooked breakfast for both of them the next morning. She was cheerful and sweet, chattering away about her new laptop and how she was thinking of reaching out to a girlfriend or two in New York.

He tried not to stare at her with his tongue hanging out, not to picture her naked. He didn't succeed.

That night, he ate his dinner fast and made excuses about having some work to catch up on. She didn't argue or try to stall him to keep him with her longer.

"I'll clean up," she said with a bright smile. "You go ahead."

And suddenly, *he* wanted to argue with *her*, to pick a fight, even. Anything for an excuse to stay downstairs and watch her bustling around his kitchen, wiping down counters and putting things away.

Somehow, he managed to turn and leave her there.

Upstairs in his home office, he sat at the desk and stared at his laptop, doing squat for a really long time. Eventually, he went through his email and checked his calendar for tomorrow.

Then he played video games until ten, at which time he got up and poked his head out the door.

Everything was quiet. The lights were off downstairs and the door to her room was shut, a sliver of golden light showing underneath.

Disappointment dragged at him. He'd wasted the evening hiding in his office when he could have been with her.

Except it was too dangerous, being with Aly. Every day it got harder to keep his hands to himself.

Every day, all the reasons he shouldn't have her in his bed again became a little less clear to him—less clear and more wrong somehow, just sad, weak excuses not to get closer when getting closer was all he longed for.

He wanted her. She wanted him. So why the hell not?

Yeah, okay. She wouldn't be here forever. Valentine Bay just couldn't contain her. He would lose her again, same as he had seven years ago.

But in the meantime, why shouldn't they just do what came naturally? She seemed to want that—she'd made it more than clear with her smoking hot kisses. She'd even said it right out loud. She was pretty much pulling out all the stops, actively trying to drive him out of his mind with lust.

And damn. It was working. He burned for her, always had. He wanted her so bad.

That night, when he finally did get to sleep, she filled his dreams. He dreamed of the two of them rolling around naked—on the floor, on the bed, up against the wall. In his dreams, they made love everywhere, including several hazy encounters outside.

In the forest on a bed of lacy ferns. In the crashing waves near the shore on Valentine Beach…

The next morning, he woke sporting serious wood. With a groan, he rolled out of bed and headed for the bathroom to take care of the problem.

He stood outside the walk-in shower, fiddling with the controls to get the side jets and the rain shower exactly to his liking, when she spoke from behind him, "Good morning."

He whirled to face her. She lounged in the doorway that led to the bedroom. Her hair was a sexy, wild tangle and she wore itty-bitty sleep shorts and a clingy cropped T-shirt that showed a tempting slice of her upper belly. No bra…

His heart rate accelerated. *"Boundaries."* He growled the word at her. "You lack them."

Those eyes, forget-me-not blue, did a lazy pass from his face, down his naked body to his feet and back up again. "Aw. You've been thinking about me, haven't you?" And she straightened, grabbed the hem of the sleep shirt and ripped it up and off over her head, revealing those beautiful, heavy breasts of hers. She dropped the shirt to the floor and then shoved down the shorts.

They stood facing each other, both of them naked as the day they were born. Slowly, shamelessly, making a show of it, she licked her lips.

"You're pushing it," he muttered, the words scraping like sandpaper in his throat, his body aching so bad for her he was approaching the detonation point.

"Oh, really?" she taunted. "You always longed for a shy girl, all sweet and submissive, the modest type? Hmm. And yet you married me…"

"Aly," he said. At that moment, every other word in the English language seemed to have deserted him.

She stalked toward him. "Go ahead. I dare you." And she stopped right in front of him. "Tell me no. Say you don't want me. Ask me to leave."

"Aly." It came out on a rough husk of breath. "Are you sure?"

Chapter Seven

"I am so sure," she whispered, her voice tender now, her eyes soft and hopeful, trained on his. "Never have I ever been more certain of anything in my whole life, I promise you that."

She was so close, inches away. So close he could count every shining black eyelash, so close the tips of her breasts brushed his chest with each breath. So close that all he had to do was reach out and gather her in.

She was all he'd ever wanted, too much to deny.

He stuck out an arm and wrapped it around her. A hungry little sigh escaped her.

Yes.

He put his other arm around her, too, bringing her in, until all that softness and beauty was plastered to the front of him. The sweet scent of her engulfed him and his erection was pressed right where it needed to be, against the giving curve of her smooth belly.

"Connor." She bent her head and scattered little kisses across his chest. Her scent mingled with the steam from the shower he'd left on behind him.

"Get that mouth up here." He took a big fistful of all that midnight hair, the long strands knotting, coiling down his arm. Pulling, he tipped her head back and crashed his mouth down on hers.

There was nothing in this world as good as holding Aly, kissing Aly...

He stepped backward, taking her with him into the open stall. The wide rain showerhead poured water down on them, drenching them. The side jets made certain they were wet head to toe.

She groaned into his mouth, a sound that turned into a gleeful, throaty laugh.

He deepened the kiss and she wasn't laughing any more. Her hands were all over him. He returned the favor, managing to extricate his fingers from her soaked, tangled hair so he could skate his palms out over the lush curves of her shoulders, down her strong, soft arms.

Everywhere.

He needed to touch her everywhere.

He cupped the full globes of her bottom, pulling her in, pressing his hardness more firmly against her belly. She gave a low, pleasured moan, encouraging him to go further. Holding her tight with one arm, he brought the other around to the front of her, easing his hand down into the cleft between her fine, full thighs, touching the core of her.

She was silky-wet, drenched, and not just from the shower. He dipped a finger inside and then another and a third. She moaned into his mouth, her body rocking into him as he stroked her, using his thumb right where she liked it as his fingers filled her up.

Always a true multitasker, she wasn't content to let him do all the work. Her soft hand kept moving, gliding down the center of his chest, over his belly until she found him.

Her clever fingers closed around him.

He groaned into her mouth at the feel of her holding him, stroking him.

Again. At last. After all these years and years…

He bit her lip and she bit him back. They kissed like their lives depended on it, moaning together, stroking each other.

It didn't take long. She hit the crest with a wild cry, calling his name like she was begging him.

He felt her inner muscles clutching, closing on his fingers, grabbing and releasing in the hot, insistent rhythm of her completion.

It was too much. He couldn't last.

He went over, too, losing it, shooting his finish against her soft belly, the water from the showerhead pouring down over them, washing it all away.

And then…

Well, they just stood there, clinging to each other as the water continued to cascade over them and pulse at them from two sides. They went on kissing, a desperate kiss that slowly turned lazy and teasing and sweet.

With a sigh, she let her head rest against his chest. He stroked her streaming hair, traced concentric circles on her skin, his finger spiraling down the delicate bones of her spine.

It was good. So good, to be with her like this again, to have this magic only she could make, to hold her so close in his arms, skin on skin.

"Come on." He turned off the water and took her hand.

She followed him, sweet and docile now as an obedient child, standing on the rug by the sinks, allowing him to dry her off, starting with her hair, moving lower until he knelt at her purple-painted toes. Carefully, he ran the towel over the scar on her knee and then continued all the way down the smooth curves of her calves and ankles to her little white feet.

When he rose again, she took the towel from him and returned the favor, tossing it away after she dried his hair and grabbing a fresh one, then taking forever, smiling to herself as she dried his chest, his arms and lower down.

But the time she finished, he was growing hard again.

On her knees, she leaned forward and gave him a long, slow lick from base to tip.

He caught her face between his hands. "Wait. I want to be with you this time, *really* with you."

She sank back on her heels, so beautiful that the breath fled his lungs in a long, hard sigh. "Yeah." She gazed up at him, her mouth trembling a little, her eyes deep enough to drown in. "That would be good. That would be really good."

He reached down and pulled her up to stand with him. "You still sure about this?"

"I am, absolutely. You?"

Was he? Should he stop this craziness, call a halt now?

To hell with that noise. "Yeah. I want you, Aly. So much. I always have."

"Good, then." She went on tiptoe to kiss him—a light kiss, a brush of her lips on his. "How long until you have to leave for work?"

"A couple of hours."

She kissed him again. "Let's not waste a minute."

In the bedroom, he took a condom from the bedside drawer and set it within reach. Then he pulled her down onto the bed with him.

The kissing and the long, slow, perfect caresses started all over again. He had her breasts in his hands, in his mouth, sucking hard the way she liked it, which just happened to be the way he liked it, too. She cried his name and every time she did, something deep within him answered.

"Do that again," she whispered, and then cried, "Again! Oh, Connor. Yes, that! Exactly that…"

When he reached for the condom, she took it from him the way she used to do all those years ago, took it from him and put it on him, her hands swift and sure, her cheeks pink, a tiny smile curving her kiss-swollen lips.

He rose above her. She wrapped her legs around him and pulled him down.

Everything flew away. All the doubts, the loneliness without her, the dragging sense of getting through the days, one after another, doing his time.

There was only Aly, close in his arms, holding him, surrounding him, making a glow all around them. Only Aly, showing him the world as it could be, full of sweet heat and boundless joy.

She lifted up enough to take his mouth again. Kissing him, she pulled him down to her, even closer. The kiss went on and on as they moved together, hard and fast.

He tried to hold out, to wait for her, but she urged him on, whispering hot promises against his lips. "Yes..." And "Always." And "Only you, Conn. Only ever you..."

He didn't care if they weren't really true, those things she whispered as they rocked together, joined in the way they hadn't been for much too long. For right now, for this golden chain of moments in the gray light of a foggy morning, everything she said was real. The future was theirs and they would get it right this time.

His climax took him over, the heat roaring down his spine. He tried to pull back a little, to slow it down, give her a chance to catch up and chase her own completion first.

But she just pulled him closer. "Now," she whispered, frantic, insistent, "Right now."

He gave himself up to it, let it roll through him, felt the sweet, hot magic of release as he pulsed within her, his whole body lost in her, given over, set free.

And then she let out another cry and he realized she had made it, after all. She was going over, too.

He held himself still within her as she claimed her own finish.

"Oh, yes." She bit his earlobe, buried her face under his chin. "Oh my, yes..."

He collapsed on top of her with a groan. She laughed,

pushing at his shoulder. He wrapped his arm around her and rolled so they were both on their sides, facing each other. She still held him inside her, her leg hitched over his hip, keeping him in place.

They dozed for a while. He felt wrung out in the best sort of way. All the longing and tension, that edge of need and frustration? Gone. Leaving him easy and satisfied, completely relaxed for the first time in so long.

When he pulled back enough to look at her gorgeous face, her eyes were shut. He brushed a kiss between her eyebrows. "You awake?"

She pulled him closer, wrapping her leg a little tighter across his hip. "Shh…"

He stroked her still-damp hair, kissed the tip of her nose, wished that this moment could go on indefinitely.

At some point, he must have drifted off to sleep.

When he opened his eyes again, it was almost nine. "Hey." He tipped up her chin. Her eyes fluttered open. She smiled at him. He kissed her, a quick one. "I'm going to be late for work."

She made a reluctant little sound in her throat as she shifted away from him.

About then, he remembered the condom. Glancing down, he saw that it was halfway off and leaking.

She was watching him. "I guess we need to have the talk, hmm?"

He guided a thick lock of hair behind the shell of her ear. "I'm really hoping that you're on the pill."

"I am." Her lips curved in a lazy smile. "And except for when we were married, I've never had sex without a condom."

"Good. I always use a condom, too. I'm sure we're

fine." He took the condom off the rest of the way and left the bed to dispose of it.

When he returned to her, she was sitting up, all rumpled and gorgeous, her skin like fresh cream against his white sheets. "Kiss me," she commanded. "Just once. And then I'll go and you can get dressed."

Bending close and framing her face between his hands, he pressed his lips to hers. She tasted so good, of all the best things he'd thought forever lost to him. He longed to take the day off, spend it with her. But he had a meeting in an hour that he really couldn't get out of.

When he straightened, she jumped from the bed, grabbed her dinky shorts and cropped shirt from where she'd dropped them in the doorway to the bathroom, and left him to rush around getting ready for work.

Aly got to her mom's a little late, but Tony's wife, Lisa, was there for a visit, so no harm done.

Cat seemed fine that day. They hung out, Cat and Aly, giggling and yakking together like the BFFs they'd always been. Aly did laundry. She ran the vacuum, both upstairs and down.

In the early afternoon, while Cat was napping, Aly PMed a couple friends in New York. They messaged her right back and she responded.

As the messages flew back and forth, memories flooded her. Of how she'd met both women, of the girls' nights out at a bar they liked in the West Village, of hitting the sales at Barneys and Bergdorf's and Saks.

She wrote that her mom was doing well and even told them about the accident—not the part where she ended up with holes in her memory, just that she'd totaled the car, sustained a few injuries and had pretty much recovered. It seemed easier to save all the gory details for the next time they got together.

Later, she cooked dinner for her dad to reheat when he got home. She left the salad in the fridge and the main dish waiting on the stove, and went to check on her mom.

"Get lost," Cat said, when she entered the bedroom. "I know you're eager to get back to that impossible man you married once."

Aly *was* a little worried. She knew him so well. Odds were that he would have second thoughts about this morning. She did want to be there before he got home, kind of get her ducks in a row for when he started laying down a thousand reasons why they needed to keep their hands off each other.

"I don't want to leave you alone in the house."

Tucker, his ears perked as he sat by the bed, gave a hopeful whine. Cat patted the mattress and the dog jumped up. He cuddled in close to her.

"Oh, please." Cat stroked a hand down his back. "You're as bad as your dad and brothers. How many times do I have to say it? Everybody I've ever known, I've got on speed dial—not to mention my doctor, the hospital and 9-1-1."

Just then, they heard a car drive up out in front. Aly went to the window. "It's Marco."

"Perfect timing." Cat scratched Tuck around the ruff of his neck. "Go."

Aly got back to Connor's at a little after five.

The good news was she didn't have to cook dinner

for the second time that day. She and Connor took turns handling the evening meal, and tonight was his night.

All day, she'd been half expecting him to call or text with some lame excuse about working late, to suggest that she should just go ahead and eat with her folks. Then he could stew about what a terrible person he was, avoiding her until he worked up the nerve to tell her that this morning was a mistake.

The man had way too much guilt. He needed to get over that.

But when five o'clock came and went and he hadn't reached out, she knew he would follow through and either cook for them or show up with takeout.

She could almost get her hopes up that he wasn't going to come in looking glum and serious, spouting regrets for what had happened, insisting that it couldn't happen again.

But no.

He showed up at a little before six with burgers and the works from her favorite burger place, Raeleen's Roadside Grill. Just looking at the grease-spotted takeout bags brought her happiness. But then her heart sank at the concerned expression on his face. He set the bags on the kitchen counter.

And she made her move. Stepping in nice and close, she slid her arms around his hard waist. "Welcome home."

"Aly…" He took her shoulders in his big hands and gazed down at her regretfully.

She granted him her sweetest smile. "Please don't be a sanctimonious, self-sacrificing fool."

"Aly, it wasn't a good idea what we—"

"Stop." She put a finger against his fine lips. "You're over thirty."

"Aly, don't—"

"And I'm twenty-nine."

He huffed out a frustrated breath. "You're not listening to me."

"Oh, yes I am, unfortunately. Because you're making my ears hurt. It's really so simple. We're two grown adults, both of us single, both fully capable of making our own decisions."

"You've been injured. You're not yourself."

"I'm not?" She tried a little humor. "Who am I, then?"

His mouth was a grim line. "You could have died in that accident. What happened to you isn't something we should be joking about."

"Good. Because I am deadly serious, Conn. This morning, you and me, together again at last... It was beautiful. I for one can't wait to do it again. Are you trying to tell me you're not interested?"

"I, um..." He seemed not to know what to say next. "No. That is *not* what I'm saying."

"All right, then. What *are* you saying?"

Actually, she was feeling a tad guilty now herself—but not about having fabulous sex with the man she loved.

She should probably mention that the gaps in her memory had started filling in. *And* that she loved him still, that she'd never stopped.

But she just wasn't ready to share those things with him—or with anyone, really, except her therapist and maybe her mom. Yes, it was cowardly of her. But she couldn't be the brave one all the time, now could she?

He might send her packing if he decided she was almost "healed." And as for telling him she'd never stopped loving him...

He lived *here*. He loved Valentine Bay. The two of them had ended up divorced because he refused to leave. From what she'd recalled and pieced together so far, she had a great life in New York. And she just couldn't start talking about trying again with him. Not yet. Not until she'd decided what compromises she would be willing to make so that they could be together.

"Aly..." He still didn't seem to know what to say next. And he looked so worried that they'd somehow done the wrong thing by climbing into bed together.

She laughed; she couldn't help it. "Lighten up. We have weeks and weeks left of sharing this house." She stepped in an inch closer, brought her hands up between them and rested her palms against his heart. "Let's make the most of the time we have. Please."

He made a low, gruff sound as his concerned expression morphed into something else altogether. Something desperate. Hungry. Now, his hands stroked her shoulders instead of gripping them. "God, Aly..."

She ladled on the appropriate platitudes. "Life's too short, Connor. Nothing is for certain."

He traced the side of her neck with the back of his index finger, stirring lovely shivers in his wake. "I'm trying so hard to do the right thing here." His eyes had gone more gray than blue.

"Pushing me away is not the right thing. Whatever happens later, I want to know you *now*. We can yammer on and on about getting closure, making peace. But what I want most of all is to have this time with you, really *with* you. I want to blow the doors off, open up all the possibilities between us, however it all turns out, for as long as it lasts. We were happy once, you and me."

He looked stricken suddenly. "Yeah, we were. So damn happy."

"We can be happy together again, right here. Right now."

He eased his hands under the heavy fall of her hair and laced his fingers at her nape. With his thumbs, he tipped her chin higher. His gaze burned her, seared her to the core. "I just— If you have second thoughts, you need to tell me."

"I don't, Connor. Not a one."

He gazed down at her, his breathing a little ragged, just like hers. She waited—for him to break, to stop playing noble, to take what she longed to give him.

And then, at last, he yanked her close and slammed his mouth down on hers.

She surged up on tiptoe and kissed him right back, letting out a little cry of surprise when he scooped her high in his arms and headed for the stairs.

In his room, he carried her straight to the bed. "Everything off. Make it fast."

They stripped, eyes locked together, clothes flying every which way. She kicked off a sandal so hard, it bounced straight up and almost hit her in the forehead, but she ducked to the side just in time. The sandal flew by, ending up somewhere on the floor on the far side of the bed.

When he finally came down to her, she grabbed him

close. "I'm so glad," she whispered, fervent now, truly grateful.

"You don't know. I went back and forth all day. I felt so guilty one minute and so damn good the next…"

"I do know, Conn." She stroked his hair back off his forehead. "I know how you are." *And dear God, I do love you. I've always loved you…*

She almost said it out loud.

But then he kissed her.

They got lost in the magic of right now.

The burgers and fries were cold by the time they sat at the counter to wolf them down. Neither of them cared. They devoured the food.

They were standing in the living area, alternately kissing and discussing whether to stream a movie or just head back up to bed, when Connor spotted Maurice asleep on the rug at the end of the sofa.

"How did he get in?" she asked.

"How does he ever get in?"

His phone rang right then. It was the lady next door, asking if Connor had seen her cat.

Connor promised to bring the cat right over. He ran back upstairs to add flip-flops and a T-shirt to the khaki shorts he'd pulled on when they got out of bed. Then he scooped up Maurice and took him home.

When he returned, Aly greeted him just inside the door wearing nothing but a smile. They skipped the movie and went back to bed.

It was long after midnight before they turned out the light, wrapped their arms around each other and drifted off to sleep.

* * *

Connor woke to his phone ringing. He grabbed it off the nightstand and put it to his ear before he realized that it was Aly's cell ringing on the other nightstand.

She groaned and poked an elbow at him. "You gonna answer that?"

He leaned close and kissed her soft cheek. "It's yours."

"Huh?" She grabbed the device, dragged herself to a sitting position and put it to her ear. "Marco? What?"

Connor could hear her brother talking at the other end of the line.

"When?" she asked. "Is she okay?" Aly listened and then nodded. "Yeah. I got it. I'm on my way." She dropped the phone onto the bed and raked her hair back with both hands. "It's my mom. Her blood pressure's up. She's had back pain and some bleeding. My dad took her to Memorial." She shoved back the covers and swung her feet to the floor. "I have to go."

He got out on the other side. "I'll drive you."

She kept walking. "You don't have to."

"Wait." Catching her arm, he turned her to face him. "You're not going off to the hospital in the middle of the night all alone. I'm driving you."

She blinked up at him, eyes desolate, mouth trembling. "Connor, I have to go."

"I know. I'll meet you downstairs."

He was dressed in seconds flat and downstairs waiting for her when she came rushing down from the upper floor. "Here." He handed her the giant purse she'd left on the bench in the nook by the front door.

"Thanks." She hooked the bag over her shoulder and finished buttoning up her shirt. "Let's go."

Chapter Eight

All four Santangelo sons were waiting in the obstetrics lounge area when Connor and Aly arrived.

"There you are," said Dante.

She went straight for him. Connor hung back as they shared a quick hug.

When they broke apart, Dante started pacing. The other three brothers sat looking bleary-eyed and apprehensive. No one said anything to Connor.

Aly seemed not to know what to do. She just stood there between the two rows of chairs. Finally, she asked, "Dad's with her?"

"Yeah," said Dante. Pacing as he spoke, he explained that the doctor thought Cat had suffered something called a partial placental abruption. "The placenta comes partly unattached from the uterus," he said. "It started around midnight. She woke up with abdominal and back pain and some contractions. And she had bleeding, all symptoms of this abruption thing."

Tony said, "They're running tests, including an ultrasound, to see how bad it is and find out if they need to do a C-section."

"It's too early," said Marco.

Pascal elaborated, "He means that Mom's not quite thirty weeks along yet, so if they have to do a C-section the baby will be what her doctor called 'very preterm.'"

Aly's eyes got even wider. "So you're saying it's really bad?"

"Could be," Dante muttered darkly.

Aly seemed unsteady on her feet. She put a hand to her mouth.

Connor stepped up and wrapped an arm around her. "Come on." He walked her to the nearest chair. She sank into it. He sat beside her.

"Oh, Connor…" She groped for his hand. He clasped hers and wove their fingers together. She took it further, pulling their joined hands into her lap and wrapping her other hand around them, like he was her anchor and she needed to hold on for dear life.

He just wished there was something he could actually do in a situation like this. "It's okay," he whispered, because what else could he say? "It will be okay."

The Santangelo men were deadly silent. Connor glanced up to see tight disapproval on every face.

Apparently, Aly wasn't as out of it as she appeared. She noticed her brothers' reaction, as well. "Don't you even start. Not one word," she commanded, her voice carefully controlled, her gaze pinning each of them in turn. "Are we clear?"

Tony, Pascal and Marco had the sense not to say anything.

Dante just couldn't let it go. "He shouldn't be—"

"Shut up." Aly clutched Connor's hand all the tighter. "Now is not the time and this is not the place." She stared her brother down.

Dante caved—at least for the moment. He turned on his heel and started pacing again.

They waited, mostly in silence, for over an hour.

When Cat's ob-gyn finally appeared, they learned that she was "stabilized." The abruption was mild, he said, and so far, the baby seemed to be active in the womb and developing normally. They wanted to avoid a preterm delivery if at all possible, so they were keeping Cat in the hospital at least for the next few days. "We'll monitor her progress closely and reevaluate treatment as necessary. She'll be started on medication to help the baby's lungs develop faster, in case a preterm C-section should become necessary."

When the doctor left, Aly leaned close and asked in a whisper, "It doesn't sound too bad, does it?"

Connor pressed a light kiss to her temple and offered more reassurances. "No. She's going to be fine—the baby, too."

Dante, who'd finally dropped into a chair across from them, muttered something angry under his breath.

Aly's shoulders snapped up straight. She glared at her brother and opened her mouth to put him in his place. Connor tugged on her hand before she got a word out, which had her whirling on *him*. "What?" she demanded. "He's got no right to—"

"Aly." He leaned close again and whispered, "Let it go." They shared a little stare-down, just the two of them.

Finally, with a sigh, she sat back in her chair. "You're right. I'll take him down later."

And that only made Dante scowl all the harder. He kept his mouth shut, though. Her other brothers stayed out of it. Marco fooled around on his phone, Pascal read a dog-eared magazine and Tony just stared into space.

They waited for another hour or so while Cat was moved to her own room. And then, one by one, Aly and her brothers were allowed in to see her—for just a few minutes each.

Tony took the first turn. When he came back out, he said that Cat was resting and she wasn't in pain. The nurses had arranged for a cot in her room so that Ernesto could stay at her side.

Pascal went next, and then Dante, and finally Marco. By the time Aly had her turn, it was six in the morning and everyone but Dante had gone home to get some rest or get ready for work. They would all be taking turns keeping the hospital vigil as long as Cat stayed at Memorial.

Aly followed the nurse through the heavy metal doors, leaving Connor and Dante sitting across from each other in the otherwise empty lounge area.

Dante barely waited for the doors to shut behind his sister before he started in. "What the hell's going on?" He kept his voice low, but each word burned with angry fire.

Connor answered carefully. "I'm not sure what you're asking. And I can't see how you and me getting into it will do any good for anyone."

Dante glanced away. For a second or two, Connor dared to hope he would leave it at that. But no. Dante always had more to say. "I just want answers, that's all. The way I heard it she was staying in your guest room—something to do with you two burying the hatchet or some such crap. But get real. You know she's had a head injury. You should have seen her when she woke up the morning after the accident and you weren't there. Like you ripped out her heart and stomped on it all over again. She really did think you two were still married. The last thing you should be doing is encouraging her delusions."

"Dante." Connor had to exert considerable effort to continue to speak calmly. His ex-best friend had a real talent for hitting his weak spots. Dante could piss him off and rouse his considerable guilt simultaneously. "She *knows* we're divorced. She understands the facts. Aly's not delusional. And she's not some wilting flower. Come on, you know your sister."

"What I know is she's been staying with you for a week now. Seems to me that's way more time than you need to make your apologies, get them accepted and move the hell on."

"Look. I don't want to fight with you. Aly asked to stay with me and I'm happy to have her." Understatement of the year. He was way more than happy to have her. In fact, he wished that *having* Aly might never end. "It's not about you. What happens between Aly and me is our business."

Dante bored right through him with those dark, angry eyes. "You hurt her again, I'll…" He let the threat trail off.

Connor understood perfectly what Dante hadn't said. He tried to decide how to answer. But what was there to say? He wasn't asking Aly to leave. She wanted to stay and he wanted her there with him—wanted it a lot.

As for how it would go down when the time came for her to return to New York, who could say? Someone could very well get hurt—him. Aly. Both of them.

Dante glared at the rug between his boots. "Has she remembered anything about the last seven years?" He glanced up. Now his eyes were troubled. Evidently, he'd decided not to ream Connor a new one right then and there. He just seemed concerned, worried for the sister he loved.

Connor shifted in his chair as he thought the question over. "She hasn't mentioned any specific memories surfacing. But she seems completely accepting of reality. She's fine, you know? She's made it clear that she does believe she lives in New York now, that she's got her dream job, that she and I have been divorced for a long time."

"But she hasn't actually said she remembers anything that happened since the two of you split up?"

"No. Maybe she's said something to Dr. Warbury, though."

"If you two are getting along so great, why wouldn't she tell you if her memory was coming back?"

Maybe she wants what I want, he thought, but decided not to say. And what he wanted was for this amazing thing between them to go on for as long as possible. Talking too much about her real life would only rock the boat on this fantasy they were living out right now—the two of them, together again. *Really* together. In every way.

Connor shrugged. "You should ask her yourself."

Dante was finding the rug of great interest again. "She and I aren't getting along so hot lately."

"When was that ever news?"

Dante glanced up again. Surprisingly, a hint of a smile tugged at the corners of his mouth. "She was always a pain in my ass. The queen of the family. No one could ever tell *her* what to do."

"Cat's more the queen, if you ask me."

"I didn't ask you—but all right. That makes Aly the princess, I guess."

Connor shook his head. "Princess. I don't know…"

"Exactly," said Dante. "It's what I said. They're both queens, Mom and Aly. The rest of us never had a chance against either of them."

The double doors to obstetrics swung slowly open. Aly came through them, her steps firm, her head high. In leggings, a wrinkled shirt and a pair of dingy white Converse, she managed as always to look nothing short of regal.

All it took her was a single glance at the two of them, him and Dante, elbows on their spread knees as they leaned in, facing each other across the space between their chairs. She knew that something had gone down between them while she was with her mom—and she assumed it must be bad.

Blue eyes flashing, she hitched her big purse more

firmly onto her shoulder and marched toward them. "Okay. What's going on?"

Dante and Connor sat up straight and answered in unison, "Nothing."

She turned on her brother. "What do you think you're doing? You've got no right to—"

"Aly." Connor cut her off.

She whirled on him. "What?"

"It's okay. We were just, you know, talking."

She narrowed her eyes at him, like if she squinted at him hard enough, she could peer inside his mind. "Really?"

"Really," said Dante.

Her head swung back and forth—to Dante and then back to Connor again. "Humph," she said finally, and dropped into the chair next to him.

He put his arm around her and changed the subject fast. "So how's your mom?"

"Okay, I think. Pale. Tired. She was sleeping when I left. Dad said we should all go home and get some rest."

"Sounds like a plan to me." Dante got up. "I'll see you two later." With a curt nod, he left them.

Aly rested her head on Connor's shoulder and confessed in a small voice, "I'm kind of scared, you know?"

He tightened his arm around her. "I know."

"The nurses keep saying how it's a *mild* abruption, that it could all work out fine, with Mom carrying the baby to full term, even having a regular labor and delivery. But I looked it up on my phone. It's nothing to fool with. Mom's forty-eight. The risk of placental abruption increases when the mother is older and if she's already had several kids. Mom could die. So could the baby. And there's a lot of not-so-great outcomes short of the worst."

Connor pressed his lips into her hair and whispered, "Your mom's tough."

"She is, yeah. But—"

"Focus on that, on the best outcome. There's no win in driving yourself crazy imagining the worst."

She tipped her head back to look at him. Outside, it must be daylight already. But in the obstetrics waiting area, it felt like the darkest part of the night.

He said, "Your mom and the baby are both going to be fine."

She actually smiled at him. "Look at you. Mr. Positivity."

He kissed her, a slow kiss. Because he couldn't resist and because he wanted to distract her from dark thoughts.

She laid her head on his shoulder again. "Okay, then. My mom and the baby are going to be fine."

"There you go."

"Connor?"

"Yeah?"

"Thanks for coming with me—and for staying, too."

"*You're* here." He stroked her hair. "And that means there's no place else I'd rather be."

Connor took Aly back to his house. He had a shower, ate some eggs and went to work.

She had a long nap in Connor's bed—because it smelled like him, all warm and manly, and because she fully intended to do all her sleeping in his bed for as long as she remained in Valentine Bay. They were together, at least for now, and she refused to sleep anywhere else.

Her eyes popped open at a little after one in the afternoon. Grabbing her phone off the nightstand, she called her mom's room at the hospital.

Cat answered. "I'm okay," she assured her. "The baby's okay. Your dad's here with me. We're hanging in there."

"Great. I'll be there in half an hour." Aly got up and hustled to the other bedroom to grab a change of clothes.

She pulled the closet door wide—and let out a cry of surprise.

For a short span of seconds, she saw another closet altogether, one full of great clothes and designer shoes.

My closet in my place in Manhattan.

She fell back a couple steps and felt the bed behind her. Slowly, never taking her eyes from the open closet, she sat.

Images assailed her: her small apartment, everything about it. The art on the walls, the windows that looked out on Leonard Street. The gorgeous tatami bed she'd found online four years ago and got a guy she was dating then to help her assemble.

As she blindly stared at the open closet, she took a mental walk around her Tribeca neighborhood and hailed a cab that took her to Strategic Image.

Once there, she rode the elevator to the thirtieth floor. She waved at Glenda in reception and breezed into the office, greeting her coworkers one by one.

It was all so clear. It was her life as she'd been living it for years.

Aly fell back across the guest room bed and stared blankly up at the slanted hemlock ceiling.

Tomorrow was the two-week anniversary of the accident. Two weeks, and she was feeling good, getting better every day, remembering more and more.

She wanted to tell Connor all that she remembered, every last little thing so far.

But she wouldn't.

They had a beautiful, fragile balance going on here and she refused to disturb it in any way. She needed every moment she could have with him. If it wasn't meant to be forever, well, she'd take twelve more weeks and not waste a second regretting the truth she hadn't shared.

At the hospital, her dad looked exhausted.

Her mom was in good spirits, though. Aly sent her dad home and instructed him not to return until dinnertime, at least.

"Take a shower, maybe have a nap," she commanded. "And make sure Tucker gets his doggy chow."

Her dad grumbled that he was fine and Marco could feed the damn dog, but then he kissed Cat and left, after all.

Once he was gone, Aly texted Connor that her mom was holding steady, adding, I'm going to stick around here, so I won't be home for dinner.

He answered seconds later. I'll bring you takeout. Fish 'n' chips from Fisherman's Korner?

She smiled at his thoughtfulness. No need. I'll get something in the cafeteria. I'll be at your house by ten at the latest.

He wrote back, Counting on it. C U then. Best to Cat.

She bent to stick her phone in her purse. When she glanced up, her mom was watching her.

"Things are good with the ex, huh?" Cat asked.

"Really good." She rose and poured her mom more water. Cat drank and set the plastic glass down on the bed tray in front of her. She held out her hand— carefully, because of the IV taped in the crook of her elbow. Aly scooted her chair closer to gently clasp her mom's cool fingers.

Cat said, "Ernesto told me Connor was here with you last night."

"Yes, he was."

"All the boys were here, too. And nobody got hurt?"

Aly laughed. "There was a definite chill in the air. And later, Dante and Connor were alone together in the waiting area. I don't know what went on then, exactly. Neither of them would say."

Cat shrugged. "Sometimes you just have to leave the men alone and let them figure it out—except when there's bleeding. You might have to step in then."

That afternoon, each of Aly's brothers came by and stayed for an hour or two. Tony's wife, Lisa, and Pascal's wife, Sandy, also stopped in to spend a few minutes with Cat.

At six, Aly's dad reappeared, freshly showered and shaved, looking considerably more alert than before he'd left. He went straight to her mom for a kiss.

When he turned to Aly, he said, "That guy who divorced you is out in the lounge."

She felt a happy glow all through her. He'd come by even though she'd made it clear he didn't need to.

Her dad smirked. "Look at this girl. Like a lovesick teenager all over again."

She kissed his cheek. "Don't tease me, Daddy. It's not nice."

"You can take it—go on, he's waiting for you." He even smiled when he said it. Maybe her mom was right. The men just had to work it out between themselves.

She found Connor, Marco and Dante sitting in the waiting area. As far as she could tell, nobody was injured. Connor stood and she went to him. They shared a quick kiss.

Aly faked a frown as she stepped back. "What? No fish 'n' chips?"

"I was thinking we could find something in the cafeteria."

"That'll do." She kissed him again.

Marco groaned. "Get a room, you two."

Dante just shook his head.

After their cafeteria dinner, Connor went in with her to say hi to Cat. Then they hung around in the waiting area, with Aly popping into Cat's room for a visit around eight.

Back at Connor's house, Aly slept with him all wrapped around her. Just like old times.

Cat remained at Memorial the next day and the next, and the day after that. Aly went to the hospital after breakfast in the morning and stayed until dinnertime.

Cat was doing well, the doctors said. The abruption

hadn't worsened. The baby was active in the womb, with no signs of distress.

Connor showed up in the obstetrics lounge every night around six. By the third day, Aly's dad and brothers were actually talking to him. Aly would emerge from Cat's room to the low murmur of their voices discussing baseball or the Trail Blazers' chances for a conference final next season.

On the sixth day of Cat's hospital stay, her dad admitted to Aly that yeah, he and her brothers had decided to ease up on Connor.

"We don't like what he did seven years ago," said Ernesto. "But it's not healthy to live in the past. He's doing what he can now, to help out. And even your brothers and I can see that you're not the only one who's been carrying a torch."

In the bed, her mother laughed. "I love it when my husband finally admits that I'm right."

Ernesto went to her. "My beautiful wife is always right."

"Yes, she is. And her husband ought to remember that."

Aly groaned. "Do you two know how weird it is when you start talking to each other in the third person?"

Her parents ignored her. Cat reached up and stroked Ernesto's cheek.

On the seventh day of her hospital stay, Cat was released to rest at home.

She would have regular visits from a nurse-midwife, who would monitor both Cat and the baby for any signs of distress. Everyone was feeling optimistic. The doctor had even gone so far as to say Cat had a very good chance of carrying the baby to term.

Aly helped her mom get settled in at the house. Her dad stayed home that day, so Aly took off at three for a visit with Dr. Warbury.

She told her therapist everything, all the bits of her recent life that she'd been remembering, the stuff she'd yet to share with Connor or her family.

Dr. Warbury said, "It's wonderful that it's all coming back to you—and pretty quickly, too."

"I've read up on my kind of memory loss. It usually takes longer than it has for me, doesn't it?"

"When it comes to the human brain, no two cases are alike. Recovery is a different story with each and every individual. You're making progress, exceptional progress. That's what matters. I'm so pleased for you." Then she asked, "What about your family and your ex-husband? How's it going with them?"

"It's good. My brothers and my dad are actually getting along with Connor now, so that's a big step…"

Dr. Warbury jotted something in the notebook she kept open across her lap during their sessions. "You're hesitating. Is there something else you want to tell me?"

Aly confessed, "It's only, well, I haven't told anyone else about the things I've remembered."

Dr. Warbury waited. She was really good at that, just letting the silence stretch out until Aly decided what she wanted to say.

"I just don't want to share that with them yet," she said. "I'm not sure why—not concerning my family, anyway. But with Connor, I like how it's working out between us. I'm afraid that admitting how much I remember might have him saying it's time for me to move on—move out of his house and back to my parents' place."

"Has Connor said or done anything that leads you to believe he wants you to move out?"

"God, no. He seems happy to have me there. I think he's enjoying our time together as much as I am. Still, I don't want to tell him that my memory is returning. I don't want to tell anyone but you. Not yet."

"Then don't. Trust yourself. Don't put too much pressure on yourself. You'll know when the time is right."

The next morning Aly was in the baby's room at her mom's house, folding baby blankets and tiny onesies, feeling like a happy little homebody, getting everything ready for when the new baby came.

She'd just set a stack of receiving blankets on the open shelf above the changing table when her phone rang. She pulled it out of her pocket and checked the display. It was Jane Levelow, her immediate superior at Strategic Image.

At the sight of Jane's name on the display, Aly's heart started racing. It was beating so hard it made her ears ring. Sweat bloomed on her upper lip and underarms. And out of nowhere, she had a headache coming on.

She just couldn't answer it. What would she say? What if she somehow slipped up? She would have to explain everything—the accident, her partial amnesia, the fact that there was no guarantee she'd get all the important parts of her memory back.

Jane was a dynamo. She had no patience with colleagues who couldn't keep up.

Aly had never had a problem staying on top of her
job. She had good ideas and excellent follow-through.
She'd worked long hours and her dedication to the job
had paid off.

Answering this call could be the beginning of the
end of her career.

But then she remembered how it had been with her
New York girlfriends. As they messaged back and forth,
her memories of them had returned to her.

Plus, dealing with Jane was ultimately inescapable.
Aly would have to talk to her at some point.

She made herself take the call.

Her heart pounded wildly in her ears as Jane apolo-
gized for calling during her family leave. "If you hang
up on me now," she said, "I will completely understand."

They both knew she was joking. No one at SI ever
refused to talk to Jane.

Aly laughed and said it was fine.

And right about then, she realized that it *was* fine.
Her terror of facing her own life had vanished, along
with the ringing in her ears and her sudden splitting
headache. She felt bizarrely confident that she could
handle whatever Jane threw at her.

Jane mentioned a certain account.

Aly remembered it. She knew all the players and
exactly where they'd been on the project when she left
for Oregon.

Jane said, "I want to switch to video chat, if that's
okay, and bring Bill in on this call?" Bill Turlington
was handling the account in Aly's absence.

"Of course," Aly said. "Give me five minutes to check on my mom and grab my laptop."

Four minutes later, she was on with Bill and Jane.

Bill had some questions and Aly knew most of the answers—and if she didn't have what they needed, she did have concrete suggestions for how to get it. Jane joked that it was really impossible to get along without her at SI.

Aly felt so good, she told Jane and Bill to give her a call any time there was something she could clear up or help out with.

She probably shouldn't have done that. After all, she *was* on leave. She was supposed to be taking a break from SI, concentrating on her family.

But Jane was happy and Bill was happy.

And the call had reminded Aly of how much she loved her job. It reminded her that her real life was on the other side of the continent.

She still loved Connor. She always had. Maybe she always would.

But she needed to remember that the future didn't hold a whole lot of promise for them as a couple.

They wanted different things from life.

Chapter Nine

Something was wrong.

Connor swam up through the layers of sleep and opened his eyes. It was ten after two on Saturday morning and he was alone in the bed.

He sat up. "Aly?"

And then he saw her, huddled in the leather club chair by the window. He turned on the lamp. They both blinked against the sudden flare of light.

She'd wrapped herself in the spare blanket and gathered her knees up under her chin. For several tense seconds they just stared at each other.

Finally, he couldn't take it anymore. "What happened? What's wrong?"

She poked a hand out of the blanket and shoved her sleep-tangled hair back from her forehead. "I remembered," she said, her voice desolate. She looked wrecked, ruined, like someone she loved had died.

She also looked absolutely furious—at him.

He wanted to go to her, to hold her, comfort her. She seemed so lost and alone. But judging by the fire in her eyes as she glared at him, no way would she welcome his touch. "You remembered what?"

"It was a dream, at first. But then I woke up in the middle of it, and I *knew*. I remembered it all—how it happened, exactly how it was. How you promised you wanted to go to New York with me, how you said we would make the move together. I remembered all our plans. Years of them, yours and mine. Or so I thought..." She rubbed at her temples.

He needed to say something to make it better, make it right. But there was nothing, no excuse he could give her. No way to make it all better.

Everything she'd said so far was only the truth.

She grabbed the blanket tighter around her. "But they weren't your plans, were they? In all those years, you never said a word about what you really felt. You lied to me and lied and lied. You were lying the whole time. And then, when it came right down to the wire, out of nowhere, you burst out with the truth. You didn't want to go and you weren't going to go."

"That's true." What else could he say? "It's all true."

She went on accusing him. "You said that I should call my new job and tell them never mind. You said it didn't matter, all the money we'd put down on that little apartment in Washington Heights. It was just money and so what if we didn't get it back? You said Daniel needed you here and you couldn't go. You wouldn't talk it over. You wouldn't budge an inch. You—"

"Aly."

She scowled all the harder at him. "What?"

Gingerly, he reminded her, "I told you all this. I told you everything, what I did, what a jerk I was. Do you remember that I told you?"

She let out an angry bark of laughter. "Of course I remember what you told me. Don't you dare look at me like this is some new problem with my memory. My memory is…waking up. And it's all getting clearer, day by day. Times like right now, I really wish it wasn't."

"I'm just trying to understand exactly what you're angry about, that's all."

She scrunched deeper into the blanket and muttered, "It's not that you didn't tell me."

He nodded at her. Slowly. "Okay," he said pointlessly, on a rising inflection.

"You told me and I got over it. I forgave you, I really did. But now I actually remember it myself. And you know what?" She jumped from the chair, grabbed the blanket tightly around her and paced back and forth at the foot of the bed, a corner of the fabric fluttering in her wake. "I'll tell you what. Now I know it for myself, now I remember exactly how it was, I'm furious with you all over again. It's so much more real, to relive it as it happened, to *know* how you were, what you did. You just flat out refused to go with me. You canceled your plane ticket and stayed home. You never reached out. Two months went by. I waited to hear from you—a call. A text. A one-line email. Anything. But there was nothing. Until the divorce papers."

"Aly, come on…"

She paced all the faster. "You were such an absolute, unmitigated jackass."

He nodded. "You're right." He put up both hands in complete surrender. "I was an idiot. A thoughtless, stupid kid. I know it. I've said it was all my fault."

She sneered at him. "You don't have to be so damn… understanding about it."

"Aly. We've been through this. If I'm understanding, it's because I know I was completely in the wrong."

She stopped stock-still and faced him. "I was wrong, too," she said through clenched teeth. "I should have tried harder. But at least now I know why I didn't."

Where were they going with this? "Um. Okay…"

"You keep saying that—'okay.' With a dot-dot-dot at the end of it."

"Because I don't know *what* to say."

"You should have told me earlier that you were worried for Daniel, that you didn't want to leave him to run Valentine Logging alone. You should have been honest with me. You should have explained to me from the first all the reasons your heart was here and you just couldn't go with me. I might have felt I had to go, anyway. I might still have ended up brokenhearted without you, but at least I wouldn't have had to be so full of rage and bitterness about what you did."

"I get it. I really do."

She lifted her arms and the blanket flapped like a cape, revealing her bare body for a fraction of a second before she grabbed it close once more. "It, well, it hurts a whole lot to have to live it all over again." Her blue eyes shone with rising tears.

"Aly, come here."

Crying silently, glaring at him through her tears, she didn't budge an inch.

"Come on." He dared to hold out a hand.

She sniffed and swiped at her wet cheeks with the blanket. "I sat in that chair over there for about a half hour, watching you sleeping so peacefully, wanting to chuck a lamp at your big, fat head. I was really hoping for a fight, I truly was. But no. You have to be all *adulting* and reasonable. I ask you, what happened to the self-absorbed, inarticulate ass I once married?"

"He grew up."

"Oh, Connor..." Her tears flowed freely now.

He tried again. "Come on..."

She put a hand to the side of her skull. "My head aches."

"Come here."

She sucked in a big breath and blew it out hard. "Fine." The blanket fell to the floor, revealing her naked body again. Damn, she was beautiful. Looking at her did something to him on an elemental level. She re-arranged the molecules in his body. She made everything burn.

He caught her fingers, pulled her back onto the bed and into his arms. She sniffled some more. He just held her, rocking her.

When she'd calmed, he asked, "How's your head?"

She gave a sad little chuckle. "Still aches a little. But it's better already."

"Come on. Let's get you under the covers." He settled the blankets around them and pulled her in, spooning her.

"Connor?"

"Hmm?"

"I have a confession."

"I'm listening."

"In the past several days, it's been slowly coming back to me, about my life in New York, about my job and my friends there."

He wasn't surprised. He kissed the side of her neck. "I'm so glad."

"You're not angry that I didn't tell you?"

"Nope."

"You're not doubtful that I really did lose seven years in the accident, that I haven't been somehow faking you out this whole time?"

"I'm not, no."

"But it's all coming back pretty quickly. Sometimes I can't help but wonder if maybe it was just some bizarre trick of my own mind that had me losing the seven years we've been apart."

"You sustained a concussion. You were out for several minutes. Those are the facts. Don't go searching around for a reason to be hard on yourself."

"Oh, Connor…" She reached back, cupped her hand around his neck and turned her head to meet his lips in a quick, hard kiss.

When she let go, he scattered a few more kisses along the slope of her shoulder. "Do you remember the accident itself?"

"Uh-uh. It's a blank now, that whole day is. My brothers have told me that I remembered more at first, at the hospital right after the accident. They said I could recall everything up to when I passed Camp 18 on the

Sunset Highway. But then, when I woke up before dawn the next morning, it was all gone. I lost seven years, including that last day. I don't remember leaving New York or the plane ride to PDX. Driving home is a blank. Dr. Warbury says I might never remember the immediate period surrounding the accident."

He whispered, "So, then. Tell me about what you do remember."

"It comes in flashes. And sometimes in dreams. I wake up and the dream I just had is a memory." She took his hand and pressed it close to her heart. "Dr. Warbury advised me to get in contact with friends from New York. I reached out to a couple of girlfriends. We were messaging back and forth and it all just came back to me, the things we did, the times we've had together. Every day I feel that I understand it all better—the past seven years, what my life is like now."

Her life. Which was not *his* life. He needed to remember that, not let wishful thinking take over, not start imagining that she might decide she wanted to move home permanently, not start hoping that they would end up together.

He kept telling himself he knew that she would leave in the end. But on some deep level, he saw her as *his*. On some deep level, no matter how he'd tried over the years to deny her and her hold on his heart, she'd always remained the one who mattered, the one he couldn't forget.

"I've been afraid to tell you all I remember," she said in a small voice. "Afraid you would decide I didn't really need to be here with you anymore, that it wasn't good for us to go on the way we have been. I was scared you would ask me to move out."

He smoothed her hair away from her ear and whispered, "Never."

"I'm so happy to hear you say that." She wiggled around in his arms until she faced him. Her eyes were midnight blue, shining up at him. "I want this time together, you and me. I really do."

"And I want you here. No way I'm ever asking you to leave."

Her smile bloomed wide. "Excellent." She kissed his chin and then rolled to her back.

For a minute or two, they were quiet. He gazed up at the shadowed ceiling, wishing that this, right now, with her, could go on forever, knowing that wishes never did turn into horses and beggars rarely got to ride.

She said, "Yesterday, while I was at my mom's, my boss called from New York…" She spoke of her fear to answer the call, of her terror that she would show herself as unable to do her job anymore. "But it turned out the same as it did when I got in touch with my girlfriends. I just *knew* what I needed to know. And the memories of my years at SI flooded back, along with how much I love my job."

"I'm glad that it worked out so well."

"Me, too." She got up on an elbow and reached across him to turn off the light.

He pulled her closer. "Sleepy now?"

"Mmm-hmm. You?"

He made a low sound of agreement. She said no

more. He held her and listened to her breathing even out into the shallow rhythm of sleep.

Things were so good between them. But he needed to accept that it wasn't forever. The basic issue between them had never changed.

He was a hometown boy. He needed to be close to his family. And he was proud of what he and Daniel had built at Valentine Logging. He couldn't really see himself living anywhere but Valentine Bay.

But Aly? She was a big-city girl all the way.

For Aly, the next week and a half went by fast. Cat was doing well at home. She'd had no more bleeding and only minor contractions. She seemed relaxed and upbeat.

Aly puttered around her parents' house, cooking and keeping things tidy, enjoying the role of Santangelo family housekeeper. She'd never been big on playing the homemaker. But for now, for her mom's sake, she was more than happy to cook and clean.

Really, everything was going so well. Her mom was doing fine—and Aly's relationship with Connor just got better and better.

They spent their evenings together, she and Connor, acting like an old married couple, sharing dinner, taking long walks along the nearby beach. And then later, in bed, he made love to her as though she was the only woman in the world, urgent and yet so tender. As though he couldn't bear to waste a second of their time together.

She got to know Mrs. Garber next door. The older woman was so pleased to see that Connor had "found someone special" at last.

"And you really have to start calling me Janine," she added. "Mrs. Garber sounds like someone you barely know."

"Janine it is," Aly promised.

"Tell that young man of yours, too."

"I will, absolutely."

Two times running, Connor took her to Sunday dinner with the Bravos. They treated her like one of the family. She had a great time with his sisters.

It was already the middle of August before she realized she might have a whole new kind of problem.

It happened on a Monday morning. Connor was downstairs fixing breakfast. She stood in the spare bathroom, which she'd been using as her own.

She'd run a brush through her hair and was about to take her birth control pill. It was her second day on a new pill pack. She stared down at it, frowning. A new pack…

Last week was her placebo week.

And her period had never come. Usually, it showed up around the third day of the sugar pill week.

She set down the almost full pack and stared at herself in the bathroom mirror.

No.

Couldn't be.

She grabbed the pack again and gazed blankly at it, trying to remember…

Okay, she'd missed two pills—the day after the accident and then the day after that, which was the day they'd discharged her from Memorial. She'd been such a mess, her whole body hurting, out of her mind over Connor, so sure the two of them were still together in spite of what everyone around her said. The last thing on her mind had been keeping up with her contraceptive pills.

Marco had gone to pick up her suitcases from the totaled rental car. When she got home to her parents' house, her things were waiting in the room that had been hers when she was growing up. It was the second day she'd skipped a pill, but she hadn't realized it then.

The next morning, the third day, she was still frantic for her supposed husband to come to her, still certain that her family was lying to her for no reason she could comprehend. But that day, she *had* remembered to take her pill. She'd pulled out that pack with the day of the week clearly marked above each pill and realized she'd missed two doses.

Luckily, her phone had survived the accident. She'd auto-dialed her doctor's office in New York and asked what to do. The nurse had said to take two pills that day and two the next and she would be covered.

Had she gotten the nurse's instructions wrong?

Right then and there, she Googled the big question.

And the answer was the same as the one the nurse had given her four weeks ago. Two pills for two days and she was supposed to be protected.

She'd *better* be protected. Because the pill was the only contraception she and Connor had been using since that first time, when they fell asleep and the condom slipped partway off.

Aly popped out the day's pill, stuck it in her mouth and shoved the pack back in the bathroom drawer.

Enough with the worrying.

She *was* protected. Her periods were light, anyway,

since she'd been on the pill. And she'd certainly been under stress. It just couldn't be all that out of the ordinary that she hadn't had a period that month.

Her phone dinged with a text from the superhot guy in the kitchen downstairs. Your coffee's getting cold.

She scooped up the phone and ran down the stairs, coming up behind him at the stove, where he was frying their eggs.

Wrapping her arms around his waist, she went on tiptoe to peer over his shoulder. "Yum. Looks good."

He dropped a quick kiss at her temple. "Set the table?"

"I'm on it."

For the next couple days, she tried to forget that her period hadn't come.

Then, Wednesday afternoon, on the way to Connor's from her mom's house, she bought two pregnancy tests—the highest-rated ones that promised an accurate early result.

But by the time she got home, she decided not to go there yet. She stuck the tests in the back of a drawer in the guest room.

Because she just didn't need to know right now. She'd always wanted kids someday and the years were going by. If she was pregnant, she would be having that baby.

Yeah, there would be a lot to deal with if the result window gave her two pink lines. But for right now, she had nine weeks left in Valentine Bay and she intended to live them to the fullest.

Unfortunately, instructing herself *not* to think about pregnancy only made her think about it more.

She started wondering about the effects of the pill on her unborn baby—if there even was a baby. Should she continue to take the pill while suspecting she might be pregnant? Would that be bad for the baby?

More Googling ensued. All the usual medical sites said there was no evidence that birth control pills hurt the baby.

Still. It bothered her. If it turned out there would be a baby, it felt wrong to keep bombarding an innocent embryo with unnecessary hormones.

Her solution to that problem wasn't perfect. It entailed lying to Connor about why she suddenly wanted to use condoms again.

Aly despised liars.

But at this point, she really didn't want to go on taking the pill. And purposely going without contraception wasn't any kind of option. That would be much worse than telling a lie in order to get Connor to use a condom.

Wouldn't it?

Sweet God in heaven. This was one ethically twisted situation.

That night, after Connor carried Maurice back to Janine's house, Aly took his hand and led him upstairs.

"Got condoms?" She pushed him down on the bed and straddled his lap.

"Yeah." He licked the side of her throat. "You taste so good—and why do I need a condom all of a sudden?"

Then came the lie. She stretched her neck back to give him better access. "I didn't pack enough pills. I'm out."

He nibbled along her collarbone. She waited for him to suggest she call her doctor and get more, or to ask why she hadn't mentioned earlier that she was running low.

"Condoms it is," he said, and claimed her mouth in a bone-melting kiss.

Apparently, the man totally trusted her. He certainly didn't seem the least suspicious.

Despicable. Oh, yes, she was.

She caught his head between her hands, tipped his mouth up to her again and took those amazing lips of his in another long, deep, thorough kiss. That led to more kisses and a lot of delicious caresses. It was a stellar ending to a nerve-racking day.

And from then on, they used condoms.

August faded into September. Her period didn't come.

Cat, settled in comfortably at home, made it to thirty-five weeks without another emergency trip to Memorial. The day before she hit the thirty-six week mark was a Saturday.

Aly decided they ought to celebrate. She baked a four-layer chocolate cake with chocolate cream cheese frosting. She covered the whole thing with chocolate chips and a dark-chocolate drizzle. Her dad made his famous chicken with mustard mascarpone marsala sauce and all the Santangelos showed up for dinner, including Sandy and Lisa and the kids. Connor came, too.

There was wine. Lots of it. Most of the adults got at least a little buzzed—not Cat, of course. And nobody seemed to notice that Aly didn't finish the one glass of Prosecco her dad had poured for her. They were all too happy that Cat and the baby were doing so well to pay much attention to who was drinking and who wasn't.

At a little after eight, Cat thanked them for the party, kissed them all good-night and returned to her comfy bed. Around nine, a couple of Marco's friends showed up to take him to a bonfire down at Valentine Beach. Sandy and Lisa were eager to get the little ones home and to bed, but Pascal and Tony wanted to keep celebrating.

Aly wasn't sure who had the bright idea that Connor, Pascal, Tony and Dante ought to head over to the Sea Breeze bar. A Valentine Bay landmark, the Sea Breeze had first opened its doors shortly after prohibition ended. Last year, it had been bought and remodeled by a local celebrity named Ingrid Ostergard.

Pascal announced, "Aly, who is way too sober, can be our designated driver, and Sandy and Lisa can take the kids on home."

Apparently, her unfinished Prosecco had not gone unnoticed, after all. "As usual, the women get to do all the work," she muttered, faking a scowl.

Pascal granted her an imperious glance. "Are you in or out?"

"Fine. I'll drive."

Dante asked Connor, "What do you say?"

There was a moment. Connor and Dante locked eyes across the family table. Decades of shared history passed in that look. Aly's throat kind of clutched at the sight.

"I'm in." Connor turned to Aly. "You sure you're willing to ferry us around?"

She leaned close to him and brushed a kiss against his freshly shaved cheek. "You know I am."

The kids and their moms went on home. Aly, her brothers and Connor piled into Connor's Land Rover. Ernesto stood at the wide-open front door, shouting warnings at Aly to drive carefully and at the men to behave themselves, as if they were all a bunch of crazy teenagers again. Aly backed and turned the big vehicle and off they went to the Sea Breeze.

The parking lot was packed. She dropped the guys off at the door and drove around for a while, looking for a space. When she finally went inside, she couldn't believe the change in the place since the last time she'd been there—with Connor—eight or nine years ago.

The Sea Breeze had undergone a major face-lift. The bar itself was gorgeous, long and gracefully curving, the top tiled in a sea glass mosaic. The remodel had even included one of those roll-up doors so popular in Pacific Northwest bars. The door was up tonight, letting in the faint sound of the waves and the moist scent of the air, framing a view of the ocean. Over in one corner, a guy with a guitar played the blues.

Connor's youngest sister, Grace, was tending bar along with the Sea Breeze's new owner, Ingrid Ostergard. Ingrid, who had once been a bona fide rock star with a band called Pomegranate Dream, also happened to be Daniel Bravo's first wife's aunt—and his second wife's mother.

"Hey, Aly!" Grace leaned across the bar to give her a hug. "The guys are over there." She pointed out the two pushed-together tables Connor and Aly's brothers had managed to claim.

"Gracie, the place looks amazing."

"I know. And business is booming, as you can see."

Aly explained, "Tonight, I'm the designated driver. How about a cranberry juice and soda, with lime?"

Grace grinned. "Connor already ordered one for you. It's waiting at the table."

Aly worked her way through the crowd and took the chair Connor had saved for her. They all laughed and joked around together. It was easy and fun. No tension. Kind of like the good old days, back when she and Connor were married and Conn was as much a part of the Santangelo family as the rest of them.

Dante sat on Connor's other side. The two men leaned their heads together. Aly had no clue what they said to each other and she didn't really care. It made her feel all warm and fuzzy, to imagine that Dante and Connor were healing their friendship for the second time. She could just picture the two of them, through the years to come, having each other's backs the way best friends should.

The guy with the guitar took a break and a DJ in a booth above the bar took over. Beyond the roll-up door, out on the concrete patio under the stars, people were dancing.

Connor leaned close to her. "It's been a long time since we danced."

She met those cloudy-day eyes and her heart swooned a little. "Too long."

"Come on." He got up and took her hand.

A slow song began just as they reached the cleared space beyond the door. He pulled her close and she swayed in his arms, her mind full of memories of dancing with Connor—at some sports bar in Eugene when they were still in college, and at someone else's wedding in Portland a year or so later.

And at their own wedding, nine years ago now.

For seven long years, she'd thought it was over forever. That the two of them would never again dance together. And yet here they were, with their arms around each other beneath the crescent moon.

When they returned to the table, Dante's chair was empty. Tony said he was getting them another pitcher, and then went back to talking football with Pascal.

Aly glanced toward the bar as she took her seat next to Connor. She spotted Dante deep in conversation with Grace. Both of them leaned in close. Grace laughed at something Dante said. And the way Dante looked at her...

Connor noticed, too. He swore under his breath.

Aly put her hand over his, leaned his way and whispered in his ear, "Don't you dare."

"He's thirty-one and divorced," Connor muttered out of the side of his mouth. "He has two little girls in Portland he hardly ever sees."

"So? You're divorced, too, in case you've forgotten. And yeah, Dante might annoy the hell out of me most of the time, but that doesn't mean he's not a great dad. As for the twins, you don't know what you're talking about. Dante has shared custody. His girls are here in Valentine Bay most weekends and for the better part of the summer. He does the best he can and that's pretty darn good, if you ask me."

Conn granted her a fulminating glance. "Gracie's too young for him."

"You don't even know what's really going on over

there. The way I remember it, Dante and Grace have always gotten along—and you need to stop living in the past. Grace is all grown up now, old enough to make her own choices."

"He should know better. She's my baby sister."

"Don't you even." Aly pinned him with her hardest stare. "After all we went through to get Dante past the whole don't-mess-with-my-sister ridiculousness, now it's *your* turn to play that game?"

"Your brother is not looking for anything serious."

"Just like a lot of people—until they find the right person. And how can you be so sure that Gracie is dreaming of a ring on her finger, anyway? She's at that age when a girl wants a good time. Maybe Dante's the one in danger of getting hurt."

"Very funny."

"I wasn't joking."

"I don't want Dante to—"

"It isn't about what you want," she said, cutting him off again. "Whatever's going on over there at the bar, you need to stay out of it."

Connor just shook his head. Aly longed to give him a bigger piece of her mind on the subject, but she'd pretty much made her point, so she left it alone.

She was glad she had. When Dante returned to the table, Connor didn't say a word about whatever had just happened with Grace at the bar. For the rest of the evening, he was maybe a little withdrawn. But he kept his big-brother idiocy to himself.

Later that night, in bed with the lights out, he tipped her chin up and captured her gaze through the shadows.

"Okay. You were right about Dante and Grace. Whatever that was, it's between them."

"I am so glad to hear you say that." She cuddled closer to him, slipping one leg over his hip to draw him in, tucking her head under his chin.

She was almost asleep when he asked, "You worried about your mom?"

"No more than usual—why?"

He rolled to his back and she readjusted her position to stay close. Resting her head against his hard, warm chest, she listened to the beating of his heart.

"It's a scary situation," he said. "But Cat looked good tonight."

"Yeah."

"Is work on your mind, then?"

"Work is fine." She'd gotten into a routine of videochatting with the team at SI a couple times a week. "They're not laying a lot of demands on me and it's kind of fun, brainstorming and strategizing without having to do all the grueling follow-through. While I'm here, on family leave, I'm doing *them* a favor. That means I'm not the one on the line to produce an outcome the client loves."

He guided a hank of hair back behind her ear. "Sometimes you seem kind of preoccupied."

The man was too perceptive by half. *I love you and we might be having a baby and I was lying to you about why we needed condoms.*

She should just tell him.

But she didn't. "I don't know. The time is kind of flying by, I guess. My nieces and nephews are back in school. My mom's actual due date is only four weeks away, and in six weeks I'm expected back at work."

He pressed his lips to the crown of her head. "You want to talk about that? About the future?"

"Not yet."

"I don't want you to go."

A thrill shivered through her, to hear him say outright that he wanted what she wanted—well, mostly. She loved her job at Strategic Image and she doubted he would be eager to move across the country. But that he wanted to be with her into the future? She could totally get behind that. "So then, do you see yourself living in Manhattan?"

"I don't, no. But I'm working on it."

She chuckled. It was a humorless sound. "It's always the same problem for you and me."

He skated his palm down her arm and then trailed his fingers back up to her shoulder again. It felt so good, so exactly right every time he touched her. "Whatever happens, I'm glad, Aly. So damn glad. That you showed up at my door asking to stay with me. I'm grateful that you're here with me, right now."

"Me, too."

And for now, she was going to enjoy each moment, treasure the time with her mom and her family. And revel in this reunion with him, no matter that it would probably be temporary.

The baby—if there was a baby—would change everything. But even a baby didn't necessarily mean they would be together forever.

They could end up co-parents on opposite coasts.

That didn't sound so great. Really, would long-distance

co-parenting even be fair to the baby? Let alone to Connor, who hadn't exactly volunteered to be a surprise dad…

Aly closed her eyes. It was all too much to cope with.

And she didn't *have* to cope with it.

Not right now, anyway. She had weeks left. Surely in that time, it would all get clearer to her. She would figure out what she absolutely couldn't do without. And what she was willing to give up to get what she needed most.

Oh, and at some point, she ought to take one of those home pregnancy tests she'd bought. That would be a good idea, too…

Chapter Ten

Two weeks later, Aly had yet to take one of those home tests. She kept telling herself she would do it tomorrow. And when tomorrow came, she put it off another day.

"Is your dad staying home with your mom today?" Connor asked that Sunday morning during breakfast.

"Yeah." Cat was doing really well at thirty-eight weeks along.

"Do you need to go over there?"

Aly set down her fork. "Connor. What are you getting at?"

He poured more syrup onto his pancakes. "I want the whole day with you."

She sipped from her glass of orange juice and picked up her fork again. "Yes. I would love to spend the day with you. What's the plan?"

* * *

It was Connor's sexiest fantasy-come-true. She wore a red bikini and they went to Valentine Beach.

"Just like old times," she teased as they spread their towels back away from the water, up in the dunes. The fog had cleared, but the day was cool.

"Just like old times...only better," he clarified, as he rubbed sunscreen on her soft shoulders and down her back, remembering his younger self.

That day all those years ago, he'd had to exercise superhuman concentration to keep his hands from shaking. She'd smelled like fresh coconut and oranges from the sunscreen, and her skin was pale and smooth and perfect under his palms.

Just like now.

He chuckled to himself and didn't realize he'd done it out loud until the grown-up Aly asked, "What's so funny?"

"Just thinking you couldn't pay me enough to be fifteen again." He dropped a kiss on her shoulder.

"Yeah. Thirteen and fourteen were the worst for me."

"Why?"

She glanced at him over her shoulder. "Well, there was this guy I was crazy about who wouldn't give me the time of day."

"That guy was an idiot."

"Yes, he was—pass me the sunscreen. I'll do you."

"Best offer I've had since the last time you did me."

"Smart-ass," she muttered, and crawled around behind him to rub the sunscreen onto his back.

When she stuck the tube back in her tote, she shivered. It really wasn't bikini weather. But they stretched out side by side anyway. He inched closer and kissed her. They ended up making out like a couple of sex-starved kids—until he tried to untie her bikini top.

She shrieked and jumped up, laughing. "I'm freezing. And you're trying to take off my top!"

"Just hoping to warm you up."

"Dream on, mister."

She did have a point. It really was too cold to be running around without a shirt.

He suggested, "We should go back to the house and put on some actual clothes."

"No way." She dropped to her towel and put on her red Keds and her beach tunic. The filmy cover-up fell to midthigh and couldn't possibly keep her any warmer than that perfect red bikini. "Pull up your big-boy pants." Her blue eyes sparkled and her smile promised mischief. "The vast Pacific is calling your name."

He didn't argue, just put on his sneakers and chased her down to the beach.

They played in the waves along the shore for a while, splashing each other, bobbing and weaving, trying not to get drenched. In no time at all, both of them were soaked through. The water was way too cold to stay in long. She was shivering and so was he. Neither of them cared. They goofed around until their feet started to get numb in their waterlogged shoes and her lips looked a little blue.

Then he scooped her up in a fireman's carry and hauled her back to their towels. They rolled up the towels. He took them, she grabbed her tote and they headed for the house.

His toes might just be frozen and he had sand in his

pants. Didn't matter. He was having the best time. It was all so simple and easy and right with her. He never wanted to let her go.

And he didn't *have* to let her go. All he had to do was move to New York City, as he'd promised to do years ago.

Move to New York City and Aly would be his—maybe. Hell, *probably*. They hadn't discussed it in so many words yet. But he definitely got the vibe that she would be open to making things permanent if he relocated to the East Coast.

All he had to do was leave his home, his family and the family business he loved, and start over, find a whole new career. At thirty-one. In Manhattan, no less.

When he looked at it that way, leaving home was a crap choice.

But losing Aly again was going to be bad—worse than being a nobody starting from nothing in New York City.

He'd spent seven years without her. Seven years with an emptiness at the core of everything he did. He wasn't looking forward to going back to that again.

Aly spotted Janine Garber sitting on the top step as they approached the house.

"I've been all up and down the block," Janine said when they joined her on the porch. The lines between her eyebrows were etched deeper than usual. "No one's seen Maurice. He's disappeared."

As Connor ushered Janine inside, Aly reluctantly reported, "He wasn't around this morning."

"But he likes it here at your house," the older woman

insisted. "Maybe he's here and you just didn't notice him. You know how he is. He could be curled up in one of the closets somewhere having a nap."

Connor wrapped an arm around her narrow shoulders and suggested, "It's a definite possibility. Let's find him."

Aly took the upstairs. She looked under beds and in every closet. Meanwhile, Connor and Janine checked the lower floor and the garage.

They met up in the living area with no Maurice to show for the search.

"He'll turn up," Connor assured Janine. "And I'll bring him right to you when he does."

Aly offered, "How about coffee or a soda?"

"No, really." Janine shook her head. "I'd better go…"

Aly's tunic was still wet. She gave Janine a hug, anyway. The older woman held on tight. "Thanks," she said with a brave little smile.

"She looks so sad," Connor said, after Janine went out the door.

"Yeah. We should check on her whether Maurice shows up or not."

"She loves that damn cat, but she won't keep him inside."

"Don't blame her. You know that cat. Nobody keeps Maurice inside."

That evening, when she and Connor got back from dinner at the Bravo house, Aly went next door to see how Connor's neighbor was holding up.

Janine answered the door looking glum and distracted. "That cat drives me crazy. I miss him so much."

"Did you eat?" asked Aly.

"I'm not hungry, dear."

Aly took her by the shoulders, turned her around and marched her to the kitchen. "I'm not leaving until you at least have a sandwich."

"I just don't feel like making a sandwich right now."

"I'll do it for you. Sit."

Janine didn't argue any further. She sat at the counter and Aly puttered around until she found what she needed.

"Here you go." She set a ham on rye, a glass of milk and a single-serving bag of chips in front of Connor's neighbor, who had begun to feel like *her* neighbor, too.

Janine ate. As she polished off everything on her plate, she explained that her husband, Theo, had died two years before. "Theo loved that impossible cat," she grumbled. She said she had a daughter. "Mira is about your age, dear. She's married, lives in San Diego. I have two grandkids. I don't see them enough..."

Aly felt like crying suddenly—for Janine, who'd lost her husband and maybe her cat, and whose daughter lived miles and miles away. And for herself a little, too. It seemed so wrong to her now, not to have family nearby.

No doubt about it. She was growing sentimental as she approached the ripe old age of thirty.

Or maybe it was hormones talking, some kind of homing instinct stirred up by pregnancy.

Really, she needed to take the damn test and find out for sure.

After Janine finished her sandwich, she put her plate in the sink and got a bag of Pepperidge Farm chocolate chip cookies from the back of a cabinet. "These are my weakness," she confessed with a devilish smile.

The two of them were sitting at the counter stuffing their faces with cookies when Aly's phone bleated from her pocket with a text from Connor. What's going on over there?

She showed Janine what he'd written.

Janine chuckled. "Tell him he'd better get over here or there won't be any cookies left."

Aly texted him back and Connor joined them. The three of them finished off the bag of cookies.

They agreed that they needed to make up a flyer with a picture of Maurice to pass around the neighborhood. Janine had one of him sprawled on the kitchen floor. In it, Maurice stared straight at the camera, green eyes wide as saucers. Aly offered to put the flyer together and print plenty of copies.

Janine had other plans. "I have a computer and a printer. I'll do it myself first thing in the morning."

And she did—very early, apparently. Aly found one slipped under the front door Monday morning before she left for her mom's house.

"Wherever you are, come home," she whispered to the wide-eyed picture of Maurice. "We miss you."

Home.

She really had started to think of Connor's house on Sandpiper Lane as her home.

At her parents' house, Marco had already left and her dad was just waiting for Aly before heading to work. He dropped a quick kiss on her cheek and off he went.

As usual, Ernesto had cooked breakfast, but skipped

the cleanup. Aly cleared the table and loaded the dishwasher and then joined her mom in the bedroom.

Cat sat up in bed reading a fat paperback with a love-struck couple on the cover. She glanced up with a wicked grin. "Don't say a word. I'm at the best part."

Tucker got up from his bed in the corner and pranced over to Aly, his ratty old dog rope between his teeth. He dropped to his haunches and growled playfully up at her, shaking it.

"Buddy, you're on." She sat cross-legged on the rug as Tuck shook the rope again and growled some more. "Bring it." He took a step closer. She shot out a hand and grabbed one end of the rope. "Hah! Got it. Do your worst."

She was laughing at Tuck's antics as he growled and struggled, wrestling her for his prize, when Cat suddenly gasped. "Baby girl," she said, "I think there's a problem."

Chapter Eleven

Baby girl.

Her mom hadn't called her that in decades.

Aly let go of her end of the rope. Growling triumphantly, Tuck ran off with it as Aly jumped to her feet and demanded in a breathless whisper, "What problem?"

Her mom had set her book aside. She had her hand on her giant belly. Her face was pale, with two vivid spots of red high on her cheekbones. "I'm cramping, my panties are wet. And it *hurts…*"

For a bizarre two or three seconds, they just stared at each other. Then a strange sort of calm descended. It seemed to settle over both of them. Aly picked up the bedside landline and auto-dialed Cat's obstetrician, Dr. Sharma, as her mom threw the covers back. The book tumbled to the floor.

All modesty out the window, Cat yanked up her giant T-shirt and opened her thighs. Her fancy lace-trimmed maternity panties were soaking wet. The white sheet beneath her was also wet—and tinged with pink. "I'm guessing my water broke. There's blood, too." She tossed her head back on the pillow and let out a long, guttural moan. "And it *hurts*."

The doctor's receptionist finally answered the phone, but Aly stared at the pink sheet and knew it was no time to fool around. "I'll call you right back." She hung up and dialed 9-1-1.

Once the ambulance was on its way, Aly called the doctor again. She shared Cat's symptoms, adding, "And I called for an ambulance. They'll be here any minute."

"Good." Dr. Sharma said he would meet them at Memorial.

Aly held her mom's hand as they waited. Cat groaned in pain and practiced her breathing, while Aly kept promising that everything was going to be all right.

Because that's what you say when your mom's water breaks and there's blood on the sheets.

The ambulance got there ten minutes later. Ten minutes after that, with her mother safely loaded in back and a paramedic to take care of her during the ride, the ambulance took off for Memorial.

Aly made sure Tuck had food and water, then grabbed the suitcase her mom had all packed and ready. She locked up the house and climbed in her rented Mazda. Before she started the engine, she called her dad.

She barely got out the word *"hospital"* before her dad said, "I'll be there as fast as I can." And hung up.

Aly called Dante's cell. When it went to voice mail,

she didn't wait for the beep, but disconnected and tried Marco instead. He picked up on the second ring. Aly explained the situation. Marco promised to call Pascal and Tony and to try Dante again.

When she got to the hospital, her dad was already there, wearing the crisp navy-blue pants and shirt he always wore to work. He was sitting in the waiting area with his head in his hands.

"Daddy?" She dropped down beside him and put a palm on his broad back. "What's wrong? What's happened?"

He sat up straight and smoothed his silver-streaked black hair with both hands. "I don't know anything yet. I just hope she's okay."

"Is Dr. Sharma here?"

"I don't know. I asked at the desk. They told me to have a seat, that someone would come." He caught Aly's hand. "How did she seem back at the house?" He looked absolutely terrified.

Had he been this way at every birth? She couldn't remember; she'd been only a kid then—ten, when Marco was born. Her aunt Siobhan, who lived in San Jose, had come up to help during the last week of Cat's pregnancy. She'd stayed on for a couple more weeks after the birth. Aunt Siobhan had handled everything. All Aly remembered of Marco's birth was being allowed in the hospital room after the delivery to see the tiny, wrinkly baby and a smiling, exhausted Cat.

"Alyssa." He was glaring at her now. "I asked how your mother seemed before she left the house?"

In the interest of her dad not having a heart attack, Aly soft-pedaled her reply. "She was having cramps and, um, some pain. Her water broke, she said. It was pretty sudden. She was fine and then she was having contractions."

"So she seemed okay?" Her dad went from glaring at her to staring with pleading eyes full of hope and abject fear—her dad, who was never afraid of anything.

"Yes," Aly lied. "She's okay. And the ambulance came fast. Dad, it's all going to be fine." It had better be. Aly sent a quick prayer heavenward for the protection of her mom and her baby brother.

Marco appeared. He sat on their dad's other side and Aly explained what she knew all over again. Marco said he'd reached Pascal and Tony and Dante, too. They would all be here as soon as they could.

A few minutes later, Dr. Sharma came striding through the doors that led into the obstetrics unit. He was wearing scrubs, and a blue mask hung around his neck.

All three of them—her dad, Marco and Aly—jumped to their feet.

"Sit down, sit down," said Dr. Sharma in that gentle, cultured voice of his. "I have excellent news."

"You do? What? Tell us now." Aly's dad fired off orders as he dropped back into his chair.

"Yes, of course," said Dr. Sharma. "You see, during the ambulance ride, the baby was showing signs of increasing distress. Your wife was in severe pain."

"Oh, my God," muttered her father.

Dr. Sharma nodded sympathetically and went on, "I saw her immediately upon her arrival. My examination revealed a high likelihood that the placental abruption had become severe. Mrs. Santangelo gave her permission for an emergency C-section."

Aly's dad said a very bad word.

"I completely understand," said Dr. Sharma. "I'm sorry there wasn't time to speak with you first. The good news is that the procedure went smoothly, your wife is doing well and you have a healthy baby boy."

"What?" barked Ernesto.

"Your baby is born and doing well," Dr. Sharma said patiently. "Because speed was of the essence, the surgery was performed under general anesthesia. Mrs. Santangelo is still unconscious, but she is perfectly fine, I promise you. She should be coming around very soon now."

All three of them—Aly, her dad and Marco—just stared.

Then Ernesto shot to his feet again. "It's over?" he demanded. "Already?"

"Yes. I apologize for not keeping you informed. There simply was no time."

"But she's okay?"

"Yes."

"The baby?"

"Six pounds, five ounces and breathing on his own. Apgar scores were seven and eight, well within the normal range."

"What the…? Apgar?"

"Appearance, pulse, grimace, activity and respiration," Dr. Sharma rattled off.

"Right," Ernesto muttered. "I knew that—and I need to see them. Take me to them now."

"I think we can arrange that," said Dr. Sharma with a gentle smile.

"*Right* now," Aly's dad insisted. And then his eyes rolled back and he crumpled to the carpet, out cold.

"Dad!" Aly shouted. Her voice echoed so loudly, she clapped her hand over her mouth to silence it.

All three of them—the doctor, Marco and Aly— dropped to their knees around the unconscious Ernesto.

A second later, his eyes popped open. He blinked up at them, frowning. "Don't worry," he said. "I'm all right."

"Yes," said Dr. Sharma somewhat wearily. "Fainting spells happen quite often with new dads." He felt Ernesto's forehead and took his pulse. "It's the stress, frequently exacerbated by low blood sugar." Dr. Sharma clucked his tongue. "Have you eaten today?"

"I had a full breakfast," Ernesto grumbled. "And I've been right there in the delivery room for five births before this one, so don't call me a first-timer." Marco and the doctor helped him back into his chair. "But that damn abruption thing and the emergency C-section? That's some scary stuff." He shook his head and muttered, "Just let them be all right. This is the last one, as God is my witness. I'm gettin' clipped."

A nurse appeared with a small carton of orange juice. Dr. Sharma took it from her and gave it to Ernesto. "Drink up. You'll feel better."

Aly's dad drank the orange juice straight down and crumpled the empty carton. "Take me to my wife, please. Now." He stood without wobbling. "See? Steady as a rock."

Dr. Sharma led him off through the double doors.

Dante showed up five minutes later. Pascal and Tony

came soon after. They were allowed, one by one, to take a quick peek at Cat and the baby in recovery.

After that, they settled in to wait for Cat to get into her own room. Aly texted Connor to let him know what was going on.

I'll come on over, he texted back.

Longing filled her, sweet and hungry. For the strength of his arms around her, the solidity of his body to lean against.

But it really wasn't necessary. No. There's nothing you can do here, really. We're just sitting around waiting for Mom to get her room.

Call me if you need anything?

Promise.

Next, she called her aunt Siobhan. That call took forty-five minutes, during which her aunt alternately insisted she was catching a flight to Oregon right away, and delivered a long list of instructions for how Aly ought to be taking care of Siobhan's baby sister.

There were two other families in the obstetrics lounge. After a while, Aly worried that the long phone conversation was irritating them. She took it out to the foyer area beyond the reception counter until Aunt Siobhan finally wound down and said goodbye.

Once Cat had been moved to her own room, Aly's brothers each took a longer turn visiting her.

Aly went last and found her mom conscious but groggy, holding Aly's new baby brother. Her dad had taken off his shoes, climbed up on the bed and kind of wrapped himself around his wife and baby son, managing somehow not to interfere with the various tubes and monitoring devices attached to Cat.

Aly bent and kissed the three of them, one by one.

"We made it," Cat said in a half whisper, her voice rough, probably from the breathing tube she would have needed while under the anesthetic.

"Meet MacCormack Salvatore," her father announced proudly. The baby promptly opened his tiny mouth in a huge yawn.

"It's a big name for a little boy," joked Aly. She had her phone ready. "Smile, you guys."

Her dad beamed, her mom turned the corners of her lips up, barely—and little MacCormack yawned again. Aly snapped three pictures in quick succession.

Then she took a turn holding her new brother. The little heartbreaker even opened his eyes once and stared kind of dazedly up at her. She chuckled in delight at everything about him—his button nose and tiny mouth, his little, wrinkled, starfish hands.

Reluctantly, she handed her brother back to her mom, who reminded her to call various members of the extended family and let them know that MacCormack Salvatore had arrived.

Her dad instructed, "You tell your aunt Siobhan that your mother and the baby are fine."

"I already talked to her, Dad."

"You need to call her again. Trust me, Bella. She'll expect another call and another report on her baby nephew, on how Cat is doing now she's out of recovery. You answer all her questions and before you hang up, you make it crystal clear that your *mother* will call *her* when she's ready to talk."

"Now, 'Nesto," her mother chided. "Sibbie calls because she cares."

"She calls a *lot* because she cares."

Cat gave Aly another tired smile. "Say it to her nicely, sweetheart."

"I will, Mom. Don't worry."

Her dad suggested, "Get Siobhan to call the rest of the family. You'll be doing her a favor, giving her something to do." He smirked. "*And* you'll get rid of her faster because she'll be in a hurry to tell everyone else what she knows."

"'Nesto!" Her mom nudged him with an elbow.

Aly's dad grunted. "You know I'm right."

Plus, it was a great idea. "Thanks, Daddy. I'll do that."

When she got back out to the waiting area, Marco, Pascal and Tony had already gone.

Dante said, "Anybody mention how long they're keeping them here?"

"No, but from what I've read about having a C-section, it'll be a few days, at least."

"Well, then." Dante got up and stretched. "I'm heading out for now."

She rose and gave him a hug. "I'll stick around for a while. I'm sure we're out of the woods, but just in case."

He chucked her under the chin. "You're the best."

She looked up into his dark eyes and thought about Grace Bravo, for no logical reason. Could there really be something going on between Dante and Connor's youngest sister? It seemed so unlikely. But that was only because they'd all grown up together and she remembered when Dante was eighteen and Grace was nine. The older they got, the less the age difference was going to matter.

Dante must have seen some hint of her thoughts in her expression. He frowned. "What?"

Did she even need to know?

Probably not. And if she *did* know, she could end up stewing over how much to share with Conn. "Nothing. It's been a heck of a day, that's all."

"You should eat something. Get Connor to bring you takeout."

She bopped him one on the shoulder. "He's at work."

"Oh, come on. It's after four. And the guy's totally whipped, anyway. You know all you gotta do is call."

She would've smacked him again, but it pleased her too much to think of Connor rushing to bring her whatever she needed. "You and Conn seem to be getting along pretty well lately."

"I might be starting to think he's okay."

"Don't fall all over yourself saying good things about him."

Dante smirked. "No danger there."

She fake-punched him again, after all. "Get outta here."

"Call if you need me."

"You know I will."

After he left, she texted Connor, including one of the pictures she'd taken of her parents and baby Mac-Cormack.

He wrote back seconds later. Cute. They're both okay, then?

So far, they're doing great.

You still at Memorial?

Yeah.

Should I bring takeout?

She smiled to herself, thinking of Dante's observation a few minutes before. Definitely. Bring takeout—but bring it home. I'll meet you there. I have to make a few family calls, share the big news, and then I'm on my way. Call Janine. Tell her to come over.

Good idea. Will do.

They shared their takeout with Janine, who'd passed out a lot of flyers that day, but had no news about Maurice.

After Janine went home, Aly grabbed Connor's hand and led him upstairs, where they spent a beautiful hour crawling all over each other.

Eventually, they settled down beneath the covers. She gave him a blow-by-blow of the day's events.

"Must've been awful," he said, when she'd finished.

Stacking her hands on his gorgeous bare chest, she rested her chin on them. "Yeah. It was rough. But at least it had a happy ending."

Idly, he fiddled with her hair, taking a fat lock of it and rubbing it between his fingers, drawing the strands out and then smoothing them down her back. "You ever think about it anymore—having kids, I mean?"

Aly's heart kicked into a faster rhythm, the rhythm of guilt for what she hadn't said. Her face must have given her away.

His golden-brown eyebrows drew together and his fingers stilled in her hair. "It bothers you, thinking about having kids now?"

"No, not at all." And it didn't. What bothered her was what she hadn't told him—and she really had no reason to be bothered about that. She would tell him as soon as she knew herself.

Which would be as soon as she took the test.

And so what if she was procrastinating on taking a home test? It wasn't good to take a test too early, anyway. Early tests had a higher chance of a false negative— yeah, the tests she'd bought were pretty much guaranteed to give her a correct result at this point.

But a false negative wasn't the only drawback to testing early. Sometimes a pregnancy wasn't viable. A woman could get a positive result, become all excited about having a baby and then not have it work out.

Those were her excuses and she was sticking with them.

"Aly?" He rubbed the back of his finger along the curve of her cheek. She loved that, the way he touched her. The way the slightest contact, skin to skin, made her feel so much—aroused, cherished, wanted. Loved. "What's wrong?"

She should just tell him.

But damn it, she wasn't ready to talk about it—or even to find out for sure yet.

"Nothing," she answered. "Honestly." *Liar, liar. Pants on fire.* She turned her head and made herself look directly into his eyes. "And yeah. I do think about kids. You know I always wanted kids."

"Me, too."

"I remember," she whispered. They'd agreed they both wanted kids way back that first year they got together at OU, though they'd never discussed when, exactly, that was going to happen.

He traced the shape of her ear and lower, his finger skimming the side of her neck, drifting around to dip into the notch between her collarbones, wandering slowly down the center of her chest, distracting her, causing desire to flare across her skin, to hollow her out below.

And wait a minute…

Why did he look so sad? "You feel like you're running out of time to have kids?"

"A little. Maybe."

"Well, stop. You're a man. You've got lots of time left to become a dad." *And you just might get lucky. It could happen sooner than you think.* "Consider my Dad. Fifty with a newborn."

"Will wonders never cease?" Connor smiled and a million winged creatures took flight in her belly. He made her giddy.

And breathless. The man could steal her breath away with just a smile. "My dad swears that MacCormack's the last one."

"I'll bet your mom's in agreement about that."

Aly lifted herself up, planted a quick kiss on his sexy lips and then pulled her pillow closer. Rolling to her back, she stuck the pillow under her head. "Think

about it. When MacCormack's twenty, my mom will
be sixty-eight—and my dad will be seventy."

"Yikes." He got up on an elbow and leaned close.
His lips touched hers. They shared one of those kisses
that went on forever, the kind that made her see stars
even though it never went deep. "What were we talking
about?" he teased when he lifted his head.

She wrapped her arm around his neck. "This." And
she pulled him down for another kiss, a deliciously deep
one this time.

They let their bodies do the talking from there.

Cat and baby Mac, as they'd all started to call him,
went home from Memorial that Thursday. Dr. Sharma
released them at a little after ten in the morning.

Mac was a surprisingly easy baby, at least so far. He
had no trouble nursing. Already, he seemed a laid-back
kind of guy. When he cried, he could usually be soothed
by the basics—a diaper change, a meal or somebody
rocking him.

A nurse rolled mother and child out of Memorial in
a hospital-mandated wheelchair. Aly's dad was waiting. He had the car seat all hooked up in Cat's Chevy
Tahoe. Cat sat in back with the baby and Aly followed
them in the Mazda.

At the house, Tucker ran in circles, whining and
quivering in ecstasy to have Cat back home again. Ernesto insisted on being the one to get mother and child
settled in the master bedroom. Aly fixed lunch. Her dad
went to work after the meal and Cat and Mac curled up
in bed for a nice little nap.

When Aly peeked in on them around two, Mac was

in the bassinet by the bed and Cat was sitting up with the romance novel she'd been reading on Monday when her water broke. Tuck had curled himself close to her side. Aly would have quietly shut the door and headed back to the kitchen to start putting her parents' dinner together if Cat hadn't glanced up and spotted her.

Aly's mom smiled, marked her page with a bit of ribbon and patted the empty side of the bed.

"You sure?" Aly mouthed.

At Cat's nod, she slipped off her sandals and tiptoed over. She set the sandals on the floor, climbed onto the bed and lay on her side, facing her mom. Cat turned, too, so their foreheads were inches apart. Now they could whisper together without disturbing the baby. On Cat's other side, Tucker let out a huff of a sigh, but otherwise didn't stir.

Aly asked, "How're you feeling?"

"Like my stomach will never be flat again." Cat put her hand on her soft belly and let out a low chuckle. "Not that it was all that flat nine months ago, come to think of it."

Aly felt kind of misty-eyed. "You're beautiful, Mom."

Cat put her hand over Aly's and gave it a squeeze. "Thank you. It is clear to me that I brought you up right."

It was a sunny day, and warm for October. Earlier, Aly had opened the windows. A gentle breeze stirred the sheer curtains.

Cat said, "Whatever it is, I'm right here if you want to talk about it."

For once, Aly didn't let herself get all wrapped up in second-guessing. She just said it. "I think I'm pregnant."

"Ah." It was an invitation. Cat wouldn't pry, but she was always ready to listen.

Aly felt so fortunate to have a mom who understood her and rarely got on her last nerve. "I bought two tests, but I haven't taken either one of them."

"How far along?"

"Eight or nine weeks—I mean, if I really am pregnant."

"And Connor?" Cat asked. It was a truly vague question, yet Aly understood it perfectly.

"I haven't said anything to him yet. I want to take a test first, find out for sure."

"How do you feel?"

"Physically? Fine. No morning sickness, nothing like that."

"How do you feel in your *heart*?"

"Um, happy. Hopeful. Nervous. Wondering what will happen, how it might all work out."

"Sounds good to Grandma." Cat pressed her lips together.

Aly sighed. "Go ahead. Speak."

"You think you might move home?"

"I don't know yet."

Cat nodded her agreement to whatever decision Aly might end up making. Her parents had always accepted her choices and adapted to them. They were much tougher on the boys.

And Cat was still watching her too closely.

"What else?" Aly asked.

"Hmm. Well. I was just thinking. Eight or nine weeks along, that's a good time to find out."

Aly took her mom's hand and wove their fingers together. "I'm getting there, Mom. I really am…"

* * *

But the next day went by. And the weekend. And Monday and Tuesday—and somehow, Aly still wasn't "there" yet.

Wednesday, she had a session with Dr. Warbury at ten. She stopped in at Janine's first.

Janine already had company, a neighbor from across the street. They sat in the front room together, sipping coffee, chatting away. Lately, Janine always seemed to have something going on. In the search for the still-missing Maurice, she'd struck up real friendships with neighbors up and down the block. She missed her cat, but her life was much less solitary than it had been before Maurice vanished.

Aly stayed for ten minutes and left the two women making plans to meet at a local fitness center and try out a yoga class.

"So," said Dr. Warbury, as the session was winding down. "Things are looking good for you. No headaches in the past three weeks or so. And you have a solid understanding of the life you've led in the past seven years."

Aly didn't remember everything—but did anyone, really? She knew enough. She no longer felt that her own mind was keeping secrets from her.

Dr. Warbury asked, "How's your mother doing?"

"Really well. She had a healthy baby boy. They're both doing great. Mom's out of bed most of the time now and doesn't need me with her every day."

Dr. Warbury offered congratulations. "And I'm thinking that we won't need to schedule a next appointment. You can just check back with me any time you feel you need to talk. I want to hear from you if you feel stressed, and don't hesitate to call should your headaches return. You've come a long way, Alyssa… You'll be leaving for New York in a few weeks, won't you?"

"Two and a half weeks, yes." It was much too soon. Wasn't it? The time had flown by so fast.

"Do you want a referral—someone to talk to in New York? I can look into that for you."

"How about I'll call you if I realize I need someone?"

Dr. Warbury was silent for a couple seconds too long. "Is there something else you'd like to talk about?"

Oh, please. She did not need to talk to her therapist about the pregnancy test she couldn't make herself take.

Did she?

She blurted, "I want to move home. I miss being close to my family. But I love New York and I love my job. I won't find anything like it here. I don't want to leave my ex-husband. I'm still in love with him and I think I always have been. I have a thousand decisions to make and I don't even know where to start."

"I think you do," said Dr. Warbury.

Aly scoffed. "Well, you're wrong."

"Just remember you can't do everything at once. You need to choose one thing."

"What thing?"

"The thing that's holding you back, the thing you're *avoiding* doing."

Aly pressed her palms to her cheeks and groaned. "How do you know this stuff?"

Dr. Warbury shrugged. "It doesn't matter how I know. *Is* there something you've been avoiding doing?"

Aly looked out the window for a good count of ten before grudgingly answering, "Yeah, there's something."

"Will you do it?"

"I will."

"Excellent. When?"

Aly laughed. "Dr. Warbury, you are so pushy."

"When?"

"Okay, okay. I'll do it today, right away, as soon as we're through here."

A half hour later, Aly sat on the edge of the bathtub in the spare bathroom at Connor's house, waiting for the results to appear in the test wand window.

It didn't take long.

She stared at those twin pink lines and suddenly, everything was blindingly clear to her.

And then the doorbell rang.

It was Janine. The older woman had Maurice in her arms and happy tears in her eyes. The cat looked great, his eyes clear and alert, his coat shiny as ever. Aly had a sneaking suspicion someone had been taking really good care of him while the whole neighborhood worried that he would never come home again.

Janine stroked his sleek head and Maurice purred. "He showed up fifteen minutes ago. I opened the front door and there he was, just sitting on the welcome rug. I scolded him—not that he listened. And then I fed him and brought him right over so you could see for yourself that he's fine."

Aly grabbed them both in a hug. Maurice allowed that, but only for a moment. Then he leaped from Janine's arms and into the house. He strutted off toward the kitchen.

"I promise I'm going to keep a closer watch on him," Janine vowed. "He's an indoor cat from this day forward."

Aly glanced back at Maurice, who sat at the end of the kitchen counter, eyes low and lazy, looking like he owned the world. Keeping that cat at home wasn't going to be easy. "I think you'd better come on in," said Aly. "This calls for cookies."

Janine stayed for an hour. When she took Maurice back home, Aly walked down to the beach and strolled along the sand under the gray October sky. She watched the gulls soar above the water and listened to their plaintive cries as she tried to get her thoughts in order, to figure out exactly what to say when Connor got home.

Connor ran up the stairs from the garage and found Aly standing in the middle of the living area. She stared at him with the strangest expression on her face.

"What?" He went straight to her. "Is something wrong?" He took her by the shoulders. "Aly?"

She gazed up at him, her eyes full of…what? Worry? Secrets? Hell if he knew. "Oh, Conn. I have so much to say. We should sit down."

"You got it." He pulled her over to the sofa and they sat side by side. He took both her hands between his. "Now. What's the matter?"

She swallowed. Hard. Her face looked too pale. "I cooked dinner. Beef braised in Chianti. Just the way you like it."

"It smells great. What's going on?"

"I knew just what I was going to say…" She crumpled toward him. He gathered her in. "And I have no idea where to start." She settled her dark head on his shoulder.

He stroked her hair. "Come on. You can tell me."

She tipped her head back and puffed out her cheeks with a hard breath. "I'm pregnant."

The world seemed to stop stock-still on its axis—and then to begin turning the other way. "Say it again."

She didn't quite give him a smile, but the corners of her mouth crooked upward a little. "Sometime next May, we're having a baby, you and me."

"May," he parroted blankly, trying to wrap his mind around the enormity of it, the impossible, perfect wonder of it. "A baby in May…"

She sucked in a sharp breath and nodded. "I've suspected for a while now. I missed a couple of pills after the accident. I called my doctor and he had me make up the pills I'd missed. He said I would be protected." She gave a little shrug. "I finally took a test today."

He rubbed his hands down her soft arms. "These last weeks, the way you've been…"

"Distracted?" she asked.

"Yeah. Distracted."

"Well, I just…" Color flooded her cheeks. "It's a lot. I didn't want to say anything to you until I was sure. And then I kept putting off taking the test. But today I finally did it. Today, I finally know what I want, how I hope it can be."

"Aly…" He knew there were words he should say. He just didn't have them.

She laughed then. "You *are* happy about it, right? I mean, I know what I said after the accident, when I asked you to let me move in here—that I only wanted to make peace with you. But I wasn't completely honest. Connor, even that first day when I showed up here on your doorstep, I was hoping for more."

His heart boomed in his ears. Was he having a heart attack? Could you have one from happiness? "You were?"

"Yeah. Does that upset you? That I lied…just a little."

He took her face between his hands. "Hell, no. I felt the same. I knew I didn't deserve a second chance with you, but damn, I did want it. I wanted it all along." He kissed her.

She took his hands and cradled them between her smaller, softer ones. "I'm so glad. So very glad. And, well, as far as the baby goes, look at it this way. Now you won't have to worry anymore that you'll get old without children."

God, she was beautiful. "You're right. It's a big relief. Whew." He pretended to wipe sweat from his brow.

She laughed again and then he was laughing, too. And then he scooped her up in his arms and stood. "Whoa!" she cried, grabbing him around his neck to keep from falling. "What are you doing?"

"Taking you upstairs. We need to celebrate."

She kissed him, a playful kiss. "Okay, then. Upstairs…"

In his bedroom he laid her down on the mattress and took his sweet time, kissing her slowly and deeply, touching her everywhere, as he set about getting both of them out of their clothes.

"So, then, the condom thing…?" he asked, when he finally held her, naked, in his arms.

"Yeah. We definitely don't need them now. And when

I said we needed to start using them again, I didn't know if I was pregnant or not. But if I was, I didn't want to keep taking the pill. It's not supposed to hurt the baby, but I just didn't feel right about it. And I wasn't ready to say anything to you yet." She gazed up at him so hopefully. "Are you upset with me, that I didn't tell you all this earlier?"

He shook his head. "I'm just happy you've told me now."

She reached up and combed the hair at his temples with her fingers. "We have so much to talk about."

Uneasiness echoed through him. What *were* her plans? She still lived in New York. Would she insist on staying there?

He wasn't going to be a long-distance dad, that much he knew for certain.

"Later," he growled, and claimed her mouth again.

They put off talk of the future for a couple of outstanding hours in bed. Then, downstairs, she reheated their dinner and they ate.

So many things made sense now. Not only how preoccupied she'd seemed for the past few weeks, but she'd been avoiding alcohol, too, now that he thought about it. And coffee, as well. All those weeks taking such good care of herself, just in case she might be going to have their baby.

The woman amazed him. No wonder he'd never gotten over her. For him, no one else could ever compare.

She shared the news that Maurice had come home on his own. "He just showed up on Janine's doorstep late this morning. Janine swears she'll never let him outside again."

"Maurice may have other plans."

"My thoughts exactly…"

Things got a little quiet between them as they were clearing the table after the meal. She wiped down the counters and he loaded the dishwasher.

Finally, they ran out of ways to put off dealing with the elephant in the room.

She rinsed off the sponge and set it in the little holder under the sink. He stuck the last dish in the rack and shut the dishwasher door.

"Let's sit down." She held out her hand.

He took it and she led him over to the sofa.

They sat close together, holding hands—and spoke at the same time.

"I want to—"

"Do you think—" He shut his eyes and drew in a slow breath. "You go ahead."

"All right. Thanks." She withdrew her fingers from his and folded her hands together in her lap.

He felt…bereft, without her hand in his. And he tried not to read anything negative into her pulling away.

She said, "I've been all over the map about what to do, how to work it out. I think I put off taking the test partly because I didn't want to have to face the choices we would have to make as soon as we knew. But it was strange. The minute I saw that the test was positive, it all became so simple to me, so completely clear." She shifted, turning her body so she faced him more directly. "I love my job, Connor."

He made himself nod and answered gently, "I know you do."

"Except for the constant ache of missing you, I have loved living in Manhattan. It really is my dream-come-true."

"I understand." He lowered his head. He knew he needed to accept that his life would have to change.

She said, "But that time is over."

Wait a minute. That didn't sound so bad. He sat up straighter.

She said, "Now, my life in New York is simply no longer the life that works for me. Now we have a baby coming. The last thing I want for our baby is you and me living on opposite coasts, flying back and forth across the country for visitation. Uh-uh. That's not the way I want it to be."

He stared at her, dumbfounded, trying to think of the right thing to say.

But then it turned out she wasn't finished.

"I'm ready, Conn," she said, "to move home to Valentine Bay. I want our baby to grow up surrounded by family, yours and mine. I want our baby to know his or her cousins, day to day, to spend time with all the aunts and uncles, with Grandma and Grandpa... Conn, you said you didn't want me to go and that meant so much to me. It meant everything. I still do need to go back east, give notice, maybe train my replacement at Strategic Image, deal with my apartment, all that. But once that's handled, I want to come home to you. I want to make a life here, with you and our baby. I only hope that maybe you might want that, too."

Chapter Twelve

Speech had pretty much deserted him. How to even begin? His heart burned with happiness. But his mind?

A dead blank.

Aly chuckled. "Your mouth is hanging open." He snapped it shut and tried to formulate words—the right words, the perfect words. She watched him, her expression morphing from laughter to something anxious and forlorn. "So…that's a no, on you and me?"

He blinked at her, stunned that she could even suggest such a thing. "What—no? Hell no, that's not a no."

A tiny smile ghosted over those perfect lips and her eyes lit up, bright as a trail of stars shining on deep blue water. "So then, um, yes?"

"Damn. Aly. Are you kidding me? You're moving back home, you want to be with me *and* you're having my baby? That all adds up to a big, fat *yes*, as far as I'm concerned."

She put a hand to her heart. "Oh, Conn. I'm so glad. I mean, I thought we were on the same page, but you scared me for a minute there."

"I couldn't find the words. There aren't any good enough." He shoved at the coffee table. It squeaked against the floor as it slid away from the sofa, giving him space.

"Connor, what…?"

He dropped to his knees at her feet.

It worked. She let out another happy peal of laughter. "Okay. I think I'm getting the picture now."

He grabbed her fingers, brushed his lips to the soft skin at her knuckles, and then pulled her hand closer. He pressed it tightly against his heart. "I love you, Alyssa Siobhan. I have always loved you. It's been so lonely without you. I messed up so bad in the past, but still, somehow, here you are, like a miracle. *My* miracle. I have missed you and I never want to lose you again. Marry me, Aly. Marry me right away."

She touched him, bending closer, her fingers trailing down his cheek. How did she do that? Turn him on with a simple caress? Already, he was hard, aching for her. "I love you, too, Connor Bravo," she whispered. And she bent even closer.

Their lips finally met.

With a groan, he reached for her, pulling her off the couch and into his arms. She laughed as he stretched out on the floor, with her on top of him. Damn. She felt like heaven and she smelled like ginger and home—

like hope and all the promises he'd thought were long broken.

She gave him one of those kisses, the kind that only she could bestow. It went on and on—and still it didn't last long enough.

When she finally lifted her head and grinned down at him, her hair falling over her shoulders, making a curtain of silk to shelter them, he said, "Let's get the license tomorrow and get married this weekend."

She put a finger to his lips. "Not so fast, mister."

He frowned up at her, not getting where she was leading him now. "Okay. What's going on? Is this where you say the part I'm not gonna like?"

She kissed the end of his nose—and sat up. "Maybe."

He stared up at her from the floor. "You won't marry me this weekend?"

She chewed her lower lip and slowly shook her head. "Why not?"

"I just don't see why we have to rush things."

He caught her arm, pulled her down and stole another kiss. When she lifted herself away again, he sat up, too. "It's not rushing when you want to be with me and I want to be with you. We lost years. *Years.* I don't want to spend another minute without you."

"I just mean, can we take it one step at a time, please? I'll be back in six weeks, a couple of months at the most, and then—"

"Wait. Months? You're going to be in New York for *months*?"

She made a sharp, impatient sound and caught his face between her hands, like he was a kid with a short attention span and she needed to make him look straight in her eyes to be sure he actually heard what she was telling him. "Think about it. I don't know what kind of work I'm going to find for myself in Valentine Bay. But whatever it is, I want to know I can count on a glowing recommendation from SI and good feelings all around. I said earlier I may even be training my replacement. That takes time. And my lease on my apartment isn't up. I need to find someone to sublet it—so yes, all that's going to take a while."

"Yeah, but…" He hesitated, not the least eager to piss her off, but not happy with this plan of hers.

"What?" she demanded.

"You act like you're flying to New York tomorrow. I don't get it. There's no big rush for you to go. We have time to talk this over. You have almost three weeks left before you're due back on the job, don't you?"

"I do, yes, and if I wasn't moving home, I would take them. But my mom and the baby are doing great. She doesn't need me close by anymore. I'm two months pregnant. I want to do what needs doing in Manhattan, get back home and get settled before I'm too far along. I want to get going on our plans."

Our plans? Not hardly.

Yeah, he knew she would have to go. But for two months? Uh-uh. It was too damn long.

He didn't blurt that out in no uncertain terms the way he longed to do, though. It would only piss her off and he didn't want that. He'd already blown one marriage to her. He refused to lose her again before he even got another ring on her finger.

"The point," he said, as gently and reasonably as he

could manage, "is *us*. Together. If you're in New York, we're *not* together."

"It can't be avoided. I have a life there. Not only a job, but friends. People I care about. I'm not going to just disappear from their lives. I'm going back and I'm going to say goodbye properly. And I need to do that now, get it all taken care of before I get too far along."

Okay. What she said made sense, as much as he hated to admit it. "Would you just, please, marry me before you go?"

Her flashing eyes went soft. "Oh, Conn…" She scooted closer. He reached out and pulled her onto his lap, right there on the floor between the coffee table and the couch. With a sigh, she rested her head on his shoulder. "No. Not yet."

He squeezed her tighter, buried his face in her dark hair. "Wrong answer."

She looked up at him them. "Please try to understand. I love you, but I'm not rushing this thing with us. I'm just not."

He had to ask. "Are you trying to say you have doubts about marrying me?"

"No, I am not." She surged up and gave him a hard, quick kiss. "I have no doubts about you and me and our future together. I do want to marry you. And I will, I promise you."

"When?"

"Can we just give it a while this time around? Give ourselves a little space to work things out? I was twenty when we got married the first time. I think we rushed it. I don't want to rush it this time."

He stroked a hand down her back and toyed with a long curl of her hair. "So then, tell me…"

She snuggled in closer again. "Hmm?"

He wrapped her hair around his hand, gave the thick, silky mass a tug until she looked at him once more. Her eyes made all the right promises. He took heart. "When you come back to Valentine Bay after those proper goodbyes, will you move in here, with me?"

"Yes, I will." Her smile could light up the blackest night. "There is no place else I'd rather live than right here with you."

Connor really did hope she would maybe stick around for a week at least.

Not Aly. She booked a nonstop flight to JFK that left Portland International at 9:30 a.m. on Saturday.

Thursday night, they shared a goodbye dinner with her family. She saved the big announcement about the baby for later, though Cat knew. Aly had confided in her mom earlier that day and sworn her to secrecy. She did tell them all that she would be moving home to stay in the next couple months.

"What? Moving in with Mom and Dad?" demanded Dante.

She caught Connor's hand and wove their fingers together. "This guy here asked me to live with him. I couldn't say yes fast enough."

Ernesto raised a toast to that.

And Dante piped up with, "So, when do you plan to get another ring on her finger?"

"That's just rude," Aly muttered.

Dante shrugged. "Maybe. I still want to know."

Connor answered with a rueful smile. "I already asked her. She said, 'Not yet.'"

Pascal's wife, Sandy, fist-pumped. "Good for you, Alyssa. Don't let the man railroad you."

Everybody laughed except Connor. He was trying to be cool about it, but he didn't feel all that cool. He wanted to marry her and he wanted that to happen soon. Aly leaned close for a kiss and he felt at least a little mollified.

Friday, Aly turned in her Mazda at the car rental place in Valentine Bay, and that afternoon, Connor drove her to Portland.

For old times' sake, they stopped at Camp 18 for burgers with the works. Before they hit the road again, they took pictures of each other with the vintage logging equipment and various chainsaw sculptures that decorated the property around the log cabin restaurant. That night, they stayed at a hotel by the airport. They made love to the whooshing sounds of planes coming in and taking off.

Saturday morning came much too soon. They ate the complimentary hotel breakfast and he took her to the terminal. He would have parked and stuck by her side all the way to Security, but she insisted he drop her off at Departures. He hauled her suitcases out to the curb and grabbed her tight in his arms for one last kiss.

"I love you," they both said in the same breath.

She promised to text him as soon as she landed.

He drove home missing her, feeling antsy inside his own skin, yet at the same time knowing he could trust her word, that she would be coming home to him, that it was all going to work out right. They would marry again—as soon as she was "ready," whatever the hell that meant—marry and have a baby, and this time around what they had together would last.

Maurice was waiting on the front step when Connor turned into his driveway. As he pulled into the garage, the cat slipped in, too, and ran up the stairs into the house ahead of him.

The place felt empty without Aly. Connor dropped to the sofa, downright bereft. Maurice jumped up beside him and slithered into his lap. Connor sat there for a good hour, petting the damn cat like some hopeless emo fool, before he took the sneaky feline back to Janine's.

Aly called him a couple hours later from JFK while she was waiting to pick up her luggage. It didn't seem possible that she could be a continent away.

"The flight was perfect, uneventful," she said. "God, I miss you way too much already."

Then come home, damn it, he thought, but didn't say. Because he was no longer a selfish kid and he respected her right to do things her way. Instead, he said he loved her and missed her, too. She said she would text him when she got to her place—and she did.

Sunday, they texted back and forth randomly. She sent him pictures of her closet with the caption, My pride and joy.

He replied, Gorgeous.

She texted back an eye-roll emoji.

She seemed happy and upbeat, like everything was fine with her.

He felt like crap.

It was more than just missing her. Something somehow wasn't right.

Monday morning, he woke up—and he got it. It was like the flash of lightning in a horror movie, where the cringing coed suddenly gets an eyeful of Jason Voorhees lurking in the corner.

Only, in this case the bad news wasn't a guy in a hockey mask with a machete. In this case, the problem was his own behavior.

He really hadn't changed that much in the years they'd been apart. He was still the same selfish jerk.

That needed to stop.

Because it really wasn't right that she should give up her dream job and the big-city life she loved. He needed to step up, make a few damn sacrifices.

He needed to prove to both of them that he really had grown up, that he finally understood the meaning of compromise. And for her, he would do a hell of a lot more than just compromise. He wanted her to have everything, her dream job, their baby, her life in New York. He wanted to make that happen for her, to be there for her in the truest way.

He texted her. Did you quit your job yet?

She wrote back, Not dealing with that or even going into the office until Wednesday. Stuff to do. Why?

Long story. Talk tonight—eight o'clock, your time?

Now you're freaking me out.

It's all good. Promise. Tonight?

All right. Tonight. She sent two hearts.

He sent back four. Because love? It made a guy an emo fool—and a happy one, at that.

That morning, Daniel had a meeting with a timber owner over near Westport. He didn't get into the office until after two.

Connor greeted him with, "Got a minute? We need to talk."

They went to Daniel's private office and shut the door.

Daniel took off his jacket and tossed it on a chair. "You look like you could use a drink." He poured them each a Scotch, neat, and they sat in the two easy chairs opposite the desk. "What's going on?"

"It's Alyssa. She went back to New York to wrap things up there, then she's coming home to Valentine Bay to live—with me. We're having a baby."

"Whoa." Daniel gave him a slow grin. "I always knew she was the one for you." He raised his glass. "Good news."

"Yeah."

They drank, set down their glasses and got up to share a hug and some mutual back-slapping.

"Congratulations," said Daniel, as he sank to his chair again.

"Thanks, man."

Daniel was frowning. "So then, why the grim face?"

"She loves her job. She doesn't want to lose it. I think she just feels she should give it up and come back home, with the baby and all."

"You're moving to New York, then?"

It didn't surprise Connor that his brother had already

figured it out. Daniel was a quick study. He had to be, what with getting seven younger siblings and the family business dumped in his lap at eighteen, when their parents died.

Connor nodded. "I want to go, yeah. But I don't want to leave you scrambling."

Daniel sipped more Scotch. "There's such a thing as the internet. You can work long-distance for a while, with trips home a couple of times a month. We'll see how that plays out. And you can start bringing Andrew up to speed, giving him more responsibility." Andrew Sykes was Connor's second-in-command when it came to the money side of the business. "It's going to be very manageable. This isn't seven years ago."

Things *had* been tougher back then. Daniel and his first wife, Lillie, had had some issues. All three of their younger sisters were still living at home, teenage girls on a mission to have their own way at any cost. At the time, it was just Daniel and Connor in the office, with a shared receptionist/secretary.

"It would have worked out even then," Daniel said. "Stop telling yourself you *had* to stay."

"I'm not. Not anymore."

Daniel nodded. "Fair enough—and as for right now, we're in good shape. Go."

"Go, as in...?"

"Now. Tomorrow. As soon as you can get a flight."

"What's happening?" Aly asked when he called her that night. "Is everything okay?"

Just the sound of her voice made the world a better place. "I want to be with you. I'll be there tomorrow."

"What?" She laughed. "You're not serious."

"Check your email. I just sent you my flight information."

"Hold on." A second later, she let out a squeal.

He grinned at the sound. "I should be knocking on your door by five or six tomorrow night."

"Oh, Conn. I can't wait."

"You sound breathless. I like that."

"How long are you staying?"

"Can we talk about that when I get there?"

She made a growling noise. "I hate waiting around to find out what's happening."

"I promise, it's good. Really good. I just want to be with you when we talk."

Reluctantly, she agreed to do it his way.

Aly's five-hundred-square-foot studio was in an upscale, glass-and-slate-fronted building on Leonard Street.

Connor gave his name and the doorman ushered him right in. Aly was waiting for him in the open front door of her ninth-floor apartment. He'd barely rolled his suitcase off the elevator when she flew into his arms.

"I don't believe you're actually here." She kissed him.

One kiss was never enough. When he eased her down onto her feet again and grabbed the handle of his suitcase, she just kept on kissing him. They kind of staggered to her door, mouths fused together, with him dragging his suitcase along behind.

They'd been apart for three days, but it felt like a lifetime.

And the great thing about a studio? It wasn't far at all from the door to the bed.

They spent a couple blissful hours getting reacquainted naked, after which she ordered a pizza from a place two blocks away and put on a giant pink shirt and a pair of lavender yoga pants that made him want to get bossy, to instruct her to bend over and lift up that shirt. When the pizza arrived, she got him a beer and they sat on the rumpled bed to eat.

"Talk," she commanded, once they were both on their second slice.

He laid it on her. "I know you love your job. I don't want you to have to quit. I think it's time I did what I promised you I would do. I talked to Daniel and we worked it out. I'm moving to New York."

Aly set her second slice back on the pizza box and asked in a soft, surprised voice, "Just like that?"

"Essentially, yeah. I'll work for Valentine Logging long-distance, for a while at least. We'll see how it goes."

She tipped her head to the side, kind of studying him, a little smile flirting with the corners of that mouth he couldn't wait to kiss again. "I have always loved you. I don't even remember the time when I *didn't* love you. There were some years when I *wished* that I didn't. But now, Connor Bravo, all I want is the chance to be with you, loving you, until I draw my last breath." She was still smiling, but those blue eyes gleamed with tears.

He shoved the pizza box aside and reached for her. She scrambled into his lap. He kissed the crown of her head and stroked her beautiful, tangled hair. "Don't cry," he coaxed. "Hey. It's a good thing."

She sniffed and tipped her head back to look up at

him. He wiped a tear from one soft cheek and then the other. "I love that you're willing to move across the country for me," she said. "I love it so much, but..."

"'But?'" Somehow, this wasn't going down quite the way he'd expected. "What am I missing here?"

"Well, Connor, the thing is, I meant it when I said I want to move home."

Should he have expected that? He hadn't. He gulped. "You're sure?"

"I am. I truly am. It's time. I want to move home."

"Damn. Aly." He grabbed her close again and pulled her across his lap. "I really am ready, to move here. I'm not just saying it."

She reached up, laid her soft hand against his cheek. "Thank you. But, well, do you mind if we just move home instead?"

"Are you absolutely sure?"

She grinned. "Didn't I already answer that question?"

"You did. But I need you to know that I'm happy either way, as long as it's you and me, together."

She held his gaze so steadily. "I want to go home."

He had no words. He kissed her instead.

The pizza fell off the end of the bed. He didn't care and she didn't seem to notice.

She was his, again, at last.

And this time he was never letting her go.

Connor decided to remain with Aly in New York for the next several weeks. There were a thousand and one things that had to be dealt with as she prepared to move home. He would help with all that.

The next day, she went in to work and gave notice. Right away, Jane was suggesting she telecommute for them and that at least she ought to consider letting them get her under contract as a consultant. Aly ended up agreeing to the consulting gig.

Friday was a big day. Aly and Connor went to her gynecologist. The doctor confirmed her pregnancy and gave her a due date in early May.

As for Aly's hesitation about going ahead with their second marriage? That faded fast.

A week after Connor arrived at her door, on the ninth anniversary of their first marriage, she married him again. They said their vows right there in Manhattan at the Office of the City Clerk on Worth Street, with two of her girlfriends as their witnesses.

"I want something more, though," she insisted in bed that night. "Maybe after the baby comes. A ceremony, a big reception. A party that says we made it. We ruined everything and yet somehow, with a little help from a car wreck and the resulting partial amnesia caused by a blow to the head, we put it all back together better than ever."

He reminded her that they couldn't have another church wedding. "As far as the Catholic Church is concerned, we've never been *un*married."

"I get that. And I'm not asking for another church wedding. I just want a killer party to celebrate how beautifully it's all ended up. We made a big mess. We were a couple of pigheaded kids who blew it in the worst way. But we got past all that and found our way back to each other. Just look at us now. Happily married all over again." She held up her ring finger. The emerald-cut solitaire she'd chosen at Tiffany's sparkled in the light from the bedside lamp. "Which brings me back around to you, me, the baby, lots of Bravos and Santangelos and a celebration—yeah. I want it. We're doing it. Maybe next October, with a harvest theme. It'll be for our one-year anniversary and also the ten-year anniversary of our first marriage." She grabbed his handsome face between her hands and kissed him hard and deep.

"Works for me," he said.

"It's going to be so great."

He kissed the space between her eyebrows. "You can stop selling it. I already said yes."

"Well, all right then." Aly turned to her other side and settled under the covers with him wrapped around her, two spoons in a drawer.

She was smiling when she closed her eyes, remembering the years they'd had together and the lonely time they'd been apart. Life was full of mysteries and miracles. And she was one of the lucky ones, reunited at last with the man she'd loved all her life, the only man for her.

The one she could never forget.

* * * * *

COMING SOON!

We really hope you enjoyed reading this book. If you're looking for more romance, be sure to head to the shops when new books are available on

Thursday 17th October

To see which titles are coming soon, please visit

millsandboon.co.uk/nextmonth

MILLS & BOON

Coming next month

THEIR FESTIVE ISLAND ESCAPE
Nina Singh

An appealing, successful, handsome man was asking to spend time with her on various island adventures but his only objective was her business acumen.

That shouldn't have bothered her as much as it did. But that was a silly notion, it wasn't like she and Reid were friends or anything. In fact, a few short days ago, she would have listed him as one of the few people on earth who actually may not even like her.

"Why me?" Celeste asked. There had to be other individuals he could ask. A man like Reid was unlikely to be lacking in female companionship.

She imagined what it would be like to date a man like him. What it would mean if he was sitting here asking her to do these things with her simply because he wanted to spend time with her.

What his lips would feel against hers if he ever were to kiss her.

Dear saints! What in the world was wrong with her? Was it simply because she'd been without a man for so long? Perhaps it was the romantic, exotic location. Something had to be causing such uncharacteristic behavior on her part.

Why hadn't she just said no already? Was she really even entertaining the idea?

She wasn't exactly the outdoors type. Or much of an

athlete for that matter. Sure, she'd scaled countless fences during her youth trying to outrun the latest neighborhood bully after defending her younger sister. And she'd developed some really quick reflexes averting touchy men in city shelters. But that was about the extent of it.

Reid answered her, breaking into the dangerous thoughts. "Think about it. Between your professional credentials and the fact that you take frequent tropical vacations, you're actually the perfect person to accompany me."

Again, nothing but logic behind his reasoning. On the surface, she'd be a fool to turn down such an exciting opportunity; the chance to experience so much more of what the island had to offer and, in the process, acquire a host of memories she'd hold for a lifetime. It was as if he really was Santa and he had just handed her a gift most women would jump at.

Continue reading
THEIR FESTIVE ISLAND ESCAPE
Nina Singh

Available next month
www.millsandboon.co.uk

MILLS & BOON

THE HEART OF ROMANCE

A ROMANCE FOR EVERY KIND OF READER

MODERN

Prepare to be swept off your feet by sophisticated, sexy and seductive heroes, in some of the world's most glamourous and romantic locations, where power and passion collide.
8 stories per month.

HISTORICAL

Escape with historical heroes from time gone by. Whether your passion is for wicked Regency Rakes, muscled Vikings or rugged Highlanders, awaken the romance of the past.
6 stories per month.

MEDICAL

Set your pulse racing with dedicated, delectable doctors in the high-pressure world of medicine, where emotions run high and passion, comfort and love are the best medicine.
6 stories per month.

True Love

Celebrate true love with tender stories of heartfelt romance, fro the rush of falling in love to the joy a new baby can bring, and a focus on the emotional heart of a relationship.
8 stories per month.

Desire

Indulge in secrets and scandal, intense drama and plenty of sizz hot action with powerful and passionate heroes who have it all: wealth, status, good looks…everything but the right woman.
6 stories per month.

HEROES

Experience all the excitement of a gripping thriller, with an inte romance at its heart. Resourceful, true-to-life women and stron fearless men face danger and desire - a killer combination!
8 stories per month.

DARE

Sensual love stories featuring smart, sassy heroines you'd want a best friend, and compelling intense heroes who are worthy of t
4 stories per month.

To see which titles are coming soon, please visit

millsandboon.co.uk/nextmonth

JOIN US ON SOCIAL MEDIA!

Stay up to date with our latest releases, author
news and gossip, special offers and discounts, and
all the behind-the-scenes action
from Mills & Boon...

 millsandboon

 millsandboonuk

 millsandboon

It might just be true love...

MILLS & BOON
MEDICAL
Pulse-Racing Passion

Set your pulse racing with dedicated, delectable doctors in the high-pressure world of medicine, where emotions run high and passion, comfort and love are the best medicine.